A Gift To Celebrate Your Stay
in Mrs. Pegram's Parlour
Best Wishes
David H. Jones
Linden Row Inn
Richmond, Virginia

TWO BROTHERS

One North, One South

DAVID H. JONES

STAGHORN PRESS

Encino, California

Copyright © 2008 By David H. Jones

ISBN 978-0-9796898-5-7
Library of Congress Control Number 2007937103

Editing by Darla Bruno
Cover and Interior Design by Charles Brock/DesignWorks Group

Staghorn Press
P.O. Box 260162
Encino, California 91426-0162
www.staghornpress.com

Printed in the United States of America

RESPECTFULLY DEDICATED TO THOSE PATRIOTS
WHO SERVED WITH COURAGE AND DEVOTION

1ST AND 2ND BATTALIONS OF MARYLAND INFANTRY

6TH MARYLAND VOLUNTEER INFANTRY REGIMENT

7TH REGIMENT UNITED STATES COLORED TROOPS

Major Clifton K. Prentiss - 1865
6th Maryland Volunteer Infantry Regiment (US)

The primary characters in this story were actual persons. Their participation in significant historical events did, in fact, occur and was detailed in diaries, letters, memoirs, and newspapers of the period. Interwoven with the real people and events are several imagined characters and circumstances to benefit the telling of the story. The discourse between characters may very well have happened in a manner similar to the presentation in this fictional account. In a number of instances, the words of an actual person or contemporary observer are integrated into dialogue and narration. By these means, the author seeks to illuminate those tumultuous times and the people whose lives were so drastically altered by the great tragedy of the American Civil War.

CONTENTS

DEATH AND REMEMBRANCE

Moonlight glimmered on the distant capitol dome and cast long shadows from the gothic towers and battlements of the Smithsonian Institute. To the west, the partially completed shaft of the Washington Monument appeared like a giant white chimney protruding from the dark landscape. Between these edifices were fields filled with temporary streets and wooden buildings. Bathed in the dim light was a city transforming itself from a military bastion consumed by the business of war to a city intent on governing the once-again United States.

Within a span of six weeks, Washington had celebrated the cessation of hostilities, suffered the assassination of a president, and witnessed a grand review of the victorious Army of the Potomac. The surrender of Robert E. Lee's Army of Northern Virginia at Appomattox Court House effectively ended the War of the Rebellion. While the carnage had ceased, thousands of soldiers from both sides languished in military hospitals situated not far from where the great battles were fought.

A large, middle-aged man with a full beard and kind face, wearing a wide-brimmed hat pushed back on his head walked along the deserted street with a purposeful stride. Better known for his poems and writings, Walt Whitman was now seeking to provide solace and comfort to the maimed and the dying within the forlorn wards of Armory Square Hospital. It was to be his small part in the distinguishing event of his time, a cruel war that almost irreversibly fragmented the United States of America. Neglecting his primary vocation, Whitman held a part-time job as a clerk in the Army Paymaster's Office and used his meager wages to buy candy and writing paper for soldiers whom he visited in Washington-area hospitals.

Arriving at his destination, Whitman mounted the steps of the hospital administration building, pulled open the heavy door, and entered the reception room. Near the entrance was a large table, behind which sat a U.S. Army hospital steward busily recording entries in medical ledgers that detailed the pain and suffering of those in his charge. The hospital steward looked up and greeted him with a friendly smile. Whitman shared the horror of this place and his contribution of time and heart made life more tolerable for the patients and the hospital staff that cared for them.

"Good evening, Mr. Whitman. It's always good to see you."

"Good evening, Simpson. I've missed seeing you for several weeks. Have you been on a leave of absence?"

Edwin Simpson smiled. "Yes, sir. Thank God I was able to get a furlough and be away from this place for a short while. I was visiting with my family in Philadelphia, and I enjoyed every blessed moment of it."

"It's always grand to return to home and hearth," Whitman replied.

Simpson leaned back in his chair. "You know, Mr. Whitman, I have to be here. I'm a soldier, and it's my duty. Why do you do it? Why do you give so much of yourself to these poor fellows?"

Whitman stared at the hospital steward for a moment, lost in his own thoughts, then re-focused and spoke softly. "It began when my brother George was wounded at Fredericksburg in December of 1862. I immediately traveled to the field hospital where he was being treated and found, to my great relief, that his wound was only superficial. As I looked around me, I was horrified. Seeing the amputation, agony, and suffering of those men who had the misfortune of being wounded in battle led me to help convey them from the front to hospitals around Washington." The flickering candlelight made the solemnity of Whitman's expression even more pronounced. He searched within himself for a more complete answer. "Since that time, I've been compelled to do this work as so many men are facing a painful, lonely death. Perhaps, in my own way, I too am a soldier in this war."

Simpson was an astute observer who stayed in the background and made it his business to know what everyone was thinking and saying about others. He knew that a few female nurses were unsettled by Whitman's almost motherly affection for the wounded men, but he chose not to comment on the minority view. "Mr. Whitman, I can tell you that most of the hospital medical staff considers you to be a godsend. We greatly appreciate the kindness and consideration that you give to these poor men. The truth of the matter is that we're consumed with administering to broken bodies. We hardly have time to spend tending to their loneliness and sorrow." He leaned forward and quickly flipped through several pages of his ledger before finding what he was seeking. "There's a young fellow in Ward D, bed seventeen, who will surely benefit from your kindness tonight. He had a leg amputated above the knee at a field hospital, but serious complications have set in and his condition is steadily worsening. He probably won't last but another week or two."

Entering the ward, Whitman waved a silent greeting to the ward master sitting at his desk. He also gave a cordial "good evening" to Helen Wright, one of his favorite nurses. He knew her to be among the most competent and compassionate at Armory Square, a hospital that treated only the most severely injured soldiers. Its location near the steamboat landing at the foot of Seventh Street, S.W., and the tracks of the Washington and Alexandria Railroad meant that arriving soldiers too ill to travel far would be assigned to this military hospital. He passed nurse Amanda Akin without an exchange of greetings. Whitman knew that she could barely tolerate him and he found it easy to ignore her vexation. He continued walking down the center of the long, high-ceilinged pavilion, counting the narrow iron-framed beds lining each side.

Standing beside bed seventeen, Whitman looked down at the patient, his vision aided by both lustrous moonlight flooding through the large windows and candlelight reflecting from the whitewashed board walls. What he saw was a young man with his right leg amputated above the knee, feeble, yet restless, and apparently unable to sleep. Whitman leaned forward to peer into his morphine-glazed eyes and watched as the young man slowly began to focus on his visitor.

"Is there anything I can do for you, or get for you?" Whitman asked.

The reply was faint. "Please, some water."

Whitman picked up the pitcher from the bedside table and poured a cup. He carefully lifted the soldier's head and shoulders and gave him a drink.

"Thank you for your kindness, sir."

After lowering the soldier's head to the pillow, Whitman sat down in a chair beside the bed, lingering and not yet sure what he could do. Resorting to the simplest of human connections, he took the pale hand lying closest to him on the bed covers and held it.

The young man appeared to be about twenty years old, but Whitman knew that trauma often obscured age. Pondering over the patient's countenance, he sensed a greater maturity than he'd first perceived and confirmation of his belief that large doses of morphine retarded the healing process.

Whitman was startled when the young man began to speak. "I hardly think you know who I am. I don't wish to impose upon you. I'm a Rebel soldier. My name is William Prentiss. I was a private in the Confederate 2nd Maryland Infantry Battalion."

As he assured the young man that this made no difference to him, Whitman decided that he would stay with William through the final hours, whenever they occurred. He had witnessed hospital death many times, but knew that it would inflict great anguish and heartache upon him.

They settled into a dialogue that surged, and then waned, as William traversed from an alertness diminished by pain and medication to complete oblivion. In his conscious moments, he wanted to talk, and over the course of several hours, Whitman learned that William was a Baltimorean, very intelligent and well bred, from a good and well-regarded family. He also learned that William had a brother, a Union officer of rank, who was a patient in another ward of the hospital.

Whitman visited William every night over the next few weeks, and they talked for hours, sometimes regarding things of little consequence, but more often about his family and wartime experiences. William often held Whitman's
hand, putting it to his face, comforted by the affection so sincerely given, not
willing to let Whitman leave him alone with his pain and apprehension. An
embrace accompanied each parting.

* * *

ARMORY SQUARE HOSPITAL
WASHINGTON, D.C.
JUNE 23, 1865

William's condition had steadily declined in the ensuing weeks. When Whitman
arrived in the early evening, he could see that these would be the final hours of William's life. The medical staff had vacated the nearby beds and stopped by frequently
to see that William was as comfortable as possible. The full extent of their healing
powers had been reached and nothing more could be done to save the young man.

As the night progressed in the long, shadowy ward, William's lucid moments
became farther and farther apart until he was barely conscious. Through it all,
Whitman held the dying youth's hand, kissed him, and spoke gently to him,
letting him know that he was not alone. As dawn's first light touched the win-
dowpanes of the hospital ward, William Scollay Prentiss quietly took his last
breath. His painful journey was over.

Whitman sat still at the bedside, gathering his strength and reflecting upon
the loss of this young man who had revealed so much of himself to Whitman
over the past few weeks. He thought of his own wartime journey and how
his view of man and democracy was transformed and forever altered. At the
beginning, he was a staunch pro-Union, anti-slavery journalist and poet,
wildly enthusiastic about a war that most people believed would only last a
few short months until the Union was gloriously restored. But it was not to be.
The spectacle of the defeated Federal army pouring into Washington after the
First Battle of Bull Run in late July of 1861 foretold a long and costly struggle.

Whitman's abhorrence of slavery and his belief in the Union had endured, but his exhilaration at the onset of war had been tempered by his firsthand observation of the courage and suffering without complaint of hospitalized soldiers of both the North and South. In his mind, the humanity, manliness, bravery, and devotion of the individual soldiers was what should be remembered about the war, not egotistical generals and grand battle strategies.

Hearing footsteps behind him, Whitman stood and turned to face an army doctor and a nurse on their rounds.

"Has the young man passed away, Mr. Whitman?" the doctor asked.

"Yes, Dr. Bliss, he has, about five minutes ago," Whitman replied, his voice disclosing a deeply felt weariness from the long night spent at William's bedside.

Dr. D. Willard Bliss, chief surgeon of Armory Square Hospital and a man who Whitman respected as one of the best military doctors, looked at his gold pocket watch and made a brief notation in his record book. The nurse, after listening for a heartbeat in William's chest, carefully placed a bed sheet over his body.

"Did you know that this young man was a Rebel?" Dr. Bliss asked.

"Yes, I'm aware of that fact, but it's of no consequence," Whitman replied with a hint of exasperation in his voice.

"Then you realize that we have an unusual circumstance to deal with," Dr. Bliss remarked. Whitman merely stared at him, but the doctor pressed on. "Private Prentiss has an older brother who happens to be a Union officer and is a patient in another ward of this hospital. His name is Major Clifton Prentiss."

"I learned from William that his brother was also here, but I've not had the opportunity to become acquainted with Major Prentiss," Whitman replied.

Dr. Bliss removed his spectacles, put them in his pocket, and adjusted his coat. He continued. "When I observed that William had taken a turn for the worst several days ago, telegraph messages were sent to the elder Prentiss brothers. One is a Union Army doctor now living in Baltimore and the other resides in New York. I received a reply last night advising that they will arrive in Washington early this morning."

"That's most appropriate. I'm only sorry that they didn't arrive in time," Whitman replied.

"Would you be so kind as to accompany them when they tell Major Prentiss that his younger brother has died. Whilst I know that this request is an imposition upon you, Mr. Whitman . . ."

Whitman put up his hand to silence Dr. Bliss.

"Thank you, Mr. Whitman." Dr. Bliss began to move along with the nurse in making their rounds. "Please come to my office in an hour or so, which should be about the time of arrival for John and Melville Prentiss."

Whitman walked over to a nearby window and stared out at the narrow strip of grass between Ward D and the identical pavilion next to it. Golden early-morning sunlight reflected brightly from the upper portion of the whitewashed exterior wall, leaving the ground cloaked in dark shadows. He turned to stare at William's sheet-covered body, remembering the courage of the young man and the noble manner in which he had conducted his short life. Whitman, suddenly overwhelmed with a profound sense of loss, was unable to remain in the same ward where he spent the long night beside William's deathbed. He quickly walked out the door to visit soldiers in nearby wards, unconsciously choosing to spend time with several who were clearly not suffering from mortal wounds.

* * *

An hour later, Dr. Bliss was seated in his office in the hospital administration building. On the other side of his desk were Dr. John H. Prentiss, Jr. and T. Melville Prentiss. Well-practiced at expressions of sympathy, Dr. Bliss began this conversation as he had done so many times before. "I wish to convey my most sincere personal condolences to you both over the passing of William, your youngest brother. In the time that he was a patient here, I had the opportunity to become well-acquainted with him. He was a very good man and endured his medical difficulties with great fortitude and forbearance."

Dr. Prentiss replied with the same banal tone he had often used himself. "Thank you very much, Dr. Bliss. Melville and I greatly appreciate your kind words. We know that you and your staff provided the best possible medical care for William. I'm aware from your periodic reports and my brief visits to Armory Square

Hospital that his physical deterioration and death were due to the severity of the original wound and the surgery thereafter."

"Sadly, the dire complications that developed from his leg amputation were impossible to overcome," Dr. Bliss acknowledged. "Prior to this post, I was Surgeon of the 3rd Michigan Infantry and know the difficulties involved with amputation in field hospitals, particularly when deluged by soldiers with horrific wounds." Noting the well-styled civilian clothing worn by Dr. Prentiss and sensing a good opportunity to change the subject, Dr. Bliss asked Dr. Prentiss if he had completed his army service.

"Yes," replied Dr. Prentiss, "I mustered out several weeks ago and am in the process of establishing my private practice in Baltimore. I'm quickly learning that there is much involved. . . ."

Melville was disinclined to allow the conversation to become medical shoptalk. "What can you tell us, Dr. Bliss, about the circumstances of William's passing?"

"Ah, pardon me, Mr. Prentiss," Dr. Bliss replied, floundering for an instant. "I can address that at best with secondhand information. Walt Whitman, the noted poet and writer, was the only person at William's bedside when he passed away."

"I'm pleased to know that William was not alone when he died," Melville replied, a trace of repugnance in his voice. "Being from Brooklyn, I know who Walt Whitman is. He lived nearby for a number of years. I'm not personally acquainted with him, but I know people who are."

Dr. Bliss was taken back by Melville's disdainful tone. "You should be aware from newspaper accounts that Walt Whitman has comforted thousands of wounded, sick, and dying soldiers in a number of hospitals over the past few years. In my opinion, no other person has accomplished as much good as Mr. Whitman has for these patients with his compassionate care."

Melville responded as a man who took his religion quite seriously. "We are eternally grateful to you and to your staff, and of course to Mr. Whitman, for the splendid treatment and consideration bestowed upon our poor brother William. God bless you for all you have done to help these broken and mutilated men."

"You're welcome, Mr. Prentiss," Dr. Bliss replied. "I'm quite fortunate to have an excellent medical staff. I'll be sure to convey your appreciation."

Footsteps in the hall caused the Prentiss brothers to glance over their shoulders. Whitman appeared on the threshold of the doorway and paused for a moment, unsure of whether he was interrupting a private conversation.

"You can personally thank Mr. Whitman for his part as he is just now joining us," Dr. Bliss said as he stood up behind his desk. John and Melville Prentiss rose to greet him.

Melville was aware from comments by his associates in New York that Whitman's poetry book *Leaves of Grass* was a base and sensual work, most disagreeable to good Christian people. He had never read the book, so, to get some sense of the man, he looked closely at Whitman. He saw a large but gentle man who clearly possessed the kind spirit necessary to console dying men. Not knowing what else to do, Melville assumed a cordial face.

Following introductions, Whitman provided the Prentiss brothers with a brief description of William's last moments. The small group then made their way to the bedside of Major Clifton Kennedy Prentiss, 6th Regiment of Maryland Infantry, Sixth Corps, Army of the Potomac.

Clifton was lying flat in bed, awake and reasonably comfortable following a good night's sleep. A nurse had just changed his bandages and given him his medications. As he wasn't expecting any further attention within the hour, Clifton dozed for a few minutes until the sound of people coming through the officer's ward door caused him to open his eyes and gaze in that direction. When he saw who entered, he closed his eyes and tears spilled onto his cheeks. "William is gone," he said as they arrived at his bedside.

"Yes, he passed earlier this morning," Dr. Bliss replied. No one spoke. Clifton looked from one face to the next as he recovered from his initial shock.

Melville stepped toward the bed and took his brother's hand. "William has departed this life to be with the Lord and our dear parents in Heaven. Rest assured that he is in pain no more and now resides in Eternal Glory."

Clifton began pulling himself together. While Melville's propensity to assume the role of lay minister irritated him, the sentiments expressed on this occasion were consoling. John stepped close to the bed and put his hand on Clifton's shoulder. "Clifton, this is Walt Whitman. Mr. Whitman spent the past few weeks visiting with William and was with him at the end. He says that our brother slipped into unconsciousness and died quite peacefully."

Clifton shifted his eyes to Whitman. "I learned of your kindness from Dr. Bliss. Indeed, we're honored that a man of your renown contributed so generously to our brother's welfare."

Whitman responded quietly. "The privilege was all mine. William was a fine young man of good heart and sterling character. I shall not forget him."

As he looked eye-to-eye with the bedfast officer, Whitman was impressed with his calm, dignified demeanor. Although greatly weakened by his chest wound, Clifton Prentiss clearly possessed the magnetism of a courageous soldier and a leader of men.

"I must attend to other duties," Dr. Bliss abruptly announced. "Please take chairs around the major's bed and visit for as long as you wish." After receiving the profuse thanks of John and Melville for the many courtesies extended, he quickly departed from the officer's ward.

Whitman put on his hat and adjusted his coat to follow the doctor's lead. "Mr. Whitman, please don't go just yet," Dr. Prentiss urged. "We would be honored if you would share your conversations with William. We know very little of his experiences over the past few years and we can, in return, enlighten you on the events that brought us to this sad juncture."

Whitman hesitated, weighing whether or not he should join what might be a private family occasion against the value of what he could contribute. "It would be my privilege," he finally said as he realized that imparting his unique knowledge was a gift that only he could bestow. Whitman took a chair as the elder Prentiss brothers sat down on the opposite side of Clifton's bed.

* * *

"I'm reminded of the tender words to the song 'The Vacant Chair,'" Clifton commented. "'We shall meet but we shall miss him—there will be one vacant chair—we shall linger to caress him—while we breathe our evening prayer.' Mr. Whitman, would you be so kind as to move that chair by the wall up to the bed so that we may have our 'vacant chair' for William?"

Whitman immediately stood, stepped to the whitewashed wall, picked up the chair, and placed it beside the one in which he was sitting.

"Perhaps I should tell you about our family history," Melville said, addressing Whitman. "The Prentiss family arrived in Massachusetts with the original pilgrims early in the seventeenth century. Our father, John Prentiss, was the sixth of his line to graduate from Harvard and was an educator held in high esteem. His father was a doctor of divinity, an educator, and a man of literary achievement who counted among his friends and associates the intellectual elite of New England. Generations of the Prentiss family intermarried with the best families and enjoyed lasting ties with people of wealth, industry, political, and social prominence." Melville's stern demeanor mellowed as he spoke. "Father moved our family to Baltimore in the 1820s to serve as president of Baltimore City College. In 1841, he founded his own school, Medfield, named for his birth city in Massachusetts. Medfield Academy was a great success and our family flourished for many years."

Melville looked toward Clifton who appeared anxious to take up the narration. Clifton immediately turned toward Whitman and began to speak.

"In 1857, things began to change, sadly for the worst." That year, Amelia Kennedy Prentiss, our dear Christian mother, whose life was a benediction to our family, was called to her Heavenly Reward. I know that I speak for my brothers when I say that her memory will forever be an inspiration to her sons. We each have a great responsibility to live up to the example she placed before us." The brothers solemnly nodded in agreement with his statement.

John took a turn addressing Whitman. "Nearly a year before our mother's death, I left Baltimore to become the chief surgeon for the Pacific Mail Steamship Company in San Francisco. Thus, I wasn't present, but was kept informed by correspondence from Melville, Clifton, and our late father. Later, when war broke out, I joined the Union Army as a surgeon, serving in Arizona and New Mexico until 1863, when I came back East to serve in the Army of the Potomac. Later, I became staff surgeon on General Edward Ord's staff, Twenty-Fourth Corps, Army of the James, and was present at Petersburg when the Confederate lines were breeched."

"The assault that broke the backbone of the Rebellion," Whitman declared.

"Indeed it was," John affirmed. "The fierce battle was fought all along the siege lines that morning last April. Sixth Corps was the first to punch through, causing the collapse of the entire enemy perimeter. Later in the day, the surgeon of the 50th New York Engineers sent word to me that both my brothers had been severely wounded. I hurried to that location and found them being treated in the same tent. I hadn't seen William in eight years, although I had met with Clifton on several occasions after reporting for duty in the lines below Petersburg."

"And since they arrived at Armory Square?" Whitman inquired.

"In the past six weeks, I've traveled to this hospital twice to receive medical reports from Dr. Bliss and briefly visit with my brothers. However, our conversations were confined to matters regarding their treatment and comfort."

"My experience is similar," Melville interjected. "As it so happened, I was a member of the U.S. Christian Commission serving at Depot Hospital in City Point when Clifton and William arrived there. They were in such fragile condition that I wasn't able to talk with either of them about much at all. We spoke only of spiritual matters, and I have not seen them since."

"It's time then that we fully share our knowledge," Clifton said as he pulled himself into an upright position, revealing his painful condition. He took a moment to gather his strength. "The peace and tranquility of our lives diminished after our mother's death and things were never quite the same. Father was devastated by the loss of his wife and mourned her to an extreme degree for nearly a year. Friends and family were worried that he might become a social recluse. It was only with great effort that we were finally able to involve him again in academic, church, and social activities. On one such occasion, our father met Sarah Watson, a young woman thirty-three years of age, only one year older than his eldest son, our brother John. To say the least, father was charmed by her."

* * *

TWO BROTHERS

Three miles from the city, the imposing masonry structure and several buildings clustered behind it fulfilled two functions. It served both as the residence of John Prentiss and an exclusive preparatory school for the sons of Baltimore's most prominent families. The classrooms and corridors were vacant on this cold Saturday morning as no classes were in session. In contrast, cheerful activity abounded within the living quarters in the front portion of the house. Sunlight poured in the tall casement windows of the dining room and logs burned brightly in the fireplace as the household servants served breakfast to the Prentiss family.

John Prentiss was seated at the head of the family dining table where he had presided for years over an academic world and raised his children—four sons who survived to adulthood and one boy and three girls who died very young. From this vantage point, he contemplated those things most dear to him—the family who was his pride and joy and the academic endeavor that had made him a man of reasonable means and substantial respectability.

John gazed toward the exquisite woman seated at the opposite end of the table. He was clearly a very happy man. In their three years of marriage, Sarah had rekindled a passion in him he thought to be long since extinguished. He relished the excitement that she brought into his life. John's first marriage to Amelia had been as plain and practical as Amelia herself and her long, fatal illness had been a trial for them both. He tried not to think of it in such a way. He had loved Amelia and truly appreciated the parenthood and companionship that they shared.

The uncomplicated truth, on the other hand, was that John was as smitten by Sarah as when he met her years before and had admired her from afar on subsequent occasions. He was amazed that Sarah had remained unmarried all these years, especially since she was never without appropriate suitors coming to her door. Some time later, however, John was informed by a mutual friend that Sarah had a much younger sister named Laura whom she had taken to raising.

A year after his wife's passing, John unexpectedly encountered Sarah while visiting the home of Horace Morrison, an old and trusted friend. Horace had been John's assistant at Baltimore City College and succeeded him when he left to establish Medfield Academy. Horace eventually resigned to open his own school for young ladies where Sarah worked as a teacher.

The attraction between John and Sarah had been mutual and immediate, as if it was the right moment for each, and they both took full advantage of it. Their whirlwind courtship resulted in a wedding ceremony at her family home on Nantucket, which was very pleasing to John. He too was born and raised in Massachusetts and had many close friends and family members who were able to attend the festivities. Sarah's brothers and sisters hosted the event, as their parents were deceased.

John and Sarah made a happy marriage together, marred only by the death of an infant daughter born to them a year after they were wed. Laura Watson lived with them and blended nicely with the family. Indeed, John thought of Laura as a daughter and his sons treated her as a sister. John's life had become complete with Sarah and he marveled that this charming, attractive young woman was his wife and shared his bed each night.

Down the table from John sat his son Clifton, a twenty-six-year-old man quite set in his ways, and strident in his opinions. He had successfully completed his education and committed himself to every enterprise in which he was involved with zeal and enthusiasm. John was proud of him. He was a forthright, honest man with high moral standards and devout Christian ideals.

John looked across the room at Elijah Carter, the family servant, who was presiding at the sideboard, insuring that each dish was properly prepared before being placed before a family member. John enjoyed his talks with Elijah, finding him to be an intelligent man who possessed a quiet dignity. They had a unique bond as Elijah's emancipation, as well as that of his family, was solely the result of John's influence and effort. Elijah, along with his wife and two children, had been the slaves of an elderly man who lived near Medfield Academy.

While assisting in the preparation of his neighbor's last will and testament, John persuaded the old gentleman to free his slaves at his death. He died the following year. When the estate was settled and the slaves freed, John hired Elijah and his family as servants in his household, making them part of the largest population of free Negroes in any city in the United States, far outnumbering those still living as the property of others in Baltimore.

John shifted his eyes to Laura, who was seated beside Clifton. She shared a strong Watson resemblance with Sarah, and John often commented that the women were so alike in many respects. Laura was beautiful in a delicate, English sort of way—fair skin, sparkling blue eyes, and cascading blonde hair. It was no wonder that William, John's youngest son, practically fell over his own feet every time he was around her.

Heavy boots could be heard coming down the central staircase, drawing the attention of everyone in the dining room to the doorway connecting it to the entrance hall. No one was surprised when William walked in wearing the elaborately decorated and stylish uniform of a private in the Maryland Guard Battalion of the 53rd Regiment, Maryland Militia. He was dressed in the Maryland Guard's class-A dress Zouave uniform that consisted of a close-fitting dark blue coat embroidered in yellow, a light blue shirt with a close row of small buttons, baggy dark blue pantaloons trimmed in yellow, and white drab gaiters.

"Good morning, William. You do look splendid indeed. Are you off to do good service with the gallant defenders of Baltimore?" his father asked in a gently mocking tone.

"Certainly, sir. We are, in fact, having a regimental full dress parade today for which we have diligently prepared. We must, after all, measure up to the glorious heritage of the Maryland Militia, as they successfully defended Baltimore at North Point in 1814 against the dastardly British invaders."

John took delight in the witty repartee he frequently exchanged with his youngest son. William found joy in all things and possessed a keen, contagious enthusiasm. He saw the good in everyone and looked to the bright side of everything, making his presence always a pleasure.

William struck a heroic pose. "Indeed, sir, my regiment is forever bound to the highest traditions of the Maryland Line in the Continental Army when independence was won from that foul despot, King George III of England."

"That's certainly a weighty obligation for the young gentlemen of the Maryland Guard to assume," his father replied. "Please sit and take nourishment at our table before you sally forth."

William pulled out a chair from the table, but before sitting, addressed his stepmother. "May I?" he asked.

In the spirit of the moment, Sarah Prentiss straightened herself in her chair. "You have conquered the household with your magnificent military bearing and thus are most welcome to join us." William sat down and glanced nervously at Laura. He was concerned that she might think him a bit boyish because of the pompous-sounding banter with his father and stepmother.

"Good morning, William," Laura said, smiling sweetly.

"Good morning, Laura," he responded and quickly looked down at the cup of coffee that Elijah's twelve-year-old daughter had just placed on the table beside him.

Meanwhile, Elijah was busy at the sideboard piling a plate high with hickory-cured ham, Chesapeake Bay crab cakes, scrambled eggs, and hot biscuits with sweet butter and jam for the newest arrival. When arranged to Elijah's satisfaction, his wife, Alma, carried the plate to the table and set it before William.

"Thank you, Alma. This looks truly delicious, and I have a considerable appetite this morning."

"You always do, Mr. William," Alma happily replied as she turned back toward the sideboard.

For several moments, the only sounds heard were the quiet clinking of crystal, china, and silverware. John put his napkin on the table and decided that he would engage his family in a stimulating intellectual exchange.

"The newspapers are making much ado about the passage last month of President Lincoln through our fair city on the way to his inauguration in Washington. The drawing in Harper's Weekly was very humorous. I also thought the print by Dr. Volck to be rather funny, although not necessarily fair in characterization or exact in detail."

"With all due respect, Father, I thought them both to be extraordinarily vile," snorted Clifton. "The discovery of a plot to barricade the tracks so that the president's cars could be boarded by assassins is hardly a humorous matter."

William couldn't help himself and chuckled aloud as he remembered the satirical political cartoons.

"There's nothing funny about the fact that President Lincoln was forced to pass through Baltimore in the dead of night!" Clifton exclaimed as he glared at his younger brother. "Adalbert Volck's widely circulated print depicting President Lincoln in a nightshirt, peering out of a railroad car door, is a vicious act of ridicule. Dr. Volck would better serve his city by attending to toothaches and not creating drawings that slander the president of the United States."

"Well, Clifton, I did say that Dr. Volck perhaps went too far. It was, after all, political satire," John said in a tone intended to placate the situation.

"And I appreciate good political satire," Clifton replied self-righteously. "But he's a rabid secessionist and his obvious intention was to demean and belittle Mr. Lincoln. The very idea that it was necessary for the president-elect of the United States to take precautions on the way to his inauguration is an insult to every loyal citizen of the United States."

John sat in silence, stunned by the acrimony evident in the debate. All heads turned toward Sarah as she leaned forward in her chair and clasped her hands before her chest. "I only feel sadness that the election of Abraham Lincoln last November caused seven Southern states to secede from the Union," she said softly. "How many others will follow, I do not know, but I fear that Virginia may yet join the Southern Confederacy. I know not what Maryland will do if that is the case. I fear for all of us if a war between the states is forced upon our country."

Sarah's observation caused each of the men to ponder what price would be paid in a conflict between strident Southern secessionists and Northerners adamantly committed to preservation of the Union. But none knew the answer.

"I'm looking forward so much to the party this evening at the Cary's!" Laura exclaimed. "Hetty and Jenny are so delightful and gracious." Looking about her and receiving no response, Laura charged ahead, determined to dispel the gloom.

"Their cousin Constance Cary from Virginia is visiting and John Pegram, a member of one of the first families of Virginia, will be attending the festivities. And Bradley Tyler Johnson and his wife Jane are visiting from Frederick."

Clifton glowered at Laura for advancing such frivolity while he remained in a state of consternation. In contrast, Laura sensed that her effort was working as the expressions of the others registered interest in her words. "William has generously agreed to be my escort in his dashing uniform, but I think he is going only because a number of his friends in the Maryland Guard and the Independent Grays will be in attendance." William looked as if he wanted to disagree with that point, but remained silent.

"There's nothing wrong with William wanting to see his friends at the party tonight," Sarah commented. "I think that you'll both have a wonderful time. The Cary sisters are known to be among the very best hostesses in Baltimore and I know from experience that the food served at their parties is truly delightful." Sarah's gaze landed upon William. "Which of your militia friends will be at the Cary party?" she asked.

"I know that Edward Dorsey, William and Clapham Murray, Alexander Murdock, and Harry Carroll will be there, all of whom are members of the Maryland Guard," William replied. "And Lyle Clarke and James Herbert of the Independent Grays. There may be a few others. I really don't know for sure."

"I do believe that I have met most of those young gentlemen at various social affairs," Sarah said. "I was particularly impressed with that handsome fellow, William H. Murray, who seems to be such a nice young man and comes from a fine family in Anne Arundel County. Laura, have you been properly introduced to Captain Murray?"

"Yes, I have," Laura replied, her cheeks turning slightly crimson. A quick look passed between Sarah and Laura that wasn't noticed by the men.

William ate the last morsel on his plate and put down his utensils. He looked across the room at Alma who was standing next to her husband at the sideboard. "Alma, these are absolutely the best crab cakes I have ever put in my mouth. They've got to be the finest ever made in Baltimore County, and I know that you deserve the credit."

"My goodness gracious, thank you for saying that Mr. William," Alma replied, a bright smile lighting her face.

The family members finished breakfast and were relaxing in their chairs as the servants cleared the table. Sarah stood and spoke to Laura. "Please come upstairs. I would like to see the dress that you're planning to wear this evening." The two women walked toward the door engrossed in conversation, followed by William who would be departing shortly for the 53rd Regiment Armory.

Clifton and his father were the last to leave the table. "The party at the Cary's tonight sounds more like a gathering of secessionists than a gay and lighthearted affair," Clifton remarked. "I fear that the small talk will be less of things social and more of things seditious, which is not good conversation for Laura and William to hear."

"I agree," John whispered, but he moved quickly toward the door, wishing not to add fuel to the fire.

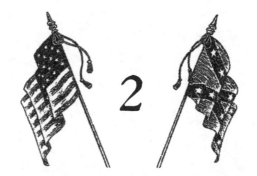

OPPOSING SENTIMENTS

In the twilight of the evening, William dismounted from the open door of his carriage and turned to hold Laura's hand as she gracefully stepped down in front of the Wilson Miles Cary home at the corner of Eutaw and Biddle. He then offered her his arm and they proceeded up the wide stone steps to the front door. Candles were aglow in each window fronting on the street and a din of happy voices could be heard coming from within the handsome red brick row house.

"Oh, William. I'm so delighted to be attending this wonderful party tonight," Laura gushed. "The Cary sisters are so elegant and always entertain the best and the most interesting people at their festivities. Hetty is so beautiful. Some say the most beautiful woman in all the Southland. And Jenny is so clever and nearly as beautiful. Don't you think so, William?"

"Laura, I doubt that any woman at this gathering tonight can possibly be more beautiful than you are at this moment. I'm very proud to be your escort."

"It's so sweet of you to say that. What a wonderful fellow you are! I'm so fortunate to arrive on the arm of my handsome brother in his Maryland Guard uniform."

William frowned. Laura, however, didn't notice as she was focused on the opening door and the flood of candlelight that greeted them.

Jenny Cary was with a small group at the far end of the spacious entrance hall. Noting the entry of William and Laura, she excused herself and made her way to greet the newest arrivals, motioning to a servant girl whose task was to collect the guests' outer garments.

"Laura, William, I'm so happy to see you both!" exclaimed Jenny, smiling brightly at two people she liked very much. "What a handsome pair you make. As soon as you have removed your wraps, please come into the parlor and warm yourselves before the fireplace. A number of guests from out-of-town are here and they're most anxious to meet you."

William helped Laura with her cape and handed it to the attentive servant girl. Noting that Wilson Miles Cary and Jane Carr Cary, the parents of the Cary sisters, were standing nearby, Laura and William showed their good manners by chatting with them for several minutes before being guided by Jenny into a candlelit parlor. The parlor was full of well-dressed people, the women wearing the elegant finery of Baltimore's upper class and the men equally well-attired, a number of them in military uniform. They were immediately approached by a servant with a silver tray of flute glasses filled with champagne. Jenny saw her aunt, Monimia Fairfax Cary walking by and stopped her in order to introduce her friends. Monimia was an exceptionally gracious lady from Virginia, the daughter of Thomas, the ninth Lord Fairfax, Baron of Cameron in the Scottish peerage, and widow of Archibald Cary, the younger brother of Wilson Miles Cary. Although aristocratic in bearing, she quickly showed herself to be warm and down-to-earth while chatting with the young people.

Soon, William and Laura were standing with their backs to the fireplace and refreshments in hand, conversing with Jenny, while watching the other guests gathered in small groups around the beautifully furnished room.

William felt a hand on his arm and turned around to see his friend and Medfield Academy classmate Daniel Giraud Wright standing beside him with an attractive young lady on his arm.

"Jero, you rascal, where have you been? I haven't seen you for at least a month!" William exclaimed as he shook the offered hand.

"Well, Willie, to tell you the truth, I've been rather busy," Giraud replied, raising his eyebrow as he patted the forearm of the young woman who appeared pleased by the implication.

After introducing the ladies to one another, the former schoolmates enjoyed a lively conversation for a few minutes until Giraud and his latest sweetheart moved on to socialize with other guests at the party.

William noticed Hetty and Jenny's older sister Sarah and her husband, James Howard McHenry, across the room in the center of a small group. He laughed to himself as he realized that the persons conversing with them were all relatives with similar and interlocking names. Just to the right of the McHenry's stood James McHenry Howard and his brother David Ridgely Howard. Standing on the other side and locked in conversation with them were Ridgely and John Duvall, classmates of William at Medfield Academy—brothers Edward Lloyd Howard, Charles Howard, John Eager Howard, and McHenry Howard, who, observing William looking his way, waved a greeting. McHenry, a grandson of Francis Scott Key, was a good friend and schoolmate. Standing nearby were two friends who William recognized with a friendly smile—Randolph Harrison McKim and his cousin William Duncan McKim. They were chatting with William Worthington Goldsborough, a successful printer in Baltimore and Francis X. Ward, an attorney, both of whom were associates of William in the Maryland Militia.

In fact, most of the people in attendance were well-acquainted with one another, creating a comfortable and convivial atmosphere for the evening. Hetty Cary's location was easily discernable as both men and women tended to glance her way from time to time in response to her highly appreciated grace and beauty.

"Jenny, who's the fine-looking gentleman so engrossed in conversation with Hetty?" Laura asked.

"He is, my dear Laura, Captain John Pegram, born into a very respectable family of Virginia planters. A graduate of West Point in the class of 1854. Commissioned as an officer of United States Dragoons. And has served at several posts out West. Despite the fact that he is not attired in his uniform, you should be able to detect his splendid military bearing from across the room."

"Is he still stationed on the frontier?" William inquired.

"No," Jenny replied. "He took a leave of absence a few years ago to observe, firsthand, the war between Italy and Austria. After returning from Europe, I understand that he served in New Mexico for a year, but most recently returned to the Old Dominion. Like many other Southern officers, he is prepared to stand with his home state of Virginia, if need be."

A sparkle gleamed in Jenny's eyes. "Whether he realizes it or not, Captain Pegram is in greater danger now than when he was fighting wild Indians on the Western Frontier as it does appear that our Hetty is out to capture his heart. Of course, Hetty desires to capture the hearts of all male creatures within her view at any given time, but handsome military officers from Virginia plantation families are particularly attractive to my darling elder sister." Turning to William, Jenny asked with a mischievous smile on her face, "Has Hetty captured your heart yet?"

"Oh no, no, no," William replied, turning red with embarrassment. "I mean to say that Miss Hetty is so pretty and charming, but I, ahhh . . ."

Jenny laughed gleefully at the sputtering youth. "Don't let Hetty hear you call her just pretty, William, or you really will be in trouble," she said, placing a comforting hand on his arm. "Hetty only accepts such laudatory descriptions as beautiful or magnificent from her many admirers and requires complete and total adoration from all men in her presence."

Captain William H. Murray, a popular officer of the Maryland Guard and a gentleman well-regarded in Baltimore society, approached the small group. Smiling directly at the young woman standing beside William, Captain Murray said, "Good evening, Laura."

"Good evening, Captain Murray," Laura replied with a delighted expression.

Captain Murray turned to William. "Private Prentiss, it's most unfair of you to completely dominate the attention of these two charming and beautiful young ladies. We're devastated by your lack of regard for your fellow soldiers who are not so well-situated. Please share their fair company with your companions of the Maryland Guard and the Independent Grays who are standing most forlorn and neglected in the corner."

"Ohhh, you complain far too much, Captain Murray," Jenny gently mocked. "Haven't you heard that all is fair in love and war? And you and your companions all outrank poor William!"

William, wanting to spare his friend and commanding officer any further pummeling by Jenny's clever wit, replied before Captain Murray could speak. "Jenny, we of the 53rd Regiment always stand together, so I'll comply willingly with Captain Murray's request and invite him and our outcast comrades to join this circle." Everyone laughed, as did William, although he was somewhat disconcerted that Laura gazed at Captain Murray in a most engaging manner. Dismay flitted across Jenny's face for an instant before she stifled it.

* * *

Captain John Pegram was thoroughly enchanted by the elegant woman who had taken an immediate interest in him upon his arrival at the Cary house that evening. Several of his Richmond friends, being familiar with Baltimore society, had informed him that the Cary sisters were quite beautiful. However, everyone always said that Hetty was in a class by herself in a city noted for its lovely women. She was of exquisite figure with shining auburn hair, warm brown eyes, and a perfect complexion. Captain Pegram found Hetty to be utterly charming and was delighted to discover that she was well-versed in current political affairs.

John had allowed his mind to wander while admiring her beauty, leaving Hetty, who had just asked him a question, waiting for an answer. He recovered quickly. "Yes, I'm aware of the Southern Party convention held recently in Baltimore." He cleared his voice to help cover his lapse in attention. "Bradley Johnson has been kind enough to keep several associates of mine in Richmond appraised of these developments. We are, as you may presume, keenly interested in what happens within our sister state of Maryland. Family and traditional bonds are too close for it to be otherwise."

Holding his attention with a steady gaze, Hetty responded. "And our hearts and minds are deeply affected by events in Virginia. As you may know, the Carys were originally Virginians, and we're proud that we descend from the Jeffersons, the Carrs, and the Randolphs. However, we're Marylanders now, and it's my observation that the people of this state are undeniably imbued with the traditions and culture of the Southern people. They will, I'm certain, stand with their Southern brethren in any political confrontation with the North."

"I'm delighted to hear that the hearts of Marylanders are similarly inclined to those of Virginians," John Pegram responded with a smile.

Hetty smiled back at her handsome guest, but was not willing to let the conversation revert to mere social banter. "Baltimore's industry and commerce have found ready markets in the North," she stated. "Nevertheless, the actions of those states to restrict and encroach upon Southern constitutional rights and freedoms are deplorable. Maryland and Virginia, and the other Southern states as well, must stand together to protect our honor and interests, which are under attack by unscrupulous Northern politicians. Whilst our agricultural products bring the most revenue to these American shores, the South is burdened by excessive tariffs placed upon manufactured goods that we must import."

"Or we're forced to buy shoddy Northern products because excessive tariffs make better quality European goods too expensive in comparison," John responded.

Unlike most women who had little interest in such matters, Hetty was not only quite knowledgeable, but fearless in expressing her opinions. This fact encouraged John to ask about her perception of the present political situation. "I'm told that substantial numbers of people in Maryland would support secession from the Union, should the question arise."

"Marylanders are typically inclined toward the Southern culture and are therefore most sympathetic to the plight of the South in the present difficulties," Hetty replied. "But please understand that many, perhaps a majority, are most reluctant to consider secession under any circumstances."

"That does surprise me. And I must admit that it's by no means certain that Virginia will join the Southern states already in succession," he said with a touch of disappointment in his voice. "In fact, many Virginians are loath to consider dissolving the Union, particularly those in the mountainous northwestern part of the state."

"There's something that I must show you!" Hetty exclaimed as she took Captain Pegram by the arm and guided him to a nearby alcove where a colorful framed print of the 1854 Great Seal of Maryland hung on the wall. "Please indulge me if you are already aware of these historical facts. There's a point at the end to justify any redundancy in what I'm about to describe."

John beamed with pleasure as he replied to Hetty. "Please continue. You have captured my complete and undivided attention."

"King Charles I of England granted the lands that now constitute Maryland to Sir George Calvert, the second Lord Baltimore. The original Calvert arms are the yellow and black quadrants of the shield in the center of the great seal."

John nodded, but his knowledgeable expression was feinted. It was something that he did not know.

"The red and white quadrants are the Crossland arms from the family of the mother of the first Lord Baltimore. Since the election of Lincoln last November, Marylanders devoted to preserving the Union have been signifying their allegiance with a display of the yellow and black colors of the Calvert arms. Conversely, those of us whose hearts are with the South identify our sentiment with the red, white, red colors of the Crossland arms, and the cross bottony incorporated in its design." Her narration finished, Hetty looked at John with a satisfied expression.

Staring at the framed great seal, John could see that if components of the state's great seal could be parceled off to represent opposing sentiments, Marylanders were indeed sharply divided, a fact that he had not fully comprehended until that moment.

* * *

Laura was standing with several young gentlemen from Harford County who vied for her attention. None were achieving much success. Across the room was Wilson Miles Cary, Jr., the younger brother of Hetty and Jenny. He was conversing with Constance Cary, his cousin visiting from Virginia. Jenny had mentioned to Laura that Constance had a flair for writing plays and short stories. Laura excused herself from her circle of admirers and crossed the room to meet her.

"Good evening, Miles," Laura said cordially.

"Why, Miss Laura, it's so good to see you," replied Miles Cary. "Please allow me to introduce you to my cousin Constance. Connie, this is Laura Watson, a good friend of our family."

"It's a great pleasure to make your acquaintance, Constance," Laura said. "Your cousins have told me nice things about you."

"And I'm delighted to meet you. Please call me Connie," Constance replied gaily. "All my family and friends do."

"Thank you," Laura responded in a delighted voice.

With the introductions made and the two young women absorbed in conversation, Miles excused himself. He was eager to sample the elegant food that filled a linen-covered table at the far end of the room. Sterling silver tureens and platters held such delicacies as scalloped oysters, crab cakes, roast lamb, turkey, cured Virginia ham, fruit pies, white mountain cake, and sand tarts.

"I understand that you live in the Virginia countryside," Laura said. "Is it difficult to be situated so far from a city?"

"I do love living at Vaucluse, our homestead in Fairfax County," Connie replied. "Everything is so lush and green in the gently rolling hills and valleys. It's so beautiful and peaceful there."

"It truly does sound like an idyllic location," Laura responded. "I sometimes miss the grandeur of Nantucket Island off the coast of Massachusetts where I spent most of my early childhood. I remember sitting for hours and watching the blue-green sea crash against the rocky shore. It's quite different from the Chesapeake Bay, which is so calm in comparison. And much is good about living in Baltimore City."

"I can certainly see that," Connie said, looking around at the assemblage of well-dressed people in the room, particularly the handsome young men. Both young girls giggled.

"I've heard that you are blessed with quite the literary ability," Laura said, shifting the conversation to suit her initial intention.

"Is that so?" responded Connie, her eyes shining brightly at the oblique compliment. "Who mentioned that?" she asked. Before Laura could speak, Connie answered her own question. "My dear cousins, of course! I suppose it's nice that Hetty and Jenny say kind things about my writings. I do love crafting words into a pleasing story or writing a play that I then imagine is acted out upon a stage." Connie took a sip of her fruit punch. "Perhaps one day that will happen. In the meantime, I take pleasure in writing about things observed in my daily activities, but in reality my life is too dull for me to create anything truly interesting to others."

"Oh! There's no excitement in that genteel country life of yours? No romance? No conspiracy or mystery?" Laura asked. "I'm always dreaming of such things, but I don't have the ability to capture such thoughts in words. In any case, there must be things in your imagination that you can write about?"

"That may be so," Connie said thoughtfully. "Whilst my life at Vaucluse has been one of unmixed happiness, the time immediately following the execution of John Brown for his attempt to incite a slave uprising certainly affected our tranquility, although few would admit it in our community."

"Why was that so?" Laura asked, sensing a shift in her mood.

Connie's face became tense as she replied. "I should explain that our family was among the first in Virginia to manumit slaves. My grandfather freed all that he had inherited. However, the people who served us at Vaucluse were hired from their owners and remained in our employ through years of the kindest relations. For this reason, one would think that we would have no reason for apprehension of a slave uprising. In the light of day, it was impossible to harbor suspicion with those familiar faces that were smiling or sad with family joys and sorrows."

Connie was almost whispering. Laura, her face revealing her own anxiety, leaned toward her so as not to miss a word. "But there was an unspoken fear, a nameless dread that I took to bed with me at night. I would sometimes awaken and be terrified by the notes of a whip-poor-will, the mutterings of a distant thunderstorm or the rustle of wind in the oaks outside my window. I know that others experienced this same fear as door bolts were drawn and guns loaded at night, things that were not done before."

Laura took the hand of her new friend and they were alone for a moment in a room crowded with people.

* * *

Bradley T. Johnson, a captain in the Frederick County militia and chairman of the Breckenridge faction of the Democratic party in Maryland, beckoned for Captain Murray, William, and Lieutenant Herbert to join him before the fireplace where he was standing with his wife, Jane, a graceful, accomplished, and attractive young woman. As they were exchanging pleasantries, John Pegram, with Hetty Cary on his arm, approached the group.

Captain Johnson, wearing the cadet-gray uniform of his county militia, bowed toward the hostess. "Good evening, Hetty. We're enjoying your fine hospitality."

"It's always a pleasure to have you and Jane in our home, Bradley," Hetty replied. "We're delighted to be here."

He turned his attention to Hetty's newest cavalier. "John, I would like for you to meet Captain William H. Murray and Private William S. Prentiss. Captain Murray commands one of the six companies of the Maryland Guard and William serves in the ranks of the same company. The other gentleman standing just beyond William is Lieutenant James R. Herbert of the Independent Grays."

"It's my pleasure to meet you all," Captain Pegram said as he shook hands with the three men. He then looked squarely at William. "Private Prentiss, you are obviously of good family and a Southern gentleman. In my view, that makes you a high private, thus distinguishing you from those men in the ranks who are not quite so welcome in polite society. Quite different, I must say, from much of the riff-raff and foreigners who serve under my command as common privates in the United States Army."

William was caught between being personally complimented and generally offended by these remarks. Captain Murray quickly spoke in his stead. "In fact, sir, I'm happy to report that many privates in the 53rd Regiment are gentlemen. They make fine soldiers and the very best companions in all situations."

"We Virginians know that to be true," John replied. "Several militia companies in Richmond and around Henrico County have a number of gentlemen in the ranks. It's a longstanding tradition that our best men serve as citizen soldiers, ready to answer the call to arms by Virginia in times of trouble."

"The noble citizen soldiers of Maryland are much the same and have always personified courage and chivalry," Hetty responded.

"This has always been so," Bradley Johnson acknowledged as the political orator in him took hold. "Soldiers of the Maryland Line in the Continental Army were at the forefront in the War for American Independence from Great Britain. They stood with William Alexander at Long Island until they were destroyed, allowing George Washington's army to escape certain annihilation. Their gallant charge at Eutaw Springs saved Nathaniel Greene's army. Their brave dash at Cowpens drove in the British line. Their bayonets at Guilford Court House broke the Grenadier Guards. These Maryland men, one and all, believed in standing by their friends, regardless of risk or consequence."

"Do you know what George Washington remarked to Israel Putnam as he witnessed the Marylanders repeatedly charge the British at the Battle of Long Island?" Lieutenant Herbert asked. Everyone reacted with an inquisitive look, so he quickly supplied the answer. "Good God, what brave fellows I must this day lose."

"Without a doubt, Marylanders have every reason to be proud of our military heritage," Captain Murray responded. "And I'm delighted to say that almost all soldiers of the Maryland Guard and the Independent Grays are ardent supporters of the South."

Jane raised her glass, capturing the attention of everyone in the circle. "Which clearly proves that Southern men are true warriors, exhibiting the finest traits of honor, duty, chivalry, and courage." Her statement was met with a chorus of agreement and all glasses were raised to toast the sentiment. As soon as they sipped their champagne, Bradley Johnson raised his glass again and proposed a salutation to Jefferson Davis and the Southern Confederacy, drawing the attention of everyone in the parlor and causing them to enthusiastically join in the tribute. This burst of patriotic exhilaration subsided after a few minutes and the guests returned to the conversations in which they had been engaged.

Hetty's thoughtful expression caught the attention of her companions and they waited for her to speak. "I pray we need not resort to war to resolve the conflict looming between the Northern and Southern states. At the same time, I simply cannot understand why Yankee politicians continue their attacks on Southern society."

"It's the abolitionists who are the most critical of us," William declared. "I personally would not be unhappy to see the institution of slavery wither and die on the vine, but its demise should not be forced upon the South by persons who lack any real knowledge of our traditions and culture."

"Your assertion that slavery is a dying institution in the South is patently false," Bradley responded scornfully. "It's the cornerstone of our economy and society."

That statement hung in the air for a moment before Bill Murray spoke. "William, I have no argument with your position. The United States was founded on the principle of state's rights with only a few specific powers designated by the Constitution for the central government. No state surrendered its sovereignty when joining the Union. However, what now drives the argument over slavery is not so much what we do within Maryland, but its expansion to states yet to join the Union, as many surely will in the years ahead."

John responded with indignation. "Regardless of all that, there's no virtue whatsoever in the North's determination to prevent the spread of slavery or to abolish the institution altogether. It's merely a matter of economics. The use of slaves does not lend itself to advantage in Northern manufacturing, whereas it is indispensable to the agricultural economy of the South. When the North moves to limit or abolish slavery, its real intent is to place the South in an economic and political stranglehold. This is a situation we cannot, and will not, abide."

"I agree entirely!" Bradley exclaimed. "The federal government has no right to declare illegal what is held to be legal under Maryland law. To threaten to impose their will upon us by force of arms is an abomination. As a soldier of this state, I will resist any such intrusion into our affairs with every fiber of my being. I will give my life if necessary to protect our liberty and independence."

Bill raised his glass. "I propose a toast to Southern self-determination."

Hetty chimed in as she raised her glass. "And to stout-hearted Southern men and women who nobly defend its honor and integrity." The others murmured in agreement as they joined in this salute.

"To speak of current matters," John said as he turned to Bradley, "I would like to know what happened when the Southern Party Convention reconvened last week. I've heard the results of the original session, most recently from Hetty, but I'm interested in learning the current details."

Bradley responded with a cynical laugh. "Perhaps you should have asked about the lack of results as that would be closer to the truth. The intent was to determine what the honor and the interest of Maryland required her to do in the impending crisis. Our brethren in several Southern states have already chosen the path of secession. It was time for Maryland to give serious consideration to the question. Sadly, no such determination was made."

"That's most unfortunate," John declared. "Northerners have shamelessly directed their best efforts toward pecuniary aggrandizement and amassing political power. The South must not allow this coercion to go unanswered."

Bradley responded with a tirade. "Our illustrious governor, Thomas Holliday Hicks, self-professed to be an ardent Southern man, insisted that Maryland should do nothing without the action of her legislature, which of course was not in session when the convention originally convened. He further proclaimed that he was in communication with the governors of other Border states and that they would devise and execute a proper means to save the Union and preserve the peace. As you know, the convention adjourned until mid-March, by which time Lincoln would be inaugurated and the direction of the federal government more apparent."

"Lincoln's inaugural address left no doubt as to his intent to recapture Federal forts, arsenals, and such within states that have seceded," John remarked.

"Exactly," Bradley replied. "Given this declaration by Lincoln, many of us attending the convention when it reconvened believed that the time for useless palaver and negotiation was long past. We insisted that the convention declare that any act of war by the federal government against the seceded states would operate *ipso facto* to dissolve the Union. However, it was not to be. Governor Hicks and other like-minded old men formed a narrow majority. The result was a set of resolutions that were nothing more than bland generalities regarding devotion to the Union and opposition to disturbance of the public peace."

"That is most disappointing," John said, his tone echoing the distaste implicit in Bradley's words.

"It certainly was!" Bradley exclaimed. "I should also point out that commissioners were sent to Richmond to learn from the convention there in session what position Virginia would take. However, they could learn nothing. Virginia, herself, does not yet know what they will do."

"Please understand that I am still a serving officer in the United States Army on furlough to visit family and friends," John replied. His back straightened and his voice cracked with emotion. "But I am a Virginian first and foremost. I will go where she goes. I stand ready to resign my commission and do whatever is necessary for the defense of Old Virginia, my home."

* * *

ARMORY SQUARE HOSPITAL
WASHINGTON, D.C.
JUNE 24, 1865

Melancholy expressions cloaked the faces of the three brothers as they recalled past events that created a schism within their family and the nation. They knew the terrible consequences that would flow from these calamities.

"William talked at length about his friends and acquaintances in Baltimore," Whitman said. "He candidly described everyone in attendance at the Cary party as staunchly in favor of the Confederacy. His own demonstration of Southern allegiance had secured his invitation to join the Maryland Guard. Within the family, he received encouragement from Laura who embraced the South as part and parcel of her social cachet. And, without a doubt, both William and Laura were greatly influenced by the Cary sisters."

"I didn't perceive the true extent of William's secessionist views!" Melville exclaimed. "Whilst I knew that he considered himself to be a Southerner, I naively assumed that this inclination only had cultural significance, not something that would compel him to join a rebellion!"

"I also failed to grasp that fact," Clifton commented with a sad expression on his face. "But I should have."

"Why is that?" John asked.

"Obvious things really. Among the sons of the wealthy and powerful Baltimore families attending Medfield Academy were a number who strongly espoused a Southern viewpoint. As fate would have it, those classmates were William's closest friends. Many of the social functions he attended were held at their homes where he met their sisters. He was quite enamored with one or two of them at various times as I remember. All of these factors no doubt were a strong enticement."

"It was always my impression that you and William got along quite well as he grew into young manhood," Melville commented sourly. "Weren't you able to counteract these unfortunate influences?"

Clifton frowned in resentment at the tone of the question. "William and I were always very close, enjoying the very best of brotherly love and a harmonious relationship. However, as discord between the states increased, what had been simple differences in political perspective grew into something substantially more ominous. I couldn't change that!"

* * *

MEDFIELD ACADEMY
NEAR BALTIMORE, MARYLAND
MARCH 25, 1861

Clifton knocked on the door of the library, knowing that his father would be in his favorite chair before the fireplace, reading a book by candlelight. "Come in" was heard through the thick, paneled door. Clifton opened the door, asking politely if he could intrude.

"Certainly, my boy, I'm always delighted to have your fine company."

Clifton took a seat across from his father, and they sat quietly watching yellow flames dance on burning logs in the fireplace. Visiting his father's library had always been a great pleasure to Clifton. He loved exploring the tall bookcases around the room and spending hours nestled in a chair, reading a selected volume. Even the musty odor of the books was pleasant to Clifton as he associated so many good memories with this room. It was truly his father's sanctuary and

Clifton was comforted by these surroundings as much was on his mind. Before he could speak, John began instead.

"You know, son, Sarah was right. The election of Abraham Lincoln last November practically guaranteed that our country would face this terrible predicament."

"Clearly, South Carolina seceded from the Union in December for that very reason," Clifton replied. "Sadly, they were soon followed by the other cotton states of the Deep South."

"And how quickly things deteriorated from that point!" exclaimed his father. "In no time at all, the Confederate States of America was formed in Montgomery, Alabama, and Jefferson Davis elected president, all before Abraham Lincoln was inaugurated in early March."

"The question now," Clifton said, "is whether or not Maryland will choose to secede from the Union. When you consider that Maryland voted overwhelmingly last November for John C. Breckinridge, the Southern democrat, with only a handful of votes going to Abe Lincoln, there is a distinct possibility that Maryland will go the way of Virginia. And I do believe that Virginia will secede if the South is threatened with war."

"Most Marylanders consider themselves to be Southerners," his father remarked matter-of-factly. "Maryland is situated below Mason and Dixon's Line and generally regarded as a Southern state. However, I believe that either Maryland will find a way to steer a middle course and stay out of the conflict, or a majority of its citizens will remain loyal to the Union."

"Maryland may remain in the Union," Clifton declared, "but our nation will be torn asunder by its sectional differences."

"Only time will tell," John replied. "As you know, I correspond with several old friends in Massachusetts who are strong abolitionists. I don't believe that they'll rest until slavery is eliminated from this continent. They'll do everything in their power to exacerbate the present difficulties between the federal government and the seceded states into a war against the evil institution of slavery."

"That does appear to be their agenda," Clifton responded.

"As you are well aware," continued his father, "I deplore both slavery and any thought of dissolving the Union. Clearly, many people in Maryland are of the same mind."

"Whilst I agree that most of our citizens do not desire secession, Maryland will not have the opportunity to do so, even if the majority of her people were so inclined," Clifton stated. "Geography and strategic considerations demand otherwise. President Lincoln cannot allow Maryland to become a Confederate state as that circumstance would surround the National Capital in Washington with foreign soil."

"If that's the case," his father said, "Mr. Lincoln will most certainly use every means at his disposal to prevent Maryland from leaving the Union, even if it means military occupation."

"And I would prefer occupation to secession," Clifton replied. Father and son, each possessed by a sense of foreboding, sat staring at the crackling fire in the fireplace.

"In his inaugural address, Mr. Lincoln stated that the seizure of federal property by states in secession would not be tolerated," Clifton remarked. "Any unfortunate occurrence at any one of these places could put the match to the magazine."

"The ramifications would be disastrous," his father agreed.

"I find myself increasingly at odds with William over these matters," Clifton said, his face clouded by a melancholy expression as he finally addressed what was bothering him. "Our debates are becoming contentious, and I fear that it will get worse in the future."

John's thoughts went back to happier times. "I cannot help but remember you and William as small boys together. You were the big brother that William always clung to and you took special care to look out for him. That bond was a beautiful thing to observe. It pains me to think that it might be imperiled by political differences."

"Childhood memories are also quite precious to me," Clifton responded. "Despite the five years difference in our ages, William and I were companions as well as brothers, growing up in a happy household. I pray that we can maintain that brotherly spirit despite the divergence in our perspectives. He will always be my little brother. Nothing can change that!"

* * *

MEDFIELD ACADEMY
NEAR BALTIMORE, MARYLAND
MARCH 31, 1861

It was a quiet Sunday afternoon. The only family members in the house were Clifton, William, and Laura, and all three were seated before the fireplace in the front parlor. Laura was intently reading a book, Clifton had his nose buried in a newspaper, and William was idly watching hot embers fall off the blazing logs to form a glowing bed on the bricks below the iron grate.

"What are you reading, Laura?" William asked as he shifted around in his chair to look at the young woman who had become the object of his innermost romantic thoughts.

"It's my very favorite book!" Laura exclaimed as she held up *Ivanhoe* by Sir Walter Scott. "I was thrilled by this story two years ago and I'm reading it again, enjoying it as much now, if not more so, than the first time. In fact, I'm at one of my most cherished parts, with my two favorite characters, Rebecca and Ivanhoe."

"Please, Laura, read a few lines to us," William invited. "Clifton, you'd enjoy hearing Laura read aloud some passages, wouldn't you?"

Clifton put down his newspaper, mildly irritated at the interruption, but not wanting to offend either William or Laura. He dearly loved William and had developed a genuine affection for Laura. Clifton was also not immune to the allure of her feminine beauty, even if he did consider her to be a silly and immature girl. "Yes, of course," he replied. "I'm at a good place to stop what I'm reading and the thought of hearing Laura's charming voice is indeed enticing, although I've little use for that particular book."

Laura smiled tolerantly at Clifton. "Allow me to read just this one part to you and then I'd be interested to learn what you think of it." Without waiting for an answer, she lifted the book and began reading. Given her love for the text, her recitation possessed both drama and emotion.

> *'What remains?' cried Ivanhoe; 'Glory, maiden, glory! Which gilds our sepulcher and embalms our name.'*

'Glory?' continued Rebecca; 'Alas, is the rusted mail which hangs *as a hatchment over the champion's dim and mouldering tomb—is the defaced sculpture of the inscription which the ignorant monk can hardly read to the enquiring pilgrim—are these sufficient rewards for the sacrifice of every kindly affection, for a life spent miserably that ye may make others miserable? Or is there such virtue in the rude rhymes of a wandering bard, that domestic love, kindly affection, peace and happiness, are so wildly bartered, to become the hero of those ballads which vagabond minstrels sing to drunken churls over their evening ale?'*

Laura looked up to see that she held the rapt attention of both young men, which pleased her greatly, so she continued reading.

'By the soul of Hereward?' replied the knight impatiently, 'thou speakest, maiden, of thou knowest not what. Thou wouldst quench the pure light of chivalry, which alone distinguishes the noble from the base, the gentle knight from the churl and the savage; which rates our life far, far beneath the pitch of our honour; raises us victorious over pain, toil, and suffering, and teaches us to fear no evil but disgrace. Thou art no Christian, Rebecca; and to thee are unknown those high feelings which swell the bosom of a noble maiden when her lover hath done some deed of emprize which sanctions his flame. Chivalry!— why, maiden, she is the nurse of pure and high affection—the stay of the oppressed, the redresser of grievances, the curb of the power of the tyrant—Nobility were but an empty name without her, and liberty finds the best protection in her lance and her sword.'

"Beautiful words and truly wonderful sentiments!" William exclaimed. "And perfectly delivered!"

"Thank you, William," Laura responded while smiling radiantly. Turning to Clifton, possibly the greater challenge, she asked, "What do you think of it?"

Clifton frowned as he pondered his reply and then spoke slowly. "Your presentation was truly delightful and that alone held me spellbound, but I remain not enamored by this book for several reasons."

"Pray tell, why you don't like it?" Laura asked as she sat back in her chair and laced her delicate fingers together over the open book in her lap.

"Well," replied Clifton, "the language form is painfully archaic and I find the manner of speaking to be unnecessarily romantic and flowery."

"Oh, Clifton, you don't have a romantic bone in your body," William said laughingly as he looked to Laura for her agreement.

"But isn't that part of the charm of the book, Clifton, to take us back to the days of yore when people spoke in beautiful prose and medieval knights in shining armor rescued fair damsels in distress?" Laura asked.

"That certainly happens in *Ivanhoe*," Clifton agreed. "I must admit that I too am influenced by expressions of noble sentiment and the accomplishment of brave deeds. But, to me, honor and duty are matters of serious consequence and not simply an indulgence in self-glorification."

"The eloquence may be excessive, but the noble actions of the characters are truly inspiring," William said, blustering a bit. "Consider the miserable conditions in England after the Norman invasion. The Saxon people suffered greatly under Norman tyranny throughout the following century."

"That was the Middle Ages, and I don't see a dime's worth of difference between Normans and Saxons. One was as bad as the other!" Clifton exclaimed while gesturing brusquely with his hands. "The Saxons would have done the same to the Normans given the opportunity!"

"Then you agree with the sentiments of Rebecca?" Laura inquired with a raised eyebrow. "She was certainly the voice of moderation and practicality in this story."

"That's probably true," Clifton conceded.

"Oh, my Clifton, you too would quench the pure light of chivalry!" William exclaimed. "*Ivanhoe* is a wonderful story about brave knights and acts of chivalry, the glorification of womanhood, the protection of the oppressed, and the defense of liberty. I understand that this is fiction loosely based on history, but

Ivanhoe captures my imagination with its grand words and deeds of gallantry. You're too harsh in your judgment of this book!"

"Perhaps," Clifton replied. "But let's consider the possibility that the motivations of Richard the Lion-Hearted and Ivanhoe were less honorable than is represented in this book. Put aside the romance, and you'll find a struggle for wealth and political power. The kings and barons, whether Norman or Saxon, were brutal rulers of the common people. In either case, it was a barbaric system built on undue reverence for rank and caste. The so-called nobles took great pleasure in their elevated position and unwarranted advantage over those of a lesser station in life."

"You can't judge those times through the prism of our enlightened nineteenth-century viewpoint," William pronounced.

"I understand that things were different in the twelfth century as human society had not yet evolved from feudalism to more modern forms of governance," Clifton responded. "But I believe that aristocracy in any form to be both repugnant and dangerous to liberty and justice."

"Putting aside what may have happened in medieval England, honor and chivalry still have currency in the world today," William retorted. "I believe that Sir Walter Scott intended for us to gain that insight from his story. *Ivanhoe* is a beautiful book, and I'm glad that he wrote it."

"So am I!" Laura exclaimed. "Sir Walter Scott often wrote about Scotland, and I think that many Southerners are attracted to his books by virtue of their kinship with the Scots. My own bloodlines are English, yet my heart is always drawn to gallant little Scotland striving to protect her cultural identity against political and military domination by mighty England."

"That's much like the South being dominated by the North," William declared.

Clifton's face twisted into a derisive expression.

Laura continued to speak, thriving on the disagreement between the brothers. "I see chivalry as the embodiment of the very best of human nature and good character. As a woman, I appreciate the generosity and courtesy shown for my sex by gallant gentlemen."

"Chivalry and honor are very much a part of the Southern way of life," William said. "It has always been so, and always will be." Their best arguments put forth, the Prentiss brothers and Laura sat back to contemplate what had been discussed thus far.

"There is a present-day parallel in *Ivanhoe* that I would like to mention," Clifton said, raising a finger in the air. "Whilst the Norman and Anglo-Saxon races finally merged into the Englishman we know today, it took a number of generations beyond the Norman Conquest for the original inhabitants to accept the newcomers. This reluctance is a common trait of human nature and the basis for the nativist movement from which Baltimore has suffered immensely in recent years."

"That's interesting, and it's something I know very little about," Laura responded. "Please tell me all about nativism, since we have a quiet afternoon to pass, warmed by good company and a nice fire in the fireplace. It may even prevent William from falling asleep in his chair." Clifton laughed and began his explanation while William was simply pleased to be the subject of Laura's quip.

"As Anglo-Saxons fought the incursion of Normans, the Nativist movement in America has strongly resisted the immigration of new ethnic groups, particularly Germans and Irish, who generally are Catholics. Over the past decade, the Nativist movement has been embodied in the American Party, the members of which are described as 'Know Nothings.' This is because their standard reply is 'I know nothing' whenever anyone questions their objectionable policies."

"I wondered about that name," Laura said. "I thought it was just because they were hateful, unintelligent people."

"Well, they are that too," Clifton conceded. "Whilst the Nativists dislike foreigners because they speak a different language and have unfamiliar customs, it mainly comes down to economic and political considerations. And there's the similarity between medieval England and present-day Maryland."

"I see where you're headed," William declared as he stood and paced before the fireplace. "The Saxons resented the fact that the Normans took the best land and controlled every aspect of life in the kingdom. The Nativists likewise fear potential loss of employment to foreigners, who will work for less money, and diminished political power, as the new immigrants will vote for their opponents, the Democrats."

"That's it!" Clifton exclaimed with a broad smile.

"What happened to the Know Nothings?" Laura asked. "I was too young to know much about elections until the one held last November, and I don't remember hearing anything about the American Party."

Clifton considered her question for a moment. "The 1850s marked many changes in Maryland's political landscape. The Whigs simply disappeared. Those from the southern counties became Democrats and those from the northern counties became Know Nothings. In the elections from 1854 to 1858, the Know Nothings dominated Maryland politics, entirely so in Baltimore because it was an industrial city with a large immigrant population to rally against. The Know Nothings captured control of the Baltimore City Council in 1854 and, two years later, ten people were killed and dozens wounded during the 1856 election in which they retained control."

"I well remember the 1856 election," William commented, leaning against the mantle. "The father of Jero Wright, my good friend and classmate at Medfield Academy, ran as a Democrat against Thomas Swann, the Know Nothing mayoral candidate."

"Robert Clinton Wright would have been a better mayor," Clifton commented, "Although Swann turned out to be surprisingly effective in creating a paid fire department equipped with steam-powered fire engines and a thirty-box fire alarm system."

"That is surprising!" Laura exclaimed, her face displaying confusion with the notion that a Know Nothing could accomplish anything of value to the public.

"Nevertheless," Clifton continued, "the Know Nothings began to decline nationally in popularity through the latter part of the 1850s. Former president Millard Fillmore ran for president on the American Party ticket in 1856 and did poorly, losing in every state except Maryland. By the 1860 election, the American Party collapsed, the Republicans emerged and the Democrats spilt into several factions."

"From what you have told me about the Know Nothings, their demise was richly deserved," Laura stated emphatically.

William, with a sly smile, responded to her remark. "Actually, Laura, you have not heard the worst of it. The American Party had a working relationship with the vicious street gangs that frequently cause murder and mayhem in the wards of Baltimore."

"In fact," Clifton commented, "the bad reputation of Baltimore for street brawls and senseless rioting dates back to the beginning of the War of 1812 when our city became known as Mob Town across the country."

"I didn't know that!" Laura exclaimed with dismay. "How awful that hooligans have caused our city to be described by that disgusting name."

"But it was richly deserved," Clifton replied. "The affiliation of the American Party with gangs like the Pug Uglies, the Rip Raps, and the Blood Tubs thoroughly corrupted our election process. These gangs are also active in other cities, New York for instance. But in Baltimore City, because of their alliance with the Know Nothings who held political power, the situation was chaotic."

"How were these awful thugs able to influence elections?" Laura asked, amazement resonating in her voice.

"It was really quite easy," William responded. "Ballots with a colorful stripe clearly identifying its origin were distributed by each party to its members in advance of the election. Whenever some poor soul carrying the ballot of another party entered the polling place, usually a saloon, he was pounced upon by gang members who used a shoemaker's awl to punch holes in the wayward voter."

"That's appalling!" Laura exclaimed.

"The gangs had another tactic on election day," William continued. "They grabbed drunks, vagrants, sailors, and farmers off the street and herded them around to the polls, forcing them to vote for the Know Nothing ticket several times over."

"Simply incredible," Laura said, turning in her chair to address her next question to Clifton. "Where were the police while this was occurring?"

"They were entirely ineffective at that time," Clifton replied. "Only in the past year or two have competent, honest men been hired, uniformed, armed, and properly trained by Mayor Brown and Police Commissioner Kane to serve as policemen in Baltimore."

William stepped away from the mantle and stood before Laura, looking into her eyes and maintaining a straight face. "It would be indelicate of me to mention within the hearing of a genteel lady of tender years the really foul tactics that the Blood Tubs employed during those desperate times."

"I'll have you know that I'm eighteen and not that much younger than you are William," Laura cried out indignantly. "I've every right to hear such things!" she exclaimed before realizing that William was teasing her.

"Since you have objected so strenuously, dear Laura, I will enlighten you about the aptly named Blood Tubs. You see, these fine fellows of the Nineteenth Ward did yeoman service for the Know Nothing cause with great regularity on Election Day." William paused for dramatic effect. "By dunking democrats in a large tub of blood and entails from the slaughterhouse."

"They have, by this means, dampened the enthusiasm of many who were inclined to vote against their party," Clifton added. The brothers carefully watched Laura for her reaction.

"Oh, that's horrible," Laura declared, covering both checks with her hands, before falling back in her chair racked by unladylike laughter to the great amusement of William and Clifton.

MOB TOWN

The Officer's Ward was hushed when Whitman and the Prentiss brothers first arrived. As the hospital staff commenced its daytime regimen, an increased level of activity could be heard, but the group around Clifton's bed hardly took notice.

"Our world turned upside down within a mere eight weeks," Clifton said in a muted voice. "All hope for peaceful resolution of the national dilemma was shattered on the twelfth of April by the shots fired in Charleston Harbor."

"The unprovoked attack on Fort Sumter caused great distress in Brooklyn!" Melville exclaimed bitterly.

"Not so in Baltimore," Clifton responded. "A perfect furor of excitement swept through the city that Friday night when the news was received. Despite the late hour, hundreds of people clustered around newspaper and telegraph office bulletin boards to learn the latest intelligence."

"William spoke of that night," Whitman said. "He told me about the circumstances in which he had obtained the news and what happened afterward."

* * *

NEAR THE 53RD REGIMENT ARMORY
BALTIMORE, MARYLAND
APRIL 12, 1861

Due to an overcast sky, the evening dusk turned to darkness earlier than usual. William had started home on horseback after a long day on duty when he noticed a commotion at the telegraph office nearby. Riding in that direction, he saw an excited crowd gathered before its bulletin board.

"What's the news?" he asked a man in the back row who appeared to be tradesman of some sort.

"The Confederates have fired on Fort Sumter," the man nearly shouted. William quickly dismounted, tied his horse to a post, and pushed his way through the milling throng of men and women. Standing in front of the bulletin board, he read the posted dispatch by the dancing light of several swaying lanterns. His heart began to pound within his chest. As he elbowed his way back through the crowd, he could hear differing opinions being expressed. While the rhetoric was becoming heated, no one had yet become violent. He quickly mounted his horse and rode back to Carroll Hall, the building that housed the 53rd Regiment Armory. Running up the steps to the regimental headquarters office, he almost collided with Captain William Murray who had just emerged from the front door.

"Captain Murray, the war has started! In South Carolina! Her state militia is firing its batteries on Fort Sumter! The news was just posted on the telegraph office bulletin board!"

Captain Murray grimaced. "Follow me, William," he replied as he turned on his heel and reopened the door. Within minutes, William was repeating what he knew to a small group of officers.

"This was certain to happen sooner or later!" Lieutenant Herbert exclaimed. "That rascal Lincoln forced the issue by attempting to resupply Fort Sumter by ship. In and of itself, that was a barefaced act of aggression against the South."

"I agree," Captain Murray responded. "But, for the moment, our first responsibility is to Baltimore. The city must be defended and the peace maintained."

William was still grappling with the news that Confederate forces were firing on a Federal fort. "Is it certain that war will erupt between the states?" he asked.

Captain Murray pondered the question, a solemn expression on his face. He was very conscious of the fact that he was the senior officer present.

"My guess is that there will be more confrontations between the federal government and the Confederacy," Captain Murray replied with an authoritative air. "However, it's by no means certain that we will have full-scale war."

"If war comes, it will be a short one!" exclaimed an exuberant junior lieutenant. "The Yankees will be sent skedaddling like whipped dogs with their tails between their legs!" The others, except for William and Captain Murray, reacted to this rash remark with confident laughter.

"In any case, gentlemen, our superiors must be advised of the situation," Captain Murray asserted. "We must recommend that the regiment be immediately assembled and stand ready to confront whatever happens."

A short time later, when the regiment's commanding officer was notified and concurred with the recommendation, a call to arms was ordered for the 53rd Regiment. Messengers were dispatched in all directions to assemble the companies.

* * *

MEDFIELD ACADEMY
NEAR BALTIMORE, MARYLAND
APRIL 18, 1861

After an early breakfast, it was the custom of John Prentiss to take a walk around the nearby village to invigorate his mind and body before immersing himself in scholarly work. Before he had gone but a few steps from the house, Clifton emerged from the front door and called out to his father.

"May I join you in your morning exercise?"

John waved Clifton to his side and they walked along Falls Road. John sensed that his son wanted to discuss something of significance. Clifton, however, said nothing for several minutes, yet John waited patiently for him to speak.

"Father, I hardly slept a wink last night. After you retired, I received a telegraph message informing me that the 7th New York Militia Regiment will respond to President Lincoln's plea for troops to defend Washington. I'll meet the
regiment as it passes through Baltimore in the next few days."

John's steps slowed. He turned his head to look at his son. "I had no doubt
that New York and New England Militias would be the first to answer the call,"
John said in a thoughtful voice. "However, the rapidity of movement is amazing
and without precedence."

"The president requires troops immediately to protect the National Capital
and quell the insurrection. There's not a moment to lose!" Clifton exclaimed.

"Mr. Lincoln must take every action necessary to preserve the Union. If the
7th Regiment has been called to arms, you must respond. It's your duty to do
so. However, I'm concerned that you serve as a private in the ranks. You're an
educated man and should seek an officer's commission."

"I appreciate your compliment, but the truth is that I'm almost entirely un-
schooled as a soldier. William knows much more than I do from his tenure in
the Maryland Guard."

"But you also have militia experience!"

"I'm embarrassed to admit that I joined the prestigious 7th Regiment of New
York Militia for purely social reasons last year while in Brooklyn," Clifton replied. "A member of the Lefferts family, Melville's employer, invited me to join
and I could not refuse. The few occasions that I was on the drill field equipped
me with only the most rudimentary skills."

"That may be true, but many gentlemen with no more experience than you
have will be clamoring for commissions."

"No, Father, I must remain a private and learn to be a soldier if I'm ever to provide
good service to my country," Clifton said, his face set with determination.

"As you wish, but keep yourself open to the opportunity when it arises, as it
surely will."

"Frankly, I'm much more concerned with the fate of the nation," Clifton
responded. "President Lincoln has issued a call to the colors for seventy-five
thousand volunteers from states not in secession. I firmly believe that if enough

good men come forward now, short work can be made of the Rebellion with a minimum of bloodshed."

"Those Southern states must be quickly returned to the fold," John agreed. "A long, drawn-out conflict would be costly and preclude any possibility of reconciliation."

John visibly shuttered as he realized that his son, perhaps all of his sons, might be going to war. The two men continued walking, each immersed in his thoughts.

"I truly fear for William," Clifton declared. "His closest associates are his fellow militiamen, and they're all rabid secessionists."

"Amidst the complexities of these times, men have sought to join militias in which they share a common political viewpoint," John said. "You have both done so!"

"That's true," Clifton conceded.

"Please understand that I share your concern regarding William's misplaced loyalties," John stated. "I also recognize that some of the Southern influence on William comes from within my household. Laura fails to comprehend the danger implicit in dissolution of the Union. Even Sarah seems ambivalent about convictions once held dear. In any case, William is a grown man. We must trust in his good judgment and pray that he doesn't do anything rash."

"Then pray that William stays in Baltimore!" Clifton exclaimed. "Rumors abound that many men have already slipped across the Potomac to join the Confederate Army. They're deserting their state and their families. It's treason, pure and simple."

"William's devotion to principle is just as strong as yours and should be respected accordingly!"

"Oh, Father, you naively trust that relations between the North and South will not deteriorate any further. William stands on the brink of making a terrible mistake. You must try to talk some sense into his head!"

Having walked completely around the small village, Clifton and his father stood before the doorstep of the family home.

"I've much to do before my regiment passes through town," Clifton said, unexpectedly choked with emotion.

John clasped his son's shoulders. Tears brimmed in his eyes. "God bless you, son."

* * *

In the afternoon, news was received in Baltimore that the Virginia legislature had passed an Ordnance of Secession. Even with the necessity that it be ratified by the voters on the twenty-fourth of May, in the minds of many people, there was no longer any question what Virginia would do. Virginia would leave the Union. And if Virginia seceded, those same people believed that it was incumbent upon Maryland to follow her sister state into the Confederacy.

The passions of the people of Baltimore were unleashed for a second time in so many days. They stormed into the streets in large numbers to loudly proclaim their allegiances and denounce any and all persons who disagreed. Hurrahs for the Southern Confederacy and Jeff Davis were heard from the state's rights clubs where they flew the Stars and Bars and the South Carolina palmetto flag. The Union clubs initially flew the Stars and Stripes over their halls, but soon pulled them down and substituted Maryland banners of black and yellow. Nevertheless, their speakers riled against the treason and treachery of those who would dissolve the Union.

* * *

53RD REGIMENT ARMORY
BALTIMORE, MARYLAND
APRIL 19, 1861

William arrived for duty at the regimental armory just before eight o'clock in the morning. He was told to immediately report to his company commander. Within minutes, William knocked on the doorframe of Captain Murray's office. "Sir, I received an order to report to you."

"Yes, William, come in please." Captain Murray inserted an official dispatch into a leather case, placed it on the desk before him, and sat back in his chair. "Do you know George Booth of the Independent Grays?"

"Yes, sir, I do," William replied as he acknowledged Private Booth who was standing before the captain's desk.

"Good," Captain Murray said. "Step forward and stand beside Private Booth to receive your orders."

"Senior officers of the regiment intend to stay abreast of what is happening in Baltimore City," Captain Murray began. "For this, we need eyes and ears on the streets. It would be imprudent to send junior officers or sergeants to gather the required intelligence, as they are too conspicuous. However, lowly privates on such a mission would not attract much attention. You two have been selected for this task because you are bright young fellows who know how to obey orders. We are correct in that assumption, aren't we?" Captain Murray inquired with a slight smile on his face.

"Yes, sir," the privates replied in unison.

"Very good," Captain Murray responded. "Here's the situation. The Federals sent a number of soldiers through Baltimore yesterday, causing some excitement when the cars were hauled along Pratt Street from the President Street Depot to Camden Station. There was a good bit of jeering from onlookers, but no real violence. However, we have received word that more Northern militia troops will be making the passage through Baltimore today. Your task will be to closely monitor the situation in the streets and provide reports to me. I must be forewarned in the event that our regiment is called out to restore order."

Captain Murray looked each private in the eye to be sure that he fully comprehended what was being said. "You will reconnoiter the streets between the two aforementioned railroad stations to gain a sense of the public attitude. You are being sent in uniform, but not under arms. This will neither provoke the Federals nor give the police or populace the idea that the militia has already been called out. Your uniforms are well-recognized by local people as those of Baltimore militia, so you won't be mistaken for Northerners. I'm sending two other privates with you to serve as couriers. You will send verbal reports to me by these couriers when and if you observe anything that suggests organized resistance to the movement of Federal troops though Baltimore. Or if you discern that the unbridled passions of the crowd are becoming such that a riot could easily ensue. In either case, you will report this information to me forthwith. I expect you to be diligent in your observations and to refrain from involvement in anything untoward. Is that understood?"

"Yes, sir," they replied, again in unison.

* * *

William, George, and the two couriers strolled around the streets for the next two hours, gauging the mood of the milling crowd. While a number of people were exhibiting an increased level of excitement, nothing indicated that anything of a planned nature was afoot.

Standing at the tracks embedded in Pratt Street, William asked George if he knew why the locomotives didn't simply pull the cars from one station to another, rather than having the cars individually hauled between stations by teams of horses.

"My Pa told me that goes back a long way," George said. "The teamsters got a municipal ordnance passed that locomotives couldn't operate on streets within Baltimore City."

"And here I figured the reason was that hissing steam and screeching locomotive wheels might scare horses and make them bolt," William said, shaking his head in disbelief. Seeing the amused look on George's face, he quickly added, "But most likely it was done just so the teamsters would get paid for transferring cars."

"Take this one, for instance," George continued, pointing at the tracks beneath their feet. "A rail car traveling from Philadelphia to Washington gets unhooked from a Philadelphia, Wilmington, and Baltimore locomotive at the President Street Depot. It's then hauled on these rails by a team of horses to Camden Station on the other side of town where it's hooked to a Baltimore and Ohio locomotive for the remainder of the trip to Washington."

William laughed. "That has always seemed silly to me," he said while the other two privates nodded in agreement.

The four young men sauntered down the street. Two were dressed in the blue uniform of the Maryland Guard and the other two were attired in the cadet-gray uniform of the Independent Grays. Believing the boys to be off-duty Baltimore militia soldiers without a care in the world, no one paid any particular attention to them.

As they approached the President Street Depot at half past ten, a Philadelphia, Wilmington, and Baltimore locomotive pulling passenger cars loaded with Federal troops lumbered into the station. A large crowd of Southern sympathizers was gathered on President Street to jeer the arriving soldiers. William and George appraised the situation and dispatched the first courier to report that the 6th Massachusetts Militia Regiment had arrived to a noisy reception. William noted that the Massachusetts militiamen wore long blue coats with gold-fringed epaulets and very distinctive shako type hats with large brass shields on the front.

Within a short time, eight of the cars, each hauled by a team of horses, departed at a rapid pace for Camden Station on tracks that ran between rows of residences, small shops, and substantial places of commerce. William and George, with their remaining courier trailing behind them, began walking in the same direction.

"Oh damnation, there's trouble ahead!" William exclaimed as they approached the Pratt Street intersection with Gay Street. The boys could plainly see that a group of men had commandeered a cartful of sand and were dumping its contents on the tracks, blocking the last two cars that had not yet passed.

"Let's get there quick," George said as the three boys began to run the remaining distance to the intersection.

"And there's even more trouble!" exclaimed William as they observed another bunch of rowdies dragging old ship anchors and chains from a nearby chandlery onto the pile of sand to further barricade the tracks. That accomplished, the crowd began to loudly hurrah for Jefferson Davis, South Carolina, and secession as they milled about the obstruction, admiring their handiwork. The commotion attracted even more men to join in the ruckus.

William turned to the remaining courier and grabbed him by the shoulders. "Get back to the armory quick and tell Captain Murray that the Pratt Street tracks are now obstructed and that the crowd is increasing in size and hostility by the minute."

The young private dashed off to deliver the message. George and William continued to move about in the excited throng steadily transforming itself into an unruly mob. As William and George watched, the teamsters of the two blocked cars unhitched the horses and attached them to the opposite ends for a return trip to the President Street Depot. While this was being accomplished, verbal abuse and occasional stones were hurled through the windows and doors at the Massachusetts militiamen. As soon as the teams were rehitched, the two cars began moving in the reverse direction.

The two privates were swept along in the rambunctious crowd that closely trailed the retreating cars. "The situation is becoming chaotic," William yelled to George, trying to make himself heard over the raging noise of the crowd.

"You're right about that," George replied. "I think they're going to do violence to these Yankees real soon."

At the President Street Depot, they watched the cars being vacated and the remaining troops formed into a column, surrounded by the howling mob. Suddenly, another crowd of hooting, shouting men surged from a side street into the turmoil. The leader of the arriving horde furiously waved a flag. It was the new Confederate Stars and Bars.

Company C of the 6th Massachusetts Volunteer Militia, under the command of Captain Follansbee, was at the head of the Federal column as the march began. They had gone but a short distance beyond the intersection of President and Fawn Streets when a shower of rocks began falling on the ranks. As the column turned left onto Pratt Street, they were ordered to march double-quick, which infuriated the rowdies attempting to block its advance. Shouts of protest and vilification were heard as the column crossed the Jones Falls Bridge.

Bam—bam—bam. William yanked his head in the direction of the shots and saw a man firing his pocket revolver into the Federal ranks. Two soldiers fell in the tightly packed column. Instantly, the nearest file of Union soldiers wheeled about and brought their muskets up to their shoulders. William turned and shoved George ahead of him. "Quick, let's get out of here," he shouted.

A ragged volley discharged behind them, blue-white smoke billowing out over the crowd as several of its number collapsed to the ground clutching their wounds, crying out in surprise and pain. The soldiers quickly rejoined the still-moving Federal column. Again, the crowd surged in close to its flanks, bellowing in rage over the exchange of gunfire, blaming only the intruders from the North for the bloodshed. Likewise, the inexperienced Massachusetts soldiers were furious at the attacking mob. A bloodbath in the streets was imminent with potential casualties on both sides many times those that had already occurred.

"Let's get past the column and back to the armory," William shouted to George. "It's too dangerous out here."

"Lead the way. I'm right behind you," George replied in an excited voice. The two young Maryland militiamen began fighting their way through the crowded street to a position where they could observe the front ranks of the Federal column. Ahead of it, the raucous mob carrying the Confederate flag howled with delight and derision that the Northern soldiers were forced to follow the secessionist flag in their headlong flight to Camden Station.

"Here comes the mayor," a chorus of rioters shouted as George W. Brown, the highly respected mayor of Baltimore forced his way through the packed bodies of the crowd. Holding out his right hand to grasp that of Captain Follansbee, Mayor Brown introduced himself and offered assistance. It was gratefully accepted. Mayor Brown marched forward at the side of the Massachusetts officer, his presence quelling the violence of the mob in their path. However, the column of soldiers behind them was subjected to greater attack, as the teeming masses grew bolder. It was a frantic melee as the excitement-crazed mob pressed in against the fast-moving column of soldiers.

"Watch out, William. They're about to shoot again," George called out.

"I see them."

The two boys shoved past rioters who were shaking their fists and shouting at the top of their lungs, away from two well-dressed gentlemen pushing through the crowd with pistols drawn and pointed skyward. When several rows back from the front edge of the teeming masses, the men raised their right arms over the heads of the crowd and pointed their revolvers at the blue ranks. Each wildly fired six shots as fast as he could cock the hammer and pull the trigger. The reaction from the Massachusetts troops was immediate. Within seconds, a volley of musket fire raked the dense wall of rioters, dropping several to the ground and splattering those around them with blood. The noise was deafening in the street jammed with angry Baltimoreans and the fleeing column of Northern soldiers. The crush of bodies against one another and the screeching vehemence of the crowd was enough to deprive many of reason and drive them to excess. Just several paces from William, a rioter jerked the sword from an officer's hand and ran him through with it. Another rowdy grabbed a musket from a soldier who had just fired it and clubbed a nearby soldier who was loading his musket.

While it seemed that the city had gone mad, not all citizens of Baltimore were consumed with hatred for the Northern troops. Police and compassionate citizens were able to pull several wounded soldiers into the doorways of stores and residences where they were sheltered from the rampaging mob.

As William pressed through the agitated crowd, he saw a gentleman snatch the flagstaff from the Massachusetts color bearer and rip the cloth from it. While making off with the torn flag, he was downed by a musket ball passing through both thighs. As the gentleman fell to the ground, William recognized him. It was Francis X. Ward, the 1st Sergeant in Company F of the Maryland Guard. William and George pushed their way over to where Ward lay on the ground, grabbed him by both arms, and dragged him off the street to the entrance of a small alley. Two members of the Maryland Guard in civilian clothes arrived to help, allowing William and George to continue on their way back to the armory. As they left the alley, the jostling, angry mob swept them along until an eddy of people moving in a contrary direction enabled the boys to force their way to the edge of the sidewalk. A Northern soldier in the column passing before them was struck in the head by a stone and landed almost at George's feet. He dropped his musket as he fell to the ground. A white-haired gentlemen seized it, raised it to his shoulder, and fired at the passing troops. The closest file of the Federal column stumbled to a stop, faced outward, and delivered a volley into the crowd, striking several citizens nowhere near the man who fired the offending shot.

"Does anyone have a cartridge that would fit this musket?" yelled the old gentleman. George hurriedly retrieved two .58-caliber rifled musket cartridges from his pocket, shoved them into the man's hand, and told him how to reload.

William grabbed George by the arm and angrily pulled him into a nearby doorway. "You damned fool," he shouted into George's ear. "We weren't supposed to get involved. We've got to get out of here!" George was still elated by the surrounding turmoil, but reluctantly agreed. The column, having moved past at the double-quick, provided the boys with the opportunity to dash across the street behind the trailing mob.

Near the intersection of Pratt and Light Street, lumps of coal, loose stones, bricks, and bottles thrown from the upper windows of adjoining houses crashed onto the swirling mass of Federal soldiers and rioters. Adding to the mayhem was the deadly effect of indiscriminate gunfire from the upper veranda of the Maltby Hotel. At that critical moment, Marshall George P. Kane and fifty Baltimore policemen with drawn revolvers rushed in from the direction of Camden Station and pushed the crowd back past the rear of the Federal column. They kept the mob at bay for the remainder of the march to Camden Station.

The bedraggled boys arrived at the armory a short time later and reported to Captain Murray. Within the hour, the 53rd Regiment of Maryland Militia marched to Monument Square in a show of force to calm the city.

The Pratt Street riot had driven the people of Baltimore into a frenzy that threatened to propel Maryland into the Confederacy. Even Baltimoreans firmly against secession were vehemently opposed to the movement of Federal forces through the city.

* * *

Later that day, rail cars packed with soldiers of the 6th Massachusetts departed from Camden Station for the remainder of the journey to Washington. The soldiers were seething with anger and indignation. Colonel Edward F. Jones, commanding officer of the 6th Massachusetts, ordered that window blinds of the passenger cars be closed to prevent further altercations.

As the Baltimore and Ohio locomotive pulling the cars began to pick up speed, a number of boys were running along an embankment beside the track, jeering at the Northern soldiers and hurrahing for the South. Other boys began throwing stones that noisily bounced off the roof and sides of the rail cars. Standing nearby were several men. Among them was Robert W. Davis of the dry-goods firm, Paynter, Davis, and Company on Baltimore Street. He had gone out of town early that morning to look at several acres of land that he was interested in acquiring. Catching the spirit of the moment, he laughingly raised his fist and hurrahed, entirely unaware of the difficulties that had occurred within the city. His motion caught the attention of two Massachusetts militiamen standing at the open door of the last rail car.

One of the soldiers raised his musket to his shoulder. "Don't shoot any of them young boys," the other soldier said. "They don't know no better."

"But that old secessionist with his fist in the air sure does," said the first soldier as he took deliberate aim.

A shot rang out and Mr. Davis lurched backward and fell to the ground. His associates gathered around his body and heard him utter his last words, "I am killed."

* * *

ARMORY SQUARE HOSPITAL
WASHINGTON, D.C.
JUNE 24, 1865

Mosquito nets hung from hooks in the high whitewashed ceiling over each bed and were tied back, giving the appearance of a towering row of tents running the length of each side of the ward. Beneath the panoply, hospital staff cared for the patients and accomplished housekeeping duties. As general visitation hours were scheduled later in the day, there were no other visitors in the ward.

"I knew that the rowdies of Baltimore had a propensity for mayhem, but it was extremely disturbing for me to learn that many tradesman and gentlemen of the professional class participated in the lawlessness," Melville said.

"The people of Brooklyn were outraged when they heard the gruesome details of the disgraceful Pratt Street riot."

This last remark caught the interest of Whitman who had resided in Brooklyn in spring of 1861. "You're quite right, Mr. Prentiss, in your assessment of the distress experienced in our town over the riotous behavior of Baltimoreans."

Melville did not immediately respond and appeared reluctant to concur with the opinion voiced by the poet. Whitman smiled as he recognized Melville's predicament and directed his next remark to John. "In fact, the reaction was equally rash by many influential persons and journals throughout the North. Horace Greeley of the *New York Tribune* called for Baltimore to be burned to the ground and *Harper's Weekly* stated that Baltimore must be secured either as a city or as a ruin. I completely agreed with them at the time."

"Without a doubt, the violence displayed during the riot was appalling," John replied. "Several regular army officers of my acquaintance in California were convinced by this event that a war between the states was inevitable. On the heels of President Lincoln's call for volunteers and Virginia's Ordinance of Secession, they could accommodate no other conclusion. Officers from Southern states, who hadn't already done so, resigned their commissions and departed for their homes."

Whitman directed an inquisitive look at Clifton. "I would assume that emotions in Baltimore remained highly elevated?"

"The aftermath of the Pratt Street riot was pure bedlam," Clifton replied quietly. "Militia companies within the city were under arms at their armories and other militias from all over the state soon arrived to aid in the defense of Baltimore. Citizens gathered in Monument Square as they have always done in times of peril and excitement. Fortunately, the presence of the 53rd Regiment, the first to be called out, pacified the crowd and prevented further civil unrest. Colonel Benjamin Huger of South Carolina, who had just resigned from the United States Army, was appointed as the new regimental commander. The city council appropriated a half-million dollars for the defense of the city to be used at the discretion of the mayor. Local banks made the money available within two hours."

"Was there a general mobilization of the citizenry?" Whitman inquired. "It seems to me that I heard something about that."

"Yes," Clifton replied. "A call was put out for citizen volunteers and fifteen thousand Baltimoreans responded, armed with pitchforks, pistols, knives, and old fowling pieces. The sounds of fifes and drums could be heard throughout the city. Railroad bridges were burnt or placed under strong guard so that no further trainloads of Federal soldiers could enter the city. Telegraph lines were cut, severing all communications with the North."

"Did William participate in this perfidious conduct?" Melville asked, his tone distasteful.

"The Maryland Guard was involved in accomplishing these tasks," Clifton replied sadly. "This circumstance completely alienated William and I. We hardly spoke a civil word during that hectic time."

"I heard that Mayor Brown and Governor Hicks negotiated an agreement with President Lincoln that no more Northern troops would be marched through Baltimore," John stated, raising an eyebrow inquisitively.

"That's correct," Clifton answered. "However, as soon as this agreement was achieved, we learned that substantial Federal forces arrived by rail cars at Havre de Grace at the mouth of the Susquehanna River and embarked on a steamboat bound for Annapolis. With the state capital in Federal hands, Northern troops could be transported to Washington without going through Baltimore."

* * *

MEDFIELD ACADEMY
NEAR BALTIMORE, MARYLAND
APRIL 21, 1861

Clifton dressed in his New York State Militia uniform for the trip to meet the 7th Regiment at Annapolis to affirm that he was not intimidated by the recent riot. His attire consisted of a gray infantry frock coat, forage cap, and trousers. He packed a small carpetbag with a few personal things and bade farewell to his father, Sarah, and Laura. Elijah conveyed him into Baltimore City in the family carriage and dropped him off at his favorite club to say goodbye to a number of friends. When he began walking toward the train station an hour later, no one on the streets took special notice of him or recognized the origin of his uniform.

As Clifton rounded a corner into Monument Square, he came face-to-face with several soldiers of the Maryland Guard, dressed in their blue class-D fatigue uniforms. One of them was William, carrying a Model 1855 Springfield rifled musket at right shoulder shift.

The brothers stood staring at one another, the stark difference in their uniforms declaring that they had chosen opposite sides in the looming conflict. Their facial expressions were a mixture of shock and dismay. After a moment, Clifton brushed by William and resumed his fast pace.

* * *

During the confrontation, Clifton was wearing a gray uniform and William was dressed in a blue uniform. Ironically, within a few months, regiments raised in the North were required to wear the regulation blue of the United States Army and regiments from Southern states adopted uniforms in various shades of gray.

* * *

Sarah sat at her dressing table in the master bedroom, brushing her long hair, an important ritual before retiring for the night. She was reflecting on the happenings of the day and contemplating what she hoped to accomplish the next. This moment of tranquility abruptly ended, however, when her husband entered the room and sat down heavily on the bed.

"What difficult and distressing times these are!" John exclaimed. "Confederates fire on Fort Sumter, so President Lincoln calls for volunteers to put down the Rebellion. This proclamation carries Virginia out of the Union. Two days later, Federal troops are attacked by a mob in the streets of Baltimore. In our own family, Clifton has gone this day with the 7th Regiment to the relief of Washington whilst William and his comrades obstruct the movement of Federal troops.

What an awful turn of events in each instance. God only knows where it will end."

Sarah moved quickly across the room and sat down on the bed beside her husband. She put her arm around him and leaned against his shoulder. He embraced her in return. "It's all so very frightening to me," she said with sadness in her voice. "Everything seems to be coming apart at the seams. Oh, John, I'm so afraid for our country and for our family."

John tightened his arm around Sarah. "I'd hoped that there would be peaceful resolution to the dispute between the states, but events seem to be driven by factors beyond anyone's control," John bemoaned. "It's like a runaway locomotive careening down the track, about to derail, and nobody can stop it."

"Despite recent events to the contrary, my perception remains that Maryland, whilst Southern in culture, is not truly inclined toward secession," Sarah responded. "Most people view with disfavor the men of the deep South who have renounced their ties to the Union."

"That's true," John agreed. "But underlying it all is the evil institution of slavery. I don't believe that resolution of this problem can be easily achieved."

"As you know, I was born and raised on Nantucket Island amidst a strong tradition of abolitionist sentiment," Sarah stated softly. "I've always deplored slavery, but not necessarily the people who practice it. My years of living in Maryland have taught me that there are slaveholders who treat their slaves with benevolence and kindness, but these are generally household slaves. I have no doubt that many field slaves on large plantations are treated terribly. My heart breaks for slave families who are cruelly split apart on the whim of an arrogant and indifferent owner. Fortunately, slavery is a declining institution. It's morally reprehensible. However, the federal government should not force the elimination of slavery on the Southern people. They will inevitably come to this decision on their own in due course."

"I must say, Sarah, that your position on this matter has greatly softened, but your friendship with Southerners cannot allow acquiescence to what is simply wrong."

"What is morally wrong in our view is not necessarily morally wrong in the view of others," Sarah stated. "We see this circumstance within our own family.

Laura arrived as a young child and grew up in Baltimore. She is more Southern in viewpoint than many who are native born. William's heart is clearly with the South. Both are loved ones, and I do not want to lose them."

"I too dread that possibility," John said, unhappiness creeping into his voice. "For the first time in my life, I feel that my intellectual powers have failed me. I have no idea what can be said or done to dissuade them from their disloyalty."

"Over the past six weeks, we have been battered by event after event that pushes our nation to the brink of war with itself," Sarah said, her expression foreboding.

"Your fears are completely justified," John replied. "The president's call for volunteers is seen by many Marylanders and Virginians as a demand that they put kinsmen to the sword and their homes to the torch."

"Then it's no longer an issue of union or disunion, but a question of invasion and self-defense," Sarah commented. "In their eyes, the president of the United States has declared war on their brethren."

"I've prayed that Maryland and Virginia remain neutral," John said. "If either or both secede, the war will surely be fought on this soil."

Sarah put her head back on John's shoulder. They sat on the bed with their arms entwined.

"Something else has been bothering me," John said. "I recently received a letter from a relative in Massachusetts accusing me of having sympathy with the Southern Rebellion. I informed him in no uncertain terms that I am proud to be among the honorable fraternity of good Union people in Baltimore. Moreover, I told him that Unionists constitute a decided majority in Maryland and at least a respectable minority in the Monumental City, or 'Mob Town' as he chose to call Baltimore."

"Please, dear husband, do not let such an absurd accusation offend you. Consider the source and pity him. You are a man of great knowledge and character, a visionary not swayed by popular emotion, but guided by intellect and principle."

Sarah looked lovingly into her husband's eyes. "You are a man to be cherished and admired, as I certainly do. Your relative who wrote that silly letter has always been jealous of your many accomplishments. You abundantly demonstrated during your eight-year tenure as president of Baltimore College that education may be effectively conducted without resort to corporal punishment. It was a bold and novel concept to reject the use of the rod and all physical infliction as a means of scholastic discipline. You justly deserve the widespread recognition that you've received as the first prominent educator to prove its practicality."

CALL TO THE COLORS

ARMORY SQUARE HOSPITAL
WASHINGTON, D.C.
JUNE 24, 1865

Bright morning sunlight reflected off the whitewashed interior of the ward, making everything appear vivid against the austere background. The clarity of vision achieved by this radiance sharpened the senses of the ward's inhabitants, even those in the weakest condition, as they awaited a bedside visit by their physicians and nurses. Doctor Bliss had exempted Major Prentiss from treatment that morning due to his bereavement and visitors.

"Were you successful in rendezvousing with your regiment at Annapolis?" Whitman asked.

"Indeed I was," Clifton replied. "But I now wish that I had immediately gone to New York when I first received the telegraph calling me to duty. I would have greatly preferred departing from the 7th Regiment Armory at Tompkin's Market with the rest of the lads."

"I was in New York when the citizens bid farewell in grand style to the 7th Regiment," Whitman declared. "April nineteenth dawned most auspiciously. Many New Yorkers knew that it was the anniversary of a date made illustrious by an earlier generation of militiamen on Lexington Green. The weather was magnificent, more like a summer than a spring day. Offices and stores closed as the whole city turned out to wish the 7th Regiment God speed. I was part of the large and boisterous crowd that lined the streets to cheer our boys as they marched to the train station for embarkation."

"Were people in New York aware of the difficulties in Baltimore?" John asked with a quizzical expression.

"Yes," Whitman replied. "We heard news of the insurrection several hours beforehand. It added much to the excitement of the moment. The very thought that the 7th Regiment would force its way through 'Mob Town' at bayonet point thrilled everyone!"

* * *

The original orders received from Lieutenant General Winfield Scott directed that the 7th Regiment proceed from New York to Washington by rail. However, when their train reached Philadelphia, the president of the Philadelphia, Wilmington, and Baltimore Railroad informed Colonel Marshall Lefferts, the regiment's commanding officer, that passage by way of Baltimore was impossible as secessionists had destroyed numerous railroad bridges and miles of track. Colonel Lefferts immediately shifted his attention to other possible routes and determined that two alternatives, both by water, were open to him. One was to sail directly up the Potomac River and the other was to transit the Chesapeake Bay to Annapolis, then complete the journey by rail or on foot. He thought it likely that Rebel batteries along the Virginia side of the Potomac would prevent his passage up the Potomac to Washington, so Colonel Lefferts chartered the streamer *Boston* for a voyage directly to Annapolis. The charter and provisioning of the vessel was accomplished with drafts drawn on his New York firm.

Brigadier General Benjamin Franklin Butler and the 8th Massachusetts Militia, having arrived in Philadelphia the night before the 7th Regiment, also sought to reach Washington at the earliest moment. He planned a journey by rail to Havre de Grace where he would seize the ferryboat *Maryland* and steam to Annapolis. Additionally, General Butler desired to bring the 7th Regiment under his command. Colonel Lefferts summarily rejected this overture as the governor of

New York granted his authority and he did not regard himself subject to the orders of a Massachusetts militia brigadier. Further, the 7th Regiment commander suspected that the ferryboat had already been either barricaded or removed by the secessionists.

With a thousand soldiers of the 7th Regiment crowded into every available space, *Boston* cast off her lines the following day and steamed down the Delaware River. She cruised overnight and all the next day before arriving after midnight off the mouth of the Severn River. The engines were slowed to make steerageway as *Boston* circled in the bay, awaiting daylight. On the twenty-second day of April, the steamboat entered the harbor of Annapolis as the fog lifted, revealing a frigate flying the Stars and Stripes with ports opened and guns run out. *Boston* was hailed and instructed to "let go her anchor," which was promptly accomplished, under the guns of the renowned USS *Constitution*, the school ship of the United States Naval Academy. Also present in the harbor was the ferryboat *Maryland*, stuck hard and fast on a mud bank, her decks crowded with frustrated soldiers of the 8th Massachusetts Militia Regiment.

Colonel Lefferts, after conferring with the Captain of "Old Ironsides," ordered *Boston* to assist *Maryland*. A tow hawser was attached to the grounded ferryboat and *Boston* commenced to tug at full engine power, but to no avail. While this was occurring, Colonel Lefferts and several of his officers went ashore and were met by the mayor of Annapolis who formally protested against the landing of troops. The colonel responded that he was obliged not only to land his troops, but to force his way through to Washington and that any effusion of blood would be the responsibility of those who opposed him.

Later that afternoon, *Boston* pulled alongside a wharf to disembark the 7th Regiment. Standing at the foot of the gangplank to greet his fellow militiamen was Private Clifton Prentiss of Company K. After the 7th Regiment and its baggage were off-loaded, *Boston* made three round trips to the grounded ferryboat to bring ashore the soldiers of the 8th Massachusetts, including a livid General Butler.

The 7th Regiment made preparations for an early march the following morning through hostile country, not knowing if Washington had already fallen. At this juncture, a messenger from General Scott arrived with news that the situation in

Washington was critical and that the president was extremely anxious that the 7th Regiment hasten to the relief of the capital. Another messenger soon arrived suggesting to Colonel Lefferts that it would also be desirable for him to reopen the railroad connection with Washington.

Two companies of the 8th Massachusetts were already at work on this task. Besides mending track, they discovered a damaged locomotive locked in a shed and set to work repairing it. One of the men of the 8th Massachusetts had worked for the company that originally built the locomotive. He and his fellow militiamen soon had it in running order.

At four o'clock the following morning, the advance guard of the 7th Regiment departed from the depot at Annapolis. Two open-platform cars were placed ahead of the locomotive. The first mounted a howitzer loaded with grape shot, manned by a gun crew and a dozen soldiers. The second contained ammunition for the howitzer and more soldiers. It was anticipated that a battle would be fought on the road to Washington given the already demonstrated belligerence of the Maryland populace.

An officer on the first platform car gave hand signals to the engineer while a sergeant watched for breaks in the track. Behind the locomotive were two passenger cars, each carrying a company of the 7th Regiment. The train ran slowly for three miles until reaching a location where the track was broken so badly that repair was required. The locomotive was unhitched and sent back, while drag ropes were attached to the platform cars so that the soldiers could haul them along the track. As its skirmishers plunged into the surrounding woods to protect their flanks and locate removed rails, the advance guard temporarily mended the road by putting back rails found nearby.

At first light, Colonel Lefferts marched along the tracks from Annapolis with the main body of the 7th Regiment under an increasingly hot sun, catching up with the advance guard by midday. They acquired a third platform car and loaded it with rails, chairs, timbers, and spikes taken from sidings to repair track as they went. Near Millersville, the regiment found a short railway bridge that had been burned. Within hours, trees were felled and hewed into timbers, new track laid, and the bridge fully rebuilt, allowing the 7th Regiment to press

onward. Throughout the evening and the moonlit night, the regiment perse-
vered, spared the ravages of the scorching sun, but approaching exhaustion
from the hard march and heavy labor.

Just as dawn was breaking, they emerged from the woods and swamps at Annapolis Junction, finding it in the hands of the federal government. A few hours
later, a train arrived and soon the entire regiment was aboard the cars bound
for Washington. Unbeknownst to them, rumors abounded that the 7th Regiment had been cut to pieces in Maryland and that the capital, garrisoned only
by the 6th Massachusetts and a few regular troops, was about to be seized by a
superior Confederate force.

When Colonel Lefferts observed the anxiety and alarm exhibited by Washington's loyal citizens, he marched his regiment down Pennsylvania Avenue to
the White House with the regimental band playing and its flags snapping in the
breeze. Inspired by the multitude of cheering Washingtonians lining the side-
walks, the soldiers of the 7th Regiment put aside their weariness and displayed
a very soldierly appearance. At the White House, a smiling President Lincoln
and Secretaries Cameron and Seward greeted them as they passed in review.
Mrs. Lincoln presented the regiment with a magnificent bouquet of flowers
from the White House conservatory.

The 7th Regiment was quartered in the chamber of the House of Representatives as the 6th Massachusetts was already housed in the Senate chamber. When
the 8th Massachusetts arrived a few days later, they settled in under the unfinished dome of the Rotunda. Musket butts rang on marble floors as 7th Regiment
soldiers in their neat gray uniforms, spotless white belts, and shining bayonets
created temporary living spaces on the House floor and in its lobbies, galleries,
and committee rooms. From necessity, the regiments marched three times a day
to Willard's, Brown's, and the National Hotels for meals.

On the afternoon of April twenty-sixth, the 7th Regiment of New York Militia was mustered into the service of the United States for a term of thirty
days during a stately ceremony before the east portico of the Capitol building. Major Irvin McDowell, a regular army officer, administered the oath in
the presence of President Lincoln, the secretary of state, the secretary of war,

and other dignitaries. Each officer and man raised his right hand and took the oath, repeating, clause by clause, the solemn obligation to be faithful soldiers of the United States. In the course of the proceedings, Major McDowell commented on the intelligence and soldierly appearance of the regiment's members. He stated to one of the captains, "Sir, you have a company of officers instead of soldiers." Those words were prophetic as a substantial number of 7th Regiment privates went on to serve successfully as officers with other regiments during the war.

For the time being, the mission of the 7th Regiment had been accomplished. The nation's capital was saved in the first hour of its greatest peril and the road was opened for Northern regiments to pour into Washington to secure its defense.

* * *

The Pratt Street riot and widespread turmoil within Maryland induced President Lincoln to suspend the writ of habeas corpus along rail lines leading to Washington. This secretive action resulted in the arrest and imprisonment without stated charges of numerous persons deemed sympathetic to Southern secession. Incarceration at Fort McHenry was soon imposed upon Mayor Brown and Police Commissioner Kane of Baltimore, many delegates of the Maryland legislature, and others including John Merryman, a prominent industrialist and militia leader who took part in the destruction of a railroad bridge.

Chief Justice of the United States Roger B. Taney, sitting as a judge of the circuit court for the District of Maryland, received Merryman's petition for a writ of habeas corpus and ruled in *Ex parte Merryman* that only Congress had the power to take this action. President Lincoln ignored the circuit court order and his officers continued to arrest anyone suspected of seditious activity. Congress formally suspended the writ for the president by passing the Habeas Corpus Act of March 3, 1863.

* * *

ARMORY SQUARE HOSPITAL
WASHINGTON, D.C.
JUNE 24, 1865

"This clearly was a very troubled time," John proclaimed. "I was far from home in 1861, so am curious about all of the circumstances. What was the military situation in Baltimore?"

"The noose was drawn tighter," Clifton replied. "On the fifth of May, Federal troops under General Butler's command occupied Relay House on the Baltimore and Ohio Railroad, about eight miles south of the city, cutting the route by which men and supplies were flowing from Baltimore to the Confederacy."

"And how long was it until Butler entered the city?"

"It was but a short time," Clifton replied. "During the evening of the thirteenth of May, a train carrying a thousand Federal soldiers rolled into Camden Station just as a thunderstorm broke. This force consisted of portions of the 6th Massachusetts, 8th New York, and Cooke's Battery of Boston Light Artillery. They marched through deserted streets in driving rain to take possession of Federal Hill, commencing a military occupation of Baltimore, which would continue until the end of the war."

Whitman spoke up in a glum voice. "Sadly, that event triggered yet another unhappy episode within your family."

* * *

MEDFIELD ACADEMY
NEAR BALTIMORE, MARYLAND
MAY 14, 1861

Early morning sunlight illuminated nearby buildings with a golden hue and heralded a new day. John stood before the carriage house, waiting patiently for Elijah to finish harnessing a horse to the family carriage. The unexpected sound of a slamming door caused John and Elijah to look toward the main house. Approaching them at a rapid pace was William, dressed in his Maryland Guard uniform and looking totally distraught. "We've been disarmed and disbanded," he shouted angrily. "Without even a fight!"

"What happened?" John asked, as he did not immediately grasp what William was saying.

"Early this morning, the damned Federals entered our armory and confiscated all our arms under an order from Governor Hicks, that treacherous, conniving turncoat!" William's eyes began to water from his agitation. "Don't you understand? The Maryland Guard and the Independent Grays have been sent home like schoolboys whilst our city has been invaded and occupied by the enemy!"

"Your brother Clifton is presently in Federal service and he is not your enemy. Please keep things in perspective, William. These are most uncertain times, but we must not turn on one another. Peace will prevail if we all remain calm."

"Can't you see what is happening?" William shouted at his father. "We've been invaded. Our laws, our destiny, our liberty are all at stake. Everything is lost if we don't have the right to govern ourselves as free men and Marylanders. We must defend ourselves against the invaders of our state."

John was stunned by the vehemence in William's voice. "Son, please control yourself—don't shout at those who love you."

William stood glaring at his father, trembling with rage, which John mistook as an opportunity to reason with him. "Maryland is part of the United States, and we are all citizens, protected by the Constitution. Our differences can be resolved by peaceful means. Secession is not the answer." William did not respond, so John tried another approach. "If you take up arms against the United States government, you will be guilty of treason."

"I am not a traitor!" William shouted. "We Marylanders are the ones who have been betrayed!"

"Not so," John responded, his tone angry. "Have you forgotten that Maryland men fought bravely for our independence from England to establish the United States? Have you forgotten that during the War of 1812 the Stars and Stripes flew over Fort McHenry, just several miles from here? Have you forgotten that throughout the British bombardment, our flag streamed over the ramparts that glorious night?"

William was livid. "It's not my country's flag that flies this day over Federal Hill and Fort McHenry," he shouted with intense emotion. "The Yankees occupying Baltimore are foreign invaders just like the British. Maryland is a Southern state and true Marylanders will fight to expel any invader that violates our border."

"Then clearly, you are a damned traitor!" his father exclaimed in a loud voice. They glared at one another, belligerence burning in their eyes, an unthinkable circumstance for an otherwise loving father and son. William turned and stalked away.

John was stunned by the sudden estrangement from his youngest son. A look of horror crossed his face—this altercation confirmed that his sons had chosen opposite sides in the inevitable conflict. "No matter what happens, never forget that you and Clifton are brothers," he cried out in anguish. John then spoke to himself as he covered his face with his hands. "Dear God, don't let them forget that they are brothers!"

Elijah witnessed the entire episode, but turned and looked away as he did not wish to intrude on the painful moment.

* * *

It was well after dark when William quietly entered the outbuilding to the rear of Medfield Academy that contained the household cooking facilities. He had not come home for supper that evening to avoid further confrontation with his father and to prevent discovery of what he was about to do.

Elijah was alone in the outbuilding. He had just completed his inspection of the larder, fireplace, and cast iron stove to insure that all was secure. Hearing the door open, he turned and peered into the darkness that cloaked that corner of the room.

He saw who had just entered. "Mr. William, we missed you at supper."

"I'm sorry that I didn't send word, but I wasn't able to be here. In any case, would you be so kind as to gather some vittles for me in a sack. I'm going on a journey and my food supply will be uncertain for a few days."

Elijah stared at William with a frown. It was obvious that the young man was leaving to join the Confederate Army. As this matter affected the tranquility of the Prentiss family, Elijah was emboldened to question William on the matter. "Have you spoken with your father about your plans?" he asked in a firm voice.

"I can't do that, Elijah. This is something that I must do. I will not burden my father anymore than I already have. I simply desire to leave without causing further disruption within the family."

The disapproving look on Elijah's face caused William to continue waffling. "I regret the awful confrontation today, but these are circumstances that I cannot change. I ask that you help, not hinder, my departure, nor inform the family of my intentions."

"Mr. William, I will prepare a parcel of food for you and I will say nothing to anyone about it," Elijah replied. "But I think that you should leave some message for your father rather than simply steal off like a thief in the night. Your father deserves better."

William stared at Elijah, taken back by the condemnation of his conduct by a Negro servant, but recognizing the truth in what was said. "I suppose that I could leave a letter with Laura to give to my father in the morning."

"That would be better than nothing," Elijah said as he turned to gather food for William to take on his journey.

* * *

William rapped lightly on the door of Laura's room. After a moment, the door opened and Laura looked out at William, surprise evident on her face that he would visit at this hour. "Laura, I must speak with you. There is no one else in the family that I can entrust with my plans."

Laura stepped aside to let him enter and then darted back into the threshold to peer down the hall in both directions. She quietly closed the door and turned to face him. "Your father was very upset over his argument with you. Dinner was a bleak affair. The silence was absolutely dreadful."

"We had a terrible disagreement," William conceded. "Father does not respect my views, and I could not endure the things he was saying without responding in kind. In any case, he considers me to be a traitor. He views my loyalty to the South as disloyalty to him."

"You're a patriot, William, a Southern patriot. Of that you can be proud." Laura wrapped her arms around him, hugging him to her breast, as tears welled up in her eyes.

William gently held Laura in his arms but struggled to keep his hands from trembling on her back. He took a breath and reduced his tone to a whisper. "Laura, I have secretly enlisted in an infantry company being formed by Lieutenant Herbert. We leave tonight for Harpers Ferry where Confederate forces are gathering. Captain Johnson is already there with his company from Frederick County, and Captain Murray and a bunch of the boys have gone to Richmond. They'll meet up with us later."

"Oh, William, I'm so afraid for you," Laura said in a plaintive voice as she leaned back away from him, but with her hands still holding his shoulders.

"It may be dangerous, but I will not shirk my duty. I'll defend the principle of states rights against Northern tyranny. That's what the Constitution is all about."

"How will you get to Harpers Ferry?" Laura asked, fear causing her voice to tremble.

"We're going cross country on foot and then take the Baltimore and Ohio Railroad at Sykesville to Harpers Ferry. There are bound to be plenty of Federal guards and detectives on the cars, so we must go now before it gets any worse. We can't take anything but the clothes on our backs—otherwise, it will cause suspicion and we'll be arrested."

"When will you be able to return home?" Laura asked, tears spilling from her eyes.

"Only when the war is over. However long that may be. Until then, every Marylander fighting for the Confederacy will be living in exile."

Laura pulled William to her breast again and hugged him. They clung to each other, both fearful of the many uncertainties ahead, until William regained his composure. "Laura, if I may borrow paper and pen, I'll write a brief note to my father and ask that you give it to him in the morning."

Laura turned and went to her desk, opened a drawer and took out her writing materials. "William, please sit where there's an inkwell," she said as she handed him several sheets of paper, a pen, and envelope.

William spent several minutes writing a message to his father. He briefly explained his actions and asked his father not to judge him too harshly. When finished, he folded the note, inserted it in the envelope, sealed it, and wrote his father's name on the face. William returned to the center of the room and gave the envelope to Laura. They stood facing one another, their eyes locked until Laura sobbed softly. She stepped forward and embraced him. William held her tightly in his arms for a long moment, and then broke away. He stepped to the door, cracked it open, and listened for sounds of movement. Satisfied that all was clear, William stepped into the hall and closed the door noiselessly behind him.

ACROSS THE POTOMAC

John was leaning forward with his elbows on his knees, his hands clasped beneath his chin. "May I assume that Laura delivered William's letter to our father the following morning?" he asked.

"Yes, she did," Clifton replied.

"How was the message received?"

"Sarah later told me that the contents did little to soothe father's pain and disappointment. He blamed himself for not being more effective at curtailing William's allegiance to the South. He had sent William to live and work with Melville and myself in Brooklyn the previous year, hoping that the separation from his Southern friends would broaden his view of the world and introduce him to Northern society."

Melville snorted and leaned back in his chair. "I assure you that his short visit with my family had little effect on William. He couldn't wait to return to Baltimore!"

Clifton spoke quickly as he wanted to prevent Melville from belaboring this point. "Father regretted not being able to convince William that both North and

South were responsible for the disaffection. His heart ached over the fact that his youngest son had voluntarily exiled himself from his state and family."

"The war brought calamity to many families," Whitman observed. "I can see that it was compounded in Border states where allegiance was split. A most unhappy circumstance for everyone involved."

John cleared his voice and spoke directly to Whitman. "Not all of the unhappy events for our family during 1861 occurred in Baltimore. Melville lost his wife, Elizabeth, from childbirth fever and the baby died the following day. Adding to his grief was the loss of his two-year-old son, Thomas, a few months later."

"The tragedy and suffering endured by my family is God's Will and not to be questioned," Melville said sharply, his facial expression tightening as he recited that foundation of his faith. "It's our Christian duty to accept these things as part of God's plan." Despite his best efforts to the contrary, tears formed in his eyes as he struggled to regain control. "But not a day goes by without anguish over the loss of my dear wife, our baby, and son," Melville said in a strained voice.

As quickly as his demeanor had softened, he sat up straight in his chair and glared at his companions. "Enough of this," he said angrily. "We're here to recall the events in William's life, not the misfortunes in mine. And that's what we shall do."

Whitman sat back and contemplated Melville's erratic behavior. He sympathized with the man, although he instinctively disliked him. Seeing Whitman lost in thought, Melville pressed forward. "Mister Whitman, tell us about William's experiences when he first arrived at Harpers Ferry. Was this something that he discussed with you in the short time that you knew him?"

"Yes, in fact he did speak of those times," Whitman replied. "He was proud of the service that he gave to his cause—to his country as he saw it. William was also proud to be a member of the 1st Maryland Infantry Battalion and its successor, the 2nd Maryland Infantry Battalion. He told me that both were commonly known in the Army of Northern Virginia as 'the Maryland Battalion.' The soldiers of the rank and file were mostly high-spirited, beardless boys like William, having great enthusiasm for army life and an ardent devotion to those things that they held dear. A large percentage of them were gentlemen by birth, education, and culture. The most prominent families of the state were represented in the ranks of the Maryland Battalion."

As he spoke, Whitman shifted his gaze between the three Prentiss brothers, and they listened attentively to his every word, although Whitman was well aware of Melville's growing hostility toward him.

"When the companies initially formed at Harpers Ferry, only Company A from Frederick County had arms and these were obsolete Hall's breech loading carbines that had been purchased in Baltimore by Captain Johnson. These weapons were not only inefficient, they were inappropriate for training soldiers in accordance with Hardee's *Rifle and Light Infantry Tactics*, the standard text approved in 1855 by Jefferson Davis, then the United States Secretary of War. Regarding other necessities of camp life, William and his comrades had rushed off from home, fired up with enthusiasm for the Southern cause, with little to sustain them. They had ridden on the cars or walked to Harpers Ferry where they commenced drilling and soldiering. Provisions were plenty, but they had no arms, accoutrements, uniforms, blankets, tents, or cooking utensils—none of the essentials that soldiers must have to take part in a serious campaign."

* * *

ENCAMPMENT OF MARYLAND TROOPS
NEAR HARPERS FERRY, VIRGINIA
MAY 22, 1861

The lushness of the surrounding verdant hillsides radiated the sweet, ripe smell of springtime. As several companies of Maryland infantry marched back and forth across the drill field, the air was filled with the shouted commands of their sergeants and junior officers. They were mostly without arms, except for the Hall Carbines of Company A, and a few old flintlock muskets that had been converted to percussion. The Marylanders were wearing an odd assortment of civilian clothing and, all in all, presented a motley appearance. Only the presence of former militiamen in the ranks provided any semblance of military bearing.

From a small knoll above the field, Captain Bradley Johnson and his wife, Jane, watched the scene below them. Captain Johnson turned to his wife, looking quite melancholy. "Jane, we have the best men that any field commander could ever hope for, but without uniforms, proper arms, and equipment, we simply cannot be an effective force in the field. I fear that our boys will merely become a resource to supply soldiers to regiments from other states. Sadly, this will most likely occur before we have a chance to establish the Maryland Line."

"It's an unfortunate circumstance that Maryland cannot support her sons in the same manner that other states are doing," Jane replied carefully. "Certainly John Letcher, Virginia's governor, has not been timid in supplying his state troops with resources even though their final vote on secession is still two days off."

Captain Johnson laughed bitterly. "I don't think that Governor Hicks of Maryland will be of any help to us. In fact, I think he'll simply become a tool of the Yankees, as he has already clearly shown that inclination. Unfortunately, that makes us orphans without the official support of our state, which is now under the control of the federal government."

The Johnsons stood silently for another few minutes, continuing to watch the Maryland volunteers marching on the drill field. "If our soldiers are ever to be of service to the Southern Confederacy under the Maryland Flag, they must be able to present themselves as a properly equipped military organization," Jane pronounced. Her husband didn't comment. "I believe that I can go to my home state of North Carolina and apply there for arms and equipment for our Marylanders. As you know, my father is a judge and a distinguished former member of Congress. With his help, I believe that I may be able to procure material assistance for a Confederate Maryland Line."

Captain Johnson stared at his wife in disbelief. A look of hope spread across his face. He smiled at her and said, "Mrs. Johnson, you may be the only hope for Maryland. I shall submit a request for advice and assistance in this matter to Colonel Thomas J. Jackson, commanding the Virginia forces at Harpers Ferry."

* * *

On the twenty-fourth day of May, Jane Saunders Johnson, with orders in hand from Colonel Jackson for transportation and safe passage, departed from Harpers Ferry on a railroad journey to Raleigh via Richmond. Two officers of the Maryland Battalion escorted her to provide protection and assistance for the mission. Upon arriving at Leesburg, they discovered that Alexandria was occupied by Federal troops. Returning to Harpers Ferry and thence by way of Winchester, Manassas Junction, and Richmond, Mrs. Johnson and her party finally arrived in Raleigh, North Carolina, during the evening of May twenty-seventh.

The following morning, accompanied by her father, Romulus M. Saunders, she applied to Governor Thomas H. Ellis and the Council of State of North Carolina for arms for her husband and his men. Just prior to the meeting, Judge Saunders suggested to his daughter that she tell her story in the fewest and simplest words possible. She did just that. When recognized by Governor Ellis to speak, the elegant and refined young woman took the floor and made her appeal in a straightforward manner.

"Governor and gentlemen, I left my husband and his comrades in Virginia. They have left their homes in Maryland to fight for the South, but they have no arms, and I have come to my native state to beg my own people to help us. Please give arms to my husband and his comrades, so that he can help you!" With that said, Jane Saunders Johnson sat down and, for a few moments, not a sound could be heard in the council chambers.

"Madam," said a venerable and gray-haired member of the council as he slapped his thigh, "you shall have everything that this state can give." The sentiment was quickly echoed by the governor and the other council members and, after brief deliberation, Mrs. Johnson was informed that she would be supplied forthwith with five hundred Model 1841 Mississippi Rifles with necessary accoutrements, percussion caps, and ten thousand .54-caliber cartridges.

As fate would have it, the constitutional convention of North Carolina was then in session. It was an illustrious body of Carolinians and its members called for a special meeting to be held in the hall of the House of Commons that night. Kenneth Raynor, a former member of Congress, addressed those assembled and paid high tribute to the patriotism and love of liberty that characterized the people of Maryland. And then he paid special tribute to Jane Saunders Johnson. "If great events produce great men, so in the scene before us, we have proof that great events produce great women. One of our own daughters, raised in the lap of luxury, blessed with the enjoyment of all the elements of elegance and ease, had quit her peaceful home, followed her husband to the camp and, leaving him in that camp, has come to the home of her childhood to seek aid for him and his comrades, not because he is her husband, but because he is fighting the battles of his country, against a tyrant."

Thunderous applause by the convention delegates shattered the silence. A substantial contribution of money was made on the spot to Mrs. Johnson for the purchase of additional equipment.

On the twenty-ninth, Mrs. Johnson left Raleigh with her escort, her rifles, and ammunition. At every town and station along the way, people gathered to see the woman who was arming her husband's regiment, and she was overwhelmed with their enthusiasm and support. When her party arrived in Richmond, Governor Letcher provided her with a supply of kettles, hatchets, axes, and other camp equipment. With the donated money in her hands, she ordered a quantity of tents made at once. On the thirty-first of May, she departed from Richmond with her arms, ammunition, and supplies. At Manassas Junction, General Beauregard ordered that she could take any train she might find necessary for transportation to Harpers Ferry.

After an absence of ten days, Mrs. Johnson arrived on the third of June at the rail station in Harpers Ferry riding in a freight car with her crates of rifles and other vital military equipage. A large contingent of Maryland soldiers met her with flags flapping in the breeze and a brass band playing "Dixie's Land." To say the very least, she had thrilled the Confederate army with her courage, devotion, and enthusiasm. Colonel Jackson, with his staff, promptly called on her and thanked her profusely.

But her task was not finished. Mrs. Johnson immediately returned to Richmond to secure cloth for uniforms from the mills that manufactured it for the State of Virginia and had the cloth made into uniforms. On June twenty-ninth, she arrived at the Maryland Battalion campsite near Winchester with tents and complete uniforms, underclothes, and shoes for five hundred men. For these things, she had paid ten thousand dollars, the contribution of enthusiastic North Carolinians and Virginians to equip the sons of Maryland who would fight for Southern independence.

* * *

THE CARY RESIDENCE
BALTIMORE, MARYLAND
JUNE 10, 1861

Tranquility descended on Baltimore as the men who were the most ardent supporters of secession were no longer present to ferment unrest and discontent. Federal Hill was fortified with substantial earthen works, and its heavy guns controlled the city.

The social activities of Baltimore's Southern elite diminished considerably when their best men crossed the Potomac. Without the distraction of parties and other such festivities, the women who were left behind focused their energies on sewing uniforms, gathering medical supplies, and exchanging news from Dixie. They showed their defiance to military occupation by adorning their hats and clothing with the Maryland secessionist colors of red, white, red. Nurses wearing white dresses and carrying infants in red and white garments were arrested and questioned by Federal authorities, as were ladies who crossed the street rather than walk under a United States flag. Despite Federal occupation of the city, not all gatherings of those faithful to the South were eliminated—they were just driven underground.

Hetty and Jenny organized a glee club composed of several enthusiastic young ladies, including Laura Watson, which met weekly in the front parlor of the Cary home. As they sang patriotic songs and exchanged news from the South, the young women sewed garments for the Baltimore boys serving in the Rebel Army. Thus, the social nature of the gathering was secondary to the industry of their nimble fingers and their desire that Maryland would someday be liberated. However, to maintain social decorum and an innocent appearance, light refreshments were served including, on occasion, some very fine apples. These apples had caused the little club to be called *"La Garde de la Pomme d'Or."* Often, at the conclusion of the meeting, Hetty and Jenny would arrange light entertainment in the form of poetry readings and songs to enthuse their group.

Jenny, the musical one in the family, eagerly searched for something new and truly inspirational to express her fervent Southern sentiments for the day's program. As she sat at her piano, she could find nothing that was intense enough to fit the mood of the young women gathered around her, and her despair was becoming quite evident. As usual, her sister Hetty came to rescue.

"I recently read something with wonderful words," Hetty said as she opened a table drawer and extracted a newspaper clipping. "It's a poem by James Ryder Randall, expressing outrage that Federal troops marched through Baltimore and that citizens were killed and wounded as a result."

Hetty read the verses aloud, choking all of the women with emotion as it perfectly articulated their anger and frustration. When she finished, Hetty placed the paper before her sister and said, "Jenny, you must find an air for this!"

Jenny sat at the piano for a full minute, repeating the poem's verses in her mind. "I've got it!" she exclaimed, and began to play *"Lauriger Horatius,"* a favorite college song that had been introduced to her by Burton Harrison, a family friend who had been a student at Yale. The refrain, as printed in the poem, had simply been "Maryland." By making the refrain "Maryland, My Maryland" at the end of each stanza, Jenny fit the heroic words with the traditional tune. The other young women sat spellbound as Jenny's contralto voice sang out the stanzas, and they soon joined in as the words naturally blended with the music. A crowd of people who had been passing on the sidewalk beneath the open window gathered to hear what would become the war anthem "Maryland, My Maryland." Within months, it would be played and sung throughout the South and around the campfires of the Confederate Army.

Hetty was totally absorbed with the birth of this song until she suddenly realized that their enthusiasm had made this moment too conspicuous, which placed the liberties of the entire party in jeopardy. Within minutes, the glee club meeting adjourned and the curtains were tightly closed.

* * *

Only Laura remained after the other women left, as she was engaged in more clandestine activities with the Cary sisters. They adjourned to another room more remote in the house where they packed money, medicines, correspondence, clothing, and supplies of all kinds that would soon be sent across the Potomac to aid the Southern cause. The room also served as a workshop and Laura was carefully finishing details of the Maryland State Seal that adorned one side of a large blue silk regimental flag with white fringe on three edges.

"Let's see how it looks!" Hetty exclaimed. Laura put down her paintbrush amid an array of small paint jars and helped Hetty lift the flag for Jenny to admire.

"It's absolutely beautiful!" Jenny declared, clasping her hands together. "Our soldier boys will be so proud of this battle flag. Laura, you have done a magnificent job!"

"Thank you," replied Laura, blushing deeply with pleasure at the compliment. "You all did such fine work sewing the flag and constructing the composition of the opposite side," Laura said as she and Hetty turned the flag around to reveal the reverse design. Arched across the flag were the words "Presented by the Ladies of Baltimore to the 1st Regiment Maryland Line."

"It's superb, truly brilliant!" Jenny proclaimed as the three young women happily admired their handiwork.

After the flag was folded and put away, Hetty turned to Jenny and their friend and motioned for them to come closer to her. She placed a hand on the shoulder of each and pulled them next to her so they could hear her muted voice. "Laura, we want to let you in on a little secret—well, really a very big secret," Hetty corrected herself, continuing to speak in a conspiratorial tone. "Jenny, Miles, and I are crossing the Potomac within the next few weeks to deliver the uniforms and regimental flag to our friends in Virginia. The journey will be quite dangerous as both the upper and lower Potomac are strictly patrolled by the Yankees."

"Oh my goodness!" Laura exclaimed as her hand flew to her mouth to cover her surprise. Her girlish nature took over and she began asking questions about the plan to run the blockade.

Hetty quickly silenced her. "Laura, it's better that you don't know the details. Don't forget for a minute that the enemy occupies Baltimore. I wish to caution you girls to be very careful in what you say. You just can't tell who might be a spy for the provost marshal's office—a servant in your house, a tradesman at the door, the merchant down the street—all might be paid informants of Yankee detectives, so please be careful in everything that you do and say."

"We'll be careful," Jenny replied, obviously annoyed by her older sister's condescending tone. "I know how important it is that these vital supplies are safely transported to Virginia," she asserted, to reinforce the notion that she was an equal participant in the plot.

"We must be very cautious in our behavior," Hetty said. "We must not draw undue attention to ourselves."

"Why, Hetty, what about the time that you waved a Confederate banner from your upstairs window when Northern troops came marching by?" Laura asked with a smile on her face.

"Well, that was when the invaders first arrived and before I knew that I would be involved in such important work," Hetty replied.

"Perhaps so," Laura said. "However, I have it on good authority that a Federal officer in that column asked his colonel if you should be arrested. They say that the colonel, after glancing up and catching a glimpse of you in your act of defiance, said, 'No, she is beautiful enough to do as she pleases.'"

"Well, that might possibly be true," Hetty replied with a coy smile. The young women, including Hetty, giggled in appreciation of the story.

* * *

The six companies of Maryland infantry formed at Harpers Ferry were under constant pressure from Virginia authorities to organize as a Virginia regiment or be parceled off to other Virginia regiments. Bradley Johnson adamantly opposed this action as he contended that Maryland did not have the opportunity to secede from the Union only because she was occupied. For this reason, he believed that Maryland should be represented in the Confederate

Army, preferably in a rebirth of the Maryland Line, a brigade composed of Maryland infantry, artillery, and cavalry.

Bradley's perseverance was rewarded when Lieutenant Colonel George Deas, Inspector-General of General Joseph E. Johnston's staff, officially mustered the six companies into the service of the Confederacy. Their organization was that of a battalion as they lacked the required ten companies to be designated a regiment. Colonel Arnold Elzey was appointed commanding officer of the 1st Maryland Battalion and Lieutenant Colonel George Hume Steuart as his second-in-command. Both were experienced career military officers and were, most importantly, Marylanders. Bradley T. Johnson was appointed as the battalion major. To supplement the strength of the battalion, the three infantry companies formed in Richmond by Captains Dorsey, Murray, and Robertson were ordered to join with the Harpers Ferry companies.

* * *

1st Maryland Battalion
Near Winchester, Virginia
June 25, 1861

The late afternoon sun was hot. Everyone was happy to fall out from the last formation after a hard day's work around camp and two rigorous periods of company drill. They were Maryland soldiers, mustered in Richmond and wearing newly issued Confederate gray uniforms. McHenry Howard and several other soldiers of Captain Murray's company sought out a nice patch of grass at the edge of the meadow shaded by a dense row of trees. It was their first moment of relaxation that afternoon. The three Richmond companies had arrived several days before to be amalgamated with the six Harpers Ferry companies that had already formed the Maryland Battalion, but found the camp empty.

"Look out for your luggage, boys. The Plug Uglies are coming," a voice cried out, causing McHenry and his friends to jump to their feet and dash a few steps out into the field.

"Will you look at that sorry-looking bunch," Nick Watkins said laughingly as they observed a ragged column winding over the hill toward them.

"I'll wager it's our missing companies," McHenry said. "I heard they'd soon be returning from a mission to Harpers Ferry."

"How'd that happen?" asked another soldier. "I thought we abandoned that place sometime ago."

"Our boys got sent back to finish the job of destroying the arsenal," a sergeant standing nearby chimed in.

Soon the column came to a halt in the meadow and was about to be dismissed. McHenry spotted William standing in the ranks and walked toward him as the order to fall out was given.

When William and McHenry clasped hands, there was an extravagant amount of backslapping and high jinks as each was accompanied by a group of friends and everyone was eager to greet their new comrades. This evolved into loud, exuberant conversation about their new way of life. Soldiering was still a fresh experience for them and they were having a grand time at it.

McHenry noted that William and his friends had the look of rough service. They were poorly clad in a hodgepodge of civilian clothing and presented an unwashed appearance from their exertions over the past few days. However, they were carrying very effective-looking rifles that left no doubt that these were soldiers engaged in serious business.

"I'm mightily impressed by that rifle you're carrying, William. It even has a fine-looking brass patch box in the shoulder stock!"

William smiled broadly as he handed it to McHenry. "It shoots right well too. These Model 1841 rifles are highly accurate and handle real nice."

McHenry threw it to his shoulder and pointed it at the nearby treetops. "Very, very nice," he said as he handed it back to William.

"They're called Mississippi Rifles as they were first used by the 1st Mississippi Regiment commanded by Jeff Davis in the war against the Mexicans," William commented.

"Didn't know that!" McHenry exclaimed, obviously impressed by that bit of knowledge.

"Where have you fellows been to?" Nick blurted out.

"We were sent by train back up to Harpers Ferry last week with instructions to burn everything," William replied. "Of course, Marylanders are more likely to do things sensibly rather than follow orders to the letter, so we brought back a whole bunch of seasoned gunstocks. I heard Colonel Steuart say that we're going to send them to North Carolina in appreciation for these fine Mississippi Rifles they gave us."

"How long have you fellows in the Richmond companies been here?" one of William's companions asked.

"We arrived just after you left on your expedition and have been busy setting up camp and drilling every day," Nick replied.

"Our train trip was apparently more of a gentleman's country excursion than yours," McHenry said. "We came up from Richmond by way of the Virginia Central to Strasburg. The ride in the cars was tiresome but a pleasant one as we enjoyed the smiles of the fairest daughters of Virginia at every station where we were showered with bouquets of flowers. From Strasburg, we rode in large, open wagons to Winchester in the boiling hot sun. Now that wasn't quite so enjoyable! It's a wonder that Nick didn't resign again from the Confederate Army."

The Richmond soldiers laughed gleefully.

"You fellows aren't going to let me forget that, are you?" Nick stated, trying to sound indignant, but not doing a very good job of it.

McHenry saw the look of confusion on the faces of William and his friends, so he explained what the levity was all about. "We were at company drill one morning in Richmond. My friend Private Nicholas Watkins," he said as he clasped Nick's shoulder, "was in a more irascible temper than usual—so he stepped a pace forward from the ranks, dashed his cap violently to the ground, and said, 'I resign!'—'Watkins,' said Captain Murray sternly, 'take your place back in the ranks,' which he did. Afterward, we called him the only private to resign from the Confederate States Army."

This amused all of the young soldiers gathered around and Nick was not unhappy, as he enjoyed the notoriety. When the laughter subsided, William asked

McHenry where their tents were set up. "Well, that's another story," McHenry said, which set his friends to start laughing again.

"It seemed like such a good idea at the time! My messmates and I purchased a wall tent in Richmond prior to our departure. When we started pitching our tent out there with the others, Colonel Elzey came riding by and demanded to know what an officer's tent was doing in the enlisted men's line, adding that we must come out of these damned Baltimore notions."

"What did you do then?" William asked, as he tried to suppress his laughter.

"Well, we rolled up our investment and sat down in a row upon it looking mighty dejected until one of our officers explained the shortage of tents to Colonel Elzey. We were finally allowed to pitch it in a hollow, out of sight of the aligned tents."

* * *

The 1st Maryland Battalion was reorganized into eight companies to equalize each company with enough men above the minimum required by Confederate military law. Captain Worthington's company was assigned as Company A, Captain Dorsey's company as Company C, Captain Herbert's company as Company D, and Captain Murray's company as Company H. The other companies were disbanded and reformed with new officers. The battalion now numbered seven hundred and twenty rifles and muskets and everyone was properly clothed as Mrs. Johnson's uniforms arrived for issue to the soldiers mustered at Harpers Ferry.

The soldiers of the Maryland Battalion were clad in a gray French kepi cap with a light blue stripe, a short, gray, tight-fitting coat with collar and cuffs bound with black braid, and matching gray trousers with a similar black stripe down the outer seams. They were among the best-dressed and drilled units in the Confederate Army.

6

FIRST BLOOD

Clifton spoke slowly as he cast his mind back to the early days of the war. "Weeks of anticipation passed as everyone waited for the initial engagement. General Joseph E. Johnston's Army was positioned in the great Valley of Virginia to block the southward advance of General Patterson's Federal forces. Likewise, the Confederate Army of General Pierre Gustave Toutant Beauregard was placed at Manassas Junction to contain the Union Army under newly promoted Brigadier General Irvin McDowell in the vicinity of Washington."

"There was much speculation as to how events would unfold," Whitman responded.

"Many, myself included, thought that one big battle, or no more than a single summer campaign, would be required to settle the issue—whether or not the United States remained intact or the Confederate States won independence. How utterly wrong we all were."

"Where were you at this point, Clifton?" John inquired.

"I had been released from service with the 7th Regiment and was back in Baltimore," Clifton replied. "Everything and everybody there seemed to be in a state of flux."

* * *

THE WATERFRONT
BALTIMORE, MARYLAND
JUNE 28, 1861

The three Cary siblings arrived early in the morning at the busy commercial wharf from which they were to embark on a side wheel steamboat bound for Leonardtown, Maryland, under the guise of a trip to visit friends in St. Mary's County. Dockhands unloaded their heavy trunks from a hired wagon trailing behind the Cary carriage and placed them beside the steamer's gangway with crates and hogsheads that were about to be manhandled aboard.

The Carys stood mesmerized by the noisy, rambunctious waterfront activity and the imposing view of Baltimore's inner harbor with tall-masted sailing ships tied up alongside steamers of every description. Small boats shuttled among the vessels, piers, and wharfs—a spectacle of thriving waterborne enterprise in the basin.

It was at that moment that the Carys' formidable array of trunks caught the attention of James L. McPail, deputy provost marshal of Baltimore. A brief confrontation ensued in which McPail was handily outmaneuvered, the trunks loaded onto the steamer and the three passengers permitted to board, their apprehension and relief barely concealed. While Wallis Blakistone, the son of former State Senator James T. Blakistone, vouched that the Carys were to be guests of his well-known father in St. Mary's, Hetty informed McPail in no uncertain terms that unmentionables such as ladies undergarments were in the trunks and that no gentleman would dare demand that they be searched.

* * *

The voyage was uneventful other than several stops at Chesapeake Bay ports to load and unload passengers and freight. In the afternoon of the following day, the Carys were joyfully met at dockside in Leonardtown by a large contingent of old family friends led by James T. Blakistone, Esquire. Several pleasant days were spent at Rose Hill, the Blakistone estate in St. Mary's, while final arrangements were made for the most dangerous part of their passage to Virginia.

On July third, the Blakistone family and their guests traveled by carriage to Colton's Point where they crowded aboard a large rowboat for the short trip to Blakistone Island near the north shore of the Potomac River. They presented the appearance of a party embarking for a daylong picnic on the scenic island. While that was certainly true, something much more serious was afoot, and those few informed of the real purpose of the day's outing carefully contained their nervous tension. They knew that the Carys and two young men from St. Mary's would attempt to run the Federal blockade that night.

Blankets were spread for a picnic on a slight knoll overlooking the river and a nice breeze coming off the water refreshed the party. During lively conversation around baskets full of good food and drink, Hetty, Jenny, and Miles learned that it was here in 1634 that the ships *Ark of London* and *Dove* landed the first English settlers to Maryland. These hardy colonists named the little island St. Clement's for they had departed from the Isle of Wright on the feast day of St. Clement, patron saint of mariners. It later became known as Blakistone Island as the family had owned and farmed it for several generations.

Conversation waned from the effects of the warm sun and a pleasant meal. Several people dozed, as others grew quiet and introspective. They watched a Great Blue Heron standing motionless near the shore for long moments before striking with lightning speed to spear a fish with its slender beak.

While the older folks relaxed in the sunshine and the children played happy games on a nearby beach, the Carys walked along the shoreline to the lighthouse on the island's southern tip. The lighthouse keeper and his wife welcomed them, and they were shown through the quaint two-story white house with a light tower rising from the ground in its center to above the roof peak.

Hetty stood in the lantern room atop the tower and silently gazed at the Virginia shore lying across a wide stretch of the Potomac River. Her concentration was interrupted when she felt a soft tug on her elbow. Hetty looked at Miles, then in the direction that he indicated with a subtle twist of his head. The United States screw sloop-of-war *Pawnee* could be seen under full sail coming up river from the Chesapeake Bay to patrol the broad expanse of water where they would be crossing that night. It was a quiet walk back to the picnic site.

Later that afternoon, amid tears, thanks, and heartfelt best wishes, the Blakistone family departed for the mainland in a boat sent to retrieve them. The Carys, the gentlemen from St. Mary's, and two watermen remained on the island at a fisherman's shanty hidden in a small grove of trees. Seated uncomfortably on trunks tightly packed with gray Confederate uniforms and medical supplies, each was tense and withdrawn as they prepared themselves for the coming ordeal.

* * *

As the last rays of sunlight faded from the western sky, the would-be blockade runners loaded the large rowboat with trunks and passengers, causing it to settle in the water until only a foot and a half of freeboard remained. In the deepening darkness, the watermen rowed the boat out from the island to observe the course and speed of the Federal man-of-war patrolling the Potomac.

Earlier in the evening, they noted from shore that *Pawnee* was operating on her steam engine as smoke belched from the single stack located amidships just aft of the foremast and her screw propeller churned the brown river water. During the several hours that they watched, she made irregular trips up and down river and alternated between full speed and bare headway, a tactic that made it difficult for observers to predict her movements.

As *Pawnee* steamed down the middle of the river past the bow of the rowboat, the watermen and the St. Mary's men began to row steadily with muffled oars for the Virginia shoreline, some three miles distant, their passengers crouched low to avoid detection. The oarsmen made good progress while the three Carys scanned the dark horizon and watched the black silhouette of the sloop-of-war grow smaller on the faint moonlit water.

Without warning, *Pawnee* came about sharply and steamed into the river current at full speed straight toward the rowboat, raising the possibility that Hetty and her companions had been sighted. For several moments, the occupants of the rowboat sat silently awaiting their fate, as they would not be able to outrun the steam-powered warship. As *Pawnee* came nearer, their eyes fixed upon the white bow wave that gleamed against the vessel's dark hull as it rushed in their direction. Abruptly, the bow wave disappeared and they heard the clattering of chain playing out through a hawse pipe as *Pawnee* dropped anchor a hundred yards downriver. Surprised by this maneuver, the men rowed with quiet intensity to keep their boat from being swept by the current into *Pawnee* as she rode at anchor. When so near the man-of-war that their muffled oars might be heard, the men stopped rowing and bent over in their seats to minimize their profile.

Hetty watched from beneath the hood of her cape as they were carried close to the Federal warship by the river flow, within easy gunshot. She could see Yankee sailors on the sloop's foredeck and officers on the quarterdeck, their attention still focused aboard the vessel, as lookouts had not yet been posted. The rowboat silently drifted by the Federal warship and, to Hetty's great relief, no alarm was raised. *Pawnee* soon receded into the darkness.

When they drifted far enough away not to be heard, the oarsmen resumed their rowing and, within another hour, they landed beneath the steep bluffs of the Westmoreland County shore. The watermen quickly unloaded the boat and bade their passengers a hasty farewell, as they wanted to be safely back in Maryland well before sunrise.

* * *

Miles tramped about unfamiliar country in the darkness for nearly an hour before he found an old black man traveling with a primitive wagon. It was drawn by the odd combination of an ox and a mule. Traveling at a snail's pace, the vehicle conveyed the ladies and luggage along a sandy farm road in now brilliant moonlight as the men trudged along behind them.

Well past midnight, they arrived at Stratford Hall, the fine colonial mansion that was the birthplace of Robert E. Lee. The occupants of the house, two old unprotected ladies, were at first reluctant to open the barred doors, but soon agreed to give shelter to Hetty and Jenny. The men spent the night in a detached brick kitchen house where they built a roaring fire in the huge chimney place and slept fitfully on planks before the open hearth.

In the morning, the ladies of Stratford Hall prepared a breakfast of beat biscuit, waffles, corn cakes, and other Old Virginia delicacies for their guests and sent them on their way to Leedstown on the Rappahannock in a large brake wagon with a stout team of horses. Buoyant with youth and high spirits, the Carys and their new friends sang "Maryland, My Maryland" and other Southern songs as they sped down country roads through green fields and dense woods.

After passing through Leedstown, they crossed at Port Micou into the flat fields of Essex County and stayed for several days at Kinloch, the magnificent home of Richard Baylor, an old friend of the family. The party next traveled to Fredericksburg on a small tugboat, then on to Richmond by rail, arriving in the new capital of the Confederate States of America on the ninth day of July. They said sincere goodbyes to the two St. Mary's men who accompanied them on the journey, as they had been good traveling companions.

The Carys first stop was the Spotswood Hotel, headquarters at the time of President Jefferson Davis and other officials of the Confederacy. In this location, they had the good fortune to meet General Robert E. Lee, who they knew as he had lived in Baltimore with his family ten years before while overseeing the construction of Fort Carroll. General Lee, now chief of staff and advisor to the president of the Confederacy, gave much attention to Hetty and Jenny and introduced them to President Davis and other important dignitaries seated in the hotel dining room. The Cary girls created quite a sensation in army and official circles during their short stay in Richmond, before traveling to Orange County Court House to visit friends. Miles stayed in the capital city, calling on family contacts, searching for the best opportunity to receive a commission and suitable placement in the Confederate Army.

* * *

1ST MARYLAND BATTALION
PIEDMONT, VIRGINIA
JULY 21, 1861

William was roused from a deep sleep at two in the morning by a shrill locomotive whistle announcing the arrival of a train on the siding below their campsite. The previous day, his battalion had marched hard from Winchester through Ashby's Gap to Piedmont, a station on the Manassas Gap Railroad, receiving neither adequate food nor sufficient rest to properly sustain them.

The 1st Maryland Battalion had been assigned to the 4th Brigade along with the 10th Virginia, 13th Virginia, and 3rd Tennessee regiments. Colonel Elzey as senior officer was designated to command it. They were part of General Joseph Johnston's army in the Valley of Virginia that had been urgently summoned to reinforce General Beauregard at Manassas. Union General Irvin McDowell was moving against him and the first major battle of the war was looming.

The Marylanders were quickly formed in ranks and marched down to the rail siding, but delays occurred in organizing the embarkation, and it was daybreak before everyone was finally aboard. The cars were filled to capacity, so William and his messmates rode on the rear platform of a passenger car for the first portion of the journey. The engine made slow progress and stopped frequently for unexplained reasons. During one such stop, William and his friends jumped down from the platform and feasted on blackberries growing alongside the embankment as they had received scanty fare over the past few days. Several cars vacated without permission as other soldiers gave in to the irresistible temptation of ripe blackberries.

A furious voice was heard and a general that William didn't recognize stormed toward the berry-picking soldiers, scattering them like flushed quail. William and his messmates climbed on top of the car, glad to have escaped the general's wrath. They later learned that this was Brigadier General E. Kirby Smith, the division commander and the senior officer bringing up this contingent of Southern troops from Winchester.

As the train neared Manassas Junction, the soldiers heard the booming of artillery and saw clouds of smoke from the discharges of thousands of muskets a few miles ahead. William and his comrades were excited by the anticipation of battle and most found ways to expend their nervous energy. Some checked their weapons and equipment, while others repacked their knapsacks. All were fidgety to some degree but strove to appear calm and collected.

"Damnation, the fight will be over before we get there!" exclaimed Billy Gannon, a sixteen-year-old drummer boy.

One of the sergeants sitting nearby laughed and replied to the youth. "Hold your horses Billy. There'll be plenty of fighting to go around for all of us."

Arriving at the railroad junction at about one in the afternoon, the troops quickly disembarked and were told to throw their knapsacks into a pile and form ranks. The brigade commander, Colonel Arnold Elzey, his eyes sparking with excitement, rode up and down in front of the ranks, urging the officers to get their troops in line.

Colonel George Hume Steuart, now commanding the Maryland Battalion, had his companies in formation and was briefing the officers when Captain Charles Snowden, the battalion's assistant commissary officer, dashed up to Colonel Steuart and rendered a hasty salute. "Sir, we just received this flag from Richmond," he said as he opened the Maryland state colors and held it up for his commanding officer's inspection. "It was recently brought through the lines from Baltimore by Miss Hetty Cary, pinned to her petticoat," he added, looking about for reaction as he was sure that the assembled officers would recognize her name. Their smiling faces verified that they admired the renowned beauty as much as the blue silk flag that they were examining. It was adorned with the Maryland Seal on one side and the inscription "Presented by the Ladies of Baltimore to the 1st Regiment Maryland Line" emblazoned on the other.

"Magnificent, truly magnificent," Colonel Steuart said as he studied the colors, then turned to Captain Snowden and asked, "Do we have a staff for it? I want our boys to go into battle today with this flag."

"No, sir," Captain Snowden replied sheepishly.

"Colonel, time is quite short," Major Bradley Johnson said. "May I suggest that we use the attached cords at the flag's top and bottom to affix it to the staff of the Frederick Volunteers Flag of Company A. There's room for two flags on that long staff."

"Excellent suggestion. We shall make it so—call the color guard over, and we'll get this done," Colonel Steuart replied. Within a minute, the Company A color bearer stood before him at attention while Colonel Steuart attached the new flag to the flagstaff. The West Pointer and former United States Army officer looked the young soldier in the eye. "Carry it well, son. On this day, we shall bring honor to our cause and the ladies of Maryland."

"Yes, sir," replied the very proud color corporal and a loud cheer went up in the excited ranks of the nearest companies, for all attention was focused on the new flag.

Farther down the line, Brigadier General Smith galloped up to Colonel Elzey as he sat on his horse before William's company. "Colonel, go where the fire is hottest," ordered General Smith, and this pronouncement brought forth more cheers from the enthusiastic Marylanders.

Soon, the entire brigade advanced under a sweltering hot sun toward the sound of battle six miles distant. The Maryland Battalion marched at the head of the column, its two flags fluttering from a single staff.

After the first two miles, General Smith dashed up on his horse and shouted at the Marylanders, "Boys, if you double-quick, you will have a chance to get in the fight." The orders were barely repeated when the Maryland Battalion moved forward at the double-quick, drawing the entire column behind them. For the remaining four miles, the brigade traveled rapidly down the dry red clay road, putting up dust so thick that it restricted vision to no more than a few feet at times and floated high above the treetops, marking the progress of the column. William's throat was parched from this exertion and he was one of many men who scooped up water as they crossed a stream bloodied by a team of dead horses. Finally, the brigade was halted to get a breath and load muskets, then marched on again at a fast pace straight toward their baptism of fire.

As the Maryland Battalion neared the front, they passed ambulances filled with dead and wounded, lurching to the rear where surgeons established crude field hospitals at any place that offered shelter, even in the shade of a large tree. The Marylanders next encountered stragglers, some slightly wounded, and many not wounded at all. A few shouted dire warnings to the new arrivals, as if to justify their own lack of courage. "We're being cut to pieces," one man shouted hysterically. Another cried out, "We're sure to be whipped, but go on in." The boys from Maryland, still fledglings at the art of war, ignored this turmoil as superior training and discipline taught them that the faint of heart are likely to say such things as they flee from the field of battle.

Elzey's Brigade marched steadily forward, twice passing over regiments lying flat on the ground. Some of these soldiers raised their heads and feebly exhorted the column to "press forward," to which the Marylanders responded with an invitation for the shirkers to join their ranks, but there were no takers. They soon came to an open field and a shell exploded seventy yards to their right, scattering a cavalry detachment near that location.

Artillery shells began falling closer as the brigade moved forward in a column of fours. A succession of sharp reports rang out and musket balls whistled over their heads, unleashed upon the brigade by a skirmish line of New York Zouaves hiding in a nearby pine thicket. General Smith, who was riding at the side of the column, was struck and fell from his horse severely wounded, as were several men in the ranks.

To William, it seemed as if he were in a dream, the whole experience being so novel and unexpected. As he looked at his friends and companions marching beside him, they seemed to move in slow motion, driven by instinct and training, their other senses suspended. As they approached the unknown, the central concern of these young men was that they not let their fellow soldiers down in the coming ordeal.

The firing ceased as the enemy skirmishers retreated and the brigade was ordered to form a battle line. It was past three in the afternoon when Colonel Elzey rode forward to reconnoiter, returning shortly to move the column first to the left oblique in column across open ground before going forward in line of battle through a stand of timber. As they approached a worm rail fence at the far edge of the wood, an unexpected volley was received from a battle line visible on high ground at the far end of the field beyond. Although this mass of troops was at no great distance, it was difficult to identify them since the opposing armies at the time were wearing a wide assortment of uniforms of various types and colors.

Colonel Elzey and his staff on horseback peered anxiously through foliage and a thick pall of smoke that lay over the field, making everything indistinct. A flag could be seen hanging close to its staff at the front of the unidentified battle line. "Is that the Stars and Bars or the Stars and Stripes?" he anxiously asked a staff officer at his side, who was equally perplexed. "Both are red, white, and blue in the same arrangement, and I'll be damned if I can tell whether it's Union or Confederate!" replied the staff officer. As it was quiet within the ranks, William could clearly hear the words of the mounted officers clustered just behind his company. He succumbed to his inquisitiveness and turned his head around to observe what was happening.

Colonel Elzey called to his *aide-de-camp*—"give me my glass, quick, quick!" As he leaned forward in the saddle and intently stared through the tube of the brass spyglass, a faint breeze momentarily blew the colors out from the flag-staff in the battle line that had just fired on them. Colonel Elzey straightened-up and shouted, "Stars and Stripes, Stars and Stripes—fire!" A rolling volley immediately erupted from the muskets of the 4th Brigade and crashed with deadly effect into the now-identified Union ranks. The Confederate soldiers re-loaded and fired a succession of volleys that caused the Yankee line to collapse and flee in confusion behind the crest of the hill.

The order "charge bayonets" was given and the brigade surged forward. In the Maryland Battalion, only Captain Dorsey and Captain Murray's companies were equipped with .69-caliber Model 1842 Springfield smoothbore muskets and bayonets. Nevertheless, William's company, armed with Mississippi Rifles, ran forward, yelling at the tops of their lungs, each striving to be the first to the summit of the hill.

As they charged up the pasture field, the Maryland soldiers discovered that it contained an abundant crop of ripe blackberries. Famished with hunger and having parched throats, the ragged battle line lurched to a halt and, for a very short time, became a crowd of blackberry pickers. The officers swore and exhorted the men to move forward, which the soldiers quickly did. However, when a particularly attractive bush was passed, they reached down and stripped off the berries without stopping and crammed them into their mouths, unconcerned that, for days afterward, they would be extracting thorns from their fingers and palms.

The battle on the banks of Bull Run surged back and forth during the long July day with the outcome in doubt until the late afternoon arrival of Elzey's

Brigade turned the Union right flank and caused the Northern battle line to collapse into a disorganized mass. The Federals made several attempts to rally, but a Confederate attack along the entire front shattered the Union forces and sent them into headlong retreat.

Captain Beckham's Newtown Battery opened fire on a thick stand of old field pines through which Federal soldiers were fleeing, adding their cannon fire to the musket volleys fired by the 4th Brigade. When firing finally ceased, the Maryland Battalion advanced though the pine thicket and found abundant evidence of the effectiveness of their small arms and artillery. Bodies of dead Union soldiers were scattered about on the ground and the trees bore fresh marks of the shot and shell that had been unleashed upon them.

Arriving at the other side, the Southern troops stopped their advance and celebrated with the wildest cheering and enthusiasm. Victory had been snatched from certain defeat and the enemy was flying before them. As Colonel Elzey rode proudly up and down before his brigade ranks, General Beauregard dashed up and hailed him for his auspicious arrival on the battlefield. President Jefferson Davis rode up with General Joseph Johnston at his side. "General Elzey! I congratulate you!" exclaimed the man who made generals—within days the promotion was made.

The rambunctious celebration subsided when the men were allowed to fall out of ranks to rest before resuming the chase. William started to follow his messmates toward a shady spot, but stopped in his tracks. Since passing through the pine thicket, he had been thinking about the .58-caliber rifled muskets with bayonets that he had seen lying by dead Yankees. The next time the order was given to "charge bayonets," William wanted to be equipped with a sharp point of steel on the end of a rifled musket. Turning about, he saw Captain Herbert, his company commander, standing nearby and made a beeline for him. Stopping short and rendering a salute, William put his thoughts into words.

"Sir, our .54-caliber Mississippi Rifles are mighty accurate, but we don't have bayonets. The Yankees left a bunch of rifled Minnie muskets with bayonets and cartridge boxes on the ground back in that pine thicket we just came through. What would you think if I got several of the boys and went back there to collect a few for our use?"

"Bring back as many as you can and place the surplus weapons in the company ordnance wagon," replied Captain Herbert. "But get back here quickly, William, because I don't know how long it will be until we move out again."

"Thank you, sir," William replied and, within a minute, he recruited several of his more energetic comrades. Walking back toward the pine thicket, they met McHenry Howard carrying his smoothbore musket with bayonet attached. McHenry apparently had the same idea as William, but was focused on the desirability of a rifled Minnie musket for improved range and accuracy.

Not knowing if any stray Yankees were hiding in the dense foliage, the small band of Rebel soldiers cocked their pieces and proceeded cautiously. It was dark and still as death among the tall pines and the thick shrubs crowded in between. They would take a few steps at a time, then stop to listen, before taking another carefully placed step, their eyes and ears alert for any sign of danger.

Within a short distance, William could only see McHenry about ten feet to his left. It seemed strange to William to be in this place with an old friend from Baltimore—they had shared many good times that were so entirely different from this moment. The two young men moved forward—one advancing while the other covered him, then vice-versa.

A voice startled them and they sought shelter behind trees while evaluating the threat. Taking the initiative, William and McHenry silently circled in the direction of the voice and found a badly wounded Union soldier, his head and shoulders propped up against a tree. He had been horribly torn about the waist by an exploding shell and obviously had but a short time to live. As the young Marylanders knelt beside him, they could see that he was a fine-looking middle-aged man of a respectable class with a dark, heavy beard and piercing blue eyes.

"I'm truly sorry to see you in this condition," McHenry gently said to the man and then asked, "Is there anything we can do for you?"

"Yes," the Yankee replied in a perfectly composed voice. "You can do one thing for me, and I wish you to do it, for God's sake. Take your bayonet and run me through, kill me at once and put an end to my misery."

McHenry and William were horrified at the request and stared at him, desperately searching for the right response. The man was in agony, but they had not been sufficiently hardened by the carnage of battle to consider doing such a thing. The boys looked at one another, then back at the grotesquely wounded Yankee, completely at a loss for words. William thought about carrying him to a hospital but knew immediately that it would be a futile effort.

"We can't do that," William replied, looking straight into the wounded man's eyes. "I can give you some water if you'd like," knowing that his sense of ethics would only cause the man to suffer more pain.

The Union soldier drank eagerly from William's canteen. As soon as he finished drinking, he again begged the young Rebel soldiers to end his suffering.

"You have but a short time left and you should spend it making your preparations for death," McHenry stated in as strong a voice as he could muster, aware that it was more fear than courage than ruled his conduct. Dismayed, the Yankee merely grunted and stared off into space as they continued to kneel beside him. The boys exchanged another glance and reached an unspoken agreement—William and McHenry stood up and walked away. The wounded man called after them, pleading with them to take his life, but that was not to be.

William and McHenry spoke very little as they found the others in their party, collected a number of rifled muskets, bayonets, and full cartridge boxes, and returned to the battalion.

* * *

BELPRÉ
NEAR CULPEPER, VIRGINIA
JULY 28, 1861

The sun was shining brightly and the summer morning air retained a trace of nighttime chill that would too quickly dissipate. Connie sat on the front porch of the charming old country house, trying to concentrate on the passages of a favorite book, but to no avail. All she could think of was the arrival that morning of the radiant Hetty, who she admired so much, and Jenny, with her delightful wit and pleasant disposition. Connie had not seen her cousins since the party in Baltimore four months before and was eager to share her multitude of thoughts and emotions.

The invitation was made when Connie's mother learned of her niece's escape to Virginia and wanted them under her chaperonage at Belpré where she and her daughter were staying with friends. Connie also knew that her mother thought her too young to be alone so much. The host family treated them well, but she was often left to her own devices while her mother attended to nursing duties at Culpeper Court House.

A carriage and driver were dispatched before dawn to meet the cars at the nearest station as military priorities on railroad scheduling made arrival times uncertain. Connie, nevertheless, was becoming anxious as each hour passed. She glanced up frequently from her book to see if the carriage was in sight, but gradually the words of the book worked their magic on her and she became engrossed in it. Thus, she was pleasantly surprised when the carriage turned in the gate and came to a halt before the porch steps. After affectionate hugging and a few happy tears shed, the next hour was spent settling Hetty and Jenny into their comfortable new quarters.

The July heat became oppressive in the house, so the girls were soon seated in rocking chairs on the porch, sipping on sweet lemonade. The sisters had changed from their traveling attire to more comfortable clothing and were chatting happily with Connie, who was eager to learn about their recent adventures. She was spellbound as Hetty and Jenny told of the happenings in Baltimore that culminated in their departure, the harrowing encounter with the Yankee warship *Pawnee* as they crossed the Potomac, and the important Confederate personages that they were introduced to during their brief stay in Richmond.

When her turn came, Connie revealed, with unexpected intensity, the recent events in her life. "Only a few weeks ago, I was living at Vaucluse with my mother and aunt, and their combined six children. When it became evident that Vaulcuse lay in the probable path of the Union Army, the youngest of the family were scattered to areas more remote, out of harm's way, and the young men were off to enter the fray. My mother and aunt then made preparations to depart for Manassas to serve as nurses for our army massing there."

"It must have been terrible for you to flee from that comfortable place under such dire circumstances," Jenny said too quickly, not realizing the pain her cousin was suffering.

"Vaulcuse is the home dearest to me." Tears began to form in Connie's eyes as she looked at Hetty, seeking the understanding of her eldest cousin. "It broke my heart to leave the seat for so many generations of the Fairfax family, but we had no choice."

"Oh Connie, there is so much sorrow for all of us in these times. I know how much you love that place. Our mother has often spoken of Vaucluse as a beautiful country home," Hetty said, trying to comfort her young cousin.

"It truly is a special place," Connie replied, the reminiscence causing a wistful tone in her voice. "A fine old white stucco dwelling, with wings on both ends, shaded by great oaks in the lawn—it was never farmed, you know, but it has attached gardens, an orchard, and dairy. Vaucluse is the perfect country estate! I love every room of that old house and every piece of furniture in it. The flotsam of Fairfax family furnishings from homes in England and Virginia—Towlston, Belvoir, Ashgrove." Connie's voice trailed off as bittersweet memories of happy years living there flooded her mind.

"Has everything fallen into the hands of the Yankees?" Jenny asked.

"Not everything," Connie replied, sitting up straight as she regained her composure. "My mother, aunt, and a nephew, with the help of an old Negro gardener, buried two large traveling trunks in the cellar containing silver candelabras, urns, tankards, bowls, dishes, and a complete Queen Anne silver service brought from England by Colonel William Fairfax in the eighteenth century. We can only pray that our family treasures have not been found."

"Did any members of your family remain at Vaucluse?" Hetty asked.

"Yes, replied Connie, unsuccessfully attempting to suppress a smile through her tears. "My mother's two maiden aunts remained in residence. The aged gentlewomen had escaped to Vaucluse only a few weeks before when Alexandria was captured by the Union Army. They decided that they would not be displaced again."

"What brave, wonderful women!" Jenny exclaimed.

"Yes they are," Connie replied. "We have since heard that Union troops ordered them to return to Alexandria in an ambulance designated for that task, but they adamantly refused."

Connie smiled with pride as she wiped tears from her eyes. "In fact, the older of the two sisters refused to move of her own accord. There she sat in her favorite chair with fire in her eyes, defying the Yankee tyrants, until an officer ordered two soldiers to lift her, chair and all, between them and place her in the ambulance for the ride to Alexandria."

The mood of the three young women became melancholy as they thought about how the established order of things had been so thoroughly usurped. Breaking the silence, Hetty asked, "Were you at Belpré when the great battle was fought at Manassas?"

"No, my younger brother Clarence and I were first packed off to safety with a relation at Millwood in Clarke County, and we spent most of the month of May at that sylvan paradise," Connie replied. "However, in early June, mother wrote from Manassas saying that we must join her at Bristoe before the military lines might shut us out. So we went by a lumbering stagecoach down the Shenandoah Valley, then by the cars to Bristoe Station, a shabby little roadside hotel on the Orange and Alexandria Railroad." She took a sip from her lemonade and sat the half-full glass on the flat railing beside her. "It was crowded to excess with officers' families. The surrounding country was treeless, the sun was blazing hot, and we were served the plainest of fare."

"That sounds like a dreadful experience," Jenny said as she leaned forward to place the empty lemonade glass that she had been clutching on a nearby table. "What did you do with your time?"

"The railway track provided our only excitement," replied Connie. "Day after day, trains came thundering by, full of eager young men going to the front. The women and girls rushed out to stand beside the tracks each time and wave our handkerchiefs at our soldier boys."

"Your mother's letter mentioned that Clarence was in the battle—how did that come about?" Jenny asked.

"A regiment from Alexandria that contained many family friends and acquaintances was camped near Bristoe Station," Connie replied. "Clarence, only fifteen years old, was invited to become a marker for the regiment. Mother sewed his white gaiters and a havelock for his cap with the neatest of stitches, tears dropping on her handiwork, but she would not tell him that he could not go."

Connie sat perfectly still. "I remember the moment when I was struck by the sudden realization of the potential for calamity within our family," she said softly. "Thank God that Clarence survived the battle and now serves on General Longstreet's headquarters staff as a courier. He plans to apply for a position in the naval service at the first opportunity."

Connie's stress was apparent, as was her need to relate the entirety of her story. Hetty and Jenny watched carefully and waited for her to speak further.

She regained her composure. "At the beginning of August, we left the cheerless railway inn at Bristoe and came to Belpré, this wonderful old place, as mother's nursing duties required her to be at Culpeper Court House. She often works from dawn to dusk, so a nearby location for me to stay was essential to her nursing mission."

"Your mother's work is truly heroic," Hetty said. "Aunt Monimia is a tireless spirit of tender sympathy, the ideal attendant for wounded, homesick boys. You have every right to be terribly proud of her."

"Oh, I am. I know that she's a stout spirit and a rock of refuge to all around her."

"Have you accompanied her to the hospital?" Jenny asked.

"No, not at Culpeper, but I did help with the nursing on the first trains coming to Bristoe Station after our victory at Manassas. By lantern light, every woman and girl in the hotel passed through the cars, distributing milk, water, brandy, and bread. We ministered to the wounded men as best we could for we had scant supplies. All we could do for those poor boys was hold their anguished hands, wipe their foreheads with wet cloths, look into their anxious eyes, and whisper a few words of encouragement. I felt so woefully inadequate!"

"What you did was kind and merciful—no one could have done more than you did under those circumstances," Hetty said.

"Dear Connie," exclaimed Jenny, "we are both of such tender years, and I am not at all certain how I would confront the pain and suffering of those men. I'm happy to know that your mother is shielding you from acceptance of such responsibilities too soon."

Jenny rose from her chair, took Connie's hands, and guided her to her feet so that they could embrace. Hetty stood, placed her empty glass on the table, and put her arms around them both. The three young women clung to each other for a time to allay their anxiety.

Connie drew back, her arms still linked with her cousin's, and smiled with a trace of sadness. "I've come to realize that my wise mother sent me here to this beautiful place to be like a little girl again, reading and studying and staying out of trouble. She thinks I have already ventured too far toward considering myself a young lady."

The amused look on Hetty and Jenny's faces caused Connie to laugh. "Alas! It's true. After all, it's wartime and the woods are full of handsome young officers and privates eager to be entertained and heartened for the fray. I've already tasted the sweets of emancipation, and there's no turning back!"

MARYLAND, MY MARYLAND

Melville cast a disapproving look at Whitman. "I really don't understand why you think it necessary to talk about the Cary women. Their mischief is of no interest to me."

"William spoke about them at length and with great affection," Whitman replied. "I cannot tell his story without relating their experiences, for they are connected."

"Then by all means we want to hear about them," Clifton said. "Please proceed."

Whitman nodded an acknowledgement with a slight smile on his face. "Following the battle at Manassas, or the First Battle of Bull Run as we know it, the Maryland Battalion went into camp near Fairfax Station."

"It's a wonder that the Rebels didn't march right into Washington following that disastrous defeat, though many on their side thought that they should have," Melville said with a grimace.

"I suspect that they were as disorganized from their victory as we were from our defeat," John opined.

"That's quite true," Clifton responded, "but both sides were new to this business and painfully inexperienced. The battle could have gone either way. Elzey's arrival with fresh forces, including our William, at just the right moment on the Federal flank helped turn the battle into a decisive Southern victory."

"William said that they couldn't believe their eyes as they followed the beaten Federals," Whitman recalled. "Particularly the overturned carriages, lunch baskets, and champagne bottles of elite Washingtonians who came out to observe the battle—it wasn't the picnic that they thought it would be. Some have called it the Bull Run run!"

"Clearly the Union Army fell apart when they were attacked on their flank. The training and experience gained within another year would have allowed them to make a more orderly retreat," Clifton said somewhat defensively.

"In any case," continued Whitman, "The following day, the Maryland Battalion accompanied Colonel J.E.B. Stuart's 1st Virginia Cavalry to Fairfax Station where they found piles of abandoned military supplies, ambulances, and artillery. The Maryland infantry remained there whilst the Virginia cavalry pursued the retreating Federals right to the outskirts of Alexandria."

"It was a terrible, terrible disaster," Melville lamented as he wrung his hands. "I thought that the war had been lost when I heard the news. Little did I know that it was only the beginning of our national misery."

"For the rest of the summer, the officers of the Maryland Battalion drilled their companies hard every day to make them even more proficient in the military arts," Whitman said. "They became exceptionally good soldiers, but off duty they yelled, shouted, and romped like schoolboys. Nevertheless, the Marylanders were widely respected as being excellent soldiers."

Whitman sat back in his chair and reflected on the story that he had just told. He recalled what else William told him about this period of time. "Oh, yes," he said with a bright twinkle in his eye as the recollection came to him. "The Cary girls were about to reappear in William's life."

* * *

BELPRÉ
NEAR CULPEPER, VIRGINIA
AUGUST 10, 1861

The first light of dawn in the eastern sky had just begun to lessen the darkness of night, not yet encroaching upon the slumber of Hetty, Jenny, and Connie in their upstairs bedroom. Indistinct sounds began to emanate from outside their window. They awoke with a start, alarmed by the noise from wheels creaking to a stop, the tramping of horses' feet, the voices of men, and the clanging of soldiers' steel.

The suddenness of this intrusion caused the worst apprehension. Was it a marauding patrol of Union cavalry? The three young women leapt out of their beds in an instant and peered cautiously from the window into the early-morning haze. To their delight, the yard below them was filled with lean, gray-uniformed cavalryman, dismounting around an empty ambulance. The girls realized at once that it was their escort and vehicle to convey them to Fairfax Station.

They had recently received an invitation from General Beauregard, couched in very complimentary terms, to visit the Confederate Army in recognition of their labors benefiting the Marylanders who had done such gallant service in his command. Within several hours, the Carys were on their way in the ambulance, seated on benches padded with army blankets, and escorted by carefully picked cavalry troopers who were proud and delighted to have been assigned this pleasant duty.

* * *

1st Maryland Battalion
Near Fairfax Station, Virginia
August 10, 1861

The presence of the young woman in camp had an electrifying effect on the soldiers. Simply put, the boys and officers were on their heads! Navy Captain Isaac Sears Sterett, a Baltimore cousin then in command of heavy guns in nearby fortifications, had prepared a large wall tent for the Cary girls.

On their first night in camp, a dinner was held to which a number of young officers were invited and afterward an outdoor levee was held in their honor. Seated on camp chairs before their tent, they were serenaded by the glee club of the Washington Artillery of New Orleans, who sang several favorite songs of the day including ones with such sentiments as "By blue Patapsco's billowy dash," and "The years glide slowly by, Lorena."

Soldiers of the Maryland Battalion, including William and his messmates, were attracted to the singing and stood listening in the shadows behind the fortunate few officers invited to the festivities. At the completion of the serenade, Captain Sterett expressed the appreciation of the girls and asked what they might render in return. Before anyone attending the levee could respond, a voice from the surrounding crowd shouted, "Let us hear a woman's voice," and everyone present quickly echoed this request.

The Carys disappeared briefly into their tent. Within a few moments, the flap was thrown open and the three young women stepped forward with Jenny standing in the middle. Complete silence fell among the onlookers. The only sound heard was the crackling of the campfire as the men stood transfixed in eager anticipation. Jenny took a breath and began to sing, her pure, sweet voice filling the moonlight air as she sang "Maryland, My Maryland." Hetty and Jenny soon joined in, followed by the Washington Artillery glee club, then the entire assemblage, as the words to the poem were well known. Following the last refrain, the large crowd, wild with enthusiasm, cheered and threw their hats in the air, shouting, "We will break her chains—she shall be free." The Washington Artillery gave three cheers and a Louisiana Tiger for Maryland.

Later, Hetty, Jenny, and Connie giggled half the night away as they reclined upon layers of cartridge flannel on the hard floor of their tent with a row of hoopskirts hanging over their heads. Finally, their excitement subsided, and they slipped into an exhausted sleep, protected by faithful sentries standing guard outside.

* * *

In the mid-morning of the following day, a young staff lieutenant rode up to a campfire around which sat a number of enlisted men of the Maryland Battalion. "I do believe that the fellows I'm seeking are all here in one place. This must be my lucky day. It certainly is yours—Randolph McKim, Duncan McKim,

Daniel Wright, and William Prentiss, you are to report forthwith to the station. Misses Hetty, Jenny, and Constance Cary are waiting there and would like to see you." With his message delivered and without waiting for a reply, the staff officer wheeled his horse and rode back to the station at a fast pace, eager to be back in the presence of the famous beauties.

The four named soldiers arose from the logs where they were seated and walked about thirty feet before stopping to confer. William's face flushed with excitement at the prospect of visiting with his good friends. He had seen them at a distance during the serenade the night before, but he and his fellow soldiers were not permitted to approach the officers' party.

Duncan McKim's face displayed a pained expression that was immediately noticed by his cousin Randolph. "Why are you so glum, Duncan? Aren't you looking forward to seeing the Cary girls?" Randolph asked incredulously.

"Well, if you must know, I'm rather uncomfortable being in the presence of ladies when I'm dressed in this crude garb," replied Duncan, motioning toward his uniform with his hands. "This roundabout jacket is a far cry from the nicely tailored coats that I usually wear during social encounters."

Jero and William were doing their best to suppress smiles, recognizing that Duncan, a Harvard College graduate and former banker in Baltimore was always impeccably dressed in the course of his previous, very civilized and successful life.

"For Heaven's sake Duncan, they know we're privates in the army!" Randolph exclaimed with exasperation in his voice.

"Look at us," Duncan said despairingly, indicating his three companions by his gesture. "We're gaunt, we're burnt dark by the sun, and we have a rough look about us."

Jero spoke up, stifling a laugh. "I don't know about you all, but I'm going to see those pretty girls. Although I might stop by my tent to freshen-up some on the way."

"A team of wild horses couldn't keep me from seeing Hetty, Jenny, and Connie!" William exclaimed. "I don't need to be wearing fancy duds for that!"

When Randolph announced his intention to go, with or without his cousin, Duncan reluctantly yielded to their persuasions. After a quick visit to their tents to brush and polish their uniforms as best they could, the four privates headed for the station. Jero and William shared another sidelong smile as they noted that the McKim cousins had donned white collars for the occasion.

The three Cary girls were on horseback in the midst of a group of well-dressed brigade staff officers and engaged in pleasant conversation with their hosts. Glancing about as the party laughed at an amusing comment made by Connie, the young lieutenant who had summoned the four privates saw them approaching at a distance. "There come your friends," he announced as he pointed toward them.

Hetty raised a hand to shield her eyes from the bright morning sunlight as she peered in that direction. "You must be mistaken. Those could not be the gentlemen that we are expecting."

The entire party stared at the approaching privates before Jenny's voice broke the silence. "In fact, dear sister, those are our friends from Baltimore."

"You're right," Hetty admitted. "I beg all of you not to let them know that I uttered such an unkind and thoughtless remark—I'm ashamed of myself." Without waiting for a reply, Hetty nudged her horse and trotted toward her friends, quickly followed by Jenny, Connie, and the staff officers.

Dismounting with William's assistance, Hetty greeted each with genuine warmth and cordiality, melting whatever discomfort and embarrassment the four privates might have felt over their appearance. The old friends from Baltimore stood in a happy group for over an hour and talked of better times in the city from which all were now in exile. The accompanying staff officers bore their impatience with forced smiles.

* * *

For a number of days, the Cary girls stayed at the camp of the Maryland Battalion, but not all of their time was spent in leisure or idle conversation. Working in concert with Mrs. Bradley Johnson, they cheered the hale and hearty, wrote letters for the illiterate, and ministered to the sick and lonely. Their gracious presence was a ray of sunshine to all of the young men, many of them gentlemen who had left comfortable homes and privileged lives to serve their country as privates in the rank and file.

* * *

Brigadier Generals Arnold Elzey, Jubal Early, and James Longstreet were meeting in an old dilapidated church a few miles away from army headquarters. This was not a council of war. It was more of an informal get-together of former United States military officers who found themselves elevated to high command in the Confederate Army. The refreshments served included a very mellow corn whisky and a good deal was consumed by the generals and their staffs. Due to the fine weather, they adjourned outdoors and took to their horses, competing against one another by leaping fences, ditches, and performing other daring feats on horseback. Fortunately, only one staff officer suffered a minor mishap with damage confined to his uniform and ego. As the group relaxed after this exercise, Elzey bragged that three beautiful young women, descendents of a distinguished old Virginia family, were visiting the camp of the Maryland Battalion in his brigade. The three generals, being gallantly inclined and slightly inebriated, decided that they must call on the young ladies to pay their respects, which they did, shutting out their staffs for a time.

As evening approached, a dress parade of the Maryland Battalion was in order and the generals were only too happy to escort Hetty, Jenny, and Connie to the scheduled event. The eight companies of the Maryland Battalion marched onto the parade field with the band playing Dixie's Land and halted in formation before the reviewing party. All of the onlookers were in agreement that the military bearing of the Marylanders was among the very best in the Confederate Army.

Colonel George H. Steuart, commanding officer of the Maryland Battalion, had also been an officer in the United States Army and was well-acquainted with the three brand-new brigadier generals. Deciding that his old friends had dominated the attention of his guests for too long, Colonel Steuart insisted that the young ladies take a position beside him when the battalion was in line. He then handed his sword to Hetty, stepped aside, and prompted her with the correct orders. Amidst monumental enthusiasm, the prettiest woman in Virginia put the Maryland Battalion through its manual of arms.

* * *

As their visit neared its conclusion, the Carys were invited to dine with General Beauregard and his staff at army headquarters located in a handsome two-story colonnaded mansion near Fairfax Court House. The general, born of a prominent Louisiana Creole family, was an excellent host and the dinner party in the spacious, candlelit dining room was a merry affair. Seated at the head of a long linen-covered table with Hetty and Jenny to his right, Connie to his left, and staff officers filling the rest of the chairs, the general entertained his guests with his usual charm and attentiveness.

"Ladies, in your honor, I am serving my last duck—my personal commissariat is now bare of such delicacies—I don't know what my French chief from New Orleans will prepare the next time you come for dinner."

"You have no reason to worry, General Beauregard," Hetty replied, a bright smile on her face. "The skills of your *chef de cuisine* are extraordinary. I have no doubt that he is capable of creating a culinary masterpiece from the flesh of any beast, fish, or fowl."

"Ahh, but the presence of three beautiful young ladies at my table demands the very finest fare!" exclaimed the general as he smiled and gestured expansively toward the three young women, before returning his eyes to rest on Hetty. Emboldened by the forthright way she was returning his gaze, he continued with his compliments. "I've always known that Baltimore was a city of lovely women, but Hetty, you are clearly the most beautiful women I have ever seen," General Beauregard pronounced with a little more reverence than he meant to reveal.

"Thank you, General, you are too kind," Hetty replied.

Jenny and Connie just smiled, tolerant of the fact that when in Hetty's company, although very attractive themselves, they were not in the limelight. Being reconciled to this circumstance, they enjoyed the delightful experiences of military entertainment that otherwise would not have come their way.

However, Connie's acceptance of this reality and her own adoration of Hetty did not restrain her independent spirit. "My mother and I were staying at Bristoe Station and had the opportunity to visit your army at Manassas before the great battle," Connie said to the general, drawing his attention back to her. "I enjoyed several impromptu entertainments at Camp Pickens during the month awaiting the enemy's advance. The dinners were cooked over open campfires, served to us by our soldier lads, and eaten out of tin plates and cups."

"What greater sacrifice could be made by Southern womanhood," Jenny said with a giggle, a remark that brought smiles to several faces around the table but was quickly overwhelmed by the general's curt response to Connie.

"I placed an engine and car at the disposal of the women and children residing at Bristoe Station with urgent advice to leave immediately for a point of greater safety," replied the general.

"That was most appreciated," Connie replied looking the general steadily in the eye, "but it was received by the ladies as a kind offer and not an order. We were sewing flannel shirts and making bandages as fast as our hands could fly and we decided to take a chance that the battle would be won."

"And win it we did," General Beauregard said, raising his wine glass in a toast, obviously glad to have regained center stage from the impertinent girl. "To the success of Confederate arms and the beauty of Southern women!"

Affirmation of these sentiments was voiced around the table as glasses were raised in salute and sips taken. Conversation hesitantly resumed afterward when it became apparent that General Beauregard had lapsed into silence. Soon, everyone was engaged in small talk except for the general who found that he was in a pensive mood. When he began speaking again in a low voice, conversation immediately stopped as those present concentrated their attention in order to hear his words.

"I must admit that there were moments during the battle when the issue was very much in doubt. By late afternoon, I knew that if reinforcements did not arrive soon, the battle, and perhaps our country, would be lost."

Everyone sat very still, the earlier merriment suspended as General Beauregard began to speak on the critical moment when everything hung in the balance.

"We could see unknown troops pressing toward our position and the colors of the mysterious column hung drooping on the staff. The day was sultry and only at intervals was there a slight breeze. I tried again and again to determine what colors they carried using my glass—I handed it to others, hoping that their eyes might be keener than mine."

The general leaned back in his chair and stared high on the opposite wall of the formal dining room, taking himself in his mind's eye back to that moment in time. His audience was spellbound, hardly breathing as he recalled the turmoil while awaiting discovery of the advancing column's identity. "I was quite anxious, but determined to hold my ground, relying on the promise of help. I knew that if it arrived in time, victory might yet be secured. I also knew that if the mysterious column was Federal, all was lost! Suddenly a puff of wind spread the colors. It was the Stars and Bars! The column had by this time reached the extreme right of the Federal lines. I turned to my staff, saying, See that the day is ours! and ordered an immediate advance by our beleaguered main battle line. In the meantime, Elzey's Brigade deployed into line of battle, smashed into the enemy's right flank, and rolled it up. Within one hour, the enemy could not be found south of Bull Run."

Hetty listened attentively to General Beauregard's candid admission of confusion on the battlefield. "General, there must be some means to prevent such befuddlement in the future. It's an intolerable circumstance for our field commanders not to be able to quickly identify Yankee formations or, worse yet, allow our soldiers to inadvertently shoot one another."

"You are quite right, my dear lady. I'm presently taking steps to alleviate that difficulty. There is no question that dust raised by marching troops and smoke billowing from guns on the battlefield renders it nearly impossible to differentiate between opposing flags of similar appearance. For this reason, I am recommending the creation of a special battle flag for our army."

"Somehow, General, I just knew that you would find a solution to this terrible problem," Hetty replied, looking at the general admiringly.

"Well, there are others involved. General Joseph Johnston and I have discussed the matter at great length and I have been in consultation with William Porcher Miles. He's the congressman from South Carolina who served on my staff during the battle at Manassas. He heads the congressional committee responsible for such matters. In any case, he supplied the flag design that I prefer—a red background with a white-edged blue diagonal cross of Saint Andrew emblazoned with white stars representing each Confederate State."

"What brilliancy! It's handsome, yet quite distinctive!" Jenny exclaimed.

"Yes it is, Miss Jenny, and the officer seated next to you, my quartermaster, Major William L. Cabell, who is a very practical fellow in all matters, has suggested that the flag be square in order to conserve cloth."

Jenny turned to Major Cabell and put her hand on his arm. "That too would enhance the uniqueness of its grand appearance."

"Absolutely," Connie concurred.

"Major, you are to be congratulated for making that excellent suggestion," Hetty said.

"Thank you—I'm honored that you all think so," replied Major Cabell, smiling broadly. "Coming from young ladies whose spirit and devotion to the cause could not be subdued by Yankee tyranny is quite a compliment. From what I have heard of your exploits on behalf of our country, I do believe that the Carys are invincible."

"That's it!" General Beauregard exclaimed. "Henceforth, Hetty, Jenny, and Connie shall be known as the Cary Invincibles!"

This declaration delighted everyone around the table and, for the next half hour, Connie prolonged their amusement by scribbling on a piece of blue scrap paper the troop organization of the Cary Invincibles. Of course, the girls held the exalted ranks and other notables of the day were placed in inferior positions. Two senior staff officers exchanged a look of concern that the young ladies were taking this concept far too seriously, but General Beauregard was thoroughly charmed by the entire exercise.

In any case, the naming of the Cary Invincibles achieved broad circulation throughout the South, a compliment not only to the ardent zeal of their patriotism but also to their widely acclaimed beauty.

* * *

MEDFIELD ACADEMY
NEAR BALTIMORE, MARYLAND
AUGUST 21, 1861

John Prentiss had a tendency to misplace things. Some time ago, he removed his prized all-brass Powell and Lealand compound microscope from the basement storage room to conduct a scientific experiment. Once the findings were summarized for presentation to his students, he promptly forgot about the microscope until it was again needed. A quick search of his library was unfruitful, and he decided that Sarah must have returned it to the shelf where it was usually stored.

As John searched the shelves, he found hidden behind sundry household items a large bundle of letters, boxes of bandages, drugs, and other medical supplies. He pulled out the bundle and immediately noticed that the letters were addressed to Marylanders who had left the state to serve the Confederacy. His curiosity piqued, John continued searching and found a wooden case with the inscription "medical supplies" well-concealed on a bottom shelf. He plied it open and discovered six Colt Navy .36-caliber Revolvers, bullet molds, and a quantity of percussion caps.

John was stunned by this discovery and stood staring back and forth from the contraband on the shelves to the letters in his hand. Recovering abruptly from his stupor, he rushed out of the storage room, up the stairs and marched to the front parlor where he knew that Sarah and Laura were sewing. Sarah looked up as John entered the room and saw what he was holding. Her face went white as she lowered the needle, thread, and cloth to her lap, and stared at John.

He slowly walked over to Sarah. He dramatically placed the letters on the table beside her and stood back, glaring at her. "How could you do this to me, Sarah? Don't you realize how dangerous this is? Don't you realize that you are engaged in seditious activities? That you are committing treason and doing so in my household?"

Sarah regained her composure. "John, please—I'm truly sorry that I've been doing things behind your back."

John snorted angrily in response, clenching and unclenching his fists as he strove unsuccessfully to control his agitation.

Sarah stretched her arms to him in supplication. "Providing medical supplies and letters to family and friends across the lines cannot be such a bad thing. I only wanted to relieve their suffering and maintain contact with them."

John stared at her, his face revealing utter disbelief.

"Several of those letters that Laura and I have written are to your son William, keeping him informed of the health and well-being of the family."

"What of the six revolvers that I found?" John asked sharply.

Sarah winced at that question and glanced at Laura, who quickly looked away and began to quietly weep.

John picked up the letters and shook them in Sarah's face. "I have no doubt that this correspondence contains military secrets. Don't you comprehend the fact that sending such information to secessionists is a serious offense?"

Sarah looked down at her lap as the tears welled in her eyes. She spoke in an anguished voice. "John, I meant no harm and would not intentionally do anything to put our family in jeopardy. We only collect parcels from others who are sending necessities and mail to family members in the South."

"Don't you know exactly what contraband is being illegally transported through our house?" John asked incredulously.

"Not necessarily," Sarah replied, tears streaming down her cheeks. "I send Elijah out to inconspicuously gather parcels from several persons. We hold them here for delivery to others who will cross the Potomac. I meant no harm to anyone."

"Don't you understand that everyone in this household could end up as prisoners at Fort McHenry because of your conduct? This is treason! We could all be hanged for such an offense! And you have put Elijah and his family at risk too! How could you do that?"

"I'm so sorry," Sarah cried. "Elijah doesn't ask questions, but he knows what we are doing and understands the properness and innocence of it."

"Properness! Innocence! My God, Sarah, have you lost your mind!" John exclaimed with great indignation. "Your deceit and deception are not only directed against the Federal authorities but also against me, your husband. That is both despicable and unacceptable!"

He hurled the bundle of letters at the floor and stomped out of the room in a rage greater than he had ever experienced in his life. Sarah ran after John, catching up with him just inside the backdoor of the house. "John, please forgive me. I'm so sorry," she wailed.

"How could you let your foolish little sister talk you into becoming part of this outrageous conspiracy? I simply cannot fathom how you could let that happen!" John exclaimed.

"I thought that I could control the situation if I participated," Sarah replied, quite distraught. "I knew it was dangerous, and I just wanted to protect her." Nearly hysterical, Sarah leaned against the wall to steady herself as she was close to collapsing. Gathering her strength in one last effort to make her husband comprehend her plight, Sarah cried out, "Laura's not my sister, she's my daughter!" Her hands flew to cover her cheeks and her eyes widened with apprehension.

John's face was frozen in shock as they stared at one another. Breaking the strained silence, Sarah continued in a subdued voice. "When I was seventeen, I fell in love with a young man who sailed away on a whaling ship and never returned. My parents attempted to present Laura as their own, but everyone knew. That's why we eventually left Nantucket."

John's expression was one of disdain. "It's just more deceit and deception," he finally said as he turned and walked out the door, slamming it behind him.

* * *

John stormed into the yard behind the main house and made a beeline for the carriage house where Elijah was harnessing a horse to the family carriage.

"I'm living in the midst of lies and treachery," John raged loudly as he approached Elijah.

The former slave turned to face John, his initial surprise masked by an impenetrable expression—one that had been ingrained in him from childhood for such moments. John glared at him expecting an immediate response, but Elijah remained silent.

"Sarah and Laura are involved in smuggling contraband to Confederates in Virginia. And you, Elijah, in whom I have placed complete trust to act only in the best interests of the family, are a part of this foolish conspiracy. How could you do this to me?"

Elijah winced at the intensity of this verbal assault and hurriedly spoke to defend himself. "Mister John, I was only doing what Miss Sarah and Miss Laura asked me to do. There's no wrong in that, is there? It's just medicines, bandages, and letters. Some of them were addressed to your son William. How could that hurt the family?"

"There are also revolvers and God only knows what secrets included in those letters!" John exclaimed. "Elijah, we are at war. The provost marshal would consider the mere possession of such materials as providing aid to the enemy, espionage, perhaps even treason. There would be severe repercussions for all of us if this activity was discovered!"

John paced, emphasizing his points by waving his arms and gesturing, which was most unlike his usual calm and rational manner. Elijah's eyes followed every move John made. His morose expression revealed increasing comprehension of his own culpability and betrayal of the man who had secured his freedom.

"What fools they are, relying on their gentility and womanhood to protect them," John continued in a loud voice. "They have gone too far, gotten too involved. The Cary sisters have been a terrible influence on Laura who is nothing but a silly young girl. Sarah should not have allowed her to participate in such a nefarious adventure. They have deceived me, and I will not tolerate it in my household," he ranted.

John whirled around and directly faced Elijah. "Don't you understand, Elijah? Members of my household have been aiding the enemy. There is no other way to say it. And you of all people should recognize that this war will inevitably be about slavery. The major issue of states' rights is the perpetuation of slavery. Sooner or later, that will come to the forefront."

John stopped to take a breath. His voice began to quaver from overexertion. "The crushing defeat of the Union Army at Bull Run last month only proves that this will not be a single summer campaign. Our nation is going to bleed oceans of blood before the fighting is over. Believe me when I say that this terrible war will become a struggle for the nation's soul."

"Mister John, I didn't mean to do wrong—!"

"For God's sake, Elijah, you've been helping the cause that supports slavery and will continue to hold your people in bondage. Can't you see that? Have you forgotten what it was like to be a slave?"

Elijah was rendered speechless by questions he could not answer.

"Give me the reins, and get out of my way!" John shouted. "I need to be by myself! I'm going to ride through the countryside, perhaps into Baltimore, to clear my head of this painful betrayal."

Elijah quickly recovered his wits. "Please, Mister John, let me drive you where you want to go."

"No damn it, give me the reins!" John shouted. With that, he grabbed the reins from Elijah's hand, mounted to the driver's seat of the carriage, took the whip, and snapped it above the horse's back. The mare started immediately and John guided the carriage through the gate and onto the Falls Turnpike. He drove recklessly through the surrounding village until its boundary was behind him, and then urged the horse to a full gallop, causing the carriage to lurch wildly. His mind was full of indignation and rage. His life was in chaos and there was little he could do about it. The nearly out-of-control ride that John was experiencing had the adrenalin pumping in his system. It was the distraction he sought. As he entered the outskirts of Baltimore City, he slowed the carriage, but was still traveling at an excessive speed as he approached a blind curve that included a railroad crossing.

The engineer of a locomotive approaching the same crossing was engrossed in conversation with his fireman and failed to sound the whistle, as was the usual practice. He didn't see the horse-drawn carriage until it was too late.

John almost made it. The horse got across the tracks just in time as did most of the carriage, but the locomotive's cowcatcher caught a rear wheel and flipped the carriage over on its side. John flew through the air and hit the ground head first, breaking his neck in the process. He died instantly.

8

GALA DAYS OF WAR

The discussion of the accident that took their father's life cast a pall over the brothers. This was the first time that they had been together since happier pre-war days. While they had shared their grief through letters at the time, now, in the presence of the other surviving sons, each was struck with a profound sense of loss.

John was the first to regain his composure. "Mr. Whitman, when did William learn of our father's death?"

"It was in late October, I believe. He received a letter from his stepmother that contained the bad news. She was quite open about her role in the chain of events, but William didn't place blame upon her."

"Conversely, I was quite angry with Sarah," Clifton admitted. "In retrospect, nothing was gained by my bitterness toward her—in fact, much was lost. I'm ashamed to have been so harsh in my judgment. Our father died in an accident caused by his own recklessness."

"Not in my view," Melville snarled. "I am forever estranged from that woman and her misbegotten daughter—I will have nothing to do with them!"

"You forget that our father loved Sarah," John responded sharply. "That simple truth is not erased by the awful calamity that occurred. If father had lived, he would have forgiven Sarah for her wrongdoing. It's our duty, as his sons, to do so."

Melville snorted dismissively at his elder brother and leaned back in his chair. John scowled at Melville and made no effort to diffuse the tension.

"John, have you visited with Sarah and Laura since your return to Baltimore?" Clifton asked.

"Yes, I have," John replied. "On two separate occasions. I'd not met them prior to my first visit last month, so we made an effort to get to know each other. Sarah talked mostly of her desire to live abroad. In my opinion, crossing the sea won't distance either of them from the sources of their melancholy."

It was apparent to Whitman that it would be injudicious for the brothers to dwell further on this topic. "The fall of 1861 was quite a time for the 1st Maryland Battalion!" he exclaimed. "Their success at Manassas gave them a great deal of confidence and they made the most of it. When General Beauregard wanted to seize Federal posts along the Potomac that overlooked Alexandria, he sent Colonel James Ewell Brown Stuart's cavalry and the Marylanders to do it. And it was accomplished with great dash and élan!"

* * *

J.E.B. Stuart was so impressed with the speed and endurance of the 1st Maryland that he dubbed the enthusiastic Marylanders his "foot cavalry" and they had many opportunities to develop their soldiering skills on his forays. For nearly a month, the Maryland Battalion manned picket lines on Munson's and Mason's hills where they could see the crane atop the United States Capitol used to hoist cast iron sections of the new dome into place. They also observed the disposition of Union forces in front of Alexandria.

When the usual three-day tour of duty for pickets expired, the Marylanders petitioned to take the place of their relief and this curious request was granted several times over. The young soldiers of the battalion gained proficiency in military skills from this duty, but there was more to it than that. Union forces held an orchard out to their front that was full of ripe peaches. As the boys from Maryland liked peaches, they pushed the Federals out and ate the peaches. From their hilltop position, they observed cattle and pigs within the Union lines, so the impertinent Marylanders drove in the Yankee pickets, took the livestock, and cooked fresh beef and pork over their campfires. Confident in their prowess and unafraid of their adversaries, they foraged wherever they desired. An area between the lines contained a large cornfield. In early September, when the roasting ears are very fine but require selection to get the tender kind, the entire battalion deployed as skirmishers every morning, swept the field clear of Yankees, and picked the ears of corn at their leisure.

* * *

A committee of Congress asked the Cary Invincibles to make the first battle flags for the Confederate Army, furnishing Hetty, Jenny, and Connie with sketches and money for necessary materials. The girls immediately recognized the flag design as the one described by General Beauregard and his staff over dinner at Fairfax Court House.

The Carys conducted an extensive search for silk in flamboyant hues of poppy red and vivid dark blue, but were not pleased with the quality they found on the depleted shelves of Virginia's dry goods merchants. Making do with what was available, the flags were soon completed by the industrious girls. Gold fringe was sewn around the edges as permission had been received for the Carys to present them to their preferred generals as headquarters flags. Hetty had first choice and sent hers to General Joseph E. Johnston. Jenny dispatched her flag to General Beauregard. Connie's flag was destined for General Earl Van Dorn, a cavalry commander highly regarded early in the war. Connie soon thereafter made a flag for the Washington Artillery, composed of gentleman from New Orleans who had awoken the enthusiasm of many daughters of Virginia.

As the year came to a close, the war dominated every aspect of the Carys lives and those of their kith and kin. Connie's brother Clarence was a midshipman in the Confederate Navy aboard the cruiser CSS *Nashville*, under the command of Captain Robert Baker Pegram. Hetty and Jenny's brother, Miles Wilson Cary Jr., was serving as an officer on the staff of General Joseph E. Johnston. Numerous cousins had rallied to the flag and were serving in posts throughout the army. Most young men of class and stature had willingly answered the call to arms. Those lukewarm or not ambitious for military glory fared poorly in the presence of the average Confederate maiden.

* * *

CLIFTON HOUSE HOTEL
RICHMOND, VIRGINIA
FEBRUARY 6, 1862

As her mother was still needed at the hospital in Culpeper, Connie was sent to Richmond to be under the care of her uncle and aunt. Doctor Fairfax and his wife had abandoned Cameron, their elegant mansion in Alexandria, and fled southward in the first months of the war. In stark contrast to their previous abode, the austere quarters at Clifton House were scarcely adequate, but the Fairfaxes were happy to share their rooms with loved ones.

Hetty and Jenny soon arrived from Charlottesville where they had been visiting relatives and joined the growing refugee band at Clifton House. Before long, the girls took possession of a vacant office a few doors down the street. It was connected to the hotel by a dark and dingy underground passage, through which they passed by the flickering light of a bedroom candle on rainy days. In their improvised sitting room, the Carys gave contribution suppers. They provided a roast turkey or ham, loaves of bread, plates, utensils, and glassware. The invited guests brought other delicacies. Many a dignitary of state or army came through the door, lugging a bottle of brandied peaches, sardines, or French prunes to join a democratic commingling of officials, officers, and "high privates" having a fine time.

William attended several of these suppers while on furlough and special attention was lavished on him. The Carys had been informed by underground correspondence of his father's fatal accident and they comforted him with their kindness. The parents of Hetty and Jenny sent letters, as well, telling of the difficulties for Southern sympathizers living under Federal occupation. The authorities had searched their house on several occasions and far fewer students were attending Mrs. Cary's Southern Home School for Young Ladies.

* * *

The inauguration of Jefferson Davis as the Confederacy's first president was held on the twenty-second day of February, 1862. The date selected was symbolic as it was George Washington's birthday. The children and grandchildren of Virginia's Revolutionary War patriots thought it fitting as they too were engaged in a fight to liberate themselves from a tyrannical power. Davis took the oath of office during a ceremony conducted beneath the towering equestrian statue of General Washington in Richmond's Capitol Square. The shivering attendees huddled beneath umbrellas in a deluge of rain.

* * *

The Carys' circle of friends expanded rapidly within a short time as more people, particularly young men, became aware of their glamorous presence. Among the callers at Clifton House was Burton Norvell Harrison, a gentleman born in Louisiana of Virginia lineage. He was acquainted with Hetty and Jenny from gatherings of Episcopalians while visiting his uncle, the rector of St. Mary's Church near Edmonton, Maryland, during vacations from Yale. Having graduated with the class of 1859, Burton was teaching at Oxford University in Mississippi when hostilities broke out. He immediately returned to New Orleans and was on the brink of enlisting in the Washington Artillery when summoned to Richmond to serve as the president's private secretary.

The Carys frequently visited the home of Mrs. Virginia Pegram. She lived with her daughters, Mary and Jennie, in Linden Row on Franklin Street and conducted a school for young ladies on those premises. Her parlor was a favorite gathering place for the Cary girls and other prominent young women, and it was here that Hetty became reacquainted with Lieutenant Colonel John Pegram, the eldest of the Pegram sons, who had just returned to Richmond on parole. While he suffered the humiliation of being the first former United States Army officer to be captured during the war, his fortunes changed as Hetty, already the most sought-after belle in the wartime capital, responded positively to his ardent pursuit. Before his departure a few months later to serve as chief engineer in Beauregard's Western Army, their romantic involvement had developed into a betrothal.

Spring opened in Richmond with a burst of greenery, magnolia blossoms, and flowering shrubs which, as always, brought joy to the hearts of the populace. Further uplifting to the spirits of the Cary girls was the arrival of Connie's mother from Culpeper, the temporary hospital having finally closed. Mother, daughter, and cousins found new lodgings in Miss Clarke's very pleasant brown-walled house surrounded by trees and a garden on Franklin Street. From this delightful location, they enjoyed rides into the surrounding countryside and walks in the woods bordering the James River and the Kanawha Canal.

Soon thereafter, Francis W. Dawson rented a room at Miss Clarke's. He was an educated and charming Englishman who had come to Virginia as a common sailor aboard CSS *Nashville* to volunteer his services to the Confederate Army. Having impressed Captain Pegram and the ship's officers, including Connie's brother Clarence, with his intelligence and perseverance, Dawson was rewarded with the rank of master's mate on arrival at Beaufort, North Carolina. After a brief assignment in Norfolk, he was ordered to accompany Captain Pegram to New Orleans to join the Confederate ironclad *Louisiana*, then under construction. They arrived within twenty miles of the Crescent City where it was discovered that New Orleans had fallen to Union General Ben Butler. Returning to Richmond immediately, Dawson was assigned to the floating battery, *Drewry*, that lay at Rocketts, below Richmond on the James River.

* * *

Hetty, Jenny, and Connie were visiting the army camps of friends and family when they were unexpectedly treated to the stirring spectacle of a Confederate division on the march. Along a red clay road winding through the Virginia countryside came rank after rank of marching men dressed in gray and butternut, beneath banners of scarlet crossed with blue, accompanied by the beat of drums and a jaunty Irish tune played by fifers.

From the dust behind the infantry column emerged horsemen, then sixteen caissons and guns of the Washington Artillery. As the leading officer passed the Cary Invincibles, he recognized them and started a chant that was caught up along the line. "She breathes, she burns, she'll come. Maryland, My Maryland".

Hearing the chant, a military brass band in the column swung into the tune that was now well-known throughout the Confederate Army. As the mounted officers passed the girls, they saluted with their swords and the colors of the Washington Artillery were dipped in their honor. These were no holiday soldiers. They were veterans on the way to the front, where the call of duty never failed to find the flower of Louisiana. The Carys, standing bareheaded by the roadside, joined in the refrain, laughing and crying at once in their delight, a moment never to be forgotten in their lifetimes.

* * *

The achievements of the Maryland Battalion brought promotion to Brigadier General for Colonel George H. Steuart and Major Bradley T. Johnson was elevated to the rank of Colonel, assuming command of the battalion. However, all was not well in the ranks as the companies had been mustered into service at different times and places for inconsistent terms. Companies A and B, being "twelve-months men," reenlisted for the war and were granted thirty to sixty-day furloughs. The soldiers in companies C, H, and I also enlisted for twelve months, but many of them preferred to be mustered out so that they could join the cavalry or the artillery. Soldiers of the other companies were disgruntled as they enlisted for the war and were not entitled to either the furloughs or the opportunity to join a different service branch.

Orders were received by General Richard Ewell near the end of April to move his command, which included the Maryland Battalion, over the Blue Ridge to join General Thomas J. Jackson in the Shenandoah Valley. The news was well-received as Ewell's troops were delighted to serve under the famous "Stonewall" Jackson and be in the beautiful Valley of Virginia rather than the swamps of the Chickahominy. After a comfortable march over the mountains, they observed from the final summit the campfires of Jackson's army in the valley below. The following evening, the soldiers of General Ewell's division bivouacked beside General Jackson's division, but were amazed to wake up the next morning and find his camp deserted. Stonewall Jackson had quietly moved his division in the dead of night. Several days later, he attacked and defeated Union forces under General Robert H. Milroy at McDowell.

In mid–May, the enlistment of Company C of the Maryland Battalion expired and they clamored to be discharged, which was reluctantly allowed by Colonel Johnson. This occurrence revived the term of service question and caused dissatisfaction to fester within many soldiers who thought that they had been treated unfairly. To Colonel Johnson's chagrin, more and more men of his battalion refused to perform duty, believing that they too were entitled to discharge.

General Jackson returned with his division and ordered that both divisions march toward Front Royal as Federal forces occupied it. Knapsacks were placed in wagons so that the soldiers of the two divisions could move quickly to attack the enemy. The malcontents of the Maryland Battalion were disarmed and forced to march at the rear of its column under arrest. As they neared Front Royal, Colonel Johnson questioned the company sergeants and heard the opinion that only about half of the men could be depended upon in the upcoming battle.

* * *

1ST MARYLAND BATTALION
NEAR FRONT ROYAL, VIRGINIA
MAY 23, 1862

William and several of his messmates from Company D were assigned under Color Sergeant Joseph T. Doyle as guards for the dozens of disarmed soldiers at the end of the marching column. Their muskets were loaded, but each guard wondered if he could shoot a fellow battalion member if the situation required. Thus far, it had been a hard march under a hot sun, but the disarmed and disgruntled soldiers kept pace and caused no trouble.

The column came to a halt where the heavily treed hillsides descended steeply to the dirt road on which they marched. William walked out a few steps from the column and looked toward the head of the battalion. Color Sergeant Doyle stepped up beside him and inquired, straightforward as always, "What's going on up there, Prentiss?"

"I can see a mounted staff officer handing a message to Colonel Johnson," William replied as he squinted, and looked out from under the shade of his left hand. Color Sergeant Doyle grunted an acknowledgement and walked back toward the column.

The order was passed for the battalion to face right and each company commander quickly complied. Shortly thereafter, Colonel Johnson rode to the center of the battalion line and wheeled about, holding a piece of paper in his left hand. His face revealed both excitement and determination as he rode back and forth, gathering his thoughts. The eyes of every soldier in the battalion closely followed his movements.

Colonel Johnson reigned in his horse and stood in his stirrups. "Men of the Maryland Battalion! We have received an order," he shouted in a voice loud enough to be heard by all of the companies. He waved the paper above his head, brought it down before his face, and read the order verbatim.

"*Colonel Johnson will move the 1st Maryland to the front with all dispatch and, in conjunction with Wheat's Battalion, attack the enemy at Front Royal. The army will halt until you pass.*" Looking up from the paper, Colonel Johnson shouted "It is signed Jackson!"

Colonel Johnson sat down in his saddle and looked from one end of his small battalion to the other before speaking again. "You have heard this order from General Jackson and you are in a pretty condition to obey it. Shame on you— shame on you! I shall return this order to General Jackson with the endorsement that the 1st Maryland refuses to face the enemy, for I will not trust the honor of the glorious old State to discontented, dissatisfied men. I won't lead men who have no heart. Every man who is discontented must fall out of ranks, step to the rear, and march with the guard."

There was a hush along the line. Not one soldier moved a muscle as they stood in the ranks, their attention riveted on their commanding officer. Colonel Johnson rode back and forth before several companies as he looked into the eyes of his soldiers to gauge their heart and fortitude. Seeing that these soldiers returned his look with steady eyes, he wheeled about and rode to a position in front of the disgruntled soldiers under guard at the rear of the column.

"Before this day, I was proud to call myself a Marylander, but now, God knows, I would rather be known as anything else. Shame on you to bring this stigma upon the fair fame of your native state. Marylanders you call yourselves? Profane not that hallowed name again, for it is not yours! What Marylander ever before threw down his arms and deserted his colors in the presence of the enemy, and those arms, and those colors, too, placed in your hands by a woman?"

William could hear murmuring among the soldiers that he guarded. He gripped his musket more tightly and turned to look at the ranks of the discontented. He noticed that Doyle and the other guards were doing the same.

It was evident to the soldiers of the Maryland Battalion that Colonel Johnson's tirade had just begun as his face turned red from a hot rush of anger. Every man stood motionless, each row in perfect alignment, as the intensity of his words pummeled them. "Never before has one single blot defaced her honored history. Could it be possible to conceive a cruelty more atrocious, an outrage more damnable?"

William studied the soldiers under arrest. He could see facial expressions that had been sullen for days turn to shock and, in some cases, bewilderment. The eyes of a few began to tear as they received this verbal broadside from their commander. Even Colonel Johnson's warhorse sensed the anger coming from the man in the saddle and tossed his head in agitation as he pranced in place along the roadway.

"Go home and publicize to the world your infamy. Boast of it when you meet your fathers and mothers, brothers, sisters, and sweethearts. Tell them it was you who, when brought face to face with the enemy, proved yourselves recreants and acknowledge yourselves to be cowards!" From his vantage point, William could hear barely audible denials escape from the mouths of the stunned men of the nearest companies as each reacted to the condemnation being heaped upon them.

Colonel Johnson reigned in the excited motions of his horse. He spoke loudly and glared at the soldiers under arrest, but he wanted the entire battalion to hear what was said, as he knew discontent lingered within many men still under arms.

"Tell them this, and see if you are not spurned from their presence like some loathsome leper and despised, detested, nay, abhorred, by those whose confidence you have so shamefully betrayed. You will wander over the face of the earth with the brand 'coward'—'traitor'—indelibly imprinted upon your foreheads and, in the end, sink into a dishonored grave, unwept for, uncared for, leaving behind a heritage to your posterity—the shame and contempt of every honest man and virtuous woman in the land!"

His denunciation complete, Colonel Johnson stared coldly at the reluctant soldiers who looked back at him in pained silence. These were proud men. They were veterans. They had performed brilliantly during the past year and were celebrated in the Army of Northern Virginia for their accomplishments. Each man, now thoroughly chastised, confronted his own shortcoming.

Not a split second had passed when the surrounding hillsides rang with an explosion of cheers by the entire battalion and exclamations loudly declaring that they were still in the fight. William shouted joyfully with the rest, his arms flung over his head, waving his musket excitedly in the air. Regiments on the road ahead and behind the battalion heard the uproar, yet no one was surprised as the enthusiasm of the Marylanders was legendary. The disarmed men under guard broke ranks and crowded around Colonel Johnson, begging to be reinstated as soldiers of the Maryland Battalion. Colonel Johnson immediately released them from arrest. They ran to the ordnance wagon with a wild yell, seized their muskets, and buckled on their equipment, as they were eager to regain the respect of their commander.

With colors flying, the Maryland Battalion marched at a quick step past the halted columns of Ewell's and Jackson's veterans to the almost deafening cheers. "The Marylanders are going to the front," shouted one crusty, old corporal in a Virginia regiment. "They'll make the fur fly for sure," shouted another Virginian as the boys from Maryland tramped by with their rapid, swinging step, their hearts bursting with pride, their honor intact, as they pressed forward to meet the enemy.

Within a mile, the Maryland Battalion debouched from the wooded road into an open field, struck the Union outposts and quickly drove them in toward Front Royal. They were supported in the attack by Roberdeau Wheat's Louisiana Tigers, who were dressed in dark blue waist-length jackets, red wool fezzes, red shirts, red woolen sashes, baggy blue-and-white-striped cotton pantaloons, and white canvas leggings. The Tigers were armed with Mississippi Rifles and each carried a wicked-looking Bowie knife. They had the reputation of being formidable fighters, although they were also notorious in the Confederate Army for their unruly behavior.

"Old Jack" was always mysterious in his stratagem. He kept his army hidden as he sent the small force to fight it out with the Yankees without additional infantry support. One can only guess at his reasons. He did, however, send two regiments of Virginia cavalry around the Federal left to attack its flank. General Jackson's confidence was based on his knowledge of the size and nature of the Union forces in Front Royal. Before the battle, accompanied by Captain Henry Kyd Douglas of his staff and General Richard Ewell, he had ridden ahead of his column to survey the ground leading to the town. While they were observing great confusion in the enemy camp, a young woman wearing a dark blue dress with a fancy white apron was seen running up the hill toward them, waving her white bonnet. General Jackson sent Captain Douglas galloping forward to intercept her. As he drew near, he was surprised to hear the young woman calling his name. He found that she was Belle Boyd, who he had known from childhood. After taking a moment to catch her breath, Belle reported that the Yankee force defending the town consisted of just one regiment of Maryland infantry, a few artillery pieces, and several companies of cavalry. She encouraged an immediate attack to bag them all. Captain Douglas raised his cap in salute and galloped back to General Jackson who immediately issued orders for the attack.

As the Confederate Marylanders and Louisianans swept through the town of Front Royal, they discovered that they were up against the Federal 1st Maryland Infantry Regiment, commanded by Colonel John R. Kenly. The Federal soldiers made two valiant stands. However, greatly outnumbered and eventually outflanked, they were routed with a large number being made prisoner. This minor Confederate victory forced Union General Nathaniel P. Banks to abruptly retreat from Strasburg and set the stage for a major Federal defeat at the first Battle of Winchester several days later. Because of the tremendous amount of military supplies captured at Winchester, the Confederates dubbed the defeated general "Commissary Banks."

* * *

On the thirty-first day of May, 1862, General Joseph Johnston attacked a Federal army under Major General George B. McClellan that had advanced up the Virginia Peninsula to the village of Seven Pines, near Fair Oaks Station. Professor Thaddeus Lowe provided McClellan with early warning of advancing enemy troops by telegraph from his balloon *Intrepid*, but the Union commander believed that the Confederates were feigning an attack. Johnston's assault, although poorly coordinated, initially inflicted heavy casualties and pushed the Union forces back. During the two-day battle, each side fed additional reinforcements into action, but neither made much headway, and both claimed victory. It was a costly stalemate, fought within six miles of Richmond, where the thunder of artillery could clearly be heard.

Nearly all women in Richmond had husbands, sons, brothers, or nephews in the battle at Seven Pines, yet they turned their attention to preparing for a flood of wounded men by making bandages, scraping lint, and improvising beds with whatever materials they could find, even sewn-together cushions from church pews. As anticipated, a procession of ambulances and other vehicles pressed into service brought droves of wounded and dying soldiers into the city during the night following the first day of the battle. Connie's mother was in her element and her daughter and nieces were pressed into service to care for men in every stage of mutilation. Many were suffering intensely and all were in need of attention. Wine cellars of private residences were opened and priceless quantities of Madeira, port, sherry, and brandy were sent to the hospitals. White-jacketed servants carrying silver trays with dishes of fine porcelain, covered with white damask napkins, containing soups, creams, jellies, biscuits, eggs a la crème, and other delicacies darted down the street to feed the wounded. Doing their part in an effort that encompassed the entire community, the Cary girls spent several days and nights toiling in stifling-hot hospital wards until they nearly reached the point of exhaustion.

The Battle of Seven Pines concluded the Union offensive that pushed up the Virginia Peninsula to the gates of Richmond and cost a frightful amount of precious blood on both sides. The battle was tactically inconclusive. The Union advance was halted and the Confederates fell back to the defensive works around Richmond. Among the seriously wounded was General Joseph E. Johnston, whose loss prompted President Davis to appoint General Robert E. Lee as the new commander of the Confederate Army in Virginia.

* * *

MISS CLARKE'S HOUSE
RICHMOND, VIRGINIA
JUNE 6, 1862

The late afternoon sun was still warm as Master's Mate Dawson trudged up to the house where he was boarding. He sat on the porch bench before going to his room, as he wanted to think in the open air about his present circumstances. The fact of the matter was that Dawson was less than pleased with his assignment and generally disappointed with his prospects in the Confederate Navy. He just needed to figure out what he was going to do about it.

As much as he appreciated the kindness and consideration extended to him by Captain Pegram and other navy officers of his acquaintance, his original intent had been to join the Confederate Army. Dawson's current duty station was aboard *Drewry*, a lighter about eighty feet long and fifteen feet wide, with neither power nor sails to maneuver during an engagement. Situated at one end of this floating battery was a v-shaped wooden shield covered with heavy iron bars. In the angle of this shield was a porthole for her one heavy gun.

His thoughts were interrupted by the voices of Hetty and Jenny Cary in animated conversation, walking up the street and mounting the porch steps. "Good afternoon, ladies," Dawson said as he got to his feet to greet the two fellow boarders at Miss Clarke's.

"Good afternoon, Mr. Dawson," responded each of the sisters in turn.

"It's such a delightful day," Hetty said as she stopped before him. "Have you just returned from duty?"

"Yes, indeed," Dawson replied. "I'm pleased to report that *Drewry* fended off an attack this afternoon by three beavers and two rather large muskrats. Our stout defense of the capital city was conducted with intrepidity and in accordance with the highest traditions of the naval service. Richmond remains safe from depredations along the James."

"Oh Mr. Dawson, that's so silly," Jenny giggled while Hetty bestowed an amused smile upon him. The two young ladies opened the door and entered the house.

"Quite right," Dawson said as he sat back down and resumed his self-indulgent contemplation.

That evening, in the parlor, Dawson joined the other boarders and a few friends who had come to call. Among the gentlemen present were Charles Ellis Munford, a private in the Letcher Artillery, and his friend and University of Virginia classmate, William Ransom Johnson Pegram. Willie, the younger brother of John Pegram and nephew of Robert Pegram, whose ship had brought Dawson to the Confederacy, was the captain of the Purcell Battery of Richmond. He wore gold-rimmed spectacles befitting the boyish simplicity of his appearance. Dawson had been waiting for the right moment to reveal to Willy his plan to leave the navy and join the army. When an attractive young lady drew Ellis Munford away from the conversation the three men were sharing, Dawson broached the subject.

"Willy, I haven't had an opportunity to tell you of my recent adventure," Dawson said.

"What, pray tell, have you gotten into this time, Francis?" Willy inquired with an amused tone.

"On the first day of the fighting at Seven Pines, I obtained a leave of absence from *Drewry* after ascertaining that there was no threat along the river," Dawson replied. "I hoisted my navy sword to my shoulder and hastened to the field of battle."

"My Goodness, what an ambitious fellow you are!" Willy exclaimed.

"Most assuredly," Dawson replied. "As it was late afternoon by the time I got there, I fell in with a Georgia Regiment and asked to be given a musket and go in with them in the morning. They gave me the musket and I took my place in the ranks. The next morning came, but the fight did not, as it turned out that the Georgians were held in reserve. Quite a poor choice on my part, but after committing myself, I couldn't simply leave when it became evident that they would not be engaged."

"No, that would have been most inappropriate," Willy agreed, before taking another sip from his cup of tea.

"So I traipsed back to Richmond, quite dejected by the outcome, or lack thereof. In any case, this debacle of my own making convinced me that I should leave the navy in order to join the army."

"That's a drastic step, Francis, one not to be taken lightly. Have you discussed this matter with my uncle?"

"No, I haven't. Whilst I'm most grateful for everything he's done for me, I do believe that he would object strenuously. Rather than subject either of us to that difficulty, I intend to go straight to the Navy Department within a fortnight and hand in my resignation, stating that I'm doing so in order to immediately join the army as a private soldier."

Willy peered at Dawson with a slightly bemused expression. "Francis, I'm in need of more tea. Are you ready for another cup?" Without waiting for an answer, Willy turned and walked to the silver tea service on a nearby table. Dawson followed him and stood waiting as Willy filled his cup.

Dawson was undeterred. "Willy, I want to join Purcell's Battery as a private. Will you permit that?"

"Oh Francis, it would be such a waste to put you back into the ranks, even in the artillery. I encourage you to look around a bit before making such a decision. Something better will surely turn up if you just wait."

Jenny swooped in between Willy and Dawson. "You two gentlemen should talk less of manly things and do more to entertain the ladies in this room." By the look on her face, they could tell that anything less than full compliance was

futile. Dawson liked Jenny and found her to be unfailingly amiable in all circumstances, but having too great a tendency to expand on things. This trait he
disliked, mainly because he was prone to do the same.

Willy, always a Southern gentleman, quickly surrendered to her terms
with a pleasant smile. He also had a look of relief on his face. Jenny linked
arms with both men and escorted them into the circle that revolved, as usual,
around Hetty.

Earlier in the evening, Dawson had shared with Willy his belief that the Cary
girls would be the center of attention at any place and time. He had stated that
the celebrated Baltimore beauty was even more beautiful in her noble mind
and generous disposition than in her charming face. Dawson had also opined
that Hetty overshadowed Jenny, who was exceptionally bright and perceptive.
He had heard Jenny joke that the only inscription necessary for her tombstone
would be "here lies the sister of Hetty Cary, the lady who presented the Confederate colors to Beauregard's troops at Manassas." Connie, attractive in her own
right and several years younger than her cousins, nevertheless possessed a very
clear sense of self and a strong, independent spirit.

Jenny herded her two prisoners into the circle where they listened to Connie
discuss the shortage of morphine, quinine, and other critical medical supplies
at Richmond's hospitals in the aftermath of Seven Pines.

"I read in the newspaper recently that there has been criticism of some young
lady visitors to hospitals who are partial in their attentions to dashing, romantic, wounded officers," Dawson interjected. All heads turned in his direction.
Dawson was undaunted by the frowns directed at him by the women.

"One such young woman is quoted as asking a noble-looking cavalry officer
'Is there not anything that I can do for you?' 'No,' he'd replied wearily. Baffled,
the persistent young woman said, 'Do let me do something for you—will you let
me wash your face?' To this request the sad response was, 'Well, if you want to
right bad, I reckon you must, but that will make seven times that my face has
been washed this evening.'" Dawson was confident that he would be rewarded
with laughter and winced as soon as he realized it wasn't forthcoming. The
women glared at him and the men merely smiled in embarrassment.

"That's hardly representative of the skill, hard work, and devotion provided to wounded soldiers by the vast majority of women working in hospitals!" Connie exclaimed, her eyes burning with indignation. "Whilst our efforts cannot compare with those of my mother, my cousins and I worked hard to properly care for every soldier assigned to our responsibility by the surgeons."

"Please forgive me, Miss Connie, for I did not mean to impugn your contributions or motives, nor those of your cousins. If I have done so, I apologize for my thoughtlessness. It was not my desire to offend anyone, but merely to relay the humorous story that I read in the newspaper."

"I'm sure that you didn't aspire to assail our good intentions," Hetty responded before Connie could speak. "In fact, I must admit that I too laughed at the description of that silly young woman's encounter with the heroic appearing cavalry officer."

The tension created by Dawson's faux pas quickly dissipated and a relaxed ambience was restored in the parlor. Willy gave Dawson a "you should have known better" look. Dawson was careful to be a good listener as he moved about the room and participated in other conversations.

A young officer was discussing with Hetty the recent wounding of General Johnston and the appointment of a new commander of the army defending Richmond. "I was really quite surprised when Robert E. Lee was given command of the army," the young man asserted.

"And why is that?" Hetty inquired, her eyes slightly narrowing.

"Well, due to his age and background as a military engineer. He's been superb at organization of our forces over the past year, but his only field command fizzled badly in western Virginia. And since taking over the army, his propensity to entrench has earned him King of Spades as a nickname."

"The Cheat Mountain Campaign was a disappointment due to the failings of General Lee's superiors and continual bickering among three inept, political generals who were his subordinates," Willy forcefully responded. "His effectiveness and courage under fire in the Mexican War is well-documented in official records. In my opinion, President Davis selected the right man to serve as our commander."

The talkative lieutenant hesitated. He was reluctant to contradict the artillery captain glaring intensely at him. Before he could speak, Hetty weighed into the fray, locking eyes, and speaking directly to the young man.

"I trust that you are aware that Robert E. Lee is the son of Light-Horse Harry Lee, a hero of the American Revolution. He is married to Mary Ana Randolph Custis, the granddaughter of Martha Washington. General Robert E. Lee is, first and foremost, a Virginian and a gentleman of impeccable character. He possesses great intelligence, dignity, and integrity. I can think of no better qualifications for the general to whom we entrust the defense of our country in these perilous times."

The young man was entirely subdued by this retort. He slipped into the background and was the first to take his leave as the evening's festivities wound down. After the departure of the last caller, Hetty stopped Dawson before he retired to his room and informed him that she was sending letters the following morning to Baltimore by a person prepared to run the blockade. Knowing that Dawson wrote to his mother in England, she suggested that he compose an epistle to go by this clandestine channel, to be posted in Baltimore and cross the ocean by regular steamer. Dawson wrote a long letter that night by candlelight telling his mother about his recent adventures and high hopes for his future in the Confederacy.

* * *

Following the inconclusive Battle of Seven Pines, McClellan's army sat passively on the outskirts of Richmond for nearly a month while General Lee reorganized his army and prepared an offensive to drive the invaders away from the capital. To augment his forces defending Richmond, Lee sent for Major General Jackson's Army, which had just completed its successful Valley Campaign. Additionally, in mid-June, Lee dispatched Brigadier General J.E.B Stuart's cavalry on a three-day reconnaissance that rode for one hundred miles completely around the Federal army. Stuart's mission was to discover the Federal army's points of weakness in preparation for Lee's attack on it.

General Jackson was directed to have his army near Richmond by the twenty-fifth of June, 1862. A week prior to his scheduled arrival, he began moving his army from the Valley, in his usual secretive manner. Colonel Bradley Johnson was riding along a street in Staunton when he happened upon General Jackson who asked him if had received his orders. When Colonel Johnson replied that he had not, General Jackson told him, without disclosing the destination, to march his battalion immediately to the station with Lawton's Georgia Brigade and go in the cars. After arriving at Frederick's Hall on the Virginia Central, Colonel Johnson was able to determine the railway arrangements. They were going to the defense of Richmond.

* * *

Prior to the first of the Seven Days Battles in late June, Dawson resigned from the navy and journeyed to the camp of the Purcell Battery, then on the Mechanicsville Turnpike. He reported to his friend Captain Willy Pegram who, when confronted with a *fait accompli,* relented and Dawson was enlisted as a private soldier.

The Purcell Battery, attached to Field's Brigade of A. P. Hill's Division, was soon in motion. This was the first time that Dawson had observed large numbers of Confederate troops marching to meet the enemy. The scene before him was an exhilarating and imposing blend of sights and sounds—rows of gleaming bayonets and waving flags—the steady tramp of the infantry—the rumbling wheels of caissons and guns of the artillery.

As the Purcell Battery neared Mechanicsville on June twenty-sixth, 1862, the order rang out "Attention, Battery! Forward! Trot! March!" With a loud cheer, the artillerymen rattled along the road and came into battery in an open field within full view of the enemy. The guns were instantly loaded and firing began. Willy remained in his saddle, shouting orders to his men, no more concerned at shells plowing up dirt about him than if he had been lounging on his mother's porch in Linden Row.

Dawson was not yet assigned to a gun, so he tied his horse behind a nearby corncrib and waited to fill any vacancy caused by the furious return fire from Union batteries. It wasn't long before a solid shot bowled past him and killed one man, tore a leg from another, and threw three horses into a bloody heap.

Dawson, energized by the fierce excitement of battle, stepped to the gun as Number Five, bringing ammunition from the limber to Number Two at the gun.

As the engagement continued into evening, the force of an exploding shell knocked Dawson to the ground, his leg pierced by a fragment below the knee near the femoral artery. It was an ugly wound, but Dawson tied a handkerchief around his leg, returned to his post, and remained there until the battery was withdrawn after sunset. Four men of the battery had been killed and forty-three wounded out of the seventy-five engaged. Dawson hobbled in the darkness on the road to Richmond for several miles before catching a ride on an ambulance.

* * *

1ST MARYLAND BATTALION
NEAR GAINES' MILL, VIRGINIA
JUNE 27, 1862

The morning broke bright and beautiful over Jackson's army. They had been on the march since long before sunrise on their way to reinforce the defenders of Richmond. The Maryland Battalion, which had not been assigned to a brigade due to its depleted condition, was situated at the head of the column. The veterans knew what was forthcoming as they marched toward the distant thunder of artillery. Word passed up and down the ranks that Old Jack smelt blood.

As William tramped along, he noticed a nearby cluster of mounted officers scrutinizing a large column of infantry several hundred yards to the right on a parallel road. The consternation of the officers was evident when these troops halted and turned toward them in line of battle. Jackson's column was also halted while the staff officers, including General Jackson and Colonel Johnson, conferred close enough for William to overhear their conversation. When the unidentified force deployed skirmishers, General Jackson ordered his column into line of battle as he supposed them to be the enemy. William, facing the advancing troops, saw battle flags before their front ranks that were impossible to identify at such distance. He noted that their uniforms were darker than he had seen on other Confederates and most were wearing white gaiters, something entirely unknown in Jackson's command.

A young staff officer rode away from the group, reined in his horse beside William's company, and sat in the saddle staring at the approaching battle line. It was George Booth, William's old friend from Maryland militia days. He had recently accepted a lieutenant's commission and was acting adjutant of the battalion. Several of William's fellow soldiers had received commissions in recent months. William, on the other hand, had made the decision not to do so. His education and background provided the same pathway to higher rank, but he spurned every well-intentioned offer. William was committed to do his duty for God and country, but not as a leader responsible for the lives of others.

The approach of the unknown formation continued and brought William's attention back to the present. He had heard George contend to the senior officers that the unidentified force was Confederate, but they were not of the same opinion. Knowing that George could be impetuous, William watched to see what he would do as the battle line came closer and conflict seemed imminent. He was not surprised when Lieutenant Booth, no longer able to restrain himself, dug his spurs into his horse, and galloped forward without orders to meet the rapidly approaching skirmish line. All eyes were upon the lieutenant as he reached the skirmishers, spoke briefly with them, and then galloped back to report that the approaching force was General Maxey Gregg's South Carolina Brigade. An hour had been consumed by this affair when no time was left to spare. Later, guides sent to lead them through a dense pine forest chose the wrong road and more valuable time was lost retracing steps. Meanwhile, the battle to relieve Richmond was underway miles ahead, much to General Jackson's frustration.

The Confederate Army, under General Lee, renewed its attack that morning against Brigadier General Fitz John Porter's Fifth Corps, which was entrenched in a strong defensive line behind Boatswain's Swamp north of the Chickahominy. The Union line held fast throughout the long afternoon, inflicting heavy casualties on a series of disjointed attacks. At dusk, Rebel forces prepared for yet another charge.

The volume of artillery and musketry steadily increased as General Jackson's column finally approached the raging battle and its lead elements became hotly engaged. As Jackson prepared to attack, the Maryland Battalion was ordered to guard artillery batteries and arrest stragglers behind the lines. Colonel Johnson, not satisfied with this assignment, decided to offer his small but dedicated band of veterans for what he considered to be more appropriate work.

Spotting General Jackson on a hillside overlooking the battlefield, Colonel Johnson galloped up the hill and found the general and his staff completing plans for the pending attack. As he rode up, Johnson called out a greeting. "Good evening, General."

"Good evening, Colonel," General Jackson replied curtly.

"If you want me, I am here," reported Colonel Johnson, his teeth clenched and his eyes blazing with excitement as he reined his horse into place beside the general.

"Very good, Colonel," General Jackson replied and turned his attention back to his staff officers. When orders had been issued and couriers dispatched, the officers listened intently to the roaring inferno of fire that rolled back and forth across the battlefield.

General Jackson suddenly turned in his saddle toward Colonel Johnson and spoke to him in a calm voice. "Colonel, take all your infantry in—I shall support the batteries with cavalry. And Johnson, make your men shoot like they are shooting at a mark, slow and low, hit them here and here," General Jackson said as he thrust Johnson in the waist with his forefinger.

"Where shall I go in?"

"Over there," Jackson replied, pointing to the left.

"When I break them, which way shall I push?"

"Press that way!" Jackson exclaimed, swinging his arm to the right.

William was standing in the ranks with the rest of the battalion awaiting the return of their commanding officer. Soon Colonel Johnson rode up and reigned in his horse before the center company in the battalion line of battle. Standing in his stirrups, he shouted, "Men, we alone represent Maryland, here. We are few in number, but for that reason our duty to our state is greater. We must do her honor!"

The attention of every man in the battalion was concentrated on Colonel Johnson, and they heard his orders immediately echoed by the company commanders. "Shoulder arms! Right shoulder shift, arms! Forward, march!" The battalion advanced smartly until it reached a patch of undergrowth impassable by the mounted officers. Here the soldiers halted and dressed their ranks as the horses of the field and staff officers were sent back. The battalion plunged into the heavy brush and, emerging on open ground on the other side, reformed ranks and moved ahead in line of battle. A half-mile to their front, a thick curtain of smoke lay across the field, illuminated by incessant flashes of musketry and from which a tremendous roar erupted.

As they tramped forward, William could see an occasional frightened man or small groups of wounded soldiers emerge from the smoke, headed for the rear. Shells burst overhead and musket balls whizzed through the air. Surgeon Richard P. Johnson, Assistant Surgeon Thomas S. Latimer, and the hospital attendants were thirty paces behind the line of battle as shot and shell tore through the ranks. Wounded soldiers were attended to on the spot by the battalion's doctors, who were as close to the line as the field officers.

Union batteries were raking the field with devastating fire from the right. Colonel Johnson gave the order, "Battalion right wheel!" and it swung around like an arm toward the foe. The little band of Marylanders advanced all alone across the storm-swept field, soon overtaking Lawton's Georgia Brigade. Enemy fire became intense and the Georgians were ordered to lie down. Colonel Johnson marched his battalion beside the prostrate Georgians who broke into hearty cheers as the Maryland Battalion pressed on in perfect order. Only a short distance was traversed before fragments of other regiments emerged from the smoke and raced toward the rear in great confusion. As retreating soldiers rushed past and nearly swept the men of the Maryland Battalion off their feet, the Marylanders became unsteady for the first time, treading on each other's heels as alignment of the ranks was broken.

"Halt!" cried out Colonel Johnson. "On the colors, dress! Order arms! Shoulder arms! Present arms! Shoulder arms! Forward! March!" Despite canister shot screaming over their heads, each order was given in a slow and deliberate manner and obeyed as if the battalion was on dress parade. The effect was immediate. The Marylanders recovered their composure and restored their ranks. Soldiers of other regiments running to the rear observed their steadfast formation and rallied on the flanks of the Maryland Battalion. The color-bearer of Hampton's Legion planted his colors on their left and men of the legion rallied around it. Fragments of other retreating regiments whose officers had been killed or wounded lined up with them and soon Colonel Johnson gathered a small brigade that would otherwise have been lost.

Brigadier General Winder observed what was happening and dispatched Lieutenant McHenry Howard of his staff to Colonel Johnson with orders to wait until he could send up the 1st Virginia Brigade to join the attacking force. Within a very short time, the Stonewall Brigade came up on the right flank of Colonel Johnson's line. At his command, the battle line swept forward toward Union batteries supported by infantry under cover of the road embankment and a breastwork of knapsacks. Heavy musketry and artillery fire was unleashed upon the advancing Confederate battle line, but it was unstoppable. The Union line collapsed and the Battle of Gaines' Mills was won.

* * *

Additional battles were fought during the Seven Days Campaign at Savage's Station, White Oak Swamp, Frayser's Farm, and Malvern Hill, but General McClellan had been unnerved by Lee's victory at Gaines' Mills and the erroneous notion that his forces were badly outnumbered. He ordered his army to retreat, precipitously ending the Peninsular Campaign of 1862.

The sanguinary battles during the siege of Richmond were fought nearby and the townspeople were immediately stricken by the sacrifices of their defenders. The family of Lieutenant Charles Ellis Munford of the Letcher Battery was sitting on their front porch, engaged in quiet conversation, enjoying the cooler temperature that falls after sunset on a sultry summer day. His body, lying across a caisson, was brought home from Malvern Hill and delivered to his parents and siblings, who, until that moment, were unaware of their loss.

WOMEN AT WAR

John shook his head in wonderment. "Whilst I've thought of the Rebels for years as the enemy, it's impossible not to admire their courage in battle. William and his comrades were excellent soldiers and devoted to their cause."

"Well, after all, the Rebels were Americans just like us, although their primary loyalty was to their state rather than the Union." Clifton responded. "Because of that perspective, they saw us as the 'Yankee race'—as foreign invaders. And secesh women were just as adamant as the men about the defense of the Confederacy. That's what made the war so bloody—so hard fought."

"Major, I've been meaning to ask if you knew Hetty Cary that well?" Whitman asked.

"Not really," Clifton replied. "I had met her on a few occasions before the war. She knew that I was William's brother and was aware of my strong Union sentiments. That made her somewhat distant, but still cordial. Our father was acquainted with her parents as they were all in the business of education in Baltimore."

"What was your impression of her?" Whitman pressed.

"As was widely acknowledged, her beauty was simply breathtaking," Clifton replied. "Despite my better sense, I found myself to be utterly captivated by her. She was, without a doubt, the most beguiling woman I have ever met. You could easily make a fool of yourself in her presence."

"William was very fond of Hetty and appreciative of her kindness and consideration," Whitman commented. "But he was not infatuated with her. He somehow understood that beneath the dazzling beauty there was a nice but fragile woman."

"Did William remain enamored with Laura throughout the war?" John inquired.

"She was the woman of his dreams," Whitman replied matter-of-factly.

"Jenny Cary was more attractive and appealing to me," Clifton said to no one in particular. "Her sensible nature and humor were charming—although she too had little use for a pro-Union man such as me."

Melville sat quietly in his chair listening to the conversation, an incredulous look on his face.

* * *

MISS CLARKE'S HOUSE
RICHMOND, VIRGINIA
JULY 10, 1862

During several weeks in the hospital, army surgeons treated an infection in Dawson's leg before determining that there was no danger of serious complications. He was released with orders to recuperate in his personal quarters. Shortly after the departure of the attendants who delivered him to his room, two soldiers knocked on the open door and asked permission to enter. Dawson, recumbent on the bed with his leg elevated by a pillow, recognized neither of them but welcomed them anyway, pleased to have the company of fellow soldiers. They introduced themselves as Captain William Murray and Private William Prentiss of the Maryland Battalion. Following an exchange of pleasantries, Captain Murray explained that he had a message for Dawson from Miss Hetty

Cary, causing Dawson to sit up in his bed. The captain proceeded to deliver the message with a stern expression. "Hetty would have come down to your room with her sister to see you, but because you criticized so sharply the conduct of young ladies attending to wounded soldiers, she would not think of doing violence to your feelings by giving you any personal attention."

Dawson was rarely struck speechless, but he had no response to this pronouncement until he noticed that the private was suppressing a smile. Before he could speak, Hetty guessed that the game might be up and stuck her head around the doorframe. "Well, Mr. Dawson, I sense that you are floundering in uncertainty as we failed to elicit an immediate rejoinder. I'm happy to have turned the tables on you for once. You richly deserve to endure such a dilemma, brief though it was!"

The sound of laughter behind her revealed the presence of Jenny and, a second later, the two young women entered the room. All was forgiven and the Cary sisters, their Aunt Monimia and Cousin Constance treated Dawson royally over the next several weeks as he recovered from his wound. The inflammation in his leg gradually subsided, in part due to an arrangement that Captain Murray rigged to drip water on the bandages, keeping them moist and cool. Dawson was pleased that the Marylander was a frequent visitor to Miss Clarke's and realized that Captain Murray was deeply attached to Jenny Cary, although the couple was quite circumspect about it.

* * *

PIZZINI'S

RICHMOND, VIRGINIA

JULY 12, 1862

The young people seated around a table on the veranda were delighted to be sharing a beautiful summer afternoon with the dearest of friends. For Captain Murray and Private Prentiss, this was a refreshing change of pace from camp life and a rare opportunity to be in the company of pretty young women. Hetty, Jenny, and Connie were pleased to be visiting the shop of the most famous Italian confectioner in the city for strawberries, ice cream, and lively conversation with two favorite soldiers.

"I've taken quite a liking to Jefferson Davis," Hetty said as she placed her ice cream dish on the table. "I often see him walking from the president's mansion through Capitol Square to his executive office. He's become a familiar figure on the streets each day and he never fails to be courteous and cordial to everyone he meets."

"And he has such a dignified, soldierly bearing," Jenny chimed in.

"The fact that he spent several years at West Point and served with distinction in the Black Hawk and Mexican Wars might have something to do with that," Captain Murray responded with a gleeful smile on his face.

Jenny smiled back at him and said, "No doubt that's true. But it's his stately demeanor and dedication to our country that means the most to me."

"Did you know that I met President Lincoln just after his inauguration?" Connie asked, surprising every one. All quickly let it be known that they were unaware of the occurrence.

"It happened when I was on my way back to Virginia from Baltimore in the spring of 1861, before I became such a fierce partisan. I was not yet fully aware of the important issues of the day," she added apologetically.

"That's truly fascinating," William commented. "How did this event come about?"

"I stopped in Washington to visit my aunt, Mrs. Irwin, whose husband was a strong supporter of the Union," Connie replied. "He insisted that I should see, as an epoch in my life, the new president at one of the frequent White House levees. The opportunity presented itself within the next few days. There was a terrible crush of people of all sorts and conditions. Everyone, from foreign ministers and great ladies to backwoodsmen in flannel shirts and Sunday coats, stood in a reception line to meet President Lincoln."

"And what was your impression of Mister Lincoln?" Hetty asked with a trace of sarcasm in her voice.

"Although a budding secessionist, I distinctly remember that I was quite impressed by the power of his personality and his commanding presence."

"Did you actually have the opportunity to speak with him?" Jenny inquired.

"Yes, indeed I did," Connie replied. "Suddenly I was standing before the towering apparition of the new president at the entrance to the Blue Room. Everything else faded from my vision. My hand was engulfed for a moment in his enormous palm, clad in an ill–fitting white kid glove. He said something kind to me, I cannot remember what, and over his rugged face played the momentary flicker of a summer-lightning smile. I responded, but I know not what. And then I was past him as he greeted the next person in line."

"Well, I'm certainly glad that he's not my president," Hetty said. "Jefferson Davis is the George Washington of our time. He'll lead our country to independence from the tyranny of Mr. Lincoln and his Yankee minions."

"I've no doubt that he will," William remarked as he smiled at Hetty's outspoken defense of anything and everything that she held dear. It was a phenomenon that he had witnessed on many occasions.

* * *

After returning to their rooms at Miss Clarke's later that evening, Hetty and Jenny revealed to family and close friends that they would run the blockade to Baltimore in early August. Arrangements to cross the Potomac into Southern Maryland had been coordinated with Captain William Norris of the Confederate Signal Corps, an organization heavily involved in clandestine work. Although the sisters declared that a visit with their parents was their prime intent, circumstances suggested to the listeners that there were more serious reasons for the trip, although no one put that suspicion into words. According to plan, once Hetty and Jenny were hidden at the home of Colonel John H. Sothoron in St. Mary's County, they would write a letter to their father, asking him to come to them and advise whether or not they could safely return to Baltimore.

Burdened by this portentous news, the parting of Hetty and Jenny that night with the two Williams was tearful and sad, particularly for Jenny and Captain Murray. Hetty was also distressed by the fact that she would not see John Pegram before her departure as duty had long since called him to his new posting on Beauregard's staff.

* * *

Months of arduous service had sapped the strength of the Maryland Battalion until there were less than two hundred fifty men fit for duty. Withdrawn from active service, the battalion arrived in Charlottesville on the eighteenth day of July for recruiting and reorganization. During the next few weeks, the Marylanders enjoyed an easy camp routine and a warm welcome by the hospitable people in a locale not yet marred by war. The unmarried men began courting the local girls and having picnics on the lawn of a dilapidated Monticello.

The hard-earned tranquility came to an abrupt halt on August fourteenth with the receipt of a Confederate War Department special order disbanding the 1st Maryland Battalion because of its depleted condition and doubts regarding the enlistment terms of its companies. Several days later, Colonel Johnson stood before a final formation and read the order. Amid tears of anguish and disbelief, the battle-tattered flag was furled and later presented to Mrs. Johnson by the battalion sergeants in appreciation of her many contributions for the soldier's welfare.

Having attached themselves to the fate of the Confederacy, the Marylanders could not go home, so most went to Richmond to enjoy their newfound freedom. It wasn't long before the novelty of idle time wore off. A few joined the artillery, some joined the cavalry, but most kept themselves available for the formation of a new battalion of Maryland infantry.

* * *

MISS CLARKE'S HOUSE
RICHMOND, VIRGINIA
SEPTEMBER 2, 1862

Connie was seated on the porch bench, engrossed in the writing of a short story, and struggling with a paragraph that would not come together. She scratched through several lines already written and rearranged the words for better expression and flow. Not yet satisfied with her wordsmithing, she read the troublesome paragraph through again and made several minor changes.

At the age of seventeen, Connie submitted her first story, a tale of lurid and melancholy love, to *The Atlantic Monthly*. When it was returned as expected, she was pleased that a note was scrawled across the first page in red ink stating that it was far better than average. However, at this moment, words were not satisfactorily flowing from her mind to the paper and she was relieved to look up at the sound of William Prentiss approaching.

"Hello William, please come join me on the porch and save me from my writer's misery."

William laughed as he mounted the steps and sat down beside her on the bench. It was the first time in a long while that Connie had seen him wearing civilian clothes, but his soldierly bearing remained evident.

"Are you enjoying the life of an ordinary citizen?" Connie inquired, knowing full well what his response would be.

"Of course not," William replied. "Thankfully, it will be but a short time until Captain Murray has me back in harness. He is busy reorganizing his company, with the permission of the war department of course. We were sworn into Confederate service several days ago and will report next week to Camp Lee at the Old Richmond Fairgrounds, just west of the city."

"What would we do without patriots like you?" Connie asked admiringly.

William blushed at the compliment. He liked Connie and considered her to be a good friend. Her grayish-blue eyes and regular features made her pretty, not beautiful and, like all Carys of her generation, she had auburn hair just escaping red, a legacy of the Jefferson family. In William's view, it was Connie's vibrant spirit and engaging personality that made her special.

"Have you heard from Hetty or Jenny since their return to Baltimore?" William inquired.

"Yes, we received a letter last week from Jenny informing us that they are safety back at their parent's home," Connie replied. "Their passage across the lines was uneventful and happily, thus far, they have not been harassed by the Yankee authorities."

"That's good to hear," William responded. "I was concerned for their well-being as their departure from Baltimore last year reportedly caused some embarrassment to the Federal authorities."

Connie put aside her writing materials and turned on the bench to face her guest. "Jenny said that she has spoken with Laura and Sarah. She reported that they are in good health, although both remain despondent over your father's demise."

Connie carefully watched William, as she knew this was a painful subject. William looked down before speaking, wrestling with his emotions. He had grieved during the past year over his father's unexpected death and suffered great anguish whenever he thought of their disastrous last encounter. Yet he was not about to attribute fault to others without accepting his share.

"Sarah heaped considerable blame upon herself in a letter she sent me after father's death. I wrote back and told her that it was an accident, that I knew my father truly loved her, and that his disappointment with me may have contributed to his erratic state of mind." William could feel his eyes starting to tear and fought to control it. "I'll always live with that."

"Jenny's letter also reports that your brother, Clifton, has received a captain's commission in the Federal 6th Maryland Regiment of Infantry and will be taking to the field soon. Were you aware of that?"

"No, I wasn't," William replied. He paused and then smiled. "Clifton will be a good officer, of that I have no doubt."

"It's frightening to think that you two might meet on the field of battle."

"That's not likely to happen. The battlefield is a big place and your view is confined to the immediate vicinity. There's not much possibility that my battalion will ever be anywhere near his regiment." Seeking to change the subject, William asked if Francis Dawson was still residing at Miss Clarke's.

"No," Connie said. "Frank—he wants to be called that now—moved out last week after being commissioned as a first lieutenant of artillery. He looked quite dashing in his new gray uniform with scarlet cuffs and collar."

"Well, in any case, Frank is a nice fellow," William commented and then chuckled to himself. "Last I spoke with him, I noted that his English accent had evolved nicely into one that sounded much like the Old English tongue of born and bred Henrico County folks."

"That hadn't occurred to me, but it's true, now that I think about it," Connie replied.

The two friends lapsed into silence and adjusted their positions on the hard wooden bench.

"What are you going to do with your last few days unencumbered by military duty?"

"Well, believe it or not, there is a purpose for my visit with you today," William replied. "Other than enjoying your delightful company, of course," he added.

Connie looked at William coyly and waited to hear what he had in mind.

"I recently saw an old friend serving in the 1st Maryland Cavalry and admired a cross bottony pinned to his uniform jacket." William opened his shirt pocket and produced a small piece of paper. He handed it to Connie. "I took a rubbing and want one made just like it." Connie examined the impression as William continued to speak. "It's about an inch high and the same wide with a pin and keeper on the back to affix it. Can you recommend a jeweler who can make one for me in silver?"

"Most assuredly," Connie replied. "In fact, it's not a long walk to his shop. Would you like to go there now?"

William agreed and within minutes they were walking to the jeweler's shop several blocks away on Main Street. Connie's selection was ideal as the jeweler proved to be a gifted artisan and displayed impressive examples of his work. This was enough to convince William to place an order to have one made. The price was improved by virtue of Connie's decision to commission the making of two more bottony crosses, one for her and another for Hetty. She was enchanted with the fashion possibilities, much to William's amusement.

As William walked Connie home to Miss Clarke's, they came across a slave family in the midst of being broken-up, not an uncommon sight in the South. The father and two older children, in chains and with tears streaming down their faces, had just been sold to a new master. As they were being loaded into a wagon, the wailing mother and two smaller children stood by, restrained by an overseer. William and Connie slowed their steps momentarily as they took in the melancholy scene, and then hurried on without looking back.

The two friends walked in silence until Connie finally spoke in a sorrowful voice. "Did you know that a Negro preacher marrying a slave couple does not include in the vows the phrase, 'til death do you part, but says instead, 'til death or distance do you part?"

"No, I didn't," William replied quietly.

"I detest the curse of slavery!" Connie exclaimed. "It's the bane of our beautiful Southern land and may well lead to the undoing of our country." William walked on beside her in embarrassed silence. Glancing over at William, Connie spoke earnestly to him. "Early in my life, I found and devoured every word of *Uncle Tom's Cabin,* that mischievous, incendiary book, as some of our friend's called it. I was inwardly terrified by the news of John Brown's raid at Harper's Ferry, for I thought that it was God's vengeance for the torture of Uncle Tom and his people."

When William said nothing, Connie continued to vent her feelings. "Slavery is as damning to us as it is terrible for the slaves. When the reign of my French governess ended, I was sent to the boarding school of M. Hubert Pierre Lefebvre. This experience introduced me to girls from the higher classes of Southern society. I became convinced that being surrounded by slave service neither inspires energy of body or spirit—both of which are indispensable to a successful life. These girls were pretty, languid creatures that never put on a shoe or a stocking for themselves." Reconsidering for a moment, Connie added, "Although I must admit, many of them have come out grandly since the war began, after their circumstances were greatly reduced."

* * *

CAMP LEE
NEAR RICHMOND, VIRGINIA
SEPTEMBER 11, 1862

Excitement raced through the camp of Captain Murray's company when it was announced that Lee's Army had crossed the Potomac into Maryland a few days before. Despite the boisterous celebration, the soldiers loudly deplored the fact they were not in the forefront to liberate their home state. Speculation was rampant among the jubilant Marylanders that the Yankee occupiers would be expelled and that the state would soon be free to join the Southern Confederacy.

As the companies were just formed with many new recruits, recent days had been spent drawing quartermaster and commissary stores to provide basic equipment for soldiering and essential creature comforts. The weapons issued lacked uniformity and the veterans were now selecting them based on the ease of cleaning in preparation for inspection. There was an assortment of Mississippi Rifles and rifled muskets made by Enfield and Springfield. The rifled musket barrels were highly polished and required the greatest effort, while the Mississippi Rifles had browned barrels and were easiest to keep in good condition. William was the only one of his messmates to select a rifled musket. He still favored being armed with a bayonet when charging the enemy.

Several companies of Marylanders took the cars to Gordonsville on September sixteenth and traveled on to Culpeper Court House the following day. On arrival, they learned that General Lee had fought a bloody battle at Antietam. Within the week, they were aware that Lee's army was withdrawing from Maryland, which considerably dampened their fervor.

The five companies of Maryland infantry converged at Staunton, drew rations of hard bread and salt shoulder pork, and trekked down the Valley Turnpike to Winchester. As they approached towns along the way, it was their custom to close ranks and march through in style to the music of fife and drum, which lifted the spirits of the soldiers as well as those of the secessionist citizenry. The Marylanders arrived in Winchester on the twenty-eighth of September and found the town full of wounded soldiers from Antietam. Lee's army was still in the vicinity.

The companies were formally organized into the 2nd Maryland Battalion and Captain James R. Herbert was elected major on the first ballot. By mid-November, the Confederate Army departed from the Winchester area, leaving only the 2nd Maryland to protect the many townspeople loyal to the South from marauding Yankee cavalry. On December fifth, 1862, the battalion abandoned Winchester to approaching Union forces and marched to their winter quarters in knee-deep snow.

* * *

OFFICE OF THE ADJUTANT-GENERAL
BALTIMORE, MARYLAND
MARCH 28, 1863

Colonel William H. Chesebrough mopped his brow with a handkerchief as he listened to the verbal report presented by Captain Henry P. Goddard, standing before his desk. Distracted by the unseasonable weather and unable to concentrate on the routine report, the colonel turned in his chair and squinted through his spectacles at the wall thermometer behind his desk. Reading a temperature much higher than usual for this time of year, he swore under his breath at his misfortune to be stationed in such an infernal place.

The sound of footsteps in the hallway caused him to turn in time to see Major General Robert C. Schenck, commander of the Department of Maryland, enter the office. He started to get to his feet, but General Schenck waved him back into his chair.

"From all reports that have come to me, Colonel Chesebrough, I think that if Miss Hetty Cary continues to be so active in communicating with her Southern friends, we shall have to send her South."

"Yes, sir," replied the adjutant general. "I have read those same reports. You would be fully justified in ordering that course of action."

"But if I do," General Schenck avowed, "I shall have to forbid the officer who escorts her through our lines not to look at her, much less speak to her, for that woman could bewitch the Angel Gabriel."

A smile flitted across the face of Captain Goddard as he listened to the conversation between the two senior officers. He had seen Miss Hetty Cary and was willing to risk being bewitched by the beautiful Rebel.

"Colonel, I want you to investigate this matter and report back to me as soon as possible," General Schenck said as he stepped back into the hall.

* * *

Colonel Chesebrough reported his findings to General Schenck the following morning. Detectives working for the Provost Marshal's Office had acquired testimony from a reliable witness that Hetty Cary uttered treasonous statements in his presence. The informant also suggested that she was in league with suspected Confederate operatives in Baltimore City. Her parents' home was thoroughly searched as a result of these allegations, but no incriminating evidence was found. After careful consideration of the matter, General Schenck decided to abandon his plan to return Hetty to Virginia on a flag-of-truce boat and ordered her immediate arrest. When the provost marshal arrived at the Cary home with a warrant in hand, she was not to be found.

* * *

On Chesapeake Bay
Between Maryland and Virginia
April 1, 1863

The small sailboat glided slowly through the water, a steady rain shower masking all sounds of its tedious passage. Hetty stared into the mist as she sat with her arms wrapped tightly around herself to keep warm under layers of clothing topped by a mariner's rain slicker. Beneath her was the hard contour of a trunk packed with morphine, quinine, and secret correspondence for delivery to the Confederate government.

Despite her discomfort, sitting atop the trunk and enduring a cold, damp wind in her face, Hetty savored the thought that she would soon surprise her fiancé with an unannounced return to Richmond. Adding to her pleasure was the fact that she found room in the large trunk for an elegant new dress in the latest style from her favorite Baltimore dressmaker, sure to be a sensation in the Confederate capital where women had long been deprived of such luxuries.

A night crossing from the Eastern Shore to Virginia was originally planned, but the waterman retained for the purpose postponed the trip for a day due to an unforeseen storm. However, he agreed to run the blockade in daylight when a continuous rain and thick fog settled over the bay during a lull in the worst weather. As the old, decrepit-looking sailboat was being loaded for the passage, Hetty feared that it wasn't seaworthy. However, any thought of finding a replacement was nullified by news that Union detectives were in hot pursuit, compelling her immediate departure. Hetty was glad that her parents persuaded Jenny to remain in Baltimore to assist in the operation of the Southern Home School.

Midway across the wide bay, the wind picked up and soon the hull of the old sailboat was creaking from strain as it plowed through each wave. Hetty noticed her shoes becoming wet as the boat took on water and she turned to look at the elderly waterman struggling with the tiller to hold his course. He had a grim look on his weathered, white-bearded face.

Looking over his shoulder, Hetty saw two Yankee guard boats overhauling them on the central expanse of the turbulent bay where improved visibility had exposed their presence. The thump of a small cannon was heard and a waterspout marked the spot where the solid shot landed in their wake. As the guard boats drew closer, rifle shots cracked and bullet splashes came ominously close. Without warning, the waterman put the tiller hard to starboard. The sailboat darted toward the western side of the bay where a fearsome thunderstorm rampaged along the Virginia shore. Heavy rain, driven sideways by powerful winds, enveloped the little boat as they sailed through the storm. They evaded their pursuers after a harrowing hour of battering by sharp wind and white-capped waves. Hetty would later tell friends that it was almost a miracle that she was spared from shipwreck on Chesapeake Bay.

* * *

MRS. PEGRAM'S PARLOR
RICHMOND, VIRGINIA
APRIL 3, 1863

The party hosted by Mary and Jennie Pegram in their mother's home on Linden Row was in full swing with plenty of ice cream, cake, and officers, guaranteeing that the young women in attendance were having a fine time. Several of the girls were from the boarding school and others ranged from longtime intimates of the Pegram's to recent acquaintances who had achieved prominence in the wartime capital. Furniture had been pushed to the walls to create space for dancing in the high-ceilinged room aglow with candlelight and smiling faces. The Pegram sisters were giving the soiree in honor of their brothers, John and William, who were home on leave from the army. The returning warriors were the center of attention, not only from close friends and family, but also from the officers present as both had achieved rank and acclaim for their valor on the field of battle.

As the evening progressed, polite conversation gave way to the clatter of flying feet accompanied by merry tunes played on banjo and fiddle. At the conclusion of a dance while everyone was selecting new partners, the unexpected apparition of Hetty Cary appeared in full panoply, wearing a beautiful Baltimore ball dress, surprising everyone including John, who thought that she was in Maryland. He fell back, almost fainting with joyful emotion over the return of his beloved Hetty. The party resumed with dancing and celebration until three o'clock in the forenoon.

* * *

THE CARY RESIDENCE
RICHMOND, VIRGINIA
APRIL 4, 1863

Their portion of the dwelling on Third Street, kindly leased to them by a friend, was much more spacious and appealing than the boarding house rooms at Miss Clarke's. The bedrooms and bath were upstairs and they had a large sitting room of their own on the main floor to receive visitors and take meals prepared in the backyard kitchen by a Negro cook. Their pantry was situated behind the sitting room. On this damp, overcast afternoon, Monimia, Connie, and Hetty were seated before the fireplace, immersed in intimate family conversation.

"I can't thank you enough for taking me in on such short notice," Hetty said to her aunt. "My hasty departure from Baltimore provided no opportunity for making any preparations other than for the journey itself."

"We're delighted to have you under our roof again," Monimia replied. "You're always welcome to stay with us."

"All that matters is that you are here safe and sound," Connie chimed in enthusiastically. "It terrifies me every time I think of your dangerous voyage through the blockade. I would have died of fright halfway across the bay in that ancient sailboat, pursued by Yankees and tossed about in a fierce storm."

"The things I was transporting had to get through and I kept that foremost in my mind," Hetty replied with a brave smile that did not entirely succeed. "And, of course, thoughts of my loved ones in Baltimore and Richmond."

"The war has displaced you from the home and hearth of your dear mother and father—always consider us to be your safe haven when you cannot be with them," Monimia said.

Tears welled in Hetty's eyes. "I'm blessed to be in your capable hands, Aunt Monimia, and thankful for the opportunity to live in the warmth and happiness of your home."

Monimia acknowledged Hetty's appreciation with a gentle smile. A crackling log in the fireplace drew the women's attention and they silently watched tiny red-hot embers burst from the burning bark.

"Life in wartime Richmond is difficult for refugees," Connie said. "We live in other people's rooms without our familiar trappings. The daily commodities that we took for granted in our previous life are now scarce and dearly bought—a far cry from our pampered existence of bygone years."

Hetty smiled sadly. "I have heard it said that a citizen now goes to market with his money in a market basket and brings home his provisions in his pocketbook. Our Confederate bluebacks don't go very far these days, making us all paupers of one kind or another."

"We're far better off than most people who have sought refuge in this overcrowded city," Monimia replied. "There are many women whose husbands and sons have gone off to war who must, for the first time in their lives, seek employment to shelter, feed, and clothe their children."

"I should not have made light of the suffering of those less fortunate," Hetty replied with contrition. "I'm painfully aware that many wives and children of our common soldiers are in desperate straits."

"You were not demeaning those people—you were simply acknowledging the reality of these times," Monimia stated emphatically. "Sadly, this problem manifested itself by rampage in our city streets just before your return to Richmond."

Hetty sat upright in her chair, confusion written across her face.

"That's right, you don't know about the bread riot!" Connie exclaimed. "A mob of women of the poorer class armed with axes, knifes, horse pistols, and hatchets gathered in Capitol Square demanding that food and other necessities be made available to them at government prices."

"A few weeks before our bread riot, a similar situation, although of much smaller proportions, occurred in Salisbury, North Carolina," Monimia said. "Soldier's wives and mothers went in search of food being hoarded by unscrupulous speculators. These women were hungry and couldn't pay the inflated prices demanded for flour and other necessities. They raided those stores and confiscated many barrels of flour."

"Oh my!" Hetty exclaimed.

"What occurred in Richmond is so much worse," Connie said, her face flushed with excitement. "When the demands of the mob in Capitol Square were rebuffed by Governor Letcher, they streamed in silence to the retail district around Main and Cary streets. The store windows of known speculators were broken and the merchandise looted. Wagons and drays were commandeered to haul the plundered goods away."

"At first, mainly meal, flour, and clothing were taken from profiteering merchants by the rioters," Monimia said, her voice tinged with strong disapproval. "But their attention soon turned to jewelry, silks, shoes, hats, and other luxuries. Street ruffians joined in the mayhem to take advantage of the chaos. The mob probably numbered a thousand miscreants at this point."

"What happened then?" Hetty asked.

"Mayor Joseph Mayo read the riot act to the reckless throng, but he was largely ignored," Connie replied. "Soon Governor Letcher arrived with the Public Guard and threatened that his soldiers would fire on the crowd if it did not disperse within five minutes. He drew out his watch and held it over his head to show everyone that he was serious."

Monimia leaned forward and placed her hand on Hetty's arm. "The sharp rattle of bayonets being fixed was convincing—the crowd moved away from the line of state soldiers. However, they did not retire to their neighborhoods as directed and began to mill about uncertainly on nearby streets. The potential existed for it all to start over again. A tall, dignified figure then appeared on the scene and climbed onto a dray. It was our president, Jefferson Davis, and he made an eloquent appeal in conciliatory terms that people should end the riot and go to their homes."

"What did he say?" Hetty asked wide-eyed.

"President Davis told them that looting would only intensify food shortages and hold troops in town that should be available to fight the enemy," Monimia responded. "As he was speaking, a woman threw a loaf of bread at him. Mr. Davis remarked that bread can't possibly be scarce else it wouldn't be parted with upon such small provocation. He urged the crowd to bear its burdens bravely."

"Was that the end of it?" Hetty asked, still struggling with the idea that Southern women, even of the poorer class, would act with such a lack of decorum and patriotism.

"Yes, it was," Monimia answered. "Thankfully, the mob finally dispersed and the streets again became quiet."

"I can't imagine how such a thing could happen and who would be responsible for it," Hetty declared as she looked from her aunt to her cousin.

"Yesterday's *Richmond Examiner* stated that the perpetrators were a handful of prostitutes, professional thieves, Irish and Yankee hags, and gallows birds from all lands but our own," Connie replied with no mirth in her tone. "That was a rather presumptuous assertion to be published in a newspaper. Certainly those elements might have been present, but to declare the entire constituency of the riot as such is patently absurd. There was more to it than that."

Monimia sighed wearily as she looked off into space before commenting. "I have witnessed the evolution of our national dilemma in hospitals where I have served. In 1861, it was the gentleman and their sons who marched off to fight, but the family plantations, large farms, and commercial endeavors continued to function. As the war progressed and many of our gallant men were killed or maimed in battle, more and more of the yeomanry have been conscripted into the army. Their women are hard-pressed to keep the farm together and the family fed with the men gone."

As Monimia continued, her voice betrayed a faint note of despair. "Our ports are closed by the Yankee blockade, our roads are clogged with military vehicles, and those few farm wagons not already taken for army service find it difficult to deliver their produce to market. It's no wonder that so many people are starving, particularly in our towns and cities."

"That certainly explains why the bread riot happened," Connie said. "It's an awful predicament."

"But our country is at stake!" Hetty exclaimed gesturing with her hands. "Everyone must keep faith to overcome such adversity. Surely God will bestow victory upon our arms so that we may achieve independence—but only if we all do our part."

* * *

The refugees, or "fugees" as they were called by the townspeople, had abandoned their homes in the face of approaching Union forces and flocked to Richmond. Others were expelled from occupied areas when they refused to take an oath of loyalty to the United States. This influx contributed significantly to a population explosion that tripled the city's pre-war census of thirty-eight thousand souls and stretched to the limit the resources of what had been a provincial capital.

As no one knew, at the time, how long the conflict would last, refugees fled with limited household goods and few personal possessions, inflicting deprivation and uncertainty upon themselves for the war's duration. Their real property in areas controlled by Federal forces was often sold at public auction due to laws requiring that taxes be paid in person. The dispossessed knew neither the date when they could return to their homes or what they would find when they got there.

Decent lodgings in Richmond were difficult to obtain at any price. Those with strong family connections in the city were able to rent adequate rooms. Those without such ties lived tenuously in crowded, uncomfortable accommodations. Families that had been landowners for generations now found themselves as tenants for the first time in their lives. Confederate currency depreciated rapidly and a limited amount of goods in the marketplace resulted in raging price inflation. Heirlooms were often pawned to pay for basic necessities. While many felt driven from pillar to post by these circumstances, most of the middle and upper classes maintained their faith in the cause of Southern independence. As the war progressed, a sense slowly grew among the poorer classes that they were carrying the burden of a war that could not be won.

MY POOR BOYS

A parade of doctors, nurses, and hospital stewards treaded lightly along the central aisle and to the bedside of each patient. The staff changed bandages, gave medications, and assisted the sick and wounded officers with their morning ablutions. This was a routine that changed little, making each day seem very much like the last to caregivers and patients alike.

Irritation was evident on Melville's face as Whitman completed his commentary on the refugee situation in Richmond. While John and Clifton were curious about the conditions experienced by their youngest brother and his friends in the Rebel capital, Melville clearly wasn't. He took this opportunity to confront Clifton on another issue. "I cannot comprehend why you wanted to join the Federal army when you were already a member of the most highly esteemed militia regiment in the United States."

"I had a perfectly good reason for my decision!" Clifton exclaimed angrily. "The 7th Regiment was called up only for a brief time to secure Washington. Afterward, the regiment returned to New York where its soldiers resumed their ordinary lives. Despite the fact that our country was at war!"

"You need not have forsaken the honorable militia membership that I arranged for you," Melville complained. "You thoughtlessly forfeited substantial benefit that we both would have enjoyed had you remained in the regiment of Colonel Lefferts!"

"As was my right," Clifton replied curtly. "And I did remain with the 7th Regiment until I realized that it would not see the active service that I sought."

"Weren't you with another Maryland regiment prior to joining the 6th Maryland Infantry?" John inquired.

"Yes," Clifton replied as he regained his composure. "I enlisted as a private in the 5th Regiment of Maryland Volunteers in March of 1862. The regiment was encamped at Lafayette Square in Baltimore City where it had been thoroughly prepared for active field service. When I learned that it would soon move to Fortress Monroe on the Virginia Peninsula, I saw this as my best opportunity to get into the fight."

"Did you ever see battle while serving with the 5th Maryland Infantry?" John asked as he adjusted his back on the hard chair.

"No," Clifton replied. "Other than being occasionally shelled by the ironclad CSS *Virginia*, the next several months were tedious as we were not engaged with the enemy. However, all was not wasted as I became acquainted with Captain John W. Horn, commanding officer of Company F. When he suggested that I be mustered out in order to accept a commission as a captain in the 6th Maryland Regiment of Infantry, I did not hesitate to accept the offer."

"You were right to avail yourself of that opportunity. I know that our father would have been pleased that you earned an officer's commission," John stated with certainty.

"It's ironic that following my departure, the 5th Maryland bore a conspicuous part in the battle of Antietam and compiled a splendid record during the remainder of the war."

"Somehow I had the idea that you were at the Battle of Antietam," Melville remarked.

"We were nearby, but did not confront the enemy," Clifton replied. "The 6th Maryland was assigned the task of guarding a supply train to the front whilst the battle was fought. On that occasion, in the distance for the first time, I heard the thundering roar of artillery and musketry. But we did not see action that day."

"So, changing regiments every whipstitch proved not to be such a profitable endeavor," Melville countered smugly.

"My haste was motivated by a strong desire to do my part," Clifton replied icily to his brother's taunt. "I could not stand aside while the outcome of the war was in question."

"Clifton's alacrity was not unusual early in the war as no one knew that it would last nearly four years," Whitman interjected. "Many brave men who I've interviewed in hospitals told a similar story of their rush to arms and their eagerness to see action against the enemy."

A smile flitted across Clifton's face. "The soldier's expression for having been in battle was to say that he had 'seen the elephant.' Before war's end, the 6th Maryland Infantry had 'seen the elephant' on many, many occasions."

"Your regiment compiled a brilliant record of which every officer and man can justifiably be proud," John affirmed.

"It did indeed," Clifton said as he adjusted the pillow behind his back. A fleeting grimace revealed the discomfort of his bandaged wound. "The 6th Maryland was raised during August of 1862 to serve three years in response to President Lincoln's call for three hundred thousand volunteers. The companies were recruited in the counties of Carroll, Cecil, Frederick, Washington, and Queen Anne's. Two companies were recruited in Baltimore City, and I was given command of one of them as I had recruited most of its members. They were all first-rate men."

"What characteristic of these soldiers contributed most to the success of the 6th Maryland Volunteers?" John asked.

"The key attribute was quite obvious to those of us in command," Clifton replied. "The majority of men in our regiment were related as brothers, cousins, friends, neighbors, and respected citizens in their home communities. They enlisted to serve together. They would not, under any circumstances, let down their fellow soldiers or bring dishonor to their names."

"Are you suggesting that there were no deserters from your regiment?" Melville asked.

"We suffered few desertions during the war, except for a handful of bounty jumpers recruited as replacements in 1863," Clifton replied emphatically. "The soldiers that enlisted early in the war were generally much better soldiers than those recruited at a later date. Many who joined for money or were drafted either deserted or were skulkers, not worth their salt."

"I imagine that the strength of William's Rebel battalion was similarly based on the high character of its individual soldiers," John opined.

"There's no doubt in my mind that's true. They were mostly men of honor and integrity, although wayward in their loyalty," Clifton replied.

"When was the first time that you and William were both on the same battlefield?" Melville inquired.

"I later ascertained that we were both present for the battle at Winchester in mid-June of 1863. It was a running fight over a large area, so I doubt that we were ever in close proximity."

"And later?" John asked.

"During the spring and summer of 1864, the 6th Maryland Regiment and the 2nd Maryland Battalion participated in the same major battles in Grant's Overland Campaign. These were times when the Army of the Potomac and the Army of Northern Virginia stood toe to toe and hammered it out on broad battlefields before settling into a siege below Petersburg."

"I thought the initial commitment of your regiment was within Maryland to defend the Baltimore and Ohio Railroad. How did you end up at Winchester in 1863?" John asked.

"It's true that our first assignment was to the Maryland Brigade," Clifton replied. "However, in March of that year, we were assigned to 3rd Brigade, 2nd Division of Eighth Corps. Our new brigade, under the command of Brigadier General A. T. McReynolds, was composed of 6th Maryland Infantry, 1st New York Cavalry, 67th Pennsylvania Infantry, and Alexander's Baltimore Battery of Light Artillery. We soon found ourselves manning a forward outpost in the Shenandoah Valley."

TWO BROTHERS

* * *

6TH MARYLAND VOLUNTEERS
NEAR BERRYVILLE, VIRGINIA
JUNE 12, 1863

During the previous evening, scouts reported to General McReynolds that the enemy was advancing in force toward his camp. The brigade departed early in the morning for Winchester, leaving four companies of the 6th Maryland Infantry, a section of guns of Alexander's Battery and one hundred-fifty troopers of the 1st New York Cavalry as the rear guard. Alexander's four guns were placed on the road, two companies of the 6th Maryland stood in line of battle on each side, and mounted troopers were deployed out front as skirmishers. When the Confederates appeared, the section of guns delayed their advance for an hour until a flanking maneuver forced an orderly retreat. After crossing Opequon Creek, the rear guard made a stand on advantageous ground and repulsed a Rebel cavalry charge. Their accurate fire emptied many saddles.

On arrival at Winchester at nine o'clock that night, Alexander's battery was ordered inside the star fort while the 6th Maryland Infantry was placed in entrenchments outside its walls. The forces of Brigadier General Robert H. Milroy occupied four forts in the defensive perimeter at Winchester.

The next morning, fourteen Rebel battle flags were sighted as the Confederates moved into position and opened fire on the Federal defenders. Milroy belatedly realized that he was fighting the entire Second Corps of the Army of Northern Virginia, not a reconnaissance in force as he had originally thought. After battling throughout the day, General Milroy ordered his forces to make a silent retreat up the Martinsburg Road in the darkness of night. Everything with wheels was abandoned. The guns were spiked, numerous supply wagons were parked, and the sick and wounded were left behind with their attending surgeons.

Once again, the 6th Maryland Infantry was called upon to serve as the retreating column's rear guard. At first light, a Confederate force sent around to cut off the retreat struck the head of the Federal column. In the ensuing fight, several Union regiments fell apart and thousands of fleeing men were either killed or captured. By virtue of its superior leadership and discipline, the 6th Maryland Volunteers remained intact and brought out many stragglers from other regiments. The battered remnants of Milroy's command arrived at Harpers Ferry that night.

* * *

2ND MARYLAND BATTALION
NEAR WINCHESTER, VIRGINIA
JUNE 12, 1863

The battalion numbered about six hundred officers and men when they joined the campaign to attack Milroy at Winchester. During their march northward in the valley, nature's cycle filled the woods with locusts. At night, the perpetual singing of the insects kept the soldiers awake despite their fatigue from the long march. They suffered another discomfort before arrival at Winchester when they slept throughout the night in a cold, drenching rain, covered with India rubber cloths and wool blankets. Early the following morning, the 2nd Maryland Battalion drums beat to colors and its soldiers rushed into the streets of the town to fight in a series of bloody skirmishes that lasted into the evening.

The next day, the Marylanders double-quick marched through town at first light with bread rations stuck on the ends of their bayonets. When they reached the star fort, they found it abandoned by its defenders, but containing a number of injured and ailing Yankees from the 5th and 6th Maryland regiments. Among the prisoners taken was Dr. Lloyd Goldsborough, surgeon of the 5th Maryland and brother of William Goldsborough, the Maryland Battalion's major. Captain Murray and Sergeant Major Laird pulled down the United States flag and raised the battalion's flag in its place.

Large amounts of Federal commissary and quartermaster stores, artillery, small arms, knapsacks, and sutler's wagons were scattered about in every direction. A whole brigade of ragged Confederate soldiers smoked fine Havana cigars as they appropriated other useful things from the bounty relinquished by Milroy's hastily departed forces.

* * *

ARMORY SQUARE HOSPITAL
WASHINGTON, D.C.
JUNE 24, 1865

Reciting his recollections of the debacle painted a glum expression on Clifton's face. "General Milroy faced a board of inquiry soon thereafter," he said. "Lieutenant Colonel McKellip of the 6th Maryland was called as a witness in the proceeding."

"I suppose that with a defeat of this magnitude, someone had to be blamed—Milroy was the obvious scapegoat," John observed.

"That's true enough," Clifton responded. "Although in his defense, I must admit that he received conflicting orders from both General Halleck, the army chief of staff, and General Schenck, the military district commander. Nevertheless, he compounded the problem with his own false sense of security. He should have withdrawn when he had the opportunity as the terrain surrounding Winchester makes it a difficult place to defend."

Didn't the town change hands something like seventy-two times during the course of the war?" Whitman asked.

"That number sounds about right," Clifton responded.

"Whatever became of General Milroy?" Melville asked.

"He was eventually exonerated by the board of inquiry and, later, with a new command in the western army, regained his military reputation," Clifton replied.

"I can see that Ewell's victory at Winchester opened the door for Lee's second invasion of the North," John commented as he visualized a map of the region.

"Milroy's force was all that stood in their way," Clifton declared as he turned his face toward Whitman. "Did William's battalion march into Pennsylvania?"

"They did indeed," Whitman replied. "The 2nd Maryland Battalion was almost destroyed in the great battle of Gettysburg."

* * *

Following the victory at Winchester, Brigadier General George Hume Steuart's Brigade, including the Maryland Battalion, was assigned to the division of Major General Edward "Alleghany" Johnson in Second Corps of the Army of Northern Virginia. Lieutenant General Richard S. Ewell had been given command of Second Corps following Stonewall Jackson's fatal wounding at Chancellorsville several months before. The loss of Jackson was catastrophic for the South as he was Robert E. Lee's most capable and aggressive corps commander. Second Corps was still "Jackson's Corps" in the minds of many people, setting a high standard and even higher expectations for General Ewell.

The invading Rebel Army, composed of Longstreet's First Corps, Ewell's Second Corps, and Hill's Third Corps, crossed the western portion of Maryland and thrust itself into the Pennsylvania countryside. Lee's intention was to draw the Union Army of the Potomac into a major fight and defeat it on northern soil as such a victory might end the war under terms favorable to the Confederacy. Both armies were converging on Gettysburg, but neither knew the exact location or strength of the other. The Confederates were approaching Gettysburg from the north and the Federals were arriving from the south.

The gods of war were not smiling on the Army of Northern Virginia on July first, 1863 as the opposing armies were drawn piecemeal into an unexpected battle. John Buford's dismounted cavalry slowed the Rebel advance by Henry Heth's Division along the Chambersburg Pike until Federal infantry began arriving in force. Retreating before superior numbers of Southern troops, Union forces seized and held the high ground situated south and east of town. As Second Corps pressed through the streets of Gettysburg, Lee instructed Ewell to take the hills beyond the town if he found it practicable, but to avoid a general engagement until more Confederate divisions were on the field. General Ewell awaited the arrival of Johnson's division instead of attacking the lightly held Federal positions. Nightfall of the first day of battle at Gettysburg found Federal soldiers in possession of Cemetery Hill and Culp's Hill, creating a serious dilemma for General Robert E. Lee and consternation among his corps commanders.

Lieutenant General James Longstreet recommended that General Lee not attack the Federal positions, but instead move around the Union left flank. This maneuver would force the Union Army to fall back in order to stay between the Rebel Army and Washington, increasing the possibility of a fight on ground more favorable to the Confederates. Ultimately, General Lee rejected Longstreet's plan as he was loath to relinquish the gains achieved by his army in the initial day of the battle. While Ewell had failed to capture the critical hills to the south and east of Gettysburg, Lee was convinced that if he hit the enemy hard where they stood, the Army of Northern Virginia would win a decisive victory.

* * *

2ND MARYLAND BATTALION
GETTYSBURG, PENNSYLVANIA
JULY 1, 1863

The march since sunrise had been dusty and exhausting for the men of the Maryland Battalion as it was one of those sweltering dog days of summer. Arriving on the outskirts of Gettysburg in the early evening hours, Johnson's division followed an unfinished railroad bed into town and halted on a side street where they were allowed to rest.

William slid his back down the side of a frame house with its shutters tightly shut. "I guess these folks won't be coming out to greet us," he said laughingly to his messmates Buck Weems, Tom Pratt, and several others who were dropping their haversacks and collapsing on the ground.

"Don't reckon they will," Tom responded while glancing at the house, "but frankly, I don't care much for Yankee hospitality anyhow."

Billie Gannon, the drummer for Company A, approached the reclining soldiers with the battalion's mascot, Grace, prancing close on his heels. She was a nondescript mongrel dog that had been with them for over a year. Billie was assigned primary responsibility for her care. Grace moved among the young soldiers sprawled on the ground, her tongue hanging out and her tail wagging furiously. She collected the affectionate petting and scratching behind the ears from all who would pay attention to her, and there were always many who were happy to oblige. Billie set his drum down and sat on the ground beside it. "Could you fellows look after Grace for a while?" he asked. "I've been told to report to the battalion commander. I suppose I'll be following him around for a while 'til they decide what's next."

"Sure thing, Billie, we'll be glad to look after her for a while," Buck responded. He reached out and grabbed Grace as she moved by him and began patting her dusty back. Billie, who looked considerably younger than his sixteen years, grunted his appreciation, got back to his feet, picked up his drum, and disappeared into the throng of soldiers milling about on the street.

The boys relaxed and drank from their canteens. They were thankful to be off their feet and quenching their thirst after a long day of tramping through the enemy countryside, following nearly a week of such hard marches.

Tom popped off his left shoe and sock and picked at a blister on his foot, drawing the idle attention of the soldiers relaxing around him. William took a long drink from his canteen, pushed the stopper back in, and set it on the ground beside him. "Those shoes look pretty shabby, Tom, how long have you been wearing them?"

"About two months," Tom replied. "They don't have much life left in 'em. Why do you ask?"

William's face took on an inquisitive look. "Did you see ole Charlie break ranks back there in the railroad cut as we were marching along?"

"I surely did. He's been shoeless for two days since his last pair fell apart and those Federal bodies scattered over the ground were too great a temptation. Charlie figured they wouldn't be needing shoes anymore, and he knew for certain that he did."

"Then why did he come back so quick and empty-handed?"

Tom chuckled. "When he got back in ranks, I asked him the very same question. Charlie told me that while he was pulling a shoe off the first Yankee he came to, the fellow sat up and said 'Mister, I ain't dead yet.' That upset poor ole Charlie so bad that he dropped the shoe and skedaddled back to the column."

The battle-hardened soldiers, just boys aged beyond their years by war, enjoyed a quiet laugh at Charlie's expense as they sat by the wayside. Buck took a drink and turned his empty canteen upside down. "Let's find us a well and get more water before our officers have us marching down the road again." William grumbled at the suggestion as Buck looked directly at him, but agreed that this was a good idea. The boys got to their feet and collected the canteens of their messmates. Grace trotted along with them as they moved to the center of the street, looking about to get their bearings in the small Pennsylvania town.

Gettysburg had a prosperous look to it. A number of well-kept houses lined the street interspersed with mercantile establishments and commercial structures that served a community of twenty-five hundred people and the rich farming region that surrounded it.

"Let's check behind that brick house on the corner," William said as he started in that direction. "There's got to be a decent well behind such a nice house."

As they trudged down the street with Grace following close behind them, William and Buck began noticing Federal prisoners being taken to the rear, many of them badly wounded. There were also wounded Confederate soldiers being treated under the shade of a nearby tree.

William led the way behind the brick house where they found, as expected, a well with an iron pump. Before starting to work, the boys filled a tin plate with water for Grace who lapped at it most appreciatively. Buck worked the pump, and William held empty canteens under the flowing water, filling all of them in a short while. Just as the task was completed, they heard a long drum roll calling the Maryland Battalion into formation. The boys hurried back to the street and distributed the canteens to their friends as they fell into ranks.

The Marylanders marched eastward through the town past rows of dead bodies clad in blue and gray, casualties of heavy fighting that raged through the streets of Gettysburg earlier that day. Two hours later, the Maryland Battalion was formed into a line of battle along the Hanover Road with their picket lines well advanced, but they were going no further in the darkness. The exhausted men of the Maryland Battalion slept soundly on their arms that night.

* * *

The Confederate battle plan for the second day at Gettysburg called for attacks on both Federal flanks by the Army of Northern Virginia. Lee anticipated that Longstreet would make his attack on the Union left flank in the morning, but Longstreet dawdled while positioning his troops and the attack was not made until late afternoon. Unfortunately, for Ewell, who was to simultaneously attack the Union right flank, the Federal troops on Culp's Hill spent the morning and early afternoon hours reinforcing and improving their entrenchments, making any attempt to capture the hill later in the day a much costlier affair.

* * *

2ND MARYLAND BATTALION
BELOW CULP'S HILL
JULY 2, 1863

Steuart's Brigade had been formed in line of battle since nine o'clock in the morning awaiting the order to assault Culp's Hill at the sound of Longstreet's guns. The soldiers expected delays as a usual part of military life, but when morning passed into afternoon without the attack being launched, the men grew more anxious. They could hear the Yankees felling trees and digging deeper into the hillside forest. At four o'clock in the afternoon, the long-awaited rumble of Longstreet's artillery was heard.

Colonel Herbert stood tall in his stirrups with two pistols strapped to his waist. "Mount your horses quickly. We're going in," he called out to his staff. He cantered to the front of the battalion and then gave the order to advance. The Maryland Battalion line of battle passed through a cornfield and drove Federal skirmishers that they encountered across Rock Creek. The Marylanders waded the waist-deep creek and attacked up the densely timbered slope. Their path brought them into a broad depression leading to a saddle between the two summits of Culp's Hill. An orderly advance became difficult as they encountered large rocks and boulders randomly scattered about the rough terrain. The Rebel battle line groped its way up the hill and caught up with its skirmishers. Instead of maintaining separation, the two advancing lines inadvertently merged and continued to move forward in the growing darkness. Without warning, the flash of a thousand muskets disclosed that Steuart's Brigade had stumbled onto Federal breastworks. The point-blank volley decimated its front ranks. The Confederate battle line staggered from the heavy blow, soon compounded by friendly fire from the 1st North Carolina coming up to aid them in the twilight. The officers of the brigade quickly rallied their men and reformed the line of battle. The brigade dashed forward in a charge to capture the first line of works, now abandoned, while taking fire from the second. In the midst of the attack, Lieutenant Colonel Herbert was struck down, badly wounded in the arm, stomach, and leg.

The Marylanders dropped into the captured trenches. In the moonlight, they could see Federal soldiers behind breastworks to their front rising to fire down on them. It was certain death not to move forward and dislodge the enemy. Coordinating with Lieutenant Colonel Simeon Walton of the 23rd Virginia, Major Goldsborough shifted the three left companies of the Maryland Battalion under his direction and, in concert with the Virginians, charged and captured the second Federal line.

The soldiers of Maryland Battalion quickly settled into the captured works. Although the uphill attack had worn down the men, the sounds of picks and shovel soon filled the air as they began fortifying the backside of the entrenchments. In the midst of this activity, a stranger rode up to Major Goldsborough in the dim light.

"How's the fight going?"

"I don't know," Goldsborough replied as he walked over to the man on horseback and seized the horse's bridle.

"What corps is this?" the man asked, surprised by this brash action.

"A Confederate corps, and you are my prisoner, sir!" the new commander of the Maryland Battalion replied as he pointed his revolver at the mounted man. Lieutenant Harry C. Egbert, a staff officer of the Union First Corps, climbed down from his horse to surrender.

* * *

General Lee ordered coordinated attacks against both Union flanks and the center on Cemetery Ridge to commence at daybreak of the third day of battle at Gettysburg. Again, a reluctant General Longstreet was slow in positioning several divisions under the command of General George E. Pickett for a massive attack on the Federal center.

Richard Ewell and Ambrose Hill advanced their forces on schedule that morning. They attacked Union positions strongly reinforced with troops from the interior lines as Pickett's attack was not made simultaneously. A half hour after Edward Johnson's attack began, Ewell learned that Pickett's attack had not begun. Johnson was attacking alone. Through it all, General Lee was unruffled. He believed that his army could accomplish great things under the most difficult of circumstances as they had so many times in the past.

* * *

2ND MARYLAND BATTALION
CULP'S HILL
JULY 3, 1863

Sporadic musket fire continued throughout the middle hours of the night—neither side suffered much other than a loss of sleep. This was about to change. At half-past four in the morning, guns of the Federal Twelfth Corps opened up on the Confederate positions. The whole hillside was enveloped in a blaze of shells ricocheting and exploding among the trees, tearing off limbs and splintering trunks. Shell fragments and Minnie balls struck the Maryland Battalion's log breastworks like hailstones upon rooftops.

As the destructive barrage of cannon and musket fire continued, Major Goldsborough made his way to the right of the battalion to see how it was faring. The three right companies, with the 3rd North Carolina to their right, were beyond both the shelter of the east slope, as well as the protection afforded by the captured works and stonewall. They faced a draw leading into the saddle between the lower and upper peaks of Culp's Hill, placing them in full view of several Federal batteries and infantry entrenchments. Major Goldsborough could see that these troops were exposed to devastating fire and had suffered dreadfully over the past few hours. He found Captain Murray and several other Marylanders huddled behind a large boulder. Major William M. Parsley of the 3rd North Carolina and about a dozen of his men had also found shelter there.

Major Goldsborough crouched down on the ground behind the boulder and surveyed the situation. A very distressed Captain Murray crawled over to his side. "Major, my men are being slaughtered in this open position."

"I can see the problem, Captain—I'll do everything in my power to relieve this difficulty," Major Goldsborough said with chagrin. "I didn't realize that your position was so vulnerable to enemy fire. The left of our line is well-sheltered, and we have suffered few dead or wounded this morning."

Turning to Major Parsley who was sitting nearby with his back to the boulder, Major Goldsborough asked, "Where are your men positioned?"

"Beyond the few that are here with me now, most of the others are scattered behind rocks and boulders on the hillside to our right," replied the distraught North Carolinian. "We have been unable to move since before daylight due to the intensity of enemy fire."

"Has the 3rd North Carolina suffered many casualties?" Major Goldsborough asked, still trying to precisely ascertain the circumstances on the far right of the brigade.

"Very many indeed," Parsley replied. "I have but thirteen men left here." At that moment, a shell burst in the air, forward of their position, causing them to press against the sheltering granite. A shell fragment struck a North Carolinian, unlucky enough to be firing over the rock in that instant. He fell toward Captain Murray, who caught the falling soldier and eased him to the ground.

"And now I have but twelve," Major Parsley tensely added.

Seconds later, a spend ball ricocheted off a nearby tree and struck Major Goldsborough in the forehead, momentarily stunning him. As soon as he had shaken off the dizziness, he cautioned Sergeant William J. Blackistone to keep a low profile when firing his musket around the side of the boulder. As he spoke, a bullet tore through the sergeant's arm, inflicting a mortal wound.

Several soldiers tended to the wounded sergeant. Captain Murray reported to Major Goldsborough that his men were almost out of ammunition and that their muskets were clogged from so much firing. "My boys are dispirited by the constant pounding and the fact that our return fire seems to be ineffective against the Yankee breastworks," Captain Murray said. "And my men have not eaten for two days."

Major Goldsborough, his face creased by concern, considered the situation for a moment. "Captain, you may pull one company at a time out of the line—only for an hour, though—so that they may clean their guns and get food, water, and cartridges."

"Yes sir, and thank you," replied Captain Murray. He raised himself to a crouching position and dashed away to arrange the rotation of the three companies under his immediate command.

In the mid-morning, Captain George Williamson, acting adjutant-general of Steuart's Brigade, arrived at the Maryland Battalion's position. Williamson wore a grim expression as he approached Major Goldsborough. He knew the message he was about to deliver would not be well-received. "Sir, we have received orders from Major General Johnson for 2nd Brigade to form in line of battle for an assault on the Federal line. You are to move your battalion to the left and unite with the right of the 37th Virginia. This will place the Maryland Battalion astride the stone wall with the Virginia regiment to the left in a strip of woods."

Major Goldsborough immediately saw the adverse implications of this positioning and was outraged. "It's nothing less than murder to send men into that slaughter pen! We'll have to attack downhill across an open field for more than two hundred yards against strong entrenchments firing directly into our front and right flank!"

The captain remained motionless—he could see the veins standing out on Major Goldsborough's neck. "When the attack starts, we'll be quickly out of the woods and in an open field—there will be a total absence of surprise! The Maryland Battalion will be shot to pieces! I strenuously object to this order!"

Captain Williamson waited for the major's anger to subside. "Major Goldsborough, I agree with you. I can tell you, sir, that General Steuart strongly disapproves of this plan and voiced his concern to the division commander in no uncertain terms—but the order stands—it is imperative."

The two men stood with eyes locked. Major Goldsborough took his time before responding with the utmost control in his voice. "Captain, you may report to General Steuart that the Maryland Battalion will do its duty."

Captain Williamson drew up and saluted, then quickly moved back toward the brigade staff.

Major Goldsborough turned to a nearby corporal. "Find Captain Murray post haste and have him report to me." The corporal saluted and dashed off. As soon as Captain Murray arrived at his side, Major Goldsborough outlined the imperative order. He directed Captain Murray to command the right of the battalion—he was senior captain and the veteran soldiers in Company A were among the best in the battalion. Major Goldsborough would command the left of the battalion as it contained the less-experienced companies.

Captain Murray was the first to break eye contact—he looked toward the treetops, then down at the ground, without saying a word. Major Goldsborough reached out to clasp his shoulder. "Bill, this is a desperate undertaking, and I'm sorry that our battalion is being used so recklessly."

Speaking softly, Captain Murray replied, "It can't be helped. It is ordered."

Before an hour passed, the Maryland Battalion was formed just within the woods in line of battle, straddling the stonewall—three companies to the right, five companies to the left. The Marylanders, veterans of many a charge, could clearly see the difficulty of the situation and they were tight-lipped and somber.

As they stood in formation, Captain Murray moved up and down the ranks, having a few quiet words with each man in his company. At the end of each conversation, he would say goodbye, shake the soldier's hand and wish him well in the coming battle. Standing next to William, David Ridgely Howard came to attention as Captain Murray arrived before him. "Are you ready for this fight, Private Howard?" Captain Murray asked.

"Yes, sir. I've been praying that I will do my duty and not bring disgrace on my family name."

"Ridgely, your family name has been honored in Maryland from its earliest times, and I have every confidence that you'll maintain that fine reputation in this trying time."

"Thank you, sir," Private Howard said as he shook hands with his company commander.

Captain Murray stepped over in front of William, and they looked one another in the eye, each remembering better times before the war.

"Goodbye, William. It's not likely that we shall meet again."

"Let us hope that we shall both live to return triumphant to our homes in Baltimore, Captain Murray—I know that has always been a dream of yours," William replied.

"Perhaps so," said Captain Murray with a wistful smile.

* * *

Steuart's Brigade was given the order to fix bayonets. The momentary metallic rattling sound disrupted the unnatural silence blanketing the woods. Only an occasional distant musket shot or shell burst was heard. Each soldier's face displayed grim determination—it was unmistakable that something momentous was about to happen.

William heard heavy footsteps as General Steuart, Captain Williamson, and Lieutenant McKim took position behind Company A. Their general was taking part in the brigade assault even though the prospects for success were at best forlorn. Unsheathing his sword, General Steuart raised it high above his head and commanded, "Attention! Forward, double-quick! March!" The nine hundred men of his brigade moved forward with their muskets at right shoulder shift.

As they stepped off, William heard Captain Murray say, "Use your bayonets, boys. Don't fire 'til you're in real close." Once through the narrow strip of woods, Steuart's Brigade emerged into the field and was immediately struck with galling fire from three federal brigades. So intense was the fire that scarcely a leaf was left on the surrounding trees.

As they marched down the open slope, the Virginia and North Carolina regiments to the left of the Maryland Battalion fell to ground, the men refusing to go forward, despite the plodding and pleading of their officers. As the Marylanders glanced over at the prostrated soldiers, expressions of contempt covered their faces as they stayed in ranks and pressed forward.

With support on the left flank gone, the Maryland Battalion was subjected to concentrated musket fire from the front and both sides. A Federal battery opened up with an enfilading fire from the left, yet they marched forward in formation at a controlled double-quick step. The Maryland Battalion officers called out, "Steady boys, steady," and they advanced as if on dress parade. The front rank was torn by shot and shell, but still the Maryland Line did not waiver. Soldiers from the rear ranks dashed forward to take the vacant places as the battalion moved forward with their faces to the enemy.

The thinning battle lines neared the Federal breastworks, and the Marylanders surged forward at a run. Weaving through the ranks and racing up to the Union entrenchment was Grace, the battalion mascot. She had pulled free of a rope attached to her collar before the attack. Grace danced along the entrenchment for a short way, barked defiantly, and returned to dash among her boys as if they were engaged in a foot race and she was part of the sport.

On the left, Major Goldsborough felt a violent shock as a Minnie ball passed through his lung and he went down. Rising on an elbow, he watched his battalion being shattered before his eyes. Captain Murray, leading the right companies, was waving his sword in an attempt to get his company to fall back when a bullet struck his neck. He toppled to the ground and died within moments. Now leaderless, the attack of the Maryland Battalion collapsed into chaos and confusion. As he turned to retreat, Private Howard was shot in the thigh. The ball broke his leg and he was left for the Union Army to take as a prisoner.

The survivors staggered, then turned to flee for cover from the relentless hail of fire, leaving behind a field strewn with the bodies of their comrades. Grace was hobbling about on three legs searching for someone she could help among the dead and wounded. She was licking the hand of a wounded soldier when a stray bullet struck her. She died among the boys that she loved so much.

Back within the shelter of the woods, a few Maryland Battalion soldiers, including William, formed a sparse battle line to meet any counterattack that might occur. Alongside them was a distraught General Steuart, wringing his hands, saying, "My poor boys, my poor boys." Tears coursed down his sun-burnt cheeks. More than half of his brigade had fallen on the steep slope of Culp's Hill.

* * *

Behind the Federal entrenchments, several soldiers of the 147th Pennsylvania Regiment peered out at the field before them covered with bodies—most lay still in death—only a few showed any signs of life.

Just a few yards in front of the Union breastworks, a young Maryland soldier, obviously gut shot, raised himself to a sitting position, picked up the muzzle of the musket lying across his body, removed the bayonet, and slowly withdrew the ramrod from beneath the barrel.

"Hey, Johnny Reb," yelled one of the Union soldiers. "We'll have to shoot you if you keep doin' that."

The Rebel took no notice of this threat as he laid the ramrod on the ground beside him, reached into his cartridge box, pulled out a paper cartridge and bit off the end.

"Stop it now or we'll shoot you sure enough," shouted another Union soldier as he and several of his companions raised their muskets and pointed them at the wounded Southerner.

An officer of the Pennsylvania regiment attracted by their shouts came up behind his soldiers. "Don't shoot unless he tries to shoot at us," he ordered.

The wounded Marylander poured black powder from the paper cartridge into the muzzle of his musket. He poked the remainder of the cartridge containing the Minnie ball into the muzzle. Taking the ramrod in hand, he pushed it down the muzzle until the ball was firmly seated atop the powder charge. He slowly removed the ramrod from the barrel and dropped it to the ground beside him. He lifted the musket until it lay across his lap, cocked the hammer, extracted a percussion cap from the cap box on his belt, and placed it upon the musket's nipple.

The young man's face seemed calm as he turned and looked at the Union soldiers watching him from behind the wall of their entrenchment. Not a word was spoken. He then laid the butt of the musket on the ground and scooted it way from him until he was grasping the muzzle end. With his other hand, he picked up the ramrod and placed the large end on the trigger while moving the muzzle beneath his chin. There was a moment's pause, and then the musket went off, shattering the stillness that had descended upon the hillside.

THAT OTHERS MIGHT BE FREE

Armory Square Hospital
Washington, D.C.
June 24, 1865

A rush of visitors converged at the ward door, signaling the commencement of public visiting hours. The commotion caused John, Melville, and Whitman to pull their chairs closer to Clifton's bed as family and friends of other patients streamed past them. The long ward absorbed the onslaught, and the hushed atmosphere was soon restored.

"The news of Lee's defeat at Gettysburg must have stunned the people of Richmond," John speculated.

"It was devastating to them," Whitman replied. "They took immense pride in the charge of Pickett's Virginians, but they were equally dismayed by the seemingly endless newspaper listings of the dead and wounded. They had expected great things from the invasion of the North."

Clifton grunted. "My division took part in the pursuit of Lee as he retreated toward Virginia, but we never got close. A more aggressive chase by General George Meade may very well have ended the war in 1863."

"I'm not qualified to expound on military matters, but I know people who would agree that Meade's pursuit of Lee was dilatory at best," Whitman responded.

"Meade took command of the Army of the Potomac just prior to the Battle of Gettysburg," John protested. "That was the reason why he was unable to move the army as quickly as everyone wanted after the battle."

"In any case, William told me of the Southern people's anguish over the casualties suffered at Gettysburg," Whitman continued. "The Cary's were grief-stricken when they learned that Captain Murray and nearly half the young men of the Maryland Battalion were lost on Culp's Hill.

"Those boys were wasted in a futile charge—William was fortunate to have come through that fight unscathed," John muttered, as much to himself as to the others.

Whitman's brow furrowed as he became more contemplative. "Misery tightened its grip on the South after receiving the sad tidings. Gone forever were the glorious times when Southern arms appeared to be invincible—when victory after victory was achieved on the battlefield."

"Things were going poorly for the secessionists, not only in a military sense, but in every aspect of civilian life," John commented. "The pinch of the Union naval blockade was ravaging their economy. The material and manpower resources of the Confederacy were dwindling rapidly from the unrelenting strain of war."

"William said much the same thing," Whitman replied. "It seemed to them that the North possessed endless quantities of both material and men in contrast to their lack of almost everything."

"This no doubt tore at the very fabric of Confederate society," John said.

"It did indeed, Dr. Prentiss, but William noted an interesting permutation that might surprise you." Whitman earned inquisitive looks from his companions, which caused him to smile. "There was a subtle shift in the traditional gender roles of Southern society. And, as you might expect, his friends Hetty and Connie were at the forefront of this progression."

"From what little I know of Miss Hetty Cary, she was always a very independent sort," Melville interjected. "She was in her late twenties. A respectable woman would have married and had several children by that age."

A subtle smile again played on Whitman's lips.

"I have no doubt that her remarkable beauty and aristocratic background gave her more latitude than an ordinary woman might have had," John replied sternly. "But you are injudicious to imply that she was not respectable."

"That woman openly defied Federal authority in Baltimore!" Melville exclaimed derisively. "She ran the blockade like a common smuggler! She flaunted herself throughout Confederate society!"

"Which makes my point," Whitman answered. "Social change occurs during times of upheaval and the war created just that circumstance. Many upper class women of the South embraced the opportunity to become more active in the public realm."

"Truth be told, this was also a phenomena in the North as well, although to a lesser degree," John said thoughtfully. "The exigencies of war clearly placed much greater pressure on the Southern social structure. Indeed, the war was often fought in their backyard, whilst Northern women were generally spared that inconvenience."

"What about women of the poorer classes?" Clifton asked.

"That's a different story—their choices were limited and the responsibilities forced upon them were a serious burden," Whitman conceded. "But I have no doubt that privileged Southern women such as the Carys relished the moment and the independence it bestowed."

"In times past, women spent their entire lives in the domestic sphere," Clifton observed. "They were submissive first to their fathers and then to their husbands. In the South, the patriarch was the absolute ruler over all supposed inferiors in his realm—the family women and children—and the slaves."

"It's a fair bargain for women!" Melville exclaimed. "They're protected from the harsh realities of the world and permitted to devote their full attention to family and to God. It suits their nature and is in accordance with the Almighty's plan for mankind."

"In your view, that might be so," Whitman said dismissively as he turned in his chair to address his remarks to Clifton and John. "Southern women were able to step outside traditional roles using the Confederate cause to shield them from public scorn. Through acts of patriotism, they successfully entered the public sphere as nurses, writers, and community leaders."

"If that's so, it's hard to imagine these women allowing themselves to again be defined as passive members of society," Clifton remarked. "At least not to the degree that their mothers and grandmothers gracefully acquiesced."

"It will not last," Melville declared with a self-satisfied smile. "Hierarchies are a natural aspect of all human relations—'twas ever thus and always will be."

* * *

THE EXECUTIVE MANSION
RICHMOND, VIRGINIA
AUGUST 20, 1863

Once Richmond became the capital of the Confederate States of America, officials made arrangements to accommodate its new responsibilities. They reconfigured Federal buildings to house clerks and functionaries of the Confederate government and the Virginia legislature shared its capitol with the new Congress. The City of Richmond purchased a recently remodeled, fully furnished, three-story house and rented it to the Confederate government as the official residence of the president. The mansion had all the modern conveniences, including gaslights in every room and a water closet.

Varina Howell Davis, the president's wife, had sent for the Cary girls to spend the day at her home. Connie entered the mansion from Clay Street, thanked the elderly butler who admitted her, and paused briefly to admire the life-sized statues of Comedy and Tragedy that sat in niches on either side of the parlor door. Each classical female figure, composed of plaster and painted to resemble bronze, clasped a gas lamp to illuminate the entrance hall. Comedy held a smiling theatrical mask, which was especially endearing to Connie and evoked a smile every time she saw it. She walked across the large parlor toward the pocket doors connecting it to the drawing room. These doors, when fully opened, provided a commodious venue for public receptions. The adjoining rooms were decorated en suite with matching crimson draperies, the richest upholstery, and finely flocked wallpaper.

From the moment she entered the executive mansion, Connie noted the presence of senior army officers and government officials, most of whom she was acquainted with in local society. Guessing that a council of war was in progress in the state dining room, she took a detour and peeked in. The long table was covered with maps and papers of all sorts and was surrounded by gray-uniformed men and a handful of civilians.

A slim servant woman emerged from a narrow stairway coming up from the basement, brushed past Connie, and made her way into the dining room with a tray of teacups and saucers. Connie took little notice as her gaze found the president's secretary sitting at the far end of the table. She made eye contact and discreetly waved her hand, keeping it low in front of her midriff. They exchanged a flirtatious smile before Connie turned in the doorway and walked with a light step to the drawing room.

Seated to the left of President Davis, Burton Harrison returned his attention to the conversation regarding Meade's slow advance into Virginia. As everyone was in accord on the matters under discussion, the young man's considerable poise and restraint, often used to placate either his chief or another strong personality, had not been called into play. Burton recorded minutiae of the meeting in his journal, occasionally adjusting his posture, and straightening his frock coat. He made a note on a question raised by General Lee, who was standing at an easel illustrating troop dispositions on the upright map. A hand passed by his shoulder and placed a teacup and saucer on the table in front of him. Burton attempted to acknowledge the servant, but her head was down and she had a look of concentration on her face as she set the teacup and saucer for the officer sitting beside him. The household residents found her to be an able but dull-witted and illiterate slave who had been "hired out" by her owner for service in the executive mansion. With the last teacup and saucer on her tray, she moved along the table and stopped near General Lee. She waited for him to sit down, as he had just concluded his briefing, before placing a teacup and saucer for him. After momentary scrutiny of the table, she let the tray down to her side, and exited the room.

Born into slavery in Richmond, the woman had been owned by a wealthy hardware merchant. Upon his death in 1851, she was given her freedom by the merchant's ardent abolitionist daughter, but remained as a servant with the family for several years. Eventually, her keen intellect was noted and she was sent to be educated at a Quaker school in Philadelphia. Mary Elizabeth graduated days before the war began and returned to Richmond to marry Wilson Bowser, a free black man.

Elizabeth Van Lew, the woman who emancipated Mary Elizabeth, had by then been dubbed "Crazy Bet" for her deranged appearance and incoherent mutterings, all part of a facade of erratic behavior to conceal her covert work. She successfully managed a Union spy ring in Richmond, helped escapees from Libby Prison find their way north, and orchestrated the placement of her former servant into the household of Jefferson Davis under a bogus name. Mary Elizabeth's photographic memory of unguarded documents and word-for-word retention of overheard conversations were fully utilized in her new capacity.

Thomas McNiven, a baker who was the Union spymaster in Richmond, regularly delivered fresh bread to the executive mansion. Each day, without causing suspicion, the ostensibly ignorant slave woman made her way to his bakery wagon parked by the old brick kitchen on the east side of the property. The valuable intelligence gleaned by Mary Elizabeth Bowser was encoded and sent through the lines directly to the highest levels of the federal government.

* * *

Connie quietly slipped onto the crimson and gold brocade sofa next to Hetty who had arrived at the executive mansion a half hour beforehand. Mrs. Davis, having just finished an amusing story, paused to graciously welcome Connie, as did Mary Boykin Chestnut, who was also very fond of her. The president's wife and her longtime friend spent the next hour reminiscing about Washington social life. During the time that her husband served in the House of Representatives, the Senate, and as secretary of war in the Franklin Pierce administration, Varina enjoyed life as a prominent hostess in Washington's high society. Mrs. Chestnut, whose husband had been a senator from South Carolina, contributed a few

stories of her own. The two young women listened attentively as both were fascinated by the episodes.

Their conversation was interrupted by ringing laughter as the three Davis
children—Margaret, Jefferson, and Joseph—dashed into the room and bee-
lined for their mother. The hubbub of childish prattle and Varina's delight at
being surrounded by her little ones marked the end of Washington society recollections. For several minutes, Mary, Hetty, and Connie sat back to enjoy the
happy chatter between a mother and her brood.

The sound of boots moving toward the front entrance hall announced that
the counsel of war had adjourned. Hetty excused herself from the group and
hurried from the room, but Connie sat still until Varina gave her a knowing
smile and granted permission for her to excuse herself. Connie was quickly
on her feet, headed for the hallway. As she approached the spiraling staircase
that would take her to the second floor, Connie passed General Robert E. Lee
standing in the hallway, resplendent in his best uniform with gold sash and
dress sword. He was holding Hetty's hands, bowing over them, absorbed in
conversation with the reigning belle of Richmond. As Connie placed her foot
on the first stair step, she turned her head to observe General Lee kissing Hetty
on the check as they were about to part. He usually kissed girls who he had
known since childhood and greatly enjoyed innocent flirtation with pretty,
clever young women.

Connie climbed the stairs to the second floor and crossed the large landing that served as an anteroom for the president's home office. She stepped
softly on the carpet in her approach to the open interior window of a former airing closet that housed the office of the president's secretary. The top of
his head was barely visible about the sill as he sat reading a report. Biting her
lip to repress a smile, she stepped up to the opening and deliberately looked
to the side instead of directly at him. He instantly looked up and she turned
her head haughtily toward him. His delighted expression when he saw her
was so pleasing to Connie that she felt her own emotion bloom on her cheeks.
He jumped to his feet to greet her, but she had already stepped around and into
the doorway. Burton, circumspect about all things, glanced about to see if anyone

else was upstairs before guiding her into the office that contained his writing desk, storage cabinets for official documents, a small drop-leaf table, and several chairs. The nattily dressed young man helped Connie take a seat and then took one close to her.

Connie reached over and touched the back of his hand. "I'm forever in your debt for the beautiful package of cream laid paper with envelopes to match."

"I was merely protecting myself against excuses for non-response to my notes," Burton replied playfully.

"It replaces a pile of prescription blanks given to me by a hospital surgeon—with envelopes made of wallpaper, the pattern side within," Connie said with a smile.

"Are you going to be here at the executive mansion for the day?" Burton asked.

"Yes, I am. Varina invited us to participate in several activities. She has planned a luncheon this afternoon and then time spent relaxing on the portico, gossiping and the like."

"That sounds like a very nice time. I fear that I've so much work to do that I'll spend the day confined to this office. What a pity for me," he added jokingly.

"Perhaps, from time to time, I'll come rescue you from your despondency."

"That would be delightful."

* * *

Varina, her sister, Margaret, and friends, Mary, Hetty, and Connie spent the afternoon in the shade of the high-columned portico on the backside of the mansion. It was the perfect spot to while away the warm afternoon hours. The portico overlooked a garden of fruit trees, roses, heliotropes, and beds of pansies and violets. They sat in a circle to accommodate chitchat and handiwork, crafting straw bonnets from previously made long ribbons of plaited straw. Today, the women were sewing the plaits together edge to edge to fabricate the headpiece. Later, the bonnets would be pressed into shape and decorated with ribbons and flowers or covered with fabric. The paucity of reasonably priced millinery eclipsed all former dictates of fashion. None of these women would have otherwise worn a straw hat that they made with their own hands.

"Here's a question I often ask my married friends," Hetty said, addressing the president's wife. "When and where did you meet Mister Davis?"

Varina leaned forward and laughed cheerfully. "Well, that's quite a story! When my father first moved to Natchez, Mississippi, Joseph Emory Davis, who was a well-established lawyer in town as well as being Jefferson's older brother, befriended him. In my seventeenth year, as I was becoming a young lady about to be introduced to society, my parents sent me to visit Hurricane Plantation, the home of Joseph Davis. I had stopped the day before at the home of his eldest daughter. That's where I met Jefferson. He curtly informed me that I was to be at Hurricane the next day."

"My goodness. What was your first impression of him?" Hetty asked with a slight frown.

"I found myself both fascinated and affronted," Varina replied. "He had a way of taking for granted that everyone agrees with him when he expresses an opinion."

"He hasn't changed much in that regard," Mary said with a smile.

"No, he hasn't," Varina replied. "At first, I thought it was his age and station in life. He was eighteen years older than me—a widower who had lived in seclusion for many years after the death of his first wife."

"Her name was Sarah Knox Taylor," Mary chimed in. "Her father was Zachary Taylor, Jefferson's commanding officer in the Old First Infantry during the Black Hawk War. Of course, you know that he later became a general, commanded an army in the Mexican War, and was elected president of the United States."

"Did she die in childbirth?" Connie asked, her face sorrowful.

"No," replied Varina. "She died of a malarial fever that they both contracted on the bridal tour to Louisiana—just short of their three-month wedding anniversary."

"Oh my, what an awful tragedy!" Connie exclaimed.

The hat making slowed and the conversation halted. It took nearly a minute for the activity to resume. When it did, the women's eyes were fixed on the sewing motions of their hands.

"Please tell us about your courtship by Mr. Davis," Hetty said.

A smile crossed Varina's face. "My parents could not have been more delighted when they learned of our mutual fondness. However, the greatest impediment to a marriage between us was my own affinity for Whig politics, not a likely thing for a young girl at that time. I was, in fact, quite outspoken about it."

"Varina, you have always had an impetuous tongue, despite having a warm heart," Mary said. She glanced at the Carys and then added, "If she thinks it, she says it!"

Varina's eyes danced with merriment. "I cannot deny that. It's a lifelong habit and too many people are already well aware of my proclivity. But to continue the story, Mister Davis was an ardent Democrat and would soon run against the Whigs for a seat in Congress. I struggled with that knowledge to the point of making myself deathly ill. Gradually, however, I put aside my pride and Whig views, regained my health, and married him on the twenty-sixth day of February, 1845, in a small ceremony at the Briers, my parents' home. It was the best thing I've ever done. Each of us is the keeper of the other's heart."

The women looked up at the sound of the door opening onto the porch. Jefferson Davis appeared, followed by Judah Phillip Benjamin, the secretary of state, a man known for his exceptional oratorical skills and sharp intellect. The men were locked in serious conversation as they walked down the steps and into the garden where the confidentiality of their words was assured. The president looked as if he bore the sorrows of the world on his shoulders as he conferred at length with his trusted advisor.

Varina lowered her voice. "Are you aware that Mr. Benjamin, a Whig from Charleston, South Carolina, was the first Jew elected to the United States Senate?"

The younger women murmured negatively in response.

"That was in 1852," Mary added. "He was reelected as a Democrat in 1858 and became an eloquent defender of Southern interests."

"I also doubt you know that during his first term he and Mr. Davis disagreed frequently on the Senate floor in glacial, yet polite phrases that barely masked a disdain for one another. Based on a suspected insult during one such exchange, Senator Benjamin challenged my husband to a duel."

"My goodness! I didn't know that," Connie gasped and turned to eye the two men in deep conversation at the far end of the garden.

"Fortunately, Mr. Davis had the good sense to quickly and publicly apologize," Varina continued. "Thus satisfied, the incident was put behind them. As the debate over Southern rights and Northern tyranny intensified over the next few years, these very different men found themselves to be political allies. They built a relationship of mutual respect and trust."

"Did you know that our silver-tongued secretary of state has a wife and daughter living in Paris?" Mary asked the Carys, her voice tainted by disapproval.

"No," they replied simultaneously with shock written across their faces.

"Her maiden name was Natalie St. Martin, the daughter of a prominent Creole family in New Orleans. Following the marriage—it was one of strategy for both—they acquired a large sugar plantation but lived there just a few years. When their only child was born, Natalie and the infant moved to Paris. Thereafter, he saw them but once a year. She rejoined her husband after his election to the Senate, but quickly returned to France because of the scandalous rumors about her that circulated in Washington."

"That's ancient history," Varina said pointedly. "What matters is that Judah Benjamin is the 'right hand' of the president and works twelve to fourteen hours a day at his side for the good of this administration and the Southern Confederacy."

"Wasn't Mr. Benjamin your husband's secretary of war for a short time?" Hetty asked.

"He was indeed. And he accepted, in silence, the scathing public condemnation directed at him over the fall of Roanoke Island. In fact, Judah Benjamin was merely carrying out the president's orders—Roanoke Island was sacrificed because we had not the resources to defend it and we dared not reveal our weakness to the enemy. His resignation ended public scrutiny of the situation. Jefferson later appointed him to his present post in appreciation of his loyalty."

The partially completed straw bonnets and sewing paraphernalia were forgotten on the women's laps as they sat in silence. Varina's younger sister Margaret spoke up. "I understand that Secretary Benjamin has been a strong advocate of a cotton diplomacy intended to bring England into the war on our side."

"He has worked tirelessly to achieve that goal," Varina replied firmly. "There is, of course, a major hurdle as the British abolished slavery a half-century ago.

For this reason, I believe there is little chance that they will ally with us in this war, or break the blockade, no matter how desperate their mills are to obtain our cotton."

"Secretary Benjamin is also a proponent of emancipation for slaves willing to bear arms for the Confederacy, but thus far has found little support in Congress," Mary commented in a neutral tone, looking to Varina for confirmation.

However, Varina did not reply. Her attention was focused on the garden. President Davis and Secretary Benjamin were walking toward the steps to the portico. Moments later, with a polite nod in the direction of the ladies, the two officers of state entered the mansion. Shortly after they disappeared across the threshold, the women returned to making hats and launched a conversation regarding the fact that Richmond's streets and drawing rooms had filled over the past six weeks with army officers.

Hetty quickly warmed to this subject. "We can be thankful for the inaction of General Meade. He has been so slow following the Confederate Army back to Virginia that our boys will have a much-deserved rest before embarking on another campaign."

"It's such a pleasing spectacle," Connie said. "They arrive from the field wearing long cavalry boots splashed with mud and soon emerge from where their dress uniforms are stored, ready for courting and social activity."

"Hetty, I suppose this means that you will soon be having another starvation party?" Mary asked.

"Of course," Hetty replied. "Is there some reason I should not?"

Mary ignored the question and tilted her head toward Hetty as she spoke to Varina. "These young ladies give parties that are entirely without food or drink. They will give thirty dollars for music and not one cent for a morsel to eat!"

"That's why they're called 'starvation parties,'" Hetty responded with a tight-lipped smile. "A cavalier recently remarked to me that the only intoxicant and sustenance necessary at these affairs is a woman's voice and her eyes—and dancing until dawn."

"Would that cavalier possibly be General James Ewell Brown Stuart?" Mary asked sarcastically. "You do know that he is a happily wedded man with children?"

"No, it was not him who made the comment—and yes, I am well aware of his wife and children," Hetty replied in an icy tone.

"He's devoted to Hetty—they're just good friends!" Connie exclaimed indignantly. To break the embarrassed silence that followed, Connie added a comment. "Besides, Hetty likes them that way, you know—gilt-edged and with stars."

* * *

MEDFIELD ACADEMY
NEAR BALTIMORE, MARYLAND
OCTOBER 3, 1863

It was something that Sarah often did on a Saturday afternoon. She took refuge in her late husband's library among the books and scientific devices that had been the tools of his profession. This comforting time lessened the pain caused by her complicity in the events leading to his fatal accident. Laura frequently joined her in the library as the trauma of John's death had increased their emotional dependence on each other.

Sarah now openly acknowledged Laura as her daughter and, after a brief but emotional transition, Laura embraced the new relationship. The infrequent letters received from Clifton and William only reminded her of the family's disintegration and she did little to encourage further correspondence. Adding to Sarah's burden was the struggle required to keep the academy in operation during uncertain times.

She was knitting while Laura sat opposite her reading a book. The only sound heard was the crackling of a fire in the fireplace until a soft knock on the library door brought Sarah out of her lassitude.

"Come in," she said. The servants were the only other ones in the house as the academy was vacant on weekends. Her back was to the door so she glanced at Laura for some indication as to who was entering the room. There was a look of surprise on Laura's face. Sarah quickly stood, knitting in hand, and turned to see who was there. Entering the room was Elijah, followed closely by his wife, Alma. He was dressed in a blue uniform of the Union Army.

Sarah's mouth flew open with a sharp intake of air. "Elijah, did you really join the army?"

"Yes, Miss Sarah, I most certainly did." The tone of Elijah's voice might have been contrite, but his bearing declared that he was quite pleased with himself. "I'm sorry to have misled you about having business to attend to last week, but I needed the time to enlist. The army gave me the oath, put me in uniform, and kept me at the recruit camp 'til now. I've got just a few hours before I must go back."

"But you're over forty years old," Sarah cried out, her hands spread in a beseeching manner. "There's no need for you to serve in the army. You have a wife and two daughters."

"Miss Sarah, I'm a free man and I want others of my race to be free. Mr. John got me my freedom and told me that this war was going to be about ending slavery. He was right and I want to do my part."

Laura's eyes were open wide and her heart palpitated in her chest. She was fond of Elijah and his family, yet the notion of Negro troops fighting to preserve the Union horrified her and increased her anxiety over the course of the war. Her belief in the righteousness of Southern independence had been tempered in recent months by mounting evidence that it could only be achieved, if at all, at a frightful cost. Laura had been heartbroken to learn of Captain Murray's death at Gettysburg and her prayers for William's safe return were frequent and fervent. She even prayed for Clifton's deliverance from harm, although most often as a guilty afterthought.

Laura's attention, despite her conflicting emotions, was drawn to Alma who was standing behind her husband. She could see that Alma was terrified by the drastic turn of events, yet very proud of her man. The confluence of these emotions contorted Alma's face and caused her body to tremble. Laura went to Alma's side and placed an arm around her shoulders.

"Yes, ma'am, I was recruited by Colonel William Birney into the 7th United States Colored Troops, Maryland Volunteers. They've signed up mostly slaves, some over at Snow Hill and near Rehoboth, which didn't make the owners none too happy," Elijah said, smiling broadly. "That's not supposed to happen. There were a few fistfights between slave owners and the recruiting details. But most of the volunteers are runaways from plantations on the Eastern Shore. They even recruited a bunch of colored men from the oyster fleet lying off the mouth of the Patuxent River. Those fellows and me are about the only freemen to have joined the regiment thus far."

"When will your regiment be at full strength?" Sarah asked.

"There are three companies now and more should be raised in the next few weeks," Elijah replied. We don't have muskets yet, but we drill every day anyhow. We'll be moving to Camp Stanton at Benedict for instruction next week."

"Oh my goodness," Sarah said, still recovering from the surprise.

"So, I'm off to war!" Elijah exclaimed while carefully watching Sarah's face for some sign that she was angry about his decision.

"Elijah, I understand your reasons for joining the army. Nevertheless, it makes me sad to see you go. So many of our men have gone off to fight."

"I know that," Miss Sarah," Elijah replied.

Tears welled in Sarah's eyes. "The thought of Clifton and William serving on opposite sides breaks my heart. My own dear brother, an officer in a Massachusetts regiment, was wounded at Gettysburg. It's not easy for those of us who must wait and pray for our loved ones."

"I'm sorry to have added to your burden, but this is something that I had do," Elijah responded evenly.

"And I accept that premise, Elijah," Sarah replied.

* * *

6TH MARYLAND VOLUNTEERS
NEAR BRANDY STATION, VIRGINIA
DECEMBER 8, 1863

Major Joseph Hill, Captain Clifton Prentiss, Lieutenant Charles Damuth, and Chaplain Joseph Brown sat on camp chairs around a log fire, sharing conversation and companionship prior to bedding down for the night. The sound of a horse walking in the darkness drew their attention just before the rider entered the circle of flickering light.

"Good evening, gentlemen," Lieutenant James Touchstone said as he brought his mare Flora to a stop between a row of tents and the campfire. The seated officers cordially responded to the regimental quartermaster's greeting. Lieutenant Touchstone dismounted and handed the reins to Hazlett Owens, his commissary sergeant, who stepped out of a nearby tent and led the horse away.

"Our wagon train was late arriving this evening, so the supplies will be off-loaded after sun-up tomorrow. The regiment did receive some mail. On brief inspection, I found a copy of the Cecil Whig, my home county newspaper with which I generally disagree. However, it sometimes contains local news worth reading, much to my surprise of course."

The men seated around the campfire chuckled, knowing that the former blacksmith from Port Deposit, despite being an unfaltering Union man, was a strident Democrat who often took umbrage with the actions of the Lincoln administration. On numerous occasions, he wrote seething rebukes to the editor of the Cecil Whig for his unqualified support for the policies of the nation's first republican president.

Lieutenant Touchstone chortled in response. "I noticed an excellent letter in this edition written by one of our 6th Maryland boys to Mr. Ewing, the esteemed editor. It very nicely describes our recent action at Locust Grove. With your permission, I'll read it aloud for everyone's edification and enjoyment."

"Please do, James," Major Hill directed.

"It will be my great pleasure," Lieutenant Touchstone replied as he put on his spectacles, opened the newspaper, and began to read.

> *Friend Ewing:*
>
> *Presuming you would like to hear of the trials and tribulations of the Boys of My Maryland, who are trying to find the road to Richmond with the Army of the Potomac, I drop you a few lines. There are a number of the 6th Maryland at present in the hospital, suffering from their wounds received in that skirmish, as the press called it, on*

the 27th ultimate. Now if that was a skirmish, I hope never to see a battle. By-the-by, I believe a fight which does not last for four or five days is not termed anything but a skirmish. But such as it was, it has caused many a happy fireside a mournful Christmas, and left many a gallant youth a cripple for life.

"That was a sharp fight, there is no doubt!" exclaimed old Mr. Brown, as he was known in the regiment. "We lost many good lads on that day."

"It was also the first time the entire regiment fought a pitched battle within a brigade formation," observed Captain Prentiss.

"True enough," Major Hill replied. "Please proceed with your reading, Quartermaster Touchstone."

But I am digressing. On Thanksgiving Day, while our friends were enjoying the dainties of life, we were nibbling hard tack, and marching to pay our respects to the Johnnys. At night, we crossed at what is called Jacob's Mills, five miles above Germania Ford. On Friday, the second division of our corps took the advance. We did not expect we would meet much opposition, but soon skirmishing commenced, and we knew that some of our misguided brothers were in the vicinity. The firing grew faster, and we took up our line of march to take a hand at the game in which death was the dealer. We did not have long to wait, for a few minutes walk soon brought us to within 300 yards of the Butternuts.

"I like the way this young fellow writes," Captain Prentiss remarked.

"Well, after all, he's from Cecil County," replied Lieutenant Touchstone. "We're a very literate lot you know," he quipped with a sly smile as he resumed reading aloud.

Nothing but a small clearing intervened between the enemy and ourselves. The woods were so thick that artillery could not be brought in to advantage, but a section of the 6th Rhode Island battery soon began to talk and the Johnnys, not to be outdone in exchanging iron compliments, brought on a section also, and the way the canister flew among the trees was a caution to the gray squirrels. Here and there, a comrade would drop. Some would crawl to the rear, while others had fought their last fight, and their proud spirits took their upward flight to appear before the Great Chieftain of us all. Peace to their remains. Memory will drop a tear on their rude graves in the wilderness.

The listeners around the campfire stared into the dancing flames with somber expressions as memories of the bloody battle were conjured up by the newspaper account.

Night soon drew her sable robe over the scene, and friend and foe rested. Now came strategy, which as a writer says, is a fine thing when one does not understand it. The Johnnys tried to flank us, but not succeeding in that, they fell back. When morning broke, the bird had flown, and we left the field to join the main body of our army. The Rebel dead and wounded were left, as we had not enough transportation for our own. At four on Saturday afternoon, the army came up to Lee, who had fell back to Mine Run, a small stream some five miles from Orange Court House. Here, they worked like beavers, throwing up entrenchments. A flank movement was in contemplation, when an order came to fall back. On Tuesday, after having escaped nearly freezing to death, we recrossed the Rapidan at Culpepper Mine Ford, reaching Brandy Station on Thursday. And then, after escaping starvation and being jolted to death in the ambulances, we took the cars for Alexandria, and here our trouble for a time ended. The deed was done. Lee was scared, and the army has gone into winter quarters. And now the old telegram will be "all quiet along the line."

"I don't think either side accomplished much in this battle or, for that matter, in the entire Mine Run campaign," Major Hill commented. "The Rebs stopped us from going farther south, but weren't able to chase us back to the Rapidan." He waved a hand. "Read on James, sorry I interrupted."

Quartermaster Touchstone adjusted his spectacles and picked up where he had left off.

> But, I fear, I am trespassing on your valuable columns and, as the surgeon is coming, I will, for the present, close.

> All honors to Old Cecil. Her sturdy sons have been tested, and their wounds show it today. The 6th Regiment of Maryland Volunteers has won its place in the pages of history. Long may it stand an emblem of its country's rights. The noble flag, the presentation of the loyal ladies of Elkton, floated over us while we met the traitors and put them to flight.

"It's signed Cripple from Cecil County," Lieutenant Touchstone said as he removed his spectacles.

"I wonder which of the boys wrote that letter?" Major Hill asked. The major was from Elkton and knew every man enlisted in the regiment along the east bank of the Susquehanna River, above Chesapeake Bay.

"Don't know," Lieutenant Touchstone replied. "Could have been any one of several from the three companies raised in Cecil and wounded in that fight."

Captain Prentiss turned toward Chaplain Brown. "Mr. Brown, I saw you up front for a while at Locust Grove."

"'Tis true," replied Chaplain Brown. "I was feeling a deep interest in the fate of our boys, so I rode forward into the line as they were moving forward. Then things suddenly got very hot and my good friend Major Hill ordered me, in terms that I readily understood, to get back behind the lines. Suiting the action to the command, I retired at the double-quick and scarcely reached the rear when the first of our wounded were carried back."

"I saw you moving to the rear right smartly," Lieutenant Damuth remarked with a chuckle.

Ignoring him, Mr. Brown continued. "For over two hours, there was a continuous roar of musketry. Surely, I thought, no man could come out of that fight without being killed or wounded, but the God of Battles was with us!" he exclaimed, sweeping his arms outward, sounding and appearing much like he was preaching one of his sermons. "And the 6th Maryland was in the midst of it, led by Colonel Horn, the bravest of the brave and, in the worst moments, steadied by the calm, deliberate Major Hill," Chaplain Brown declared as he dramatically unfolded his arm toward Major Hill. "The Colonel's horse received a shot and a ball passed through the Major's coat, hitting his saddle, but doing him no harm."

Major Hill lifted the left side of his blue frock coat, stuck his right forefinger through the bullet hole, and wiggled it.

BELLES, BEAUX, AND BATTLES

ARMORY SQUARE HOSPITAL
WASHINGTON, D.C.
JUNE 24, 1865

Clifton's hands gripped the side rails of the bed as he carefully shifted his hip to find a more comfortable position. Once resettled, he looked up and saw that his brothers and Whitman were watching him. He hurriedly resumed talking about his regiment. "We went into winter quarters following Locust Grove and remained there until the beginning of the spring campaign of 1864—the roads in Virginia are impassible in the wintertime," he said as he shook his head.

"Essentially, it was the same for William and the 2nd Maryland Battalion," Whitman said. "They too went into winter quarters, but there were some memorable moments that I can relate, if you're interested." Seeing assent on everyone's face, Whitman sat back in his chair and crossed his arms. "The long-touted Maryland Line was finally formed the previous November. All Maryland infantry, artillery, and cavalry units in the Army of Northern Virginia were ordered to rendezvous near Hanover Junction under the command of Colonel Bradley T. Johnson. The Maryland Line numbered about fifteen hundred men at the time, the m Marylanders ever assembled in Confederate service under the Maryland fla soldiers of the 2nd Maryland Battalion built a camp of sturdy log huts, a la house, and even a handsome little church. Many of the young Marylanders were playing the beaux for pretty girls in the vicinity and numerous applications for church membership were received from the young ladies."

"I can readily imagine William being a part of that activity," Clifton said with a chuckle. He noted that John was puzzled by the quip. "Going to church regularly, that is," he added.

Clifton and John both laughed, as did Whitman. Melville smiled, despite himself.

Whitman was pleased by the light moment and pressed on with the reminiscence. "During this period, the soldiers built fortifications, stood guard duty, drilled, and intensified their military training. As the Baltimore Light Artillery was situated in a nearby camp, William and a select group of fellow infantrymen were drilled in loading and firing artillery pieces so that they could turn captured guns on the enemy when they overran their works. In return, the infantry taught the cavalry and artillery to fight as foot soldiers in skirmish and battle lines."

"Cross training in arms was a good idea for a mixed brigade like the Maryland Line," Clifton interjected. The others nodded politely as military science was not their forte. "This was something that we should have done." His voice trailed off.

"It was a cold winter and there was much snow, precipitating on more than one occasion a large-scale snowball fight. The exuberant boys of the infantry would attack the cavalry troopers and the artillerists would join in on the side of the cavalry. Fortunately, nothing more than a few black eyes and bloody noses resulted from the fracases."

"And I have no doubt that William was in the middle of this activity as well," John commented with a sad smile on his face.

"I can confirm the truth of that," Whitman replied. "However, picket duty away from camp in the extreme weather was a miserable affair. The men suffered from exposure to severe cold, high winds, snow, and rain without adequate clothing, boots, or tents."

"It was a mean winter," Clifton added as he pulled the sheet higher on his waist.

"There was one small, bright spot from that period that I remember William mentioning," Whitman said. "Much to everyone's delight, orders were read at dress parade in March authorizing every soldier of the Maryland Line to wear the cross bottony as a badge of distinction. In fact, most of them already wore the small silver crosses, but were nevertheless gratified that it was now official- ly sanctioned. A number of ladies in Richmond were also wearing the emblem as it seemed to be quite the fashion."

"I noticed that ornament on his jacket for the first time whilst in the hospital tent at Petersburg," Clifton remembered.

"With the beginning of spring weather, the tempo of military operations in- creased," Whitman said. "The Union Army, under a determined General Grant, moved south and Lee's Army of Northern Virginia maneuvered to block any threat to Richmond. The Maryland Line functioned as intended on several oc- casions in minor actions, but expediency soon brought an end to the dream. The Maryland cavalry rode off on other assignments, the Maryland artillery batteries were parceled off to other commands, and the 2nd Maryland Infantry Battalion was assigned to the division of Major General John C. Breckenridge."

"Wasn't this the same man who was a former congressman, senator, vice president, and Democrat candidate for the presidency in the 1860 election?" Melville inquired sarcastically.

"Of course, he is one and the same—and in January of 1865, he became the last secretary of war of the Confederate States of America," replied Clifton dryly.

"William spoke about attending an event at the home of George Wythe Ran- dolph, one of Breckenridge's predecessors as secretary of war," Whitman com- mented with an artful smile. "Always being available for his friend Connie, William was drafted to work behind the scenes in one of her theatrical produc- tions. He found himself in very interesting company."

* * *

THE RANDOLPH HOUSE
RICHMOND, VIRGINIA
JANUARY 9, 1864

Six weeks beforehand, Mrs. General Randolph, the beautiful, oriental-looking wife of Connie's cousin, appealed to her to arrange the entertainment for a party that she was giving for social and official Richmond. Connie accepted the assignment and planned a series of pantomime charades to liven what was otherwise becoming a dreary winter season. She threw herself into the enterprise with her customary enthusiasm, energy, and creativity.

Once the scripts were written, Connie called upon her friends to paint scenery, make costumes, gather props, and become the actors. To accomplish several of these formidable tasks, she drafted Frank Vizetelly, the correspondent and artist for the *London Illustrated News*. A big, red-bearded Bohemian, he was a treasure trove of knowledge in stage device, theatricals, tableaux, and charades. William was assigned to be his assistant and painted several backdrops while on furlough.

The much-anticipated evening finally arrived. President and Mrs. Davis, cabinet members and their wives, and other important personages were seated in rows within the ample space of the Randolph's parlor to view the performance. "Knighthood" was the first word depicted in a set of verses penned by John R. Thompson and spoken by Miss Mary Preston, costumed as a Greek chorus. The allusion it contained was to General John Bell Hood, who happened to be in the audience, much to Connie's surprise, as he recently lost a leg in battle. A burst of applause after the verses were read caused him to rise on his crutches and bow, blushing from the unexpected attention. The next word was "Pen," taken from a Dickens novel and pantomimed by Miss Josephine Chesney, as Fanny Squeers, cajoling Major Francis X. Ward, as Nicholas Nickleby, to sharpen her quill pen. In "Eye" Mr. Forbes, as Uncle Toby, peered into the face of Miss Herndon, portraying the Widow Wadman, who held a handkerchief to her eye while pretending that she had something in it. "Tent" was represented by several young women in jewels, spangles, and scarves lolling on sofa cushions and admiring Mrs. Russell Robinson as the *Light of the Harem*, taken from the painting by Lord Frederick Leighton. Miss Lizzie Giles posed in the garb of a novice for the word "Penitent" with tears painted on her rose-colored cheeks. Mr. Robert Dobbin, appearing too anxious to find a mat upon which to kneel before Miss Pollard, performed a pantomime for the word "Mat."

Hetty, in a charade for the word "Rye" was dressed as a Scottish lassie and paraded around the stage before a field of oats painted on a backdrop. The spectacle that she created was so pleasing that the audience demanded that it be repeated several times as the piano played "Comin' Thro' the Rye." As Hetty was about to leave the stage, it was necessary for Connie to quell a disturbance by volunteer stagehands J.E.B Stuart and Fitzhugh Lee behind the scenes. General Stuart loudly declared that he wouldn't stay by himself in a stuffy place next to the butler's pantry unless Hetty would come and talk to him. Connie directed him to remain alone, as his duty required that he hold one end of a stepladder serving as a garden fence stile in the next scene. She then returned to the stage to play a country maiden in "Money," perched coquettishly on the stile, dividing her smiles between Colonel John Saunders, playing a humble swain, and Frank Vizetelly, as a plumed cavalier, offering a purse of gold. The curtain went up as Connie sat down on the stile. It gave way and Connie slid to the ground as the audience laughed uproariously. The country maiden was instantly transformed into an irate stage manager. She darted behind the scenes to scold the guilty party. Despite abject penitence, his position was forfeited for gross negligence and he was banished to the audience for the remainder of the show. Fitzhugh Lee virtuously declared that no young lady could make him forget his responsibility and took Stuart's post. Standing at his post to raise and lower the curtain, William was awestruck as he observed the hierarchy of the Confederacy in a playful moment.

* * *

The next morning, despite fatigue, Hetty and Connie went for a long horseback ride in the brilliant winter sunshine with General Fitzhugh Lee and Colonel Heros von Borcke, a Prussian cavalry officer serving in the Confederate Army. The young women rode in English park style and had no trouble keeping up with the men as they bounded across fields glistening with melted frost. The men could not keep their eyes off Hetty in a riding habit that fit her graceful figure like a glove.

While resting the horses under a large oak tree, Connie entertained her companions with anecdotes of her amateur theatrical productions staged that winter, including the charades of the previous evening. In the pleasant afterglow of its success, she confided to her friends that she would love to go upon the real stage, but laughingly said that if she did, all of her grandfathers and great-aunts would rise from their graves in horror. Her companions were amused by this confession. It wasn't many years before that members of the Episcopal Church in Virginia risked excommunication for waltzing, going to the theater, fox hunting or horse racing.

* * *

Within days, Hetty was on horseback again, although dressed quite differently and under much more hazardous circumstances. Her return to Maryland was again accomplished with the assistance of the Confederate Signal Corps. She easily eluded the Potomac patrol and reached the river's northern shore. However, Federal agents arrested the driver retained to take her by wagon to the next way station and she could only assume that her itinerary was compromised. Hetty disguised herself in the uniform of a Union cavalryman and rode past enemy guard posts pretending to be a courier, a subterfuge that, if discovered, could have been fatal.

* * *

THE CHESTNUT RESIDENCE
RICHMOND, VIRGINIA
MARCH 15, 1864

Connie knocked on the door more insistently than was considered ladylike. It was a cold, rainy day and she was in no mood to endure further discomfort. However, the previous evening, Mary had sent an urgent appeal for help in creating a new hat. Connie's knack for making "something out of nothing" was well-known to her friends and her concept of friendship obliged her to honor such requests. She considered Mary Chestnut a close friend, despite the age difference, and both enjoyed their conversations full of fun and nonsense. While Mary's caustic wit annoyed her at times, Connie admired her friend for being an intelligent woman full of life and vigor.

"Do come in!" Mary exclaimed as she opened the door just wide enough for Connie to quickly squeeze through. "You'll catch your death of cold out there!"

Mary chattered nonstop as she helped her young friend remove a sopping wet cape and hustled her before an iron stove radiating waves of welcome heat. "Connie, I can't tell you how much I appreciate your assistance in my crusade to construct a new chapeau. I've been whimpering about my lack of bonnet to wear in full dress. My poor husband runs from the room in despair every time I mention it. You'll earn our undying gratitude if you can fabricate something that'll relieve my unbridled discontent."

Currency devaluation and an effective embargo of Southern ports caused milliners in Richmond to ask five hundred dollars for a hat made of the cheapest and homeliest of materials. Inspired by this travesty, the two women went to work to create a new hat superior to one that could be bought. Within the hour, Mary's bed was strewn with the wrecks and relics of her Washington finery as they searched for bits and pieces that could be blended into something new. The selections made, Connie ripped up an old mignonette green velvet bodice and a point lace barbe. She cut patterns from the fabrics, sewed them together, shaped the result over an old bonnet frame, and adorned it with sprays of artificial pale yellow and old gold nasturtiums. A very stylish and becoming headpiece evolved, much to Mary's delight, and she relished the thought of wearing it to upcoming formal functions.

As their mission was accomplished, the two women sat on a couch in the parlor to enjoy the last of Mary's horde of imported tea. "We are a society on the brink of ruin," Mary lamented. "How can decent people conduct their business sipping faux tea? It tastes so awful. The advancement of civilization will come to a halt. Women will no longer gossip. Men will struggle and youth will blunder. Where will it all end?"

"Well, I pray it doesn't stop all courting and flirtation," Connie replied with pretended trepidation.

"No, that's the one thing that will not be stopped, Mary declared with a smile. "It seems to me that war leads to an overabundance of lovemaking. Soldiers do more courting here in a day than they would do in ten years at home without a war to motivate them."

"That may be true," Connie agreed.

"When men are about to go to the front, they say their say desperately to the young women," Mary said. "They want to be heartened by their lady love—for her to be as nice as she can be—before they enter the fray. I've heard all about it from the Preston girls."

Connie merely smiled at her comments.

"I've been wondering," Mary said, letting her words hang in the air for a moment. "Why doesn't your cousin marry General Pegram who is daft about her? She's engaged to him. But that doesn't seem to have slowed down her social life!"

"How can you say such a thing? Hetty is having a good time—you know that she is so much admired."

Mary thought about that for a moment. "Then he's in love with her and she's grateful—or she's being sympathetic and kind. She wouldn't refuse to marry just because she's having a good time—because she's so much admired?"

Connie turned this over in her mind. "If Hetty hears that we doubt her devotion to General Pegram, she will be very angry with us."

"Forgive me," Mary replied, more amused than contrite. "I'm just being spiteful. My husband's brash declaration still rings in my head." Bending forward in her chair, Mary precisely imitated Colonel Chestnut's manner of speaking. "If there was no such word in the English language as 'fascinating,' it would be necessary to invent one to describe Hetty Cary."

* * *

DISPATCH BOAT *GREYHOUND*
ON CHESAPEAKE BAY
MARCH 17, 1864

Major Henry Kyd Douglas leaned over the rail and watched a fast-flowing groove of white water slide along the hull as the sleek vessel raced southward toward Virginia. His odyssey since being wounded and captured at Gettysburg involved many a twist and a turn, but he was now homeward bound.

Well-treated by his captors at a makeshift hospital in a private home, Major Douglas convalesced for nearly two weeks and was visited by Northern friends and acquaintances who came to view the battlefield. His mother and sister drove a buggy through both armies when they heard of his wounding and stayed at his bedside for several days as he recuperated.

In mid-July, he was moved to a hospital at the theological seminary where he found himself in the company of other captured Confederate officers, including Generals Trimble and Kemper. When able to travel, he was sent for imprisonment on Johnson's Island near Sandusky, Ohio. Months later, he was transferred to Point Lookout in Southern Maryland to be exchanged for a Union officer of the same rank.

Lifting his eyes, Major Douglas looked toward the Virginia coastline and smiled. It was evident to him that General Butler's dispatch boat was worthy of her name as they would arrive at Fortress Monroe within the hour. He was quite fortunate to have gotten this far. The previous day, Major Douglas had been removed from the flag-of-truce boat without explanation at the last possible moment prior to departure. Before leaving the boat, he dashed off a note to Major John E. Mulford, a Federal exchange officer who treated him civilly during his transfer from Baltimore to Point Lookout, the final leg in the journey from Ohio. The flag-of-truce boat captain accepted the note and promised to deliver it to Major Mulford at Fortress Monroe.

Upon return to the prison hospital ward, Major Douglas learned that the commandant of Point Lookout had selected him to be put in irons and solitary confinement in retribution for a Union officer subjected to this treatment in Richmond. Utterly dejected, he went to sleep on his cot, but was awakened at three in the morning when lantern light flashed in his face. A Federal staff officer told him that he was to leave shortly for Fortress Monroe. Major Mulford had received the note, General Butler had seen it, and a reprieve had been immediately issued.

Safely aboard *Greyhound*, Douglas joined a dozen Federal officers on deck and was offered several libations. He took "morning bitters" with one group, "an eye-opener" with another, a "preprandial *apéritif*" with a third, and all together they imbibed in an "appetizer." When breakfast was ready at daylight, so were the officers. A few hours later, *Greyhound* came alongside the pier at Old

Point Comfort, below Fortress Monroe. Moored on the opposite side was the flag-of-truce boat that had left him behind at Point Lookout. Within minutes, he was shaking hands with Major Mulford.

* * *

Despite an auspicious start, General Benjamin F. Butler's military career had been a series of calamities, but in each instance his political clout guaranteed another prime assignment. Early in the war, he was chastised for occupying Baltimore without orders, as well as for failing to return runaway slaves found within Union lines in contravention of the Fugitive Slave Act. Without authorization from Washington, he classified slaves as contraband of war and put them to work, building fortifications. He was fired in December of 1862 for his excesses while in command of the Department of the Gulf. The impervious political general was next given command of the Department of Virginia and North Carolina headquartered at Fortress Monroe on the tip of the Virginia peninsula. As a collateral duty, he was appointed Federal commissioner of exchange, and in that capacity engaged in frequent negotiations with Judge Robert Ould, chief of the bureau of exchange for the Confederacy. Despite the acrimonious tone of their public correspondence, they had a private agreement to parole any prisoner specifically requested. The previous week a letter had been received from Judge Ould asking for the exchange of two officers—Captain Cabell Breckinridge, the son of General Breckinridge, and Major Henry Kyd Douglas. This request thwarted the plan devised by the commandant at Point Lookout to hold Major Douglas in retaliatory durance vile.

* * *

As mooring lines were slipped to allow the flag-of-truce boat to depart for Dixie, Major Douglas was placed in the vessel's hold with other paroled officers and men. Within minutes, a guard escorted him and Captain Breckinridge to the salon where they were greeted by Major Mulford and given comfortable quarters in a stateroom. Later in the voyage, Major Douglas was introduced to Mrs. Martha Todd White of Alabama, the half-sister of Mary Todd Lincoln.

He accepted an assignment by Major Mulford to escort Mrs. White to Richmond after disembarking at City Point, Virginia.

Six weeks beforehand, Mrs. White came through the lines on a presidential pass to handle business and personal matters, but without an invitation to visit the White House. She sought admittance on several occasions, but permission to call on her sister and brother-in-law was denied in each instance. President Lincoln was suspicious of her motives and concerned that her outspoken Confederate sympathies would ignite a scandal that he could ill-afford. When his fears regarding her conduct were confirmed, the president threatened through intermediaries to have her arrested and confined in Old Capitol Prison unless she immediately returned to the Confederacy. A pass was provided to accommodate her passage home, but Mrs. White sent it back with a request that her trunks be declared exempt from examination. The president refused and returned the original pass with an ultimatum that she depart from Washington or face incarceration within twenty-four hours.

When Mrs. White arrived at Fortress Monroe, General Butler was confronted with a sensitive situation. He suspected that her thirteen large trunks contained contraband, the discovery of which would involve her arrest and public disclosure of her crime. This would be an enormous embarrassment to President Lincoln. He would be vilified in the Democrat press of the North. Being a shrewd lawyer and consummate politician, General Butler simply let her proceed without searching the trunks.

On arrival at City Point, Major Douglas telegraphed ahead to Richmond for a carriage and baggage wagon to meet them at the wharf below Drury's Bluff on the James River. Unaware that such luxuries had disappeared in his absence, he expected to see a nice Landau and a sturdy wagon at dockside. What arrived instead was a dilapidated turnout, driven by a polite old Negro freeman wearing a burnished silk hat, followed by a crude baggage wagon driven by his grandson. The two carriage horses leaned against one another for support and those pulling the wagon weren't in much better condition. Despite these problems, Major Douglas, Mrs. White, and her trunks were safely delivered to the Spotswood Hotel later that day.

The following evening, the two were invited to the executive mansion to meet President and Mrs. Davis. In the course of a pleasant conversation in the mansion's formal parlor, Major Douglas learned that Mrs. White's trunks contained contraband, including a large quantity of quinine, strong spirits, scarce medical supplies, surgical instruments, and a new uniform for Robert E. Lee. He was also made aware of the contents of a trunk that would be turned over to him the following morning for delivery to the residence of Hetty Cary. It contained her wedding trousseau.

* * *

ARMORY SQUARE HOSPITAL
WASHINGTON, D.C.
JUNE 24, 1865

Clifton's jaw was clenched as he stared down at his folded hands. John noted his brother's aggravation. He watched for a moment to gain some clue as to what was bothering him, but finally gave in to his curiosity. "Clifton, I see that something has annoyed you. What is it?"

Clifton looked up with a furious expression on his face. "The mere mention of General Ben Butler enrages me. He was the worst of the political generals who were promoted and given assignments far beyond their military competence. The Lincoln administration tolerated far too much from him."

"I believe you're still angry that he attempted to assume command over the 7th Regiment on the way to Washington," Melville countered.

"Not so!" Clifton exclaimed before reconsidering. "Well, perhaps that was the original source of my aggravation with the man. More importantly, I have nothing but disdain for anyone who acquires or maintains his position through political power. Butler was the first major general of volunteers appointed by a grateful President Lincoln in May of 1861. That mistake had terrible consequences in terms of unnecessary casualties and opportunities lost. As a field officer, I deplore the high cost paid by the common soldier for the failures of political generals. Thank God I never had to serve directly under one."

"I've heard many criticisms of General Butler from Twenty-Fourth Corps staff officers," John commented.

"I'm not surprised as many of them, no doubt, had the misfortune to serve in one of his several commands," Clifton replied. "He failed to distinguish himself at New Orleans and as commander of the Army of the James. He allowed his army to be entrapped at Bermuda Hundred on the Virginia peninsula. Had he done a competent job in the autumn of 1864, Richmond could have been captured and the war ended. General Grant jumped at the opportunity to fire Butler following his dismal performance on the North Carolina coast."

"General Butler clearly failed to endear himself to the ladies of New Orleans," Whitman said with a twinkle in his eye. "His threat to treat them as women of the town, plying their avocation if they displayed contempt for Federal soldiers, was not well-received throughout the South."

"There was even outcry against General Butler's proclamation in the North," Melville observed. "Although it seemed entirely appropriate to me," he added with a smirk.

"The severity of his administration of New Orleans earned him the nickname Beast Butler across the Confederacy," Whitman declared.

"And Spoons Butler for his alleged habit of pilfering silverware from Southern homes," Clifton contributed with satisfaction.

"He also executed a man for tearing down the United States flag placed on the Federal mint in New Orleans," John said. "For this act, Jefferson Davis denounced him as a felon deserving capital punishment if captured."

"That's ironic," Clifton said. "Were you aware that Benjamin Franklin Butler was a Democrat before the war?"

"No I wasn't," John replied, surprise evident in his voice. "Being on the far side of America at the time deprived me of the opportunity to know such things."

"At the 1860 Democratic National Convention held in Charleston, South Carolina, Ben Butler voted fifty-seven times for the nomination of Jefferson Davis for president of the United States against the candidacy of Stephan A. Douglas. When the Davis nomination failed, Butler supported John C. Breckinridge in the ensuing national campaign."

"He's truly a man of political expedience!" John exclaimed.

"That he is! And my patience is at an end discussing him. Let's move on to a better topic," Clifton said.

"What was happening with your regiment, Major Prentiss?" Whitman inquired. "I know that General Grant reorganized the Army of the Potomac when he came east to be general-in-chief of all Union forces."

"The 6th Maryland was transferred to 2nd Brigade, 3rd Division, Sixth Army Corps in March of 1864," Clifton replied. "We were pleased to take our place in the old Sixth Corps. It had never known defeat and was the only corps in the Union Army that passed through three successful campaigns in one year. Sixth Corps was truly the bedrock of the Army of the Potomac. The 6th Maryland Regiment was known as "Little Six" within Sixth Corps and our boys proudly wore the light blue Saint Andrews cross of its 3rd Division on the top of their caps."

"Was that about the time of your assignment to the division staff," John asked.

"That occurred somewhat later," Clifton replied. "Shortly after the Battle of the Wilderness, I was temporarily assigned to be chief of engineers for Brigadier General James B. Ricketts, our division commander. I wasn't with the regiment for the battles of Spotsylvania and Cold Harbor, but was present on the same battlefields serving in a staff capacity."

* * *

6TH MARYLAND VOLUNTEERS
NEAR CULPEPPER COURT HOUSE, VIRGINIA
MAY 4, 1864

For several days, rumors circulated in camp that Lieutenant General Ulysses S. Grant was moving the Army of the Potomac south in another "on to Richmond" campaign. This time, there was optimism among the soldiers that President Lincoln had finally found a general who knew how to fight.

In the early-morning darkness, 6th Maryland soldiers were issued five days rations to prepare for their haversacks and forty rounds for their cartridge boxes. The spring campaign had begun. After the usual breakfast of hardtack, mess pork, and coffee, the regiment joined countless other Sixth Corps regiments in columns marching southward toward the Rapidan. That evening, they crossed the river at Germania Ford and camped in a clover field where the soldiers, much fatigued by the long march, slept soundly. The regiment numbered four hundred nineteen muskets and twenty-three officers.

General Lee positioned the Army of Northern Virginia to meet the new Federal campaign in a rugged area known as the "Wilderness." He had chosen his ground well. Its tangled thickets of stunted pine, sweet gum, scrub oak, and cedar concealed Lee's outnumbered forces and neutralized the advantages possessed by Grant's larger, better-equipped army. It became a battle of brigades and regiments fighting at close quarters in the dense woods.

The 3rd Division was held in reserve until early afternoon of May fifth when orders were received to proceed east on the Brock Road, first at quick-time and later at the double-quick for two miles. Guided by one of General Meade's staff officers, 2nd Brigade departed from the road, marched through scattered timber and formed into line of battle with the 6th Maryland and the 110th Ohio in the front line. One company from each of the front regiments moved forward as skirmishers under the command of Captain Clifton Prentiss of the 6th Maryland and Captain Luther Brown of the 110th Ohio. They pushed back the enemy skirmishers and engaged in a brisk exchange of musketry for several hours. At seven o'clock, the entire brigade moved forward to attack, finding the enemy on the slope of a hill in thick, scrubby forest, sheltered by log breastworks. A continuous fire was exchanged until darkness ended the first day of battle.

It was a costly affair for the 6th Maryland Volunteers. Among the one hundred fifty-eight casualties suffered by the regiment that evening were Major Joseph C. Hill, wounded; Captain Adam B. Martin, stricken with death hours after his face was mangled by a bullet; 2nd Lieutenant Alexander F. Myers, killed; Captains Albert Billingslea, Thomas H. Goldsborough, John J. Bradshaw, and John R. Rouzer, wounded; Lieutenants John R. King, John A. Schwartz, Demarest J. Smith, and Charles A. Damuth, wounded.

Sergeant Jason Damuth, a younger brother of Lieutenant Damuth, was mortally wounded in the battle. Corporal James E. Heffner and 1st Sergeant Grayson Eichelberger sat by their friend, holding his head until three o'clock in the morning when he died. Sergeant Adam Shank, shot in the left side and unable to move, remained on the battlefield all night. Just before daylight, a squadron of cavalry ran over him and the horse's hooves did serious damage to his hips and legs. Flames and sparks belching from musket muzzles ignited dry foliage. Many wounded soldiers on both sides were burned to death in dozens of small conflagrations that raced between the battle lines.

Early the next morning, the 6th Maryland Volunteers were initially held in reserve and then ordered forward as skirmishers. A desultory firing continued all day as they shot at puffs of smoke from the barrels of enemy skirmishers hiding a few rods ahead in the dense forest. At six in the evening, a great commotion was heard on their extreme right. A flanking column of Lee's veterans had crashed into 1st Division of Sixth Corps, causing the whole Sixth Corps line to collapse and retreat for about a mile with the loss of many killed, wounded, and captured.

The 6th Maryland formed in line of battle the following morning near Wilderness Tavern for a counterattack to recapture ground lost the previous day. Following a fierce artillery cannonade, they charged forward in a strong double line, well closed up, and drove the Rebels back to their original lines. The next day found the division in line of battle once again. Its attack pushed the enemy skirmishers back, but the fierce fight had run its course. Both armies disengaged and began to withdraw.

Weary Union soldiers buried their dead, packed their equipment and began the trek away from the blood-soaked woods and fields where many of their comrades had fallen. Soon, the roads were jammed with long columns of blue stretching as far as the eye could see. The 6th Maryland was at the head of the corps, its soldiers withdrawn and silent as they marched at a steady pace in the waning light of evening. The column approached a road junction where the soldiers in the front ranks noticed General Grant sitting on his horse by the roadside, smoking a cigar. Mounted staff officers motioned for the column to take the right fork that ran due south, causing the men to look at one another in surprise. Speculation ran up and down the ranks until it dawned on them what was happening. A loud, thunderous cheer rose into the air and reverberated from the surrounding pine thickets as the column turned southward. The voices of soldiers in regiments behind them joined in the tumult as they reached the road junction and realized the new direction. The Army of the Potomac was not retreating. Previous commanders had turned the army northward after each battle, regardless of the outcome. This new general was different. He was taking the fight to the enemy and meant to see it through. Common soldiers in the ranks knew little about campaign strategy, but this determination made sense to them. They simply wanted to do their duty, win the war, and go home.

* * *

It was a tedious and tiresome overnight march to Spotsylvania Court House. At every halt, the men dropped to the ground and were instantly asleep, soon to be awakened as the march resumed. When dawn's first light streaked across the sky, Union forces discovered that General Lee had won the race to this vital crossroads and had blocked the road to Richmond with strong entrenchments and earthworks.

The next few days saw heavy skirmishing as the two sides probed the other's defenses, but each declined to bring on a general engagement. Soldiers of the 6th Maryland were repositioned to a series of rifle pits where Rebel sharpshooters, firing from a great distance, hit Corporal John Henry Shields in the left arm near the shoulder. Close by, Major General John Sedgwick, commander of Sixth Corps, was directing the placement of an artillery battery. The sprinkling of fire was causing both infantrymen and artillerymen to dodge at every bullet that passed close with a long, shrill whistle. "They couldn't hit an elephant at this distance," General Sedgwick admonished a man who had ducked to the ground in front of him. Moments later, the highly esteemed general was struck by one such bullet and died with blood spurting from his left cheek just below the eye. Within hours, General Horatio Wright, General Meade's chief of staff, assumed command of Sixth Corps.

Lieutenant David G. Orr of the 6th Maryland was killed the following day on the skirmish line. His friends buried him near a fence and marked the grave with his name on a cracker box board. The next afternoon, the regiment was withdrawn from the lines and sent to guard the corps wagon train. They were spared from the wholesale slaughter that occurred at the "Bloody Angle."

* * *

2ND MARYLAND BATTALION
BEAVER DAM STATION, VIRGINIA
MAY 10, 1864

The Maryland Battalion, assigned to protect bridges in the vicinity, posted a small detachment on guard duty at the Confederate supply depot. Under their watchful eyes, two freight trains carrying bacon, rice, sugar, coffee, molasses, vinegar, and medical stores were unloaded that day. These commissary provisions were enough to supply Lee's army for several weeks.

Unbeknownst to the Marylanders guarding the depot, General Philip Sheridan's Union cavalry had moved swiftly around the flank of the Army of Northern Virginia at Spotsylvania and was headed directly for them. In the early evening, George Armstrong Custer's Brigade of Michigan cavalry swept into the supply depot, forcing the small detachment of Marylanders to flee precipitously. Within a short time, thirty-six rail cars, two locomotives, the depot buildings, and all commissary stores were put to the torch by the Yankee cavalrymen. By the time General J.E.B. Stuart's cavalry arrived to prevent destruction of these vital supplies, the raiders had departed and flames lit the sky above the burning depot.

General Stuart was concerned that Sheridan's raid would descend upon Richmond and issued orders to place his cavalry between the marauding Union force and the Confederate capital. Before joining his troopers, he detoured a short distance to visit his wife Flora and their two children at the nearby plantation of Colonel Edmund Fontaine. When his wife ran out to greet him, Stuart could not take time to dismount, so leaned down from the saddle to kiss her. They talked privately for several minutes. He then kissed her and the children goodbye and rode off to rejoin his column at Hanover Junction. Arriving there at nightfall, he learned that Sheridan's cavalry was camped only ten miles away, a mere twenty miles from Richmond. Southern bugles sounded Boots and Saddles at one o'clock in the morning. An hour later, General Stuart's column was moving on a collision course with Union cavalry at an abandoned, ramshackle stagecoach inn known locally as Yellow Tavern.

The battle was joined before noon and for three hours the cavalry clash ebbed and flowed. At four o'clock, Federal horse soldiers launched a powerful counterattack and two of Stuart's Brigades began to give way. General Stuart brought his reserves forward to stem the tide and rode into the melee of clashing sabers and cracking pistols and carbines. The dashing Confederate cavalry leader, conspicuous with his red beard, plumed hat, fancy gray coat, and golden sash, fired his LeMat revolver into the enemy cavalry ranks, helping to break their charge and sweep them from the field. A dismounted Michigan cavalryman aimed his pistol at General Stuart from thirty yards and fired, hitting him in the right side. Stuart's head bowed, his hat fell off, and he clutched the mortal wound. Two of his troopers, one on either side, held him in the saddle and took him to the rear where he was gently lowered to the ground. An ambulance carried him to the home of his brother-in-law, Doctor Charles Brewer, where he suffered great pain for a full day and died only four hours before Flora and the children arrived at his bedside.

13

GRANT MOVES SOUTH

ARMORY SQUARE HOSPITAL
WASHINGTON, D.C.
JUNE 24, 1865

Whitman scratched his beard; his brow was deeply furrowed. This drew Clifton's attention. "I suspect that you're pondering the death of General Stuart," Clifton said. "Besides being a formidable adversary, he was an interesting character and without parallel as a cavalry leader."

"He certainly was," Whitman replied. "His horsemen rode circles around the Army of the Potomac on more than one occasion—they completely outclassed our Federal cavalry for the first few years of the war."

"General Philip St. George Cooke led a hapless chase when Stuart circumvented McClellan's army in the summer of 1862," Melville commented derisively. "Many thought General Cooke's lethargy stemmed from a misplaced affection for his daughter's husband."

"Melville, you should feel compassion, not contempt for the man—his family was split into factions, just like ours," Clifton responded. "General Cooke is an honorable man, loyal to his country, and thoroughly humiliated by his failure to foil the audacity of his son-in-law on that occasion. As a matter of fact, it finished his service in the field for the remainder of the war."

"Even Cooke's son John served as a Confederate officer," Melville added, unaffected by his brother's admonition.

"Clifton, is it true that you returned to Maryland for the battle at Monocacy?" John asked.

"I was there," Clifton replied. He was dispirited by Melville's remarks. "I arrived with the first elements of 3rd Division in my capacity as Chief of Engineers. It was a hard-fought engagement before we were swept aside." Clifton paused and, for the first time, it was evident that his strength was dwindling. "Of greater importance is the fact that I completed my staff assignment and returned to 6th Maryland before Sixth Corps was sent to the Shenandoah Valley. Command of the regiment devolved to me at Opequon Creek, and I remained in that capacity until after the Battle of Cedar Creek. My promotion to the rank of major was precipitated by that circumstance."

Whitman spoke up. "As we seem to be discussing things in chronological order, please allow me to inject a note about Hetty before we get too far ahead. Something significant was about to happen in her life."

* * *

THE CARY RESIDENCE
BALTIMORE, MARYLAND
MAY 18, 1864

In the twilight, Hetty walked at a brisk pace on the opposite side of the street from her parents' home. She briefly glanced at the familiar place before discretely looking about for the object of her concern. He wasn't hard to spot. A Union detective was hidden behind the steps of a nearby row house, a vantage point that provided a good view of the Cary's front door, but not of the dark-haired woman who turned the corner and disappeared from sight. Another attempt to spend precious time with her family had been thwarted.

Unlike her previous wartime visits, this one was marked by increased restriction on Hetty's movements, and she was unable to visit with her parents and sister as often as she desired. She constantly moved between secret locations provided by Southern loyalists and wore a black wig to avoid recognition. The increased efficiency of the Federal authorities hampered her ability to carry out clandestine activities on behalf of the Confederate Signal Corps.

When news was received that General Pegram had been dangerously wounded at the Battle of the Wilderness, Hetty made preparations without a moment's hesitation to return to Richmond. Fearing detection if she traveled directly south from Baltimore, she donned her disguise and took the cars to Philadelphia. Once there, she booked passage on a steamer to St. Mary's and thence across the southern Potomac in a small boat at night. Upon arrival in Richmond, Hetty discovered that John's wound was superficial.

* * *

6TH MARYLAND VOLUNTEERS
NEAR COLD HARBOR, VIRGINIA
JUNE 1, 1864

At the conclusion of the Battle of Spotsylvania, General Grant disengaged his forces and moved relentlessly southward, forcing General Lee to stay between the invading army and the Confederate capital. During the march, the 9th New York Heavy Artillery was assigned to General Keifer's Brigade. Its soldiers, recently retrained to fight as infantry, had been in service for years, manning the heavy guns of Washington's defenses. The large, full-strength regiment had never been subjected to the rigors of an active campaign, a condition that changed rapidly as the brigade marched and skirmished the entire way from the North Anna River to Totopotomoy Creek.

The destination of the opposing armies was the crossroads at Cold Harbor. This time, Sheridan's Federal troopers were the first to arrive. They clashed with General Fitzhugh Lee's cavalry when it arrived and fought off a strong force of Confederate infantry the following day. In each instance, the Yankee horse soldiers repulsed the attackers with their seven-shot repeating Spencer Carbines. Nevertheless, the Federal hold on the vital crossroads was tenuous at best. A forced march brought Sixth Corps to Cold Harbor by mid-morning of June first to relieve the hard-pressed cavalrymen. As the day progressed, 2nd Brigade was moved a short distance to the left of its initial entrenchment and formed in four lines of battle, with 6th Maryland and 138th Pennsylvania in the front line.

In the early evening hours, the Rebel works were carried in a general assault that drove the defenders for over a mile and captured several hundred prisoners. The Union advance was checked by heavy Confederate artillery fire and eventually compelled to fall back. By the end of following day, the opposing armies were massed along a seven-mile front from Bethesda Church to the Chickahominy River. Delays in the arrival of additional Union forces prevented a planned attack from being launched. Confederate forces used this time to good advantage by constructing an interlocking series of trenches with overlapping fields of fire. The assault on June third by the Federal Second, Ninth, and Eighteenth Corps was met with a tremendous volume of infantry and artillery fire from these entrenchments. Thousands of Union troops were slaughtered in less than an hour. Sixth Corps spent the next week approaching the enemy lines with zig-zag trenches until the night of June twelfth when Grant again disengaged his army and crossed the James River to threaten Petersburg. The carnage of Cold Harbor changed the primary mode of fighting from maneuver to entrenchment for the remainder of the war in Virginia.

* * *

2ND MARYLAND BATTALION
NEAR COLD HARBOR, VIRGINIA
JUNE 3, 1864

The predominate sound heard was a steady tramp as soldiers in the Confederate infantry column put one foot ahead of the other on the hard-packed, red dirt road. They were alone with their thoughts except when somebody would say something, drawing the attention of the others for a short time until the idle chatter ran its course.

"Well, I knew the Maryland Line wouldn't last—it was just too good an idea," Buck proclaimed to William as they trudged along in the ranks of Company A.

"Buck, you might just as well let go of it," William replied with a sigh. "You've been complaining about it for the past six weeks and nobody is listening to you anymore."

"Then maybe I'll start complaining about all this damned marching or the mighty poor rations we've been receiving lately," Buck said. Hearing soldiers marching near him mutter in annoyance only encouraged Buck. "Or the fact that our battalion is in reserve and not likely to get into a respectable fight," he declared.

At the end of the day's march, the Maryland Battalion was positioned three hundred yards to the rear of a salient on Turkey Hill held by the 26th Virginia and two guns of Caskie's Battery. Stationed four hundred yards behind the Marylanders was General Joseph Finnegan's brigade of Floridians. The Marylanders retired for the night, lying in a depression from which the ground rose slowly to the plateau containing the salient they were to support. Wrapped in blankets and tent flies, the veteran soldiers slept with their muskets tight against their bodies.

William was the first of his small group of messmates to wake. Stretching on the ground to get his kinks out, he noticed that it was a particularly foggy morning with visibility restricted to a little more than a hundred yards in each direction. He could hear skirmishing going on to their front and was surprised that most of the sleeping men around him were not awakened by it. When the fire became hotter, William sat up on his elbows and looked up the hill. He saw Confederate soldiers running toward the rear in great disorder. Behind them—and barely visible in the morning mist—was a battle formation. It halted and fired a volley that killed several Marylanders still wrapped in their blankets.

A long drum roll called the battalion into line of battle, although there was confusion as to whether or not the battle line approaching in the fog was the enemy. "It's the damned old gridiron," shouted a sergeant when he saw the Stars and Stripes. Soldiers in the ranks begged Captain Crane, the acting battalion commander, for permission to charge, but he refused, saying that he did not have orders. The Marylanders could see that the Yankees were capturing the salient. Buck yelled at Captain Duval to take command, but he refused to do so with Captain Crane on the field.

Exasperated, Buck threw his hat in the air and shouted, "Let's charge 'em, boys," and ran forward without orders, igniting a spontaneous charge as the entire battalion followed him. Retreating Virginians turned and mixed in among them as they dashed up Turkey Hill. The Federals could see the tops of the Maryland battle flags cresting the hill and heard the fierce yell of charging Confederate infantry. Finnegan's men, some distance behind the charging Marylanders, began to move forward, but did not get into the fight until after the enemy was expelled from the salient.

William and other soldiers of the Maryland Battalion, having been drilled on artillery procedures while in winter quarters, manned the guns that the Union soldiers were in the process of turning on the Rebels. The guns, loaded with double loads of canister, were now rotated on the retreating Yankees and a furious volley unleashed upon them. When the smoke cleared, the ground before the works was covered with mangled bodies, afterward identified as soldiers of the 5th and 11th New Hampshire Infantry and the 7th and 8th New York Heavy Artillery. Many Marylanders were jubilant at the thought that their loss at Gettysburg was avenged.

* * *

6TH MARYLAND VOLUNTEERS
NEAR CITY POINT, VIRGINIA
JUNE 17, 1864

After several days on a crowded steamer coming down the Potomac and around to City Point on the James, soldiers of the 6th Maryland Infantry were happy to again have their feet on solid ground. After setting up camp, the weary soldiers found a beach along the river where they hoped that a much-needed bath might be enjoyed. As the first of the men splashed into the water, a Rebel battery up river lobbed a few shells in their direction. The few soldiers in the water exited quickly and dashed into the woods to dress, thus ending for the moment any hope of bathing for the regiment.

The next day, 6th Maryland resumed its march and crossed a bridge over the Appomattox. As they were in enemy country, flankers were positioned on either side of the column to prevent an ambush. When protecting the flanks of the column, these soldiers would ordinarily be out some distance, but in this instance, they came in close to the column during the bridge crossing.

Just beyond the bridge, the camp of the 175th Ohio Infantry Regiment was set up with the road running through its middle. The Maryland veterans could tell by the spic-and-span uniforms that these were "one hundred days" men who would be spending a relatively short time in the present campaign. When the Colonel of the 175th Ohio observed the approaching column of sun-burnt, battle-scarred soldiers in tattered uniforms with shot-riddled flags unfurled, he hastily lined his men up on each side of the road, facing inward.

Possessing the pride of veterans, the 6th Maryland files dressed-up, the pace quickened, and backs straightened, all without orders to do so. The regimental fifes and drums struck-up a jaunty tune as the Marylanders marched between the open ranks of the Ohioans. The 6th Maryland flankers, passing among the big airy wall tents of the 175th Ohio camp, couldn't help but notice all kinds of clean laundered clothing, underwear, towels, and wash rags hanging on lines or lying about in open knapsacks. For men who had been fighting and marching continuously for a month, the temptation was too great. The flankers appropriated as much of the clean clothes and other laundry as they could carry, later sharing the bounty with their friends who had been in the column ranks. Everyone reasoned that the 175th Ohio boys would soon be going home, so they wouldn't be too greatly inconvenienced by the appropriations.

* * *

THE MONOCACY RIVER
NEAR FREDERICK CITY, MARYLAND
JULY 9, 1864

The horrific bloodshed of Grant's summer campaign demoralized a large segment of the Northern population. In the view of many citizens, the prospects for decisive military victory were dim. Many people clamored for peace at any price and President Lincoln viewed his bid for reelection in November as unlikely to succeed. His Democrat challenger, General George B. McClellan, while not openly advocating an immediate end to the war, was more inclined to accept cease-fire terms that would recognize the independence of the Confederate States of America.

General Lee, always the great strategist and risk-taker, saw another invasion of the North as a means to foster growth of the anti-war movement as well as relieve pressure on his lines at Petersburg. He ordered Lieutenant General Jubal Early's army of twenty thousand men to clear the Shenandoah Valley, cross over into Maryland, and attack Washington from the north.

Major General Lew Wallace, federal commander of the Middle Department in Baltimore, soon learned that the Confederates had plundered Harpers Ferry and were rapidly moving eastward. Their apparent objective was either Baltimore or Washington, but he knew not which. Despite the confusion, General Wallace acted decisively. Having only sparse forces available within his department, he placed them along a line that covered the convergence of the National Pike to Baltimore and the Georgetown Pike to Washington, where the iron bridge of the Baltimore and Ohio Railroad crossed the Monocacy River. He also manned several fords around these points.

Two brigades of 3rd Division, Sixth Corps were withdrawn from the lines at Petersburg and expeditiously sent to supplement Wallace's small force of inexperienced National Guard and one hundred days men. When the brigades arrived by rail at daybreak, the 6th Maryland Infantry was not with them. The steamer carrying the regiment burst its boiler a few hours after getting underway from City Point and the ship's engineer mashed his hand before he could complete the repairs. A former engineer in the regiment was able to finish the job, get up steam, and have the transport underway within a few hours, although the greater part of the night had been lost. The following morning, the regiment took the cars to Monocacy, but arrived too late. Wallace's little army had already been pushed aside by the larger Confederate force.

Knowing that the capital was vulnerable to attack by Early, General Grant ordered the rest of Sixth Corps onto transports at City Point and rushed them to Washington. Anxious citizens cheered wildly as General Wright and two divisions of his battle-hardened soldiers marched through the streets to man the district's defensive perimeter.

Jubal Early, slowed by Wallace's stout defense at Monocacy, advanced cautiously toward Fort Stevens on the outskirts of Washington. Rebel sharpshooters shot at President Lincoln as he stood atop the fort parapet, his height and stovepipe hat making him a conspicuous target. When a medical officer standing near him was killed, aides convinced the president to move to a safer position.

General Early, seeing that veteran troops were manning Fort Stevens, commenced a retreat toward safe haven in Virginia. General Wallace, who would later gain fame as the author of *Ben Hur*, had done his job well. The Confederates won the Battle of Monocacy, but the minor defeat for the Union saved Washington.

* * *

MISS CLARKE'S HOUSE
RICHMOND, VIRGINIA
AUGUST 4, 1864

Connie sat perfectly still at her dressing table as she mulled over a letter from her cousin Victoria Ann, who everyone in the family called Nannie. It proposed that she and Hetty visit Retreat in King William County where Nannie resided with her husband and children. The letter further suggested that they bring their fiancés for a week of relaxation and fun, far from the grim realities of war. Connie felt a warm blush on her face as the possibilities of such sweet asylum danced through her mind. The invitation was particularly welcome, as Connie had just returned from a difficult time of nursing wounded soldiers at Camp Winder.

Arrangements for the trip were made within another week and, the following Saturday morning, Connie and Hetty boarded the Virginia Central cars going eastbound, each joyfully clasping the arm of their respective betrothed, Burton Harrison and John Pegram. They disembarked at the railway station near Hanover Court House where Uncle Nebuchadnezzar, an old slave from Retreat, met them. He was waiting by the tracks in a quaint backcountry wagon capable of fording the Pamunkey River at low water and passing through its surrounding swamps. Several hours later, accompanied by barking dogs, they drove through the gate at Retreat and were met in a rush on the front porch of the great house by the happy hosts, their laughing children, and smiling house servants.

That evening the couples sat down to a table heaped with the luxurious bounty of Retreat. Doctor Moore at his end, dispensing thick slices of turkey—Cousin Nannie at hers, carving a ham with cloves adorning a crust of sugar, its pink slices cut thin and the fat having a nutty flavor. The center of the table was covered with platters of spareribs and pork sausages, cornpone, biscuits with fresh butter, and pitchers of mantling cream to be served with real coffee. Desert was plum pudding with a berg of vanilla ice cream, a mould of calves' foot jelly, many little iced cakes, and rosy apples in pyramids. It was quite a departure from the standard fare in Richmond where, like the army, typical meals consisted of salt pork, rice, dried apples, and faux coffee made of dried beans and peanuts, without milk or sugar.

Conversation was brief after dinner as the young people claimed exhaustion from the day's travel. With the blessing of the host and hostess, they retired to their rooms on the ground floor in the guest wing. Sinking into lavender-scented, linen-spread feather beds, youth and happiness emerged triumphant over the darkest prospects—Elysium was attained.

After a week of immemorial bliss, the men went back to their duty stations, leaving the women at Retreat for another fortnight of relaxation. Burton Harrison returned the following weekend, so great was his desire to be with Connie. He left Richmond on horseback late Saturday evening, rode all night, swam a river where the ferryman was not present, and spent Sunday with his true love. He rode back through the night and arrived in Richmond just in time for an official breakfast meeting early Monday morning. The mystery of his weekend absence and fatigued appearance caused humorous speculation, even from his usually staid chief.

TWO BROTHERS

* * *

7TH UNITED STATES COLORED TROOPS
BERMUDA HUNDRED, VIRGINIA
AUGUST 24, 1864

Since departing from Camp Stanton, Elijah's regiment had embarked on an odyssey that included several coastal voyages, construction of fortifications, and skirmishes in Florida, South Carolina, and Virginia. In the process, the men became good soldiers. Years spent in slavery made them obedient to officer's orders, but of greater importance was their eagerness to learn their duties and prove their worthiness. For many, these were their first experiences beyond the plantation and their interest in the outside world was fully awakened. White commissioned officers taught basic reading, writing, and arithmetic to black non-commissioned officers so that they could, in turn, pass this knowledge to the privates. When the day's duties were completed, groups of five or six soldiers clustered around their corporals and sergeants to learn the alphabet or calculate simple mathematical problems. Over time, many developed sufficient skills to write letters, read books, and appreciate the value of money, enriching them with a newly found self-respect and self-reliance.

The sun was just sinking into the tops of the surrounding pine trees, allowing the men at least another hour of daylight. They were enjoying their first rest after a hard day of marching, before gathering with their messmates to cook the evening rations.

Sergeant Elijah Carter, two corporals, and several privates were sitting around a hastily constructed fire pit in which burning wet wood crackled and popped, giving off a thick cloud of smoke. No one objected as the noise was pleasant and the billowing cloud discouraged the bothersome swarms of mosquitoes that hovered in the field where Company C had set up camp.

"I's too tuckered out for da A-B-Cs tonight, Sergeant Carter," Private Noah Bailey said as he reclined on the ground.

"Won't get no smarter dat way," remarked another private who was clutching a copy of "The School and Family Primer" provided to the regiment by a Quaker society in Pennsylvania.

"I have to agree with Bailey," Sergeant Carter responded. "For once," he added, causing everyone, including Bailey, to smile. "There were no stragglers during today's march, so you all have earned a good rest. Fortunately, we won't be moving the camp for a couple of days. Captain Weiss will surely give permission for us to do some schooling in the morning."

Bailey and the other soldiers settled into a relaxed mode, which suited Elijah. He was bone-tired and not up to conducting lessons. At twice the average age of his soldiers, it took every bit of Elijah's physical stamina to do his job as the company's senior sergeant. However, his maturity, coupled with his leadership skills, gained him the respect and trust of every soldier and officer in the company. Although Elijah missed Alma and his daughters, he discovered that his role as an army sergeant was the most satisfying achievement of his life.

Since disembarking in Virginia, the soldiers of the 7th U.S. Colored Troops exuded excitement that their regiment had joined the Army of the James. Despite being under fire in several skirmishes, they had missed the big battle in Florida at Olustee. Now they were positioned to participate in a decisive battle—an attack on the lines defending the Confederate capital.

* * *

6TH MARYLAND VOLUNTEERS
NEAR WINCHESTER, VIRGINIA
SEPTEMBER 19, 1864

The Marylanders halted at a ford south of the Berryville Pike for a hurried breakfast before crossing Opequon Creek. The march had begun at two o'clock in the morning as Sixth Corps was advancing at all possible speed to provide infantry support for Union cavalry engaging the enemy.

Once across, they proceeded uphill to the head of a ravine, high above the creek. As the Marylanders filed off the road into a dense stand of timber, a flock of wild turkeys took to flight, giving those leading the column a start. Upon reaching open woods, 2nd Brigade, the extreme right of 3rd Division, formed in line of battle with fixed bayonets and moved forward with 6th Maryland and 110th Ohio on the front line. Union skirmishers pushed back Rebel skirmishers as the division advanced three hundred yards to a rise where they rested for several hours as Federal artillery pounded Confederate positions.

As 6th Maryland passed through a clearing when the advance continued, a large black snake emerged from under a brush pile and frantically slithered through the officer's line in an attempt to escape. Captain Charles A. Damuth swung his sword down to kill it, striking the ground so hard that the blade broke ten inches from the hilt, without touching the snake. He waved the stub of his weapon in the air to show that he was not deterred in the slightest. Soldiers in the ranks cheered Captain Damuth as their formation moved forward to close with the enemy.

The 6th Maryland Volunteers came under a heavy barrage from Rebel artillery. Among the first to fall mortally wounded was Sergeant Houston T. Murray, the regimental color-bearer. Lieutenant William H. Burns, the nearest man to him, picked up the regimental colors and marched forward, holding the flag high above his head. It was but a short time later that a cannon ball decapitated Lieutenant Burns, his body crashed to the ground, and a torrent of blood gushed over the folds of the 6th Maryland colors beneath him. Sergeant John L. Jones dropped his musket, dashed forward, and rolled the lieutenant's body off the crimsoned blue flag. Gripping the flagstaff with both hands, Sergeant Jones raised it before him and led the regiment forward.

The Marylanders had not yet returned fire at Confederate skirmishers peppering their line of battle with musketry from a narrow ravine hidden in high grass. When the 6th Maryland reached a point about thirty yards from the ravine, the Rebel soldiers stood, emptied their muskets into the Union ranks, threw down their weapons, and held up their hands to surrender. It was too late. The first volley from the line of battle cut down many Rebels and the few that survived turned and ran toward their lines, closely followed by furious 6th Maryland soldiers. The Federal avalanche crashed into the Confederate lines and drove them from their guns at bayonet point.

* * *

The Battle of the Opequon became an intense, desperately contested fight as Major General Phil Sheridan's Union Army of the Shenandoah, consisting of three corps, attacked Lieutenant General Jubal Early's four veteran Confederate divisions concentrated in strong positions to meet the Union assault. After capturing the Confederate guns, Colonel Horn again ordered his regiment forward, this time to attack an enemy battery that was hurling shot and canister into his ranks. Without hesitation, the Marylanders raised a yell and charged Rebel emplacements near the Dinkle Barn, firing as they advanced across an open field strewn thick with dead and wounded soldiers. Private Josiah Willhide of Company D was struck in the hip and went down in a heap. When asked by Captain John R. Rouzer if he could get to the rear by himself, the young private replied affirmatively and shouted encouragement to his company, which included four other Willhide family members, as they pressed forward under a blazing September sun.

As the charging battle line approached the Rebel position, Union soldiers saw that the battery horses had been killed and that enemy artillerymen were attaching ropes to pull their guns to safety. Just when it appeared certain that 2nd Brigade would capture the Rebel guns, its commander received orders to fall back as their flanks were exposed. During the rapid advance, a gap developed between Nineteenth Corps and Sixth Corps as Nineteenth Corps failed to maintain contact with Keifer's right. The Marylanders withdrew a short distance with the rest of 2nd Brigade. They tore down a split rail fence by a cornfield and stacked the rails to provide cover for soldiers in prone positions behind it. They ate a bite of hardtack whenever there was a spare moment, but excitement stifled most thoughts of hunger.

Charging like a whirlwind through the gap, Cullen A. Battle's Alabama Brigade smashed into the right of 3rd Division, causing Colonel Keifer to throw three of his regiments into its path to slow it. General Sheridan committed his reserves, Russell's Division, which blunted the attack in an exchange of volleys with the attacking Rebel force. Crook's Corps of West Virginians came forward to reinforce the embattled Sixth Corps. Infantry plowed into infantry, cavalry clashed horse-to-horse at a thundering gallop, and artillery fired case shot and double canister into massed formations at close range.

Lieutenant Eichelberger was wounded by a shot across the chest. While being helped to the rear by Corporal Jacob Freeze, the two passed Private Willhide returning to the front, smoking his pipe as he limped across the field. After arriving at a medical station in the rear, the young man discovered that he had been struck by a spent ball and had not been seriously wounded. He chose to rejoin his company because friends and family were still in the thick of the battle.

A violent Confederate counter-charge abruptly halted the 6th Maryland advance and a pitched battle was fought back and forth across the same ground for hours. During this time, Colonel Horn was seriously wounded and left for dead on the battlefield. When his men regained the ground, they discovered that he was still alive and carried him to the rear. Captain Rouzer fell badly wounded and was taken from the field by retreating Rebels who were driven through the streets of Winchester to the heights beyond. Sergeant Jones was shot in the left hip, the third regimental color bearer to be struck down that day. Another soldier picked up the flag and carried it forward. Captain Prentiss assumed command when Colonel Horn fell and led the regiment as they pursued the enemy until darkness ended the fighting.

* * *

6TH MARYLAND VOLUNTEERS
NEAR STRASBURG, VIRGINIA
SEPTEMBER 20, 1864

At five o'clock in the morning, the Army of the Shenandoah commenced pursuit of the retreating Rebel Army. Its forward elements reached Strasburg in the mid-afternoon where it was discovered that the enemy had entrenched itself in a strong position southwest of town on Fisher's Hill. Sixth Corps massed in a heavily wooded area and bivouacked for the night.

During the afternoon of the twenty-first, 3rd Division was moved in two columns toward the left of the enemy line. Captain Prentiss's regiment was detached from the brigade and sent to support a portion of the 2nd Division skirmish line that had broken and retreated in great confusion. An audacious charge by 6th

Maryland drove the enemy force back to a line of works constructed of fence rails. Seven enlisted men of the regiment were wounded in the action.

On the twenty-second, 6th Maryland was withdrawn from the skirmish line and rejoined 2nd Brigade as it was deployed on the enemy's extreme left. Captain Prentiss was once more ordered to move his regiment to the skirmish line where it drove the Rebels from the heights and engaged enemy skirmishers throughout the day. At six in the evening, 3rd Division moved forward in concert with Crook's Corps of West Virginians who were fully on the enemy's left flank. The swarming Federal wave dispersed the Rebel infantry and captured much of their artillery in position, bringing about a resounding Union victory in the Shenandoah Valley.

* * *

The Army of the Potomac had pressed relentlessly southward in Grant's Overland Campaign during the months of May and June. It engaged the Army of Northern Virginia in a series of bloody battles, including the Wilderness, Spotsylvania, and Cold Harbor. While the Confederate capital city was successfully defended, Lee's army was forced into a defensive line below Petersburg. Despite this achievement, Ben Butler's Army of the James remained on Bermuda Hundred, trapped by Confederate fortifications across the neck of the peninsula at the confluence of the James and the Appomattox.

In the early fall, General Grant planned and executed a two-pronged operation to break the stalemate. The Army of the Potomac further invested Petersburg by extending its lines southwestward below the city and the Army of the James made a thrust directly toward the Confederate capital.

Butler's main attack column, Major General Edward Ord's Eighteenth Corps, crossed the James before dawn on a pontoon bridge at Aiken's Landing and moved directly against an outer perimeter of fortifications around Richmond. Simultaneously, Major General David B. Birney's Tenth Corps, supplemented by Brigadier General Charles Paine's Division of colored troops from Eighteenth Corps, crossed the river on a pontoon bridge at Deep Bottom to attack Confederate works on New Market Heights.

When informed of the Union advance, the commander of Richmond's defenses, Lieutenant General Richard S. Ewell, dispatched several veteran infantry brigades and field artillery batteries, plus a City Battalion composed of clerks from the various departments of government, to reinforce his thinly held lines.

General Ord's initial objective, Fort Harrison, was attacked and captured at first light, despite stubborn resistance by its defenders. Birney's attack, spearheaded by Paine's Division, swept across obstacle-strewn fields and captured New Market Heights, suffering eight hundred casualties in less than an hour.

As the morning wore on, Union forces failed to exploit their initial successes. While General Ord's staff organized an attack against Fort Gilmer on the Rebel's intermediate defense line, Confederate reinforcements under the personal command of General Ewell arrived. He was well-aware that if Fort Gilmer fell, Rebel forts to the south, along the river, would be untenable and the way to Richmond would be open. Ewell's swift reinforcement doomed to defeat an assault launched late in the morning by two battalions of the oversized 2nd Pennsylvania Heavy Artillery.

Fort Gilmer sat on a hill half a mile ahead of Birney's and Foster's brigades. Both brigades were operating under the command of Brigadier General William Birney, an older brother of the Tenth Corps commander. The Confederate lines were plainly visible, appearing as a long, yellow slash across the fields. The lines consisted of earthworks about eight feet in height with forts and artillery redoubts positioned at quarter-mile intervals. The angle of the battery within each was such that it could sweep the ground in front of the next battery with enfilade fire. At a distance of two hundred yards from Fort Gilmer, attacking forces would be exposed to shot and shell from at least four batteries and, when in the front ditch, from its neighbors on each side.

Repulse of the morning attack with heavy losses apprised Union commanders of the reinforcement of Fort Gilmer. They surmised that the breastworks beyond Fort Gilmer were poorly supplied with infantry and might be taken by sudden assault, if the batteries could be silenced.

* * *

7TH UNITED STATES COLORED TROOPS
CHAFFIN'S FARM, VIRGINIA
SEPTEMBER 29, 1864

General William Birney received orders from General Ord to storm the breast-works in his front, silencing the enemy batteries with sharpshooters deployed as skirmishers ahead of the assault forces. General Birney directed General Robert Foster to advance his brigade in column of regiments with sharpshoot-ers in front so as to cover the two forts to the right of Fort Gilmer. Foster was to assault the Rebel works as soon as sharpshooters of the 7th U.S. Colored Troops opened fire on Fort Gilmer.

General Birney explained in detail to Colonel James Shaw, commanding of-ficer of the 7th U.S. Colored Troops, the absolute necessity of silencing the bat-tery in Fort Gilmer as the success of Foster's assault depended upon being free of heavy cannonading upon his flank. Colonel Shaw was to send four of his ten companies ahead as sharpshooters. The remaining six companies would ad-vance to the rear of the skirmish line and attack with the sharpshooters as soon as the Fort Gilmer battery was silenced. To insure complete understanding of the details, a written copy of the order was given to Colonel Shaw. It directed him to personally command the storming party. Furthermore, Colonel Shaw was not to move his regiment until the other regiments were in line. When General Birney completed this task, Captain Bailey was sent to tell Colonel Shaw to immediately advance his skirmishers.

Following a brief conversation with the brigade staff officer, Colonel Shaw ordered his skirmishers to assault Fort Gilmer, not simply silence its batteries by sharpshooting at the gun crews. Captain Julius A. Weiss, the senior captain of the four companies, pointed out to Colonel Shaw that it was suicidal to attack a strong fort with such a small force, but was told that the decision was not his to make.

The 7th U.S. Colored Troops skirmish line crossed fields from which all trees had been cut. The trees were lying on the ground to create a maze of abatis with sharpened branches pointed in their path. Approaching Fort Gilmer, cautiously at first, then in a determined rush, the four companies were subjected to heavy artillery and musketry fire from the fort and an enfilade fire of canister at close range from the artillery redoubts. Those soldiers not struck down jumped into the deep, broad ditch in front of Fort Gilmer and attempted to climb the walls on each other's shoulders. Many were shot in the head as they reached the top of the parapet. Confederate defenders in the fort rolled lit shrapnel shells with fifteen-second fuses into the ditch.

As the smoke cleared from the last discharge of canister shot, the bodies of slain and wounded soldiers in Fort Gilmer's dry moat became visible to observers in the nearby redoubt manned by Griffin's Salem Flying Battery. Two Confederate artillery officers mounted the redoubt's earthen wall with telescopes to gain a better view. While the officers watched, Rebel infantry entered the ditch to capture the few black soldiers and white officers still alive. The ambulatory prisoners were quickly rounded up and taken into the fort.

"That was as brave a charge as I ever saw," Captain Frank Dawson said to the battery commander as he lowered his telescope. "They've proven their manhood—there's no question that Negro soldiers will fight. Is it not time that the Confederacy should recruit its own black regiments?"

"We can't do that," the battery commander replied slowly. "It would dispel every justification upon which we have relied to maintain slavery." Before Dawson could respond, their conversation was interrupted by the sound of gunfire from the ditch. The officers turned to look again in that direction.

Sprawled on the ground and gut shot, Sergeant Elijah Carter watched as wounded Negro soldiers around him were summarily executed. A Rebel soldier walked up and pointed his musket at Elijah. Elijah glared at him in defiance. The Rebel cocked the musket hammer and fired a shot into Elijah's chest, killing him instantly. With the exception of one soldier, every officer and man in the four companies of the 7th U.S. Colored Troops sent forward in the skirmish line was killed, wounded, or captured.

* * *

When Captain Bailey returned, General Birney signaled the regiment to the left of the 7th U.S. Colored Troops to advance. Soon thereafter, ferocious cannon and musket fire erupted in the direction of Fort Gilmer, but quickly waned. A few minutes later, a rattle of musketry revealed that Foster's brigade was making its assault and within moments the guns on Fort Gilmer opened fire on those hapless soldiers.

As General Birney advanced with his leftmost regiment, he could only wonder what had happened to the 7th U.S. Colored Troops, but tall abatis prevented a view in that direction. It was apparent to the general, however, that the assault by Shaw's regiment never happened, that Foster's attack was beaten back, and that the untouched battery on Fort Gilmer would soon play havoc upon the flank of his left regiment if its advance were to continue. General Birney halted that regiment and made his way around the abatis to find out what had become of Colonel Shaw.

Several hundred yards away, he found the colonel and five of his companies lying flat on the ground in a hollow sheltered from enemy fire with impenetrable abatis to the front. Colonel Shaw had sent one company forward to search for the missing skirmishers. An irate General Birney demanded to know why Colonel Shaw had not attacked as ordered. In the course of intense questioning, he learned that Colonel Shaw had reduced his attacking force to four companies. The colonel claimed that this was his understanding of the order relayed by the staff officer.

It made no difference which officer was right in his interpretation of the orders given and received. Even a complete regiment attacking alone had no chance of success in an assault on Fort Gilmer. Two hundred brave soldiers of the 7th U.S. Colored Troops had been sacrificed for naught.

* * *

The summer campaign of Lieutenant General Jubal A. Early had achieved significant victories at Lynchburg, Monocacy and Kernstown. Federal authorities were kept in a state of apprehension as his troops were in constant motion and periodically feinted toward the Potomac. The crusty Confederate general had threatened Washington and burned Chambersburg, Pennsylvania, to the ground for failing to pay ransom. His successful rampage had forced General Grant to dispatch Major General Philip H. Sheridan, with an army of forty thousand soldiers from the lines at Petersburg, to defeat "Old Jube" in the Shenandoah Valley. Early's luck ran out when Sheridan learned that Kershaw's Division had left the Valley for Richmond in mid-September. Sheridan had immediately attacked the reduced Confederate force on the banks of Opequon Creek and at Fisher's Hill, causing the loss of many irreplaceable Southern veterans.

General Early needed a victory to restore his tarnished reputation and gain the success that General Lee was relying upon him to deliver. He watched carefully as Sheridan, believing that the Rebel Army had retreated far south in the valley and was too crippled to take offensive action, withdrew his forces to Cedar Creek. Sixth Corps was released to return to the lines at Petersburg as the Army of the Shenandoah settled into a camp routine to celebrate their successful campaign.

In the mid-morning of October thirteenth, the illusion was dispelled. Shells began to rain down upon Major General George Crook's Army of West Virginia from a Confederate battery on the crest of Hupp's Hill, below Cedar Creek. Two brigades of West Virginians crossed the creek to investigate. They advanced across the farm of Abram Stickley and collided with the recently returned veterans of Kershaw's Division. For the next hour, the opposing forces pounded each other until the Federal line cracked, and the greatly outnumbered Yankees were routed. Sixth Corps was immediately recalled by Sheridan and arrived back at the Cedar Creek encampment by the afternoon of the fourteenth. Early withdrew southward and the Federals again became complacent. Several days later, Sheridan departed for a conference in Washington, called to determine future operations in the Valley. He only got as far as Winchester.

* * *

6TH MARYLAND VOLUNTEERS
NEAR MIDDLETOWN, VIRGINIA
OCTOBER 19, 1864

Before daybreak, Captain Prentiss was roused from a deep sleep by the sound of heavy firing in the distance. He immediately called the regiment to arms.

Confederate forces had surprised and routed Union troops encamped to their left. The 6th Maryland was ordered by the brigade commander to fall back. Captain Prentiss moved his regiment off by the right flank and, accompanied by the 126th Ohio, formed a line of battle on the hill behind its camp. The two regiments advanced across a nearby run, toward the noise of battle, and soon discovered that Federal troops on their right had been flanked and were retreating. This compelled them to fall back to the point of departure, which they accomplished in good order despite being subjected to heavy artillery fire. When it was determined that the enemy was rapidly advancing in its direction, 6th Maryland withdrew another four hundred yards. Two guns of Captain McKnight's Battery M, 5th United States Artillery, were abandoned during the movement and fell into the hands of the Rebels. Captain Prentiss promptly advanced his battle line, retook the guns, and withdrew to a field opposite Middletown. There, Sixth Corps formed a line of battle that was appended by remnants of shattered brigades and divisions rallied by General Sheridan during a dramatic ride to the battlefield. Before the Sixth Corps counter-attack began, the feisty general rode before the growing battle line. He waved his hat in the air and shouted encouragement. The soldiers responded with tremendous cheers from one end of the line to the other. Smarting from near-defeat, they proceeded to drive Early's forces every step of the way back across Cedar Creek in a fierce fight. By nightfall, 6th Maryland reoccupied its old campsite. Losses sustained by the regiment that day totaled four officers wounded, eight enlisted men killed, thirty-seven enlisted men wounded, and one enlisted man wounded and missing.

Lieutenant Colonel Hill returned from a long medical leave in early November to assume command of the regiment. Captain Prentiss was promoted to the rank of major in early December and promptly sat for a photograph in his new uniform.

* * *

In December of 1864, the Confederate Congress passed a bill that authorized the enlistment of slaves into colored regiments. During congressional debate,

General Robert E. Lee testified as follows: "Fort Gilmer proved, the other day, that Negroes will fight—they raised each other on the parapet to be shot at as they appeared above." The law was instituted too late to benefit the South as few colored regiments were raised and none were fielded.

AT THE ALTAR OF SAINT PAULS

ARMORY SQUARE HOSPITAL
WASHINGTON, D.C.
JUNE 24, 1865

Clifton stared glumly at the whitewashed wall across the ward. "I learned in a letter from my stepmother of Elijah's death at Fort Gilmer. Later, I spoke with a staff officer who interviewed Captain Weiss at the time of his parole. A strongly worded report regarding those murders was drafted and sent to Army Headquarters."

"Which no doubt has already been lost," John commented bitterly. "Whilst I never met Elijah, I know from father's letters that he held Elijah in high esteem."

"As did I," Clifton replied.

Melville glanced toward Whitman and caught his eye. "Kindly tell us more about William during the last year of the war."

Whitman's eyebrows arched slightly. Melville's tone was almost cordial. He leaned forward in his chair, intent on remembering William's words from the final days of their conversations. "During the colder months when the opposing armies were in winter quarters and not disposed toward confrontation, William was able to get fairly frequent furloughs to visit his friends in Richmond. The Confederate capital was just about twenty miles travel northward on the cars from Petersburg. During one of these visits, he learned that Hetty's mother, Mrs. Wilson Miles Cary of Baltimore, had obtained a special pass from President Lincoln to go through the lines to Richmond for the purpose of visiting her children who resided there."

"How was this pass obtained?" John asked.

"With the help of General John G. Barnard, the Chief of the United States Army Engineer Corps."

"Ah, yes," Clifton said. "That makes perfect sense. He's married to the adopted daughter of Mrs. Cary."

"In any case," Whitman continued, "the arrival of Hetty's mother before Christmas provided General Pegram with the opportunity to urge that the marriage should be delayed no longer. Hetty happily agreed and the wedding was set for the evening of the nineteenth day of January, 1865. The invited guests anticipated the event with much enthusiasm. It was the one bright spot on the horizon during an otherwise dismal season in war-weary Richmond."

"I can well imagine how miserable those times had to have been in the Confederate capital, no matter how richly deserved," Melville stated.

"Surely, they had to realize that the end of the Confederacy was drawing near," John said. "Lincoln had been reelected the previous November, assuring that the war would go on. Jubal Early had been thoroughly beaten by Phil Sheridan in the Shenandoah Valley the preceding fall. Their economy was in shambles. There was no food. What hope did they have?"

"Many still kept the faith, certainly those in the upper echelon of Southern society like the Carys," Whitman replied. "General Lee had accomplished the impossible on the battlefield so often that many Southern patriots clung to the hope that he would do it again. But they clearly knew that it was a desperate and dangerous time."

"I have no doubt that many remained steadfast in their convictions and dedication," Clifton commented. "And that included our brother William."

"He never wavered in his loyalty to the Southern cause, his fellow soldiers or his dear friends in Richmond," Whitman said.

"I can only respect him for that," Clifton responded. "Correspondence from Laura in late 1864 informed me that William was frequently in the company of

Hetty and Connie. William no doubt thought of them as surrogate family as he could not visit what was left of his own in Baltimore."

"That's true," Whitman said. "William found comfort in the hospitality of the Carys and they obviously were rather fond of him."

"William was a dear and affectionate boy," John said, his eyes misting slightly. He shook his head to regain his composure. "Please tell us more."

"As I mentioned," Whitman began, "Richmond society was entirely fascinated by the upcoming marriage of Hetty to General Pegram, a favorite son of the city. Every occurrence regarding the nuptials was widely circulated throughout local society. For instance, two days before the wedding, Hetty brought her bridal veil to the Fairfax residence where her cousin was confined with a cold so that Connie and their two mothers would be the first to see it worn. As Hetty turned from the mirror, her elbow struck the mirror's edge and it fell to the floor, breaking into fragments. Afterward, this incident was spoken of by the superstitious as the first in a series of ominous happenings."

* * *

SAINT PAUL'S EPISCOPAL CHURCH
RICHMOND, VIRGINIA
JANUARY 19, 1865

The pews of the imposing church were filled to capacity with the cream of Confederate society, including President and Mrs. Davis, General Robert E. Lee, and many high-ranking officers of the Army of Northern Virginia. The families of the bride and groom were in their seats and the Reverend Charles M. Minnegerode was waiting before the altar to perform the ceremony. Private William Prentiss was seated just behind the family of the bride. As the minutes ticked past the appointed hour of eight o'clock, the tightly packed congregation began to murmur and fidget as they waited for the arrival of the bride and groom.

In the vestibule, Connie and Burton were positioned to receive the wedding couple. "What could be keeping them?" cried Connie as she peered out the door at the dark and empty street. "They should have been here over twenty minutes ago."

"The president's carriage was sent in a timely manner to Colonel Peyton's house to drive them to the church," Burton said as he began to pace back and forth."

"I know that the arrangements were perfectly made," Connie replied. "Mrs. Davis is so very fond of Hetty—she begged to be allowed to provide her personal carriage to convey them to the church. Oh my goodness, what could have gone wrong?"

A shabby hack drawn by an old scarecrow of a horse came around the corner at a fast pace and lurched to a stop before the church. Connie and Burton dashed out the door and down the steps where Burton helped the perturbed couple dismount from the dilapidated hack. As the party hurried up the steps and into the vestibule, the groom explained that the normally gentle horses drawing the president's carriage had become violent and could not be controlled.

"Thank Goodness that you've arrived—that's all that matters," Connie said as she guided the bride and groom forward while Burton helped them remove their outer garments. John, in the full uniform of a Confederate general officer with a sword at his side, was dispatched down the side aisle toward the altar. Connie beckoned for Captain Miles Cary, Hetty's brother, to take his place beside the bride as he was standing in for their absent father. Hetty wore her bridal veil and an exquisite silk dress over which a heavy sash of red, white, and red had been draped from behind her right shoulder, diagonally across her front to below her waist.

Stepping across the threshold into the nave, she accidentally dropped her lace handkerchief. Stooping to retrieve it before anyone else could react, she caught her fragile tulle veil on a corner of the door latch plate and tore it to almost its full length. Hetty knew that the grand interior of the church, mellow in the light of hundreds of burning candles, was packed with a hushed congregation. She quickly regained her composure and took her brother's arm. Hetty began her march to the altar with a slow and stately step. As she passed down the aisle, there were whispers of delight at her rare beauty, her pearly white complexion, the vivid roses on her cheeks and lips, the sheen of her lovely auburn hair, and the happy gleam of her beautiful brown eyes. Standing at the altar with Reverend Charles Minnegerode was the handsome John Pegram, appearing exactly as he felt, triumphant, the "prize winner" as many men called him.

A small reception following the wedding ceremony was held at the home of Colonel Thomas Peyton, one of Hetty's many cousins in Virginia. The newlyweds spent the night in Richmond and departed early the next morning for Petersburg as there was no time for a real honeymoon. Their destination was General Pegram's headquarters, located in a farmhouse about nine miles below town near Hatcher's Run, a short distance from the infantry division under his command.

A large parlor, a cooking room with cast-iron stove and dining table, and a room used as an office were situated on the main floor, while the young couple occupied the entire upper floor. Within a few days, Hetty rearranged the furniture, added a few decorative items, and transformed the humble farmhouse into a comfortable abode more appropriate for a general officer and married man.

General Pegram rode out daily to inspect his division and the fortifications that they occupied. He was often accompanied by his new bride. His soldiers gathered around them at every occasion, thrilled to see the beautiful wife of their general.

The corps commander, Major General John B. Gordon, ordered a review of Pegram's division to be held on the second day of February, 1865. The review was seen by Pegram's staff to be an excellent opportunity to honor the new Mrs. Pegram. Invitations were sent to Generals Robert E. Lee, James Longstreet, Ambrose P. Hill, Richard Anderson, Henry Heth, and several socially prominent ladies from Petersburg to meet Hetty. To everyone's delight, all invitees graciously accepted.

The scheduled day arrived and it was blessed with perfect spring weather, a rare occurrence this time of year. The sun shown brightly, towering white clouds were vivid against a deep blue sky, and the air was crystal clear and pleasantly brisk. As Pegram's division passed in review, Gordon backed his horse several paces so that he was among the other generals and staff officers clustered behind, leaving Hetty in the position of honor to the left of General Lee. Hetty's face became flushed in rich color and her eyes were alight with the triumph of the moment.

Once the troops marched by and the distinguished guests had departed, Hetty rode off the field, escorted by Colonel Henry Kyd Douglas, her husband's adjutant. She was sitting her horse like Joan of Arc. She smiled at the soldiers who gathered around her to cheer and admire her marvelous beauty. In the midst of this excitement, her horse accidentally bumped a soldier from a North Carolina regiment in Pegram's division, almost knocking him to the ground. Hetty reined in her horse and began to apologize, but the soldier interrupted her. Removing his tattered hat and holding it in hand, he straightened his back to face her. "Never mind, Miss. You might rid all over me—indeed you might!" he said.

* * *

HATCHER'S RUN
NEAR PETERSBURG, VIRGINIA
FEBRUARY 6, 1865

The period of tranquility enjoyed by the newlywed couple was disrupted several days later when Federal forces made a demonstration against the extreme right of the Confederate line, occupied by General Gordon's corps, including Pegram's division. The opposing forces skirmished all day with little advantage gained by either side. General Pegram returned to his headquarters that night and, before daybreak of the following day, was roused from his bed with news that the enemy was about to renew its attack. His wife prepared his coffee and breakfast in the gray light of a winter dawn, then bade him farewell, admonishing him to take good care and return safely to her.

Throughout the morning, as the battle surged and waned, the general's aides came and went from headquarters. Each time they reported to Hetty that the general was safe. Her mother arrived to visit in the afternoon. She brought with her letters from family members regarding Hetty's wedding. After an hour in which they relished the words of their loved ones, the two women withdrew to an ambulance parked in a small grove of trees near the farmhouse to card lint.

Later that afternoon, Pegram's and Mahone's infantry divisions were ordered to attack Federal positions that threatened the Confederate lines. When his division was drawn up in line of battle, General Pegram rode from one end to the other, giving encouragement to his soldiers for the coming attack. While they were ragged in appearance, he saw strong heart and determination in their eyes. The order was given to march at the double-quick toward the enemy. Pegram's Division closed to within one hundred yards of the Federal battle line and the Confederates rushed forward. Their general was conspicuous on horseback directly behind his charging ranks when the Federal line opened fire. A Minnie ball knocked the sword from General Pegram's hand, passing through his body near the heart. Hunched forward and clutching the left side of his chest, he slowly toppled from his saddle. Colonel Douglas jumped from his horse and caught the general in his arms, lowering him to the ground where he died within seconds. The galling Federal fire brought Pegram's troops to a halt. Their momentum lost, they became disorganized and were forced to retreat.

After assigning a guard detail to remain with the general's body, Colonel Douglas and two officers from the division staff rode to Major General Gordon's hillside position where he had been directing the battle from horseback, surrounded by his staff.

Colonel Douglas saluted the corps commander and began his report. "Sir, I regret to inform you that General Pegram was killed as we made our advance. As I'm sure you are aware, the charge failed to reach the Federal line, and the division has been withdrawn in good order from the field."

General Gordon kept his eyes fixed on the field of battle below him.

"So now," Colonel Douglas added, biting his bottom lip with increased intensity, "Who will inform Mrs. Pegram of her husband's death?"

General Gordon turned in his saddle to face the colonel. "You must do it, Colonel Douglas," he stated matter-of-factly.

"Good Heavens, General! I'd sooner lead a forlorn hope—anything that is war—but not that!" exclaimed Colonel Douglas, his voice suddenly filled with anguish.

General Gordon stared coldly at him.

"Sir, I'm a bachelor—I don't know that much about women—I cannot tell Mrs. Pegram that her husband is dead. Send Major New. He's married—he'll know what to do."

General Gordon's face displayed disgust, but he did not wish to continue the embarrassment for all concerned. He turned in his saddle toward a staff officer and told him to find Major New. After casting a final withering look at Colonel Douglas, General Gordon wheeled his horse and trotted up the wooded hillside to return to corps headquarters, followed closely by his staff.

As Colonel Douglas and the two accompanying division staff officers returned to General Pegram's headquarters, they learned from a courier that Major New had not yet arrived. Colonel Douglas deliberated briefly with the two staff officers before announcing his decision. "Tonight, we shall apprise Mrs. Pegram that the general is delayed on the battlefield and that she should retire as he will be out quite late." He dispatched the junior officer to bring General Pegram's body to headquarters after dark. Colonel Douglas and the remaining officer quietly rode up to the parked ambulance, their faces carefully set. They could hear the two women laughing merrily.

The canvas flap at the back of the ambulance opened and Hetty peered out. She had heard the light tread of horse's hooves on the grass. "Good evening, Colonel Douglas. I can tell that the sounds of battle are receding. Will my husband be home soon?" She smiled brightly at the two officers on horseback.

"No, Mrs. Pegram," replied Colonel Douglas. "The general will be unable to return until quite late and suggested that you retire for the night."

"Thank you, Colonel. I shall do just that—we've finished our carding and it has been a long day," Hetty replied. The officers immediately dismounted and helped the two women climb down from the ambulance. As soon as Hetty and her mother were standing safely on the ground, Colonel Douglas begged leave and the officers hastily departed.

After saying goodnight to her mother and seeing her off in a carriage to her nearby lodgings, Hetty retired to the upstairs of the farmhouse. Just before midnight, General Pegram's body was placed in the room used as the adjutant's office, directly beneath the bedroom where Hetty slept peacefully.

TWO BROTHERS

GENERAL PEGRAM'S HEADQUARTERS
NEAR PETERSBURG, VIRGINIA
FEBRUARY 7, 1865

It was a cold, damp morning as Colonel Douglas woke from a fitful sleep. He was slouched in the chair where he had spent the night, fully dressed in his boots and overcoat, yet chilled to the bone. The gloomy first light of dawn, passing through a small window, revealed the stark details of the room as his senses began to register the events of the previous day. His eyes finally opened. He looked at the adjutant's desk in front of him and then up at the covered body lying on the camp bed against the wall. The colonel had served on Stonewall Jackson's staff, been wounded in battle several times, and lost many friends during the war, but this circumstance had him firmly in the grip of despair. Faint noises emanating from the ceiling above his head revealed that Hetty was up and about. He continued to stare at the general's blanket-covered body.

Colonel Douglas scrambled to his feet at the sound of a horse arriving in front of the farmhouse, walked quickly to the front porch, and peered into the heavy morning mist. Major New was nowhere to be seen. An enlisted man was tying his horse to the hitching rail. As the private walked up to the colonel and saluted, Colonel Douglas noticed the small silver cross bottony on his tattered uniform jacket, which he recognized immediately as the emblem of the Maryland Battalion posted several miles away.

"Sir, I'm Private William Prentiss of the 2nd Maryland. I reported in last night at corps headquarters from a furlough and learned that General Pegram had been killed in battle. I borrowed a horse from one of the staff officers and received permission to come here to offer my condolences to Mrs. Pegram."

The colonel glared at William as he struggled to contain his frustration. "I gather that you are a longtime acquaintance of Mrs. Pegram," he declared condescendingly.

"Yes sir, we were friends in Baltimore before the war."

"Did you attend the wedding last month?"

"Yes sir, I was there."

The colonel's face took on a look of contemplation. "Private Prentiss, we have a very delicate situation here. Mrs. Pegram is not yet aware of her husband's death. I was just getting ready to call her down from her quarters, inform her of the dreadful fact, and guide her to her husband's body in the office just inside," Colonel Douglas said as he gestured toward the open farmhouse door behind him.

"Oh my," William said. "How can I be helpful?"

"Just before your arrival, I heard her footsteps on the floor above," the colonel replied. "I think that she'll be coming downstairs shortly to inquire regarding the general's whereabouts. It may be better if she is escorted down the stairs."

"I'll do it," William said calmly.

Colonel Douglas turned and walked back into the farmhouse with William following a few steps behind him. At the foot of the stairs, William stood still. He took a deep breath before slowly climbing the staircase.

Hetty heard his footsteps as he approached the landing and rushed out from the bedroom, wearing a heavy robe over her sleeping gown. "Oh John, I was so worried!" she exclaimed before seeing that it was William on the stairway. She stopped her in her tracks. "William, what are you doing here?" she asked. In a second, her expression changed from inquisitiveness to fear, then to horror as it struck her. She looked past William to see the upturned face of Colonel Douglas and his grim expression confirmed her worst suspicion.

"I'm so sorry," William said. He took the last step to the landing and pulled Hetty into his arms as sobs began to wrack her body and her knees gave way. Hetty cried her heart out and William gently held and comforted her. She finally pulled her head away from William's shoulder.

"Where is he?" she asked. Her voice broke and tears continued to roll down her checks.

"Downstairs," William replied.

"Please take me to him," Hetty said as she wiped the tears from her eyes. William helped her descend the stairs and guided her to the office door held open by the colonel.

Hetty stopped on the threshold, released William's arm, and walked unassisted to the camp bed. She knelt beside her husband's body and gently pulled back the gray army blanket that covered him. Hetty wept and tenderly caressed his face. As her grieving hands crossed his chest, she sought the wound that took her husband's life. She put her hand into the breast pocket of his coat and removed his still-ticking watch, which she had wound the morning before, as well as a miniature of her—both stained with his blood. William and Colonel Douglas quietly withdrew from the office and closed the door so that Hetty could mourn without disturbance.

Before noon, a courier arrived at General Lee's headquarters to inform Captain Miles Cary that his brother-in-law had been killed in action. Captain Cary immediately mounted his horse and rode through a cold, drizzling rain and occasional enemy fire toward Hatcher's Run. Nearly there, he met an ambulance containing his mother and sister, followed by a wagon bearing the body of General Pegram.

They spent the night in Petersburg where Hetty, crazed with grief, could not be induced to leave the body. The following morning, accompanied by her mother and brother, she sat beside her husband's coffin in a freight car taking them to Richmond. As Connie later spoke of her, "Hetty was like a flower broken in the stalk."

* * *

SAINT PAUL'S EPISCOPAL CHURCH
RICHMOND, VIRGINIA
FEBRUARY 9, 1865

Three weeks to the day after his marriage, Brigadier General John Pegram had returned to the same place before the altar of his church and Reverend Minnegerode once more officiated at the ceremony. There was no joy in the silent congregation this time. Most of it had been present twenty-one days before to celebrate his nuptials. Hetty, swathed in a black crepe dress, knelt throughout the service beside the coffin crossed with a victor's palms and adorned with General Pegram's cap, sword, and gloves.

The hearse, followed by his rider-less warhorse with boots reversed in the stirrups, led the funeral procession to Hollywood Cemetery. Next came a carriage driven by Burton Harrison carrying Hetty, her mother, Miles, Monimia, Connie, and General Custis Lee, a close friend of General Pegram. Another carriage followed with General Pegram's mother, sisters, and brothers. Behind them marched an honor guard of soldiers with arms reversed and banners crepe-enfolded. A military band followed, playing a sad dirge that wailed in the cold winter air.

The Pegram family plot at Hollywood Cemetery was situated on a gentle slope facing the nearby James River. Beside the stone that had been erected for his father, who died many years before, a freshly dug grave awaited the coffin of the eldest son. During the graveside service, Hetty stood between her brother and General Custis Lee with the Pegram and Cary families gathered close around them. White snow lay on the Hollywood hillside beneath bare tree limbs reaching skyward. The ceaseless rumble of water cascading around exposed rocks in the river gave comfort to the grief-stricken as another son of the Southern Confederacy was laid to rest.

COMMUNICATING WITH THE ENEMY

Whitman and the Prentiss brothers sat motionless. "The Pegram family ordeal did not end with the death of the general," Whitman said. "At the Battle of Five Forks on April first, his youngest brother, Lieutenant Colonel William Pegram, was mortally wounded and died a day later."

"I have heard," Clifton said, "that Willy Pegram made a prophetic declaration. 'Men, whenever the enemy takes a gun from my battery, look for my dead body in front of it.' And that is precisely what happened."

The trace of a sneer flashed across Melville's face, but he restrained it. Instead, he inquired about the disposition of the 6th Maryland at the beginning of 1865.

"The regiment was in winter quarters southwest of Petersburg," Clifton replied. "Our assignment was mostly picket duty and, in conjunction with other regiments, the building of Fort Fisher, one of the larger forts in our lines."

"Was there any adventure to this duty, or was it simply a time of cold and miserable drudgery?" Melville inquired.

"One event does come to mind," Clifton replied thoughtfully.

"And when you have finished recalling your episode, Major Prentiss, I have one of William's to offer," Whitman announced. "His battalion, like your regiment, was frequently on picket duty that winter manning rifle pits in the outer lines."

"I often wondered how William was faring," Clifton said. "I knew that he had to be somewhere across the lines, not too far from where I was located."

"He was also quite interested in your whereabouts," Whitman replied.

* * *

6TH MARYLAND VOLUNTEERS
NEAR PETERSBURG, VIRGINIA
FEBRUARY 27, 1865

Major Prentiss knocked on the plank door of a log house commodious enough for Captain Charles Damuth, Lieutenant Grayson Eichelberger, and their cook to live in relative comfort. Hearing a muffled invitation to enter, he opened the door and stood in the doorway shaking snow from his overcoat.

"Kindly close the door quickly, Clifton, or the cold draft will overcome the trifling amount of heat from our camp stove," Captain Damuth declared as he sat on a rough-hewn bench across the table from Lieutenant Eichelberger. Both were drinking hot coffee from tin cups.

"Charles, it's warm enough in here to bake bread," Clifton replied. The officers joined in laughter at this remark as he closed the door and hung his coat on a wooden peg protruding from the wall. Sam, the Negro cook, poured a steaming cup of coffee and placed it on the table as Clifton sat down on the bench beside Captain Damuth.

"Thank you Sam, this hot coffee will be well received over my frozen lips," Clifton said as he raised his cup. Sam acknowledged the appreciation with a broad smile and went back to tending the stove.

"Grayson was just telling me about his experiences whilst on a three-day picket detail, from which he has just returned," said Captain Damuth.

"Please continue," Clifton said, "This information is one of the reasons for my visit."

"My pleasure sir," Lieutenant Eichelberger replied. "I can well imagine that you're interested as we had a minor disturbance on our picket line yesterday morning. It was the result of an arrangement that I'd made with a Rebel officer to chop firewood together each afternoon in a stand of trees between the picket lines."

* * *

A cold wind was blowing hard out of the west and large snowflakes swirled in the air. Knowing that it was about time for his wood-chopping detail to venture forth, Lieutenant Eichelberger scanned the woods to his front for any sign of a Rebel detail assigned to the same task. Intermittent periods of snowfall throughout the day had left a thin, white covering on the ground and made it possible to see for some distance into the timber. All had gone smoothly on the first day of the arrangement and he was satisfied that the agreement would be kept.

"Sergeant, our Southern brethren are not out yet, but we should go before this snowfall gets any worst," Lieutenant Eichelberger said.

"Yes sir," replied the sergeant, who turned to the eight soldiers holding saws and axes in the trench below. "Let's go, fellows. It's time to cut wood for our camp fires."

Several other soldiers not on the work detail were loitering nearby and asked the sergeant if they could go out with the wood-cutting party just for the exercise. The sergeant looked at Lieutenant Eichelberger, who assented, and the entire party, without arms, climbed out of the trench and walked toward the woods.

As they crossed the open field, Lieutenant Eichelberger saw motion in the trees and quickly identified it as the Rebel wood chopping detail. When, within fifty yards, he noted that the detail was under armed guard, there to keep the Rebel soldiers from deserting.

The Rebel lieutenant saluted as the parties neared one another and said, "Good afternoon sir, it's a fine day for chopping wood."

"That it is, lieutenant," replied Lieutenant Eichelberger as he returned the salute. "There's a wind-downed tree yonder that should suit our needs. I suggest that we work on it together—there's plenty of suitable lengths of firewood to share." The soldiers of both sides approached the tree and readied their cutting tools. Soon, Northern and Southern soldiers were toiling side-by-side. As the work continued, it began to snow hard with visibility greatly decreasing. Two Rebel soldiers quietly stepped up to the Union soldiers who were not working and let them know of their desire to desert. Gathering each deserter between two soldiers, the 6th Maryland soldiers pulled the capes of their blue overcoats around them and walked back toward the Union positions without detection. Lieutenant Eichelberger observed all this and remained alert for any problem that might develop.

When the tree had been sectioned into firewood, the parties began preparations to withdraw to their own lines. Heavy snow continued to fall. As the Rebel lieutenant counted those in his charge, a look of confusion appeared on his heavily bearded face, quickly turning to a grimace, then a scowl. He threw a hasty salute in the direction of Lieutenant Eichelberger and organized what remained of his work detail for a return trek to the Confederate picket line.

As Lieutenant Eichelberger and his party were reentering their trenches, they heard a commotion from the stand of trees between the lines. A Rebel deserter could be seen running through the swirling snowflakes toward the Federal positions. A Rebel picket raised his musket to fire while ordering him to halt, but the deserter continued his desperate flight. Not fifty yards away, a Union picket stood up in his rifle pit and pointed his musket at the Rebel picket.

"Don't fire or I'll shoot you dead," shouted the Union soldier. The standoff lasted just long enough for the deserter to reach the refuge of a Union trench. Lieutenant Eichelberger sent the three deserters to brigade headquarters shortly afterward. Their war was over.

* * *

"I reckon the secesh will be less disposed to share wood chopping duty with our boys after this affair," Lieutenant Eichelberger said with a grin.

"I suppose that's true," Clifton replied. "The Rebels are obviously short of supplies and suffering greatly in this unusually cold winter weather. The famished, ill-clad condition of their deserters and prisoners all testify to this fact, but we cannot forget that the Army of Northern Virginia remains a formidable foe."

"I would not argue the point," Captain Damuth commented. "The Rebels have been short of arms, artillery, shoes, uniforms, and supplies throughout this war and yet they have done quite well, all considered."

* * *

2ND MARYLAND BATTALION
NEAR PETERSBURG, VIRGINIA
MARCH 27, 1865

William and the battalion picket detail slipped out through an opening in the Confederate main line long before sunrise and quietly moved forward to their rifle pits under cover of darkness, relieving the soldiers that had been on duty there.

The day turned out to be clear and pleasant, a welcome departure from the hard winter weather that the Maryland Battalion had recently endured. There had been sporadic sharpshooting along the picket line early in the morning, but the exchange of fire soon subsided as both sides enjoyed the first warm sunshine in many days. It was also evident from sounds heard by the Rebel pickets that the Yankees were busy burying their dead from recent heavy skirmishing.

The rifle pit that William was sharing with Private Henry Hollyday was a fairly shallow ditch just wide and deep enough for the two men to lie prone side-by-side, their heads below the heaped-up, compacted earth at the end. It faced similar enemy positions a mere seventy-five yards away. William enjoyed being on duty with Henry Hollyday because Henry was a graduate of St. James College in Hagerstown and a skilled conversationalist. As the day progressed, Henry and William took turns napping and remaining alert, periodically peeking over the low earthen wall to make certain that nothing was threatening their position.

About mid-afternoon, the stillness was disturbed by a voice calling from the nearest Union rifle pit. "Hey Johnny Reb, are you having a pleasant day?"

William smiled to himself, welcoming the distraction. He lifted his head and carefully peered over the mound of compacted earth, scrutinizing the enemy positions within sight to detect anything that might constitute danger. He saw only the top part of a face wearing a blue bummer cap showing above the front of the rifle pit opposite his position.

"I'm having a grand day, Billie Yank," William replied. "How about you?"

"It's far too nice a day to spoil by dying, Johnny Reb, that's why I'm mighty glad no one is fool enough to be shooting," the Union soldier answered as he raised his head a bit further. William could now see, even at a distance, that the Yankee was grinning as he spoke.

Henry was smiling under the cap pulled down over his eyes as he listened to the conversation.

"I most certainly agree with that notion," William called out as he lifted his head and glanced around at the Rebel positions to his left and right. Nothing indicated that anyone else was paying attention to what was occurring in this part of the picket line.

"Where are you from, Yank?" William yelled to the Union soldier who was now quite visible in his rifle pit.

"New Hampshire," came the reply. "How about you?"

"I'm a Marylander," answered William in a voice that he hoped would be loud enough just to carry between the two rifle pits.

"Why, you must be a bit confused, Johnny Reb. Maryland is part of the Union."

"Sadly, at the moment, that's true Billie Yank, but there are those of us who still intend to have Maryland in the Southern Confederacy."

The Yankee didn't answer right away. He stared back at William with a bemused look on his face.

Not wanting to let the conversation lag, William asked the Union soldier another question. "What's the name of your regiment, Billie?"

"The 11th New Hampshire Infantry, the best damn regiment that ever marched out of our state's magnificent mountains," responded the Yank, his voice booming with pride.

"That may be so, but I do believe that the 2nd Maryland whipped that Yankee regiment rather badly at Cold Harbor last June," William replied. He remembered the sight of its battle flag as the New Hampshire soldiers were routed by the audacity of the Marylanders.

"That was a stand-up fight for sure, Reb. And you might have come out better in that one than we did, but the war ain't over yet."

William wasn't sure how to respond. Both men had head and shoulders well above the front wall of their rifle pits and their voices continued to become louder.

"I have a brother in the Federal 6th Maryland Volunteers. Do you know if that regiment is anywhere near about?"

"He sure must be proud of you, Johnny Reb," replied the Yankee with amusement in his voice. "Yes, I've heard of the 6th Maryland. It's a top notch regiment in Sixth Corps. They're somewhere in the vicinity, though I don't know exactly where."

"That'll be enough of that!" shouted Lieutenant Samuel T. McCullough as he crawled up behind William's rifle pit, surprising William and causing the Union soldier across the way to quickly drop from sight.

"You know better than to communicate with the enemy, Private Prentiss—it's against general orders," ranted the lieutenant, a former lawyer from Annapolis who was a stickler for enforcing regulations. "Consider yourself under arrest, Prentiss. I'm sending you back to camp under guard."

"Yes sir," William replied.

Lieutenant McCullough twisted over on his side and called back behind him to the corporal in charge of William's section of rifle pits. "Smith, damn it, why didn't you put a stop to this misconduct. I ought to put you under arrest too."

Corporal H. Tillard Smith, who had been acting Sergeant Major of the battalion the previous year, knew better than to reply to such an irate statement. He remained silent. Lieutenant McCullough quickly forgot about him and twisted back around toward William.

"Prentiss, damn it to hell and back, this is serious business—you have no right sharing information with the enemy—I don't care if you were inquiring about your rotten Yankee brother—by God, it's against regulations and you'll pay for disobeying them." The red-faced lieutenant turned back toward the corporal and issued an order. "Smith, take Prentiss back to the battalion under guard and turn him over to Lieutenant Zollinger."

"Yes sir," Corporal Smith hastily replied, still crouched in his rifle pit.

William left his rifled musket, bayonet, and cartridge box with Hollyday and was escorted back to camp by Corporal Smith, who was delighted at the opportunity to leave the picket line. The camp commander, Lieutenant William P. Zollinger, tolerant of what he considered to be a minor infraction by a veteran soldier of high character, immediately released William from arrest. William was happy to not spend the balance of the warm day on picket duty. He was also strangely comforted by the knowledge that his older brother, Clifton, was not far away.

16

BREAKTHROUGH AT PETERSBURG

ARMORY SQUARE HOSPITAL
WASHINGTON, D.C.
JUNE 24, 1865

John stepped up to the bed and placed his hand on Clifton's shoulder. He looked closely at him with both the trained eye of a physician and the concern of a brother. "Are you too weary to continue?"

"No, I'm not tired," Clifton replied. His fatigued and fragile appearance belied his words. John noted the determined look on Clifton's face and returned to his chair.

Whitman and Melville observed the exchange. Neither spoke. They too were troubled by Clifton's weakened condition, yet understood his need to continue.

* * *

A stalemate at Petersburg had developed by March of 1865. After a siege of nearly ten months duration, the Army of the Potomac and the Army of Northern Virginia occasionally exchanged artillery fire and engaged in minor skirmishing between the picket lines. However, the stakes remained high, as Petersburg was the junction of the last two railroads that connected Richmond with the rest of the Confederacy. The fall of Petersburg would force General Lee to abandon the defense of Richmond and flush the Army of Northern Virginia into the open where it could be surrounded and destroyed.

The Union and Confederate lines were composed of extensive earthworks, trenches, and fortifications of approximately the same strength and configuration. The terrain between the lines was almost entirely devoid of trees, except for a few stands that had not yet been cut to improve fields of fire, provide logs for building fortifications, or supply firewood during the cold winter season. Sixth Corps, under Major General Horatio G. Wright, held the extreme left of the Union line opposite a series of Confederate works stretching along the Boydton Plank Road. The divisions of Cadmus Wilcox and Henry Heth of Ambrose P. Hill's Third Corps of the Army of Northern Virginia held these fortifications.

Brigadier General J. Warren Keifer's 2nd Brigade, 3rd Division of Sixth Corps, occupied a loop in the line of Federal works that included Forts Fisher, Welch, and Gregg. The enemy picket line before these forts was strongly entrenched on a small hill and manned by an unusually large number of Rebel soldiers. During the morning of March twenty-fifth, the 110th Ohio and 122nd Ohio of 2nd Brigade were ordered to support already deployed Federal pickets in driving the Confederates from this line. The attack failed and a substantial number of casualties were incurred.

As the capture of this line was imperative, the 6th Maryland Infantry was formed in ranks early in the afternoon and several companies were detached to garrison Fort Gregg. The remainder of the regiment was ordered by General Keifer to join with the 67th Pennsylvania, one battalion of the 9th New York Heavy Artillery, and the 126th Ohio to make another attempt to capture the enemy picket line. When the attack was launched, the line of battle commanded by Major Clifton K. Prentiss advanced under severe fire and overran the Rebel trenches, capturing more than two-hundred prisoners.

Color Sergeant Robert Spence of the 6th Maryland Volunteers was the first man to enter the enemy works and plant the regimental flag on an embankment; shortly after, he was wounded in the neck by an enemy bullet. Several Maryland soldiers volunteered to advance and occupy sharpshooters' pits at the front of their position, preventing the enemy from forming a skirmish line for a counter-attack. It wasn't long before a heavy concentration of Confederate artillery fire was falling on the captured position.

* * *

6TH MARYLAND VOLUNTEERS
NEAR PETERSBURG, VIRGINIA
APRIL 1, 1865

It had been raining intermittently for several days and the ground was sodden. No improvement was in sight as threatening clouds hung in the gray sky over the opposing fortifications. The camp of the 6th Maryland Infantry Regiment was situated behind Fort Welch—its straight rows of tents appeared to be floating in a sea of mud. Groups of off-duty soldiers were either huddled around fire pits trying to keep warm or seated on logs as they cooked their meals.

Major Prentiss, temporarily commanding the 6th Maryland in the absence of Lieutenant Colonel Joseph C. Hill, had directed that the officers and sergeants assemble near his tent in the late afternoon. By the time Major Prentiss and Lieutenant Colonel Hill arrived on horseback, the rain had stopped falling. They quickly dismounted and made their way behind a wooden camp table opposite the assembled officers and sergeants. Major Prentiss unfolded a large military map and draped it across the tabletop.

"I've just returned from a briefing at 2nd Brigade headquarters with Brigadier General Keifer and his staff," Major Prentiss said, addressing the assembled officers and sergeants. The veteran soldiers were attentive as they stood in a semi-circle wearing overcoats and mud-covered boots. "As I'm sure you have noted, Lieutenant Colonel Hill has returned from a fifteen-day furlough, but is serving on General Wright's staff for a few days before returning to command our regiment. He kindly agreed to come to our camp and brief us on the pending operation. I suspect that he is also happy to visit with us as there aren't many Marylanders in the lofty domain of Sixth Corps headquarters."

The remark drew what may have sounded like obligatory laughter to one not familiar with the regiment. In fact, the soldiers were delighted to see the man who, behind his back, they affectionately called "Uncle Joe." Lieutenant Colonel Hill smiled broadly and held up his hands to quiet the greetings of his appreciative audience. He turned to Major Prentiss. "Thank you, Clifton. Coming home to your regiment, even for a brief visit, is always a great pleasure for an old soldier. Sixth Corps headquarters is a fascinating place to be at times, but I would, by far, prefer to be with the 6th Maryland in the coming fight. However, higher authority has decreed otherwise, and I rest easy in the knowledge that the regiment is in capable hands."

The expressions of the listeners evidenced their concurrence with this remark, yet masked sadness that previous commanding officers had been lost along the way. Lieutenant Colonel William A. McKellip had been disabled in an accidental magazine explosion early in the war and was held in high esteem. Colonel John W. Horn, whose battlefield performance was a source of pride to everyone who had ever served in the regiment, had been severely wounded leading a charge at the Opequon. Along with Joseph Hill and Clifton Prentiss, these commanding officers provided the gallant leadership that helped make 6th Maryland a well-regarded regiment throughout Sixth Corps.

"We have shared many a hard march and a difficult campaign together," continued Lieutenant Colonel Hill, his voice beginning to waver. "I have yet to see better soldiers than those that stand in the ranks of the 6th Maryland Volunteers. I am proud of my service in this regiment and the great honor and privilege bestowed upon me to be its commanding officer. I have no doubt that this will be the greatest achievement of my life."

The officers and sergeants were mature men not easily swayed by mere words. Nevertheless, lumps formed in their throats and hearts swelled within their chests. The affection and admiration alluded to by "Uncle Joe" was mutual.

"But enough of this sentimentality. We have serious work to do. The assault on the Confederate lines is scheduled for tomorrow in the early morning hours. All three divisions of Sixth Corps, about fourteen thousand men, will be deployed for the attack. The 3rd Division will be on the left wing in echelon. The 2nd Brigade will have its right resting on Arthur's swamp, which separates 3rd Division's right from the left of 2nd Division."

Half turning and pointing in the direction of the Confederate lines, Lieutenant Colonel Hill revealed that Sixth Corps profited greatly from the assault conducted by 6th Maryland and other 2nd brigade regiments on the twenty-fifth of March. Again facing his audience, he swept his hand across the map and described how the picket lines captured on that day had previously been enabling the enemy to observe everything done for some distance within the Union lines. A smile played across his lips as he declared that their adversaries, now dispossessed of this elevated position, would not detect the massing of Sixth Corps for the attack to be made in the morning.

"It's anticipated that Sheridan's cavalry, in conjunction with Warren's Fifth Corps, will be successful today in cutting off a portion of the Confederate Army under George Pickett and Fitzhugh Lee at Five Forks. This creates the ideal circumstance for a general assault on the entire Confederate line. Major Prentiss will provide you with the specific details of 6th Maryland's important role in tomorrow's battle."

"Gentlemen, please gather around the map," Major Prentiss said assertively. The officers and sergeants moved in around the table and craned their necks forward. "The brigade will form after dark tonight in front of Fort Welch and then move forward to the picket line when directed." Major Prentiss pointed to various spots on the map to show where the 110th Ohio, 6th Maryland, and 126th Ohio were to form the front battle line of 2nd Brigade with two battle lines behind, comprised of the remaining regiments of the brigade. He also indicated the position where 1st Brigade, 3rd Division, was to be aligned in battle formation to the left of 2nd Brigade. "We have the honor to spearhead the 2nd Brigade assault which, I am confident, will decisively break the enemy line."

With backs straight and eyes focused, the officers and sergeants received the details of the battle plan. There were no light hearts among them, but there were no faint hearts. They knew the strength of the Confederate works to be assailed. Over previous months, while on picket duty, each had observed first-hand the construction and improvement of the enemy fortifications. They also understood that this was an opportunity to rapidly end the war.

"After darkness falls, 6th Maryland will pack up camp and move to its assigned place on the picket line, which will bring the regiment quite near the main Rebel line. This movement must be accomplished as quietly as possible." Major Prentiss peered sternly at the faces of his officers and sergeants to emphasize the point. "The signal to attack will be the discharge of an artillery piece on the parapet of Fort Fisher. At the beginning of the assault, the 'Little Six' will be positioned along this line and will attack in this direction. Axemen of the Pioneer Corps will accompany each regiment to clear the abatis of felled trees with sharpened limbs and assist our soldiers in crossing ditches and other obstructions."

Major Prentiss scrutinized the men standing before the table, making eye contact with each and every one. "In the best tradition of the Maryland Line of Continental Army fame, we will accomplish this charge without stopping to fire—we will initially engage the enemy only with our bayonets. By this means, we will quickly cross the open ground and close with the enemy in his fortifications. Any questions so far?"

No one spoke.

Major Prentiss revealed that a sally port in the main Confederate fortification wall had been observed from the observation tower situated directly behind them. He tapped the location of the sally port on the map. "This opening is just wide enough for a wagon to pass through. It has a shoulder wall directly in its front to shield the interior of the fort. Rebel deserters have confirmed its position and configuration."

Major Prentiss leaned back and looked around at his cadre. "As you know, a sally port is intended to allow troops to 'sortie out'—to 'sally forth' if you please. However, in this instance, the 6th Maryland shall 'sortie in' to pay our respects to the Johnnys!" His quip provoked the expected chuckles and smiles.

The mission briefing that followed gave the details of what was expected of the regiment during the assault. All companies were to converge on the sally port after sweeping up the enemy pickets and passing through the obstructions. The colors accompanying Major Prentiss would guide them directly to the opening. Once inside the main wall, half of the regiment would charge to the right and other half to the left and, in so doing, clear the walls of defenders so that other regiments of the brigade could scale the rampart walls with little op-position. Once the area around the sally port was secure, 6th Maryland would quickly reform its line of battle and attack other forts along the wall to the left.

"Are there any questions?" Major Prentiss asked.

Again, there were none.

"Very well," he said. "Final instructions will be given tonight when the regi-ment is in formation, before we march out to the picket line. As our regiment has a specific assignment, we will be placed in position several hours ahead of other regiments of the brigade and division. It's essential that our soldiers maintain absolute silence until the signal to attack is given—the enemy must not know that an assault force is gathering before its lines."

Major Prentiss scanned the faces of his officers and sergeants. He saw ex-pressions of comprehension and confidence.

"One more thing," he said as he lifted a corner of the map with his right hand. "Prior to our assembly tonight, I want each man to have three days rations in his haversack and forty rounds in his cartridge box."

Major Prentiss picked up the map, folded it neatly, and tucked it under his arm. "Gentlemen, tomorrow morning our regiment will represent the honor and dignity of our beloved Maryland in what could be the last major battle of the war. As we look back with pride on the gallantry of the Old Maryland Line during the Revolutionary War, so too will future generations of Marylanders remember how well the 6th Regiment of Maryland Infantry kept that sacred trust in the coming battle. We shall not fail them—neither our predecessors nor our posterity. I am confident that every officer and man will do his duty."

After conclusion of the briefing, the officers and sergeants returned to their companies to prepare for the assault while Lieutenant Colonel Hill departed from camp. Lieutenant Eichelberger, commanding Company G, lingered be-hind. He took a seat at the table with Major Prentiss.

"Sir, do you really think that this attack will be decisive in breaking the Rebel lines?"

"General Grant is throwing the entire weight of the Army of the Potomac against the enemy tomorrow," Major Prentiss replied. "I do not think that their lines can withstand such a blow." He lit his pipe while collecting his thoughts. "Certainly, we have learned the hard way on past occasions to never underestimate General Lee and the Army of Northern Virginia. But yes, I do think that we will be successful."

"I would certainly welcome that happening," Lieutenant Eichelberger said with a sigh. He shook his head as he looked down at his chest. "Who would have thought that the hostilities would go on for this long? Or imagine the price paid in blood and misery?"

"At the beginning, I was as nearsighted as everyone else," Major Prentiss admitted with a long face. "In my overzealousness, I saw it as short work, but it didn't turn out that way. I'm just glad that it might be over in a matter of days or weeks."

The two men held different perspectives on the prospect of peace. Lieutenant Eichelberger's thoughts were centered on operating a grain mill again, or perhaps becoming a farmer, and starting his own family. His sweetheart had died of typhoid the previous September and he had since developed an affectionate correspondence with her younger sister. In contrast, Major Prentiss wanted to remain in the army. Despite this, he yearned for reconciliation between the states and with his younger brother.

"Laura, my sister in Baltimore, recently forwarded a letter to me written by our brother William who serves in the Confederate Maryland Battalion. He is, no doubt, somewhere over there within their lines at this moment. It's been four years since I've seen him. I've learned how William is faring from Marylanders that we've taken prisoner and that he's aware of my circumstances by the same means. He's survived many campaigns without sickness or serious injury, and for that I am most thankful, but I detest his allegiance to the Confederacy."

"I have cousins on the other side," Lieutenant Eichelberger said. "It saddens me to think that we might come face-to-face on the field of battle."

"William's letter was very interesting as he described the desperate plight of the populace in Petersburg and the deteriorating conditions within the Rebel army," Major Prentiss said. "He also stated that the Maryland Battalion does most of the picket duty for its brigade as it is well known that they will not desert."

"I'm sure that's because they're better soldiers than most," Lieutenant Eichelberger said. "But there's also the fact that they cannot go home to Maryland."

* * *

At ten o'clock, a tremendous bombardment of the Confederate line by every Federal gun from the James River to the left of the Union Army shattered the stillness of the night in the greatest discharge of artillery to be unleashed during the Petersburg campaign. Confederate guns responded with counter-battery fire, seeking to silence the Federal artillery, but it was with no noticeable effect. The ground shook from the thundering roar of the barrage and a multitude of high-arcing shot and shell streaked across the dark sky, some bursting in the air above the Confederate fortifications.

The 6th Maryland Infantry Regiment was drawn up in formation and its soldiers given final instructions in muted voices. Sergeants went up and down the front ranks of the companies to insure that each soldier had loaded his musket but had not primed it with a percussion cap. In accordance with the plan of attack, a bayonet was affixed to every muzzle.

Captain William H. Abercrombie, having just learned that Private Luther Fogler had fallen-in with Company H, approached him in the dim light. "Fogler, are you sure that you're well enough to be here?"

"Yes sir, I am," replied the thirty-six-year-old private.

"You're as good and true a soldier as any in this company, Luther, but you were seriously wounded last fall at Fisher's Hill. You just returned to the regiment a few days ago, and I know that you're still suffering from your wound. That's why I told the sergeant to excuse you from taking part in this charge."

"I've never shirked my duty, Captain—if the boys are going in to finish off the Rebs, I'm going with 'em," Fogler declared. The captain and the private stood looking each other square in the eye and neither spoke for a long moment. Captain Abercrombie clapped him on the shoulder before turning away and returning to the company front.

Flashes of light momentarily silhouetted the soldiers of the 6th Maryland as they watched the sublime display passing over their heads. Within a short time, the bombardment slackened, then stopped, and the silence became intense for the sharpened senses of the soldiers in the darkness.

The order was finally received for the regiment to quietly march to its assigned place behind the advanced picket line. It took them nearly two hours in the deep darkness to cross the swampy ground, all the while enduring an annoying fire from enemy pickets. When the soldiers of 6th Maryland were assembled at the designated spot for its line of battle, the order was passed in whispers to lie down on the cold, damp ground and rest.

* * *

6TH MARYLAND VOLUNTEERS
NEAR PETERSBURG, VIRGINIA
APRIL 2, 1865

Throughout the night, Major Prentiss moved from one company to the next, his calm presence reassuring the soldiers and providing them with encouragement for the upcoming battle. As other regiments were brought forward to take position on their flanks, the soldiers of the 6th Maryland were stood up in battle formation, shivering from the hours spent on the ground. Nervous Rebel pickets fired into the darkness and a number of the blind shots found their mark. The Union soldiers stood their ground without returning fire.

Completing his circuit for a final time, Major Prentiss approached Captain Damuth, the commanding officer of Company D, who spoke under his breath in a mildly agitated tone. "Sir, it's past four o'clock. We haven't heard the signal gun for the attack."

"It's still pitch black out there, Charles," Major Prentiss replied. "I suspect that General Wright is waiting for first light, which is delayed this morning by low cloud cover. There's also some ground fog," he observed as an afterthought.

A half hour passed as the sky slowly lightened from the total darkness of night, prompting Major Prentiss to return to the front of the color company in the center of his regimental line of battle. He had just begun to discern the ground contour before them when he heard the signal gun fired at Fort Fisher, prompting him to bark a command.

Company officers repeated the order to shoulder arms in muted voices up and down the 6th Maryland battle line. "Forward, double-quick march!" Major Prentiss ordered as he drew his sword. With the regimental color bearers trailing behind him, he advanced at a steady pace in the faint light and heavy mist toward the enemy's main works, not yet in sight. Within minutes, the battle line of 6th Maryland came under a brisk fire from the enemy's picket line. Men began crumpling to the ground as they were hit. A soldier from the rear ranks immediately filled each vacant spot as the battle line surged across the rolling terrain. Forward they marched, not firing a shot, with the bayonets of the front ranks pointed straight before them. A perfect rain of Confederate shot and shell passed overhead and through their ranks, but onward they advanced, sweeping up the enemy pickets with their wall of steel points.

As the main enemy fortifications took shape in the dim light, Major Prentiss turned to his regiment. Marching backward, his sword held high, he shouted the command, "Charge bayonets!" He immediately spun on his heel and ran forward with his regiment close behind him. Through two lines of abatis and ditches, the 6th Maryland Volunteers charged with a wild rush and the old accustomed yell, slowing only momentarily as they overcame the obstacles in their path. A Minnie ball wounded Color Corporal William J. Brown as he approached the enemy works. He fell with the 6th Maryland regimental flag. Sergeant Samuel Kerney caught the falling flag in stride, carrying it forward alongside the color guard member bearing the national emblem.

Major Prentiss, looking ahead and seeing the sally port, dashed directly for it. With five or six officers, the color bearers, and about twenty men on his heels, he ran through the opening in the wall, waving his sword. Sergeant John E. Buffington was at his side, clearing the way with his musket and bayonet as the soldiers of 6th Maryland collided with North Carolinians braced to meet them. Once inside the works, the color bearers planted their flags on the enemy ramparts and pitched headlong into the fray. Other 6th Maryland soldiers coming through the sally port fired their muskets at any defender still on his feet. Major Prentiss slashed his way past several Rebels with his sword, firing his Colt .44–caliber Re-volver as he pressed into the fortification. Stopping and turning, he directed his soldiers to the right and to the left. Following instructions perfectly, they were soon delivering fusillades along the interior walls in both directions.

Most Rebel soldiers not killed or wounded by the onslaught were surrender-ing, but not all were so inclined. One Rebel officer, hiding in a log hut, stepped from behind its door and shot a Union soldier in the back. Several of the soldier's comrades formed a semi-circle with their muskets leveled at him. Surrounded, he dropped his revolver and offered to surrender. "Like Hell you will!" shouted a 6th Maryland private as he fired his musket, killing the Rebel instantly. Major Prentiss, standing a short distance away, said nothing.

Just inside the sally port, Captain Abercrombie leaned over to examine a fall-en soldier made conspicuous by being among the first to reach the enemy wall. Seeing that the chest wound was mortal, he looked to the man's pain-contorted face. It was Private Luther Fogler. A sad sigh escaped from the captain's lips. He had witnessed many acts of valor on the battlefield over the past few years to the point that it seemed commonplace. However, Fogler's courage and devotion to duty nearly overwhelmed him. This mature man, understanding his mortality and what could be lost, had chosen to return to his regiment for one more bat-tle, despite a wound not yet healed. Motioning for two nearby stretcher-bearers to relieve him, the captain abruptly stood and walked away, lest his grief might be revealed when there was still work to be done.

The rapid entry of the 6th Maryland Volunteers through the sally port, coupled with their flank fire along the interior walls, had irrevocably breeched the Con-federate line. They were among the first to do so. Sixth Corps had accomplished the breakthrough.

Major Prentiss quickly reformed 6th Maryland, turned it to the left, and moved forward in accordance with General Wright's battle plan. Other regiments of the brigade aligned on his formation as it swept to the southwest inside the Confeder-ate fortifications. Ahead, Major Prentiss could see Rebel infantry spinning ninety degrees from their works to confront the approaching Federal battle line. The day was just dawning when the headlong rush of 2nd Brigade soldiers swept aside the defending infantry and carried Fort Alexander with ease, commandeering its four guns and bagging a number of prisoners. Lieutenant Samuel W. Angel of 6th Maryland captured the colors of the Purcell Artillery of Richmond.

General Keifer and his staff arrived on horseback soon after his brigade had secured the fort. Seeing Major Prentiss, General Keifer rode over to him exclaiming, "Splendid work, Major Prentiss! A gallant charge, perfectly executed. We were on them before they could organize their defense!"

Major Prentiss proudly saluted his brigade commander. "Thank you, sir," he said.

General Keifer returned the salute from the saddle. "Reform your regiment at once behind the fort, facing southwest in line of battle. As soon as I have the other regiments of the brigade organized and formed on 6th Maryland, we'll attack the next Rebel fort down the line. They're well-supplied with artillery and are, in fact, directing fire at us now." An incoming shell streaked overhead and exploded beyond the fort, emphasizing his warning.

General Keifer wheeled his horse around after acknowledging another salute from Major Prentiss and spied Major William Wood of the 9th New York Heavy Artillery. "Major Wood, have your men position these Rebel cannons to support the assault that we're about to make," he commanded, pointing in the intended direction.

"Yes sir," replied Major Wood.

The captured guns were soon firing rapidly as Major Wood's ex-artillerymen found a substantial supply of munitions. Major Prentiss and other 2nd Brigade officers moved quickly to position their regiments perpendicular to the main Confederate works and facing Fort Davis, the next strongpoint, less than a thousand yards away. It was a smaller version of Fort Alexander—a semi-circular, outward protrusion of earthen wall with five gun positions, although only two mounted a cannon. At General Keifer's order, the 2nd Brigade battle line, supplemented by a regiment from 1st Brigade, surged forward across an open field, encountering a multitude of tree stumps and vacated camps within the Confederate lines. Shot and shell from Major Wood's guns screamed overhead to suppress artillery fire directed against the Union assault from Fort Davis. As they neared their destination, the blue-coated soldiers, holding their muskets over their heads, crossed the swampy course of a narrow creek swollen with icy water.

McComb's Confederate Brigade was positioned alongside Fort Davis and fired several volleys at the advancing Federal battle line. The Rebels fought briefly and withdrew in good order for two hundred yards, disappearing into a thick patch of woods. As scant protection was afforded from their direction, the Confederates poured a severe musket fire into Union soldiers milling about within the captured works. Federal officers desperately sought to reform their ranks and turn the fort's two guns toward the Rebels firing upon them. Before much could be done, the Rebels in the woods were reinforced and launched a violent counter-charge. The Federal soldiers hurriedly withdrew to an open field a short distance away. Shot, shell, and musket balls fired by Confederates reoccupying the fort rained on the unprotected men of Keifer's brigade as they struggled to reform their ranks for another charge. As the brigade dashed forward in what was to be its most determined and bloody fight of the day, a shell fired by one of Major Wood's captured guns at Fort Alexander burst in the air over Fort Davis and silenced its last gun remaining in action.

Once again, Major Prentiss was charging ahead of his soldiers, waving his sword and shouting encouragement as his men rushed toward the enemy line of battle that was defending the fort. In his mind's eye, it was a perfect tableau of victorious soldiers surging toward an enemy citadel—the leader with his sword held high, his color-bearers following with flags fluttering in the breeze, and his valiant soldiers charging forward to vanquish all adversaries before them. The conjured image coalesced into the reality of his headlong charge as he crashed into the disintegrating Confederate formation.

Major Prentiss entered the rear area of Fort Davis and immediately crossed swords with a Confederate officer. They slashed and stabbed, circling one another. Each was oblivious to all else. The Rebel lunged forward and they locked blades just in front of each officer's chin. The encounter ended abruptly when Major Prentiss knocked his adversary to the ground and demanded his surrender. The Confederate lieutenant attempted to draw a revolver, forcing Major Prentiss to plunge his sword into the officer's neck. He did not see the Rebel soldier, crouched behind a barrel nearby, aiming a musket at him. The ball struck his chest from the side, shattering the breastbone over his heart. He collapsed near the first gun emplacement, just yards from several dead and wounded Rebel soldiers scattered around the gun they had been manning. Among them was Private William Prentiss, his right leg shattered above the knee by a shell fragment.

* * *

Sixth Corps lost nearly eleven hundred men that April morning, but its soldiers decisively broke the Rebel lines at Petersburg, dooming Richmond and the Confederacy. Later that morning, General Lee sent a telegram to John C. Breckenridge, the Secretary of War, in Richmond. It read, in part, "I see no prospect of doing more than holding our position here until night. I am not certain I can do that. If I can, I shall withdraw tonight north of the Appomattox and, if possible, it will be better to withdraw the whole line tonight from James River. The brigades on Hatcher's Run are cut off from us. The enemy have broken through our lines and intercepted between us and them. Our only chance of concentrating our forces is to do so near Danville Railroad, which I shall endeavor to do at once. I advise that all preparations be made for leaving Richmond tonight. I will advise you later according to circumstances."

Breckenridge immediately dispatched a courier with a copy of this message for delivery to Jefferson Davis who was attending church services that morning. The parish sexton, William Irving, walked quietly to the Davis pew and handed him the message. A gray pallor came across his face as he read its contents. The President of the Confederate States of America left Saint Paul's Church shortly afterward without taking communion.

* * *

6TH MARYLAND VOLUNTEERS
NEAR PETERSBURG, VIRGINIA
APRIL 2, 1865

The fighting was over in the recaptured Confederate works. The thunder of artillery and the rattle of musketry continued in other directions, but all was quiet behind the earthen walls of Fort Davis. Those few Rebel soldiers left standing were disarmed and herded at bayonet point against the front wall of the fort. The casualties of both sides lay where they fell during the brief, but furious, hand-to-hand struggle. Some were lying still; others were clutching their torn limbs and bodies, weltering in blood.

Most Union soldiers not engaged in guarding prisoners dropped down where they could find places against the fort's embankment to rest, drink from their canteens, and savor a sense of relief that they had survived yet another charge against the enemy. Some of the older veterans began moving among the fallen, sorting them out according to the severity of their injuries, regardless of the uniform they wore. In doing so, they would determine who could be helped and who was beyond any aid. Stretcher-bearers were then summoned to move the wounded to ambulances arriving from the Union lines.

Two 6th Maryland soldiers, a corporal, and a sergeant crouched over William, who was gripping his mangled right leg. "Easy now, young fellow. We'll get some help for you shortly," the sergeant said as he motioned for a team of stretcher-bearers.

"May I have some water?" William asked. The sergeant unslung his canteen, removed the stopper, carefully lifted the young man's head, and held the canteen to his lips. William took a short drink with his eyes tightly shut. He thanked the sergeant as he opened his eyes and looked up at the bearded face. William noticed the number 6 in the sergeant's cap emblem.

"Is the 6th Maryland Infantry anywhere close about?" he asked.

"We're in 6th Maryland, Johnny Reb, why do you ask?"

"My brother is in that regiment."

"Who is he?" asked the corporal.

"Captain Clifton K. Prentiss," William replied. "Is he here?"

"He's our major now and he's lying wounded over yonder," the sergeant said, motioning with his head.

William looked in the direction indicated and said, "I would very much like to see him."

"What's your name?" the sergeant asked.

"Private William S. Prentiss, 2nd Maryland Battalion."

The sergeant glanced at the corporal who at once got up and walked over to where Major Clifton Prentiss was lying on the ground. He was about to be placed upon a stretcher by several 6th Maryland soldiers. The corporal knelt down and waited until the injured officer was situated. "Sir, there's a wounded Rebel over there who says that he's your brother, William. We're about to put him on a stretcher. Shall we bring him over to your side?"

The expression of pain on Clifton's face deepened. "I want to see no man who has fired on my country's flag," he replied and turned his face away.

The corporal exchanged glances with the men tending Major Prentiss and slowly stood up. He could see that the major had been shot in the chest and realized that it may be a mortal wound. As the corporal was returning to William's stretcher, he noticed that Lieutenant Colonel Hill and several staff officers had just entered the captured Confederate works. "Colonel Hill, might I have a word with you, sir?" the corporal asked. Lieutenant Colonel Hill stopped short as the corporal quickly walked over to him, saluted, and explained what had just happened.

Lieutenant Colonel Hill, after giving directions to have William brought over, knelt down beside Major Prentiss and pleaded with him. "For the love of God, Clifton, he's your brother. You are both badly wounded. You must see him and talk with him—he's your kin, your own flesh and blood."

Clifton lay on his stretcher, his jaw clinched in fierce determination. When William was brought beside him, Clifton glared at him for a long moment. William smiled and, with that one touch of nature, out went one of Clifton's hands and it was clasped by both of William's. With tears streaming down their cheeks, the two brothers who had each gone their separate ways, were once more brought together.

* * *

ARMORY SQUARE HOSPITAL
WASHINGTON, D.C.
JUNE 24, 1865

Clifton had finished his recollections of the assault at Fort Davis, the wounding of the brothers, and their tearful reunion. Whitman's head was tilted back. His eyes were moist as he stared at the ceiling, still immersed in the tragedy that had befallen this American family and their battered nation. John and Melville were slumped in their chairs, stunned by the inconceivable turn of events that befell their brothers.

Whitman stood and approached the bed, extending his hand to a now exhausted Major Prentiss. "Thank you for sharing with me the full breadth of what happened to your family. I'm truly honored to have known William, even for a brief time, and it's a great privilege to have met his brothers and shared these recollections."

"We're the ones honored by your kindness and shall remain forever in your debt," Clifton replied as they shook hands. They stared into one another's eyes and Whitman noted a look that he had observed in so many young men—a strong spirit slowly succumbing to a mortal wound.

Whitman shook hands and exchanged farewells with John and Melville Prentiss, who were now both standing, and quickly departed from the Officer's Ward. Greeted by the warm afternoon sun, Whitman walked away from the hospital area before spotting an empty bench situated under a shady tree. As a light breeze was stirring the leaves, the bench offered a welcome opportunity to rest and reflect on the story that he had just heard. The rending of the Prentiss family precisely represented the national trauma that pitted state against state, father against son, and brother against brother. It was ironic that the patriotism of both sides was rooted in the legacy of the American Revolution. Southerners viewed their struggle as a second war for independence and Northerners fought to preserve the union created by their forefathers. The war had begun based on these differing perspectives but, by its end, the elimination of slavery had become the greater cause.

Whitman pulled his coat wide open to fully enjoy the cool breeze and spread both arms outward on the back of the bench. What an incredible coincidence! One brother loyal to the Union, the other a Secessionist, separated for four years on opposite sides in a hard-fought war, yet both were badly wounded at the same time and place, just seven days before the surrender of Lee's army at Appomattox. This was the real war that must be remembered—the courage, character, and humanity of individual American soldiers giving all they had for their cause.

Whitman stood and began to walk, his hands tucked in his coat pockets. If the relationship of the Prentiss brothers could be restored, it was possible that the North and the South might accomplish a similar reconciliation. Perhaps the agony of this long and costly conflict had finally wrought one indivisible nation. Whitman was quite weary, but he smiled from the sense of hope for America that he felt in his heart.

EPILOGUE

On August 17, 1865, Dr. Bliss approved Clifton's transfer to the home of his brother in Brooklyn, New York. The transfer order stated that while Major Prentiss was confined to his bed, he could be moved to this location where special treatment could be obtained to save his life. This effort was to no avail. Clifton Kennedy Prentiss died of his wound on August 20, 1865, shortly after arriving at Melville's home.

Clifton and William Prentiss had been mortally wounded just yards and moments apart in one of the last battles of the Civil War. One fought for the North, the other for the South, yet they were able to reconcile their personal differences before the extent of their wounds proved fatal.

They now rest side by side at Green-Wood Cemetery in Brooklyn, New York. Each died for his cause in opposition to the other, but in final measure, their spirit of brotherhood prevailed.

APPENDIX

Two brothers, one South, one North — May 28 - 29, 1865 — I staid tonight a long time by the bedside of a new patient, a young Baltimorean, aged about nineteen years, W. S. P. (2d Maryland, Southern), very feeble, right leg amputated, can't sleep; has taken a great deal of morphine, which, as usual, is costing more than it comes to. Evidently very intelligent and well-bred; very affectionate; held on to my hand, and put it by his face, not willing to let me leave. As I was lingering, soothing him in his pain, he says to me suddenly: "I hardly think you know who I am. I don't wish to impose upon you — I am a rebel soldier." I said I did not know that, but it made no difference. Visiting him daily for about two weeks after that, while he lived (death had marked him, and he was quite alone), I loved him much, always kissed him, and he did me. In an adjoining ward I found his brother, an officer of rank, a Union soldier, a brave and religious man (Colonel Clifton K. Prentiss, 6th Maryland Infantry, Sixth Corps, wounded in one of the engagements at Petersburg, April 2, lingered, suffered much, died in Brooklyn, August 20, 1865). It was in the same battle both were hit. One was a strong Unionist, the other Secesh; both fought on their respective sides, both badly wounded, and both brought together here after a separation of four years. Each died for his cause."

WALT WHITMAN, Army Hospitals and Cases - Memoranda at the Time, 1863–1866, The Century, Vol. 36, Issue 6 (Oct. 1888), 825–30.

Note: Listed below are various accounts, some written a number of years later, relating to the mortal wounding of the two brothers when the Confederate lines at Petersburg were breeched by the Sixth Corps in the final days of the war. As can be expected, there are contradictions, but the gist of these accounts remains fairly consistent.

* * *

Walt Whitman clipped and saved the two following articles that are preserved in the Library of Congress, Feinberg Collection.

BREVET COLONEL CLIFTON K. PRENTISS. The numerous friends of this brave and seriously wounded officer, now at the Armory Square Hospital in this city, will be glad to see this recognition of his faithful and meritorious services.

At the outbreak of the rebellion, Brevet Colonel Prentiss joined the 6th Maryland regiment, and soon attracted the special notice of his commanding General Ricketts, who detailed him on his personal staff. He was conspicuous in the battles of the Wilderness, Spotsylvania, Cold Harbor, and in front of Petersburg, Va., during the spring and summer of 1864, and fought bravely in defence of his native State at the battle of the Monocacy, with the gallant 3d division, 6th corps; thence throughout the Shenandoah Valley campaign, when he rejoined his regiment, and, as its major, elicited the highest encomiums for his shining qualities as a disciplinarian, who ever did most by his own personal example.

He was thus the first officer to lead troops within the enemy's apparently impregnable works in front of Petersburg on the 2d of April, and there received in hand-to-hand conflict, his probably fatal wounds. Maryland may well be proud of her heroic son, and recognize in this brief sketch his outwardly glorious career. But friendship finds deeper and higher claims to distinction in his earnestness in the path of duty as an honest man and true Christian.

THE WASHINGTON, *D.C. Daily Morning Chronicle*, August 4, 1865.

* * *

On August 18, 1865, Clifton Prentiss was permitted to travel to Brooklyn, New York, to visit his family. He died on August 20, 1865, at the home of his brother, J.H. Prentiss, 35 Livingston Street. William and Clifton Prentiss were buried in adjoining graves at The Green-Wood Cemetery, in Brooklyn, New York.

New York Times, August 23, 1865.

* * *

DIED

PRENTISS—At Armory Square Hospital, Washington, D.C., on Saturday morning, June 24, William Scholley Prentiss, youngest son of the late John Prentiss, of Baltimore, Maryland, aged 26 years and 26 days. The relatives and friends of the family are respectfully invited to attend the funeral, from the residence of his brother, T. Melville Prentiss, 35 Livingston Street, Brooklyn, L.I., on Tuesday afternoon, at four o'clock. Boston papers please copy.

New York Herald, Monday, June 26, 1865.

* * *

DEATH OF AN OFFICER—Col. Clifton L. Prentiss of the 6th Md. Vols, died a few days since in Brooklyn. Col. Prentiss shortly after commencement of the war enlisted as a private in the company then commanded by Lieut. Col. E.M. Faehtz, and gradually worked his way up to the position of Major of the 6th

Reg't and Brevet Colonel of U.S. Volunteers. He was wounded in several actions, but never quitted the field.

Herald & Torch—Hagerstown, Maryland, Wednesday, August 30, 1865.

* * *

". . . Maj. Clifton K. Prentiss, 6th Md., according to the report of Mr. Hannah, field correspondent of the *New York Herald*, was the first commissioned officer to enter the enemy works.

"Major Clifton K. Prentiss commanding the Sixth Maryland Volunteers, was one of the first officers to enter the rebel works, but was unfortunately shot through the chest . . . we picked up a wounded rebel, who said he was Lieutenant Prentiss, of the Second Maryland rebel regiment. He is a younger brother of the Major whom he has not seen since the rebellion broke out. "They are now lying in the same tent in the Fiftieth New York Engineer's camp, and I am glad to say likely to do well. . . ."

"The Battle of Sunday: Highly Interesting Details of the Operations
of the Sixth and Ninth Corps—Honorable Mention of a Wisconsin
Brigade Commander—Incidents," Milwaukee Sentinel,
Monday, April 10, 1865 (correspondent of the New York Herald).

* * *

"Majors Wood and Lamoreaux, with men of the Ninth New York Heavy Artillery, were the first to turn and fire the enemy's guns upon him. Major Prentiss, Sixth Maryland, with a large portion of his regiment, was the first to penetrate the enemy's works, where, after a most bloody struggle, he fell severely, if not mortally, wounded. Five other officers of the Sixth Maryland were wounded very soon after entering the fortifications. Too much praise cannot be given the officers and men of this regiment.

Report of Bvt. Brig. Gen. J. Warren Keifer, commanding Second Brigade, Third
Division, Sixth Corps, of operations April 2, 1865.

APPENDIX

* * *

"It is not disputed here that my brigade was the first to enter the Rebel works and gain a position. When we first entered the works my Brigade captured eight pieces of artillery for which we have receipt by order of Genl. Meade. . . . Maj. C.K. Prentiss 6th Maryland was mortally wounded (as is now supposed) shortly after entering the works. His brother a Major in the Rebel army was wounded a few moments later & was captured. The two brothers now lie side by side in our Hospital. The Rebel Maj. has had a leg amputated and it is thought he will also die. . . ."

Joseph Warren Keifer Papers, Library of Congress, Excerpts from letters
to My Dear Wife, April 3, 1865. Courtesy of A. Wilson Greene.

* * *

"The brave Colonel Prentiss as he led a storming column over the parapet of the fort, was struck by a ball which carried away a part of his breast-bone immediately over his heart, exposing its action to view. He fell within the fort at the same moment the commander of the Confederate battery fell near him with what proved to be a mortal wound. These officers, lying side by side, their blood commingling on the ground, there recognized each other. They were brothers, and had not met for four years. They were cared for in the same hospitals, by the same surgeons and nurses, with the same tenderness, and in part by a Union chaplain, their brother. The Confederate, after suffering the amputation of a leg, died in Washington in June 1865, and Colonel Prentiss died in Brooklyn, N. Y., the following August."

Joseph Warren Keifer, Slavery and Four Years of War, Volume II,
New York, G.P. Putnam's Sons, 1900, 196.

* * *

A Pathetic Incident.

"Maj. Clifton K. Prentiss, a Baltimorian, was a man of exceptional bravery, a veritable cavalier. On this fateful morning he fell mortally wounded, as with waving sword he urged forward his men, to be the first to mount, with assistance, the enemy's works.

The following pathetic incident occurred after the enemy had been defeated. Two of the 6th Md. men like many others were going over the field ministering to the wounded without regard to the uniform they wore, came upon a wounded Confederate, who after receiving some water, asked if the 6th Md. was any way near there. The reply was, 'We belong to that regiment. Why do you ask?' The Confederate replied that he had a brother in that regiment. 'Who is he?' he was asked. The Confederate said, 'Captain Clifton K. Prentiss.' Our boys said, 'Yes, he is our Major now and is lying over yonder wounded.' The Confederate said: "I would like to see him." Word was at once carried to Maj. Prentiss. He declined to see him saying, 'I want to see no man who fired on my country's flag." Col. Hill, after giving directions to have the wounded Confederate brought over, knelt down beside the Major and pleaded with him to see his brother. When the wayward brother was laid beside him our Major for a moment glared at him. The Confederate brother smiled; that was the one touch of nature; out went both hands and with tears streaming down their cheeks these two brothers, who had met on many bloody fields on opposite sides for three years, were once more brought together. They were both carried back in the same ambulance and both died in the same hospital. I question if there was another incident of that kind happened during the whole war."

John R. King, "Sixth Corps at Petersburg. Its Splendid Assault, Which Broke the Main Line of the Rebels," National Tribune, April 15, 1920.

* * *

"In one of our wards we had an officer, Colonel Clifton J. Prentiss, of Baltimore, whose case was of such peculiar and touching interest that it ought not to be passed by. In one of the closing battles of the war he was wounded through the lungs. When I first saw him, he was brought into the hospital from the field, as we thought, fatally hurt. At the same time a lad, a rebel soldier, was lifted from the stretcher upon an adjoining bed, with a thigh amputation, having been struck by a fragment of a shell above the knee. Thus Union officer and this rebel soldier [William S. Prentiss, Co. A, 2nd Maryland Battalion] lay side by side, not knowing that they were indeed own brothers . . . that they had been striking the one against the other, and falling but ten feet apart. In the early stages of their wounds, two of their brothers—one of whom neither had seen for eight years—came down to nurse and watch with these other two, who were dying so far from home. . . . both entering the new home, where there is no distinction between the blue jacket and the gray. "The younger died first. . . . The brave and all-enduring colonel lived on . . . through many weary months he waited and suffered. . . ." (Died August 20, 1865)

William Howell Reed, Hospital Life in the Army of the Potomac
(Boston: Special Edition, 1881), 190–92.

* * *

"Here I will relate an incident that would make quite a history. Lieut.-Col. C. K. Prentiss, who was made a Colonel in the Regular Army for bravery, before his death, had a brother William, who was a Lieutenant in the Confederate army, and who had been fighting against him in several battles. They would hear of each other through the prisoners taken, and on this morning they were both hit about the same time. I do not think there was two minutes' difference in the time; in fact, I saw them both wounded within 20 yards of each other. They both died after the close of the war from the wounds received there. Col. C. K. Prentiss was, I think, as good and brave a soldier as any in the army; he was brave almost to rashness."

E. S. Norvell, "Petersburg. A Maryland Comrade's Account of the
Sixth Corps Operation," National Tribune, June 11, 1891.

* * *

"A sad tragedy was the mortally wounding of our Major Clifton K. Prentice, within a few yards of where his brother, a Captain of a Confederate Battery of

Artillery, fell also mortally wounded. Both were carried to Hospital by stretcher bearers of the 6th Md. They met each other and talked most affectionately together - but in a short time afterwards both died. Major Prentice had me read a letter from this brother only a few days before this battle. He had written to a sister in Baltimore and she forwarded the letter to the Major. In it he deplored the fate that compelled brother to fight against brother. We were assaulting a fort on the left when Major Prentice fell. His brother was in command of the battery in the fort."

Grayson M. Eichelberger Papers,
U.S. Army Military History Institute, Carlisle, Pa.

* * *

"The narrow opening utilized by the 6th Maryland is most likely the one that survives along the Breakthrough Trail at Pamplin Historical Park, but in the absence of more explicit evidence this must be considered merely informed speculation."

"An opening in the preserved Confederate works along the Breakthrough Trail in Pamplin Historical Park is mostly likely the feature described by Keiffer and Eichelberger. A traverse behind the main line, not in front of it as Eichelberger described, exists to one side of the gap, representing perhaps a portion of the parallel work built to protect the opening."

A. Wilson Greene, *Breaking the Backbone of the Rebellion—*
The Final Battles of The Petersburg Campaign, 333–334.
Note: The Pamplin Historical Park, including Breakthrough Trail,
and the National Museum of the Civil War Soldier are located
at 6125 Boydton Plank Road, Petersburg, Virginia 23803.

* * *

"He was present at the Battles of Petersburg and Richmond, and had two brothers mortally wounded. His brother, Clifton K. Prentiss, raised the 6th Maryland Volunteers in Baltimore, and became a Lieutenant Colonel. William, another brother was on the Confederate side, and both brothers were fatally wounded at the same battle within 100 yards of each other."

Excerpt from the obituary of Dr. John H. Prentiss (elder brother of Clifton and William Prentiss) from the *Baltimore Sun*, January 27, 1888. Reprinted in The Maryland Historical & Genealogical Bulletin, Volume XV, Number 4, Robert F. Hayes, Jr., Baltimore, Maryland, October 1944.

* * *

"Even now, writing of it after so many, many years, I seem to feel again the pulse of that thrilling time. And it was here that there came intimately into my life one of its strongest influences, in the radiant person of my cousin, Hetty Cary, daughter of my uncle, Wilson Miles Cary, of Baltimore, my father's elder and only brother. She, with her younger sister, Jenny, had taken the lead in the secessionist movement among the young girls in Baltimore, who, having seen all their best men march across the border to enlist with the Confederates for the war, relieved their strained feelings by overt resentment of the Union officers and troops placed in possession of their city."

Mrs. Burton Harrison (Constance Cary), *Recollections Grave And Gay*, Charles Scribner Sons, New York, 1911.

* * *

"I devote myself much to Armory Square Hospital because it contains by far the worst cases, most repulsive wounds, has the most suffering & most need of consolation—I go every day without fail, & often at night—sometimes stay very late—no one interferes with me, guards, doctors, nurses, nor any one—I am let to take my own course."

Walt Whitman, *Correspondence*, 1: 112.

* * *

"One of six model hospitals constructed in 1862, Armory Square took its name from the Old Armory on the Mall, around which the hospital was built. Its location placed it nearest the steamboat landing at the foot of Seventh Street, S.W., and near the tracks of the Washington and Alexandria Railroad, which ran along Maryland Avenue. As a result, Armory Square received the most serious casualties from the Virginia battlefields, those too ill to travel any farther. From August 1861 to January 1865, Armory Square recorded the largest number of deaths of any Washington military hospital, 1,339 out of 18,291 deaths."

Armory Square Hospital Gazette, Feb. 25, 1865.

* * *

Three weeks later, to the day, General Pegram's coffin, crossed with a victor's palms beside his soldier's accoutrements, occupied the spot in the chancel where he had stood to be married. Beside it knelt his widow swathed in crape. Again Dr. Minnegerode conducted the ceremony, again the church was full. Behind the hearse, waiting outside, stood his war charger, with boots in stirrups. The wailing of the band that went with us on the slow pilgrimage to Hollywood will never die out of memory.

Mrs. Burton Harrison (Constance Cary), *Recollections Grave And Gay*,
Charles Scribner Sons, New York, 1911.

APPENDIX

* * *

In Loving Memory of
Hetty Cary Martin
Daughter of Wilson Miles and Jane M. Carey
Born May 15, 1836
Died September 27, 1892

Married January 19, 1865 to
Brig. Gen. John Pegram CSA of Richmond VA
who was killed in battle Feb. 6, 1865

Married Dec. 20, 1879 to
Henry Newell Martin Esq. M.D. ERS
of Newby Ireland
Fellow of Christ College Cambridge and
Professor in Johns Hopkins University Baltimore

Beautiful, Brilliant, Brave
Of Pure and Noble Heart, True and Generous Soul
In the Battle of Life Heroic
In Death Triumphant

WITH GRATITUDE

There is so much that goes into crafting a book beyond the creative energy and effort of the author. My appreciation is eternal for the many contributions of those good folks who lent their talents and expertise to help me bring this book to fruition.

Art Bergeron, now of the U.S. Army Military History Institute, kindly provided me with the initial historical data on the Prentiss brothers. He also referred me to M. L. Prentiss, a Prentiss family member, who graciously shared many facts about her family that she had unearthed in her genealogical research.

Inevitably, my journey took me to the site of the Sixth Corps breakthrough, located within Pamplin Historical Park, near Petersburg, Virginia. There, Will Greene, the park's executive director, provided me not only with information, but also encouragement, and made it possible for me to stand on the hallowed ground where events portrayed in this book took place. No matter how much time is spent studying the monumental accomplishments of those American patriots, there is simply no substitute for visiting the actual sites to fully comprehend the extent of their devotion and sacrifice.

Thankfully, early in the writing endeavor, Alex Knowles provided the knowledge and guidance that made it possible for me to complete the manuscript. Without his excellent contribution, this book would not have made it past an initial outline.

I was fortunate to retain Darla Bruno whose professional editing of this book has made it the best that it can be. Her corrections and suggestions were prompt, honest, and accurate, while preserving my writing style and natural voice.

Charles Brock of the DesignWorks Group created an outstanding book cover and interior layout, utilizing the photographic skills of Steve Gardner of

PixelWorks Studios and the typesetting ability of Robin Black. All together, they have provided the book with an appearance of which I am immensely proud.

Above all, without the love, inspiration, and encouragement of my wife, Dian, this book would never have been written.